A REAPER AT THE GATES

THE EASTERN SEA

Adisa

MARINN

Ayo

USKAN
SEA

AUGURS' CAVE

THE BOWL

E V E N N E S

R A N G E

PILGRIM'S GAP

PILGRIM ROAD

NORTH GATE

EAST GATE

WEST GATE

PALACE GROUNDS

SCHOLAR SECTOR

MARINER EMBASSY

TIER 2

BLACK GUARD BARRACKS

TIER 1

MAIN GATE

ANTIUM

BOOKS BY SABAA TAHIR

An Ember in the Ashes

A Torch Against the Night

A Reaper at the Gates

A Sky Beyond the Storm

All My Rage

PRAISE FOR THE
AN EMBER IN THE ASHES
QUARTET

An instant *New York Times* bestseller
A *USA Today* bestseller
A *Wall Street Journal* bestseller
One of *TIME*'s 100 Best Fantasy Books of All Time
One of *TIME*'s 100 Best YA Books of All Time

NAMED ONE OF THE BEST BOOKS OF THE YEAR BY
Amazon * Barnes & Noble * *The Wall Street Journal* * BuzzFeed
LA Weekly * Bustle * *Paste Magazine* * Indigo * *Suspense Magazine*
The New York Public Library * PopSugar * Hypable

"This novel is a harrowing, haunting reminder of what it means to be human —
and how hope might be kindled in the midst of oppression and fear."
—THE WASHINGTON POST

"A worthy novel — and one as brave as its characters."
—THE NEW YORK TIMES BOOK REVIEW

"A captivating, heart-pounding fantasy."**—US WEEKLY**

"*An Ember in the Ashes* mixes *The Hunger Games* with *Game of Thrones* . . .
and adds a dash of *Romeo and Juliet*."**—THE HOLLYWOOD REPORTER**

"Fast-paced, well-structured, and **full of twists and turns.**"**—NPR**

"**Blew me away** . . . This book is dark, complex, vivid, and romantic —
expect to be completely transported."**—MTV.COM**

"This is a page-turner. There comes a moment when it's impossible to
put it down. Sabaa Tahir is a strong writer, but most of all, she's a great storyteller.
An Ember in the Ashes glows, burns, and smolders — as beautiful and radiant
as it is searing."**—THE HUFFINGTON POST**

"**It's addictive, and there's no way you can put it down** before you
figure out what happens to the characters you have fallen for over the
course of the 400 some-odd pages. So I didn't."**—BUSTLE**

"Spectacular."**—ENTERTAINMENT WEEKLY**

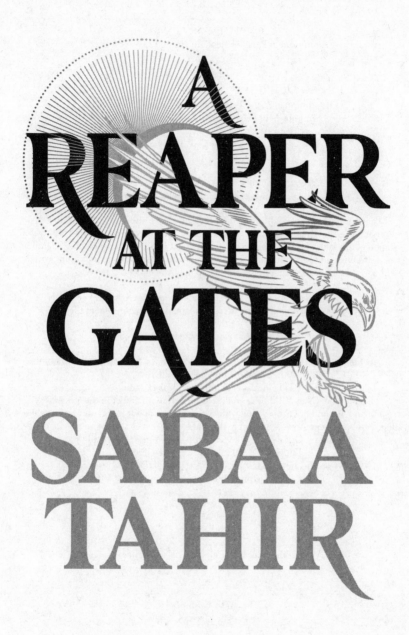

A REAPER AT THE GATES

SABAA TAHIR

putnam

G. P. PUTNAM'S SONS

G. P. PUTNAM'S SONS
An imprint of Penguin Random House LLC, New York

First published in the United States of America by Razorbill,
an imprint of Penguin Random House LLC, 2018
First paperback edition published 2020
This edition published by G. P. Putnam's Sons 2024

Visit us online at PenguinRandomHouse.com.

THE LIBRARY OF CONGRESS HAS CATALOGED THE HARDCOVER EDITION AS FOLLOWS:
Names: Tahir, Sabaa, author.
Title: A reaper at the gates / Sabaa Tahir.
Description: [New York] : Razorbill, 2018. | Series: An ember in the ashes ; 3 |
Summary: Beyond the Empire and within it, the threat of war looms ever larger as the
Blood Shrike, Helene Aquilla, Laia of Serra, and Elias Veturius all face increasing dangers.
Identifiers: LCCN 2018006968 | ISBN 9780448494500 (hardback)
Subjects: | CYAC: Fantasy. | Love—Fiction.
Classification: LCC PZ7.1.T33 Re 2018 | DDC [Fic]—dc23
LC record available at https://lccn.loc.gov/2018006968

ISBN 9780448494517

9th Printing

Printed in the United States of America

LSCC

Design by Kristin Boyle
Text set in Electra LT Std

For Renée, who knows my heart.
For Alexandra, who holds my hopes.
And for Ben, who shares the dream.

PART I

THE KING OF
NO NAME

I: The Nightbringer

You love too much, my king.

My queen spoke the words often across the centuries we spent together. At first, with a smile. But in later years, with a furrowed brow. Her gaze settled on our children as they tore about the palace, their bodies flickering from flame to flesh, tiny cyclones of impossible beauty.

"I fear for you, *Meherya*." Her voice trembled. "I fear what you will do if harm comes to those whom you love."

"No harm shall befall you. I vow it."

I spoke with the passion and folly of youth, though I was not, of course, young. Even then. That day, the breezes off the river ruffled her midnight hair and sunlight poured like liquid gold through the sheer curtains of the windows. It lit our children umber as they trailed scorch marks and laughter across the stone floor.

Her fears held her captive. I reached for her hands. "I would destroy any who dared hurt you," I said.

"*Meherya*, no." I have wondered in the years since then if she already feared what I would become. "Swear you would never. You are our *Meherya*. Your heart is made to love. To give. Not to take. That is why you are king of the jinn. Swear it."

I swore two vows that day: to protect, always. To love, always.

Within a year, I had broken both.

«««

The Star hangs from the wall of the cavern far from human eyes. It is a four-pointed diamond, with a narrow gap at its apex. Thin striations spiderweb across it, a reminder of the day the Scholars shattered it after imprisoning my people. The metal gleams with impatience, potent as the glare of a jungle beast closing in on prey. Such vast power within this weapon—enough to destroy an ancient city, an ancient people. Enough to imprison the jinn for a thousand years.

Enough to set them free.

As if sensing the armlet clinging to my wrist, the Star rattles, yearning toward the missing piece. A wrench shudders through me as I offer the armlet up, and it oozes away like a silver eel to join with the Star. The gap shrinks.

The four points of the Star flare, lighting the far reaches of the speckled granite cavern, eliciting a wave of angry hisses from the creatures around me. Then the glow fades, leaving only pallid moonlight. Ghuls swish at my ankles.

Master. Master.

Beyond them, the Wraith Lord awaits my orders, along with the efrit kings and queens—of wind and sea, sand and cave, air and snow.

As they watch, silent and wary, I consider the parchment in my hands. It is as unobtrusive as sand. The words within are not.

At my summons, the Wraith Lord approaches. He submits reluctantly, cowed by my magic, straining always to be free of me. But I have need of him yet. The wraiths are disparate scraps of lost souls, joined by ancient sorcery and undetectable when they wish to be. Even by the Empire's famed Masks.

As I offer him the parchment, I hear her. My queen's voice is a whisper, gentle as a candle on a chill night. *Once you do this, you can never come back. All hope for you is lost,* Meherya. *Consider.*

I do as she asks. I consider.

Then I remember she is dead and gone and has been for a millennium. Her presence is a delusion. Her voice is my weakness. I proffer the scroll to the Wraith Lord.

"See that it finds Blood Shrike Helene Aquilla," I tell him. "And no other." He bows, and the efrits sail forward. I order the efrits of air away; I have a separate task for them. The rest kneel.

"Long ago, you gave the Scholars knowledge that led to the destruction of my people and the fey world." A jolt of memory ripples through their ranks. "I offer you redemption. Go to our new allies in the south. Help them understand what they can call forth from the dark places. The Grain Moon will rise six months hence. See it done well before then. And you"—the ghuls press close—"glut yourselves. Do not fail me."

When they have all left me, I contemplate the Star and think of the treacherous jinn girl who helped bring it into being. Perhaps to a human, the weapon would shine with promise.

I feel only hatred.

A face drifts to the forefront of my mind. Laia of Serra. I recall the heat of her skin beneath my hands, how her wrists crossed behind my neck. The way she closed her eyes and the golden hollow of her throat. She felt like the threshold of my old home when the rushes were fresh-changed. She felt safe.

You loved her, my queen says. *And then you hurt her.*

My betrayal of the Scholar girl should not linger. I deceived hundreds before her.

Yet unease grips me. Something inexplicable occurred after Laia of Serra gifted me her armlet—after she realized that the boy she called Keenan was naught but a fabrication. Like all humans, she glimpsed in my eyes the

darkest moments of her life. But when I looked into her soul, something—
someone—peered back: my queen, gazing at me across the centuries.

I saw her horror. Her sadness at what I had become. I saw her pain at what
our children and our people suffered at the hands of the Scholars.

I think of my queen with every betrayal. Going back a thousand years, to
each human found, manipulated, and loved until they freely gave me their
piece of the Star with love in their hearts. Again and again and again.

But never had I seen her in the gaze of another. Never had I felt the sharp
blade of her disappointment so keenly.

Once more. Only once more.

My queen speaks. *Do not do this. Please.*

I crush her voice. I crush her memory. I think I will not hear her again.

II: Laia

E verything about this raid feels wrong. Darin and I both know it, even if neither of us is willing to say it.

Though my brother does not speak much these days.

The ghost wagons we track finally roll to a stop outside a Martial village. I rise from the snow-heavy bushes where we've taken cover and nod to Darin. He grabs my hand and squeezes. *Be safe.*

I reach for my invisibility, a power awoken within me recently, and one that I'm still settling into. My breath wreathes up in white clouds, like a snake undulating to some unknowable song. Elsewhere in the Empire, spring has scattered its blossoms. But this close to Antium, the capital, winter still whips its chill fingers across our faces.

Midnight passes, and the few lamps that burn in the village sputter in the rising wind. When I am through the perimeter of the prisoner caravan, I pitch my voice low and hoot like a snowy owl, common enough in this part of the Empire.

As I prowl toward the ghost wagons, my skin prickles. I whirl, my instinct rearing in warning. The nearby ridgeline is empty, and the Martial auxiliary soldiers on guard do not so much as twitch. Nothing appears amiss.

You're just jumpy, Laia. Like always. From our camp on the outskirts of the Waiting Place, twenty miles from here, Darin and I have planned and carried out six raids on Empire prisoner caravans. My brother has not forged a single scrap of Serric steel. I have not responded to the letters from Araj, the Scholar leader who escaped Kauf Prison with us. But together with

Afya Ara-Nur and her men, we have helped to free more than four hundred Scholars and Tribesmen over the past two months.

Still, that does not guarantee success with this caravan. For this caravan is different.

Beyond the perimeter, familiar black-clad figures move in on the camp from the trees. Afya and her men, responding to my signal, preparing to attack. Their presence gives me heart. The Tribeswoman who helped me free Darin from Kauf is the only reason we know of these ghost wagons—and the prisoner they transport.

The lock picks are blades of ice in my hand. Six wagons sit in a half circle, with two supply carts sheltered between them. Most of the soldiers busy themselves with the horses and campfires. Snow gusts down in flurries, stinging my face as I get to the first wagon and begin working the lock. The pins within are enigmas to my freezing, clumsy hands. *Faster, Laia.*

The wagon is silent, as if empty. But I know better. Soon, the whimper of a child breaks the quiet. It is quickly shushed. The prisoners have learned that silence is the only way to avoid suffering.

"Where the burning hells is everybody?" a voice bellows near my ear. I nearly drop my picks. A legionnaire strides past, and a tendril of panic unfurls down my spine. I do not dare to breathe. *What if he sees me? What if my invisibility falters?* It has happened before, when I am under attack, or in a large crowd.

"Wake up the innkeeper." The legionnaire turns to the aux hastening toward him. "Tell him to roll out a keg and prepare rooms."

"Inn's empty, sir. Village looks abandoned."

Martials do not abandon villages, even in the dead of winter. Not unless a plague has come through. But Afya would have heard if that were the case.

Their reasons for leaving are not your concern, Laia. Get the locks open.

The aux and the legionnaire stalk off toward the inn. The moment they are out of sight, I get my picks in the lock. But the metal groans, stiff with rime.

Come on! Without Elias Veturius to get through half the locks, I have to work twice as fast. I have no time to think of my friend, and yet I cannot quell my worry. His presence during the raids has kept us from being caught. He *said* he would be here..

What in the skies could have happened to Elias? He's never let me down. *Not when it comes to the raids, anyway.* Did Shaeva learn that he snuck Darin and me back across the Waiting Place from the cottage in the Free Lands? Is she punishing him?

I know little of the Soul Catcher—she is shy, and I assumed she did not like me. Some days, when Elias emerges from the Waiting Place to visit me and Darin, I feel the jinn woman watching us and I sense no rancor. Only sadness. But skies know, I'm no judge of hidden malice.

If it were any other caravan—any other prisoner we were attempting to break out—I would not have risked Darin, or the Tribespeople, or myself.

But we owe it to Mamie Rila and the rest of the Saif prisoners to try to free them. Elias's Tribal mother sacrificed her body, freedom, and Tribe so I could save Darin. I cannot fail her.

Elias is not here. You're alone. Move!

The lock finally springs open, and I make for the next wagon. In the trees just yards away, Afya must be cursing at the delay. The longer I take, the more likely it is that the Martials will catch us.

When I crack the last lock, I croon a signal. *Snick. Snick. Snick.* Darts hurtle through the air. The Martials at the perimeter drop silently, left insensate by the rare southern poison coating the darts. A half dozen Tribes-men approach the soldiers and slit their throats.

I look away, though I still hear the tear of flesh, the rattle of a final breath. I know it must be done. Without Serric steel, Afya's people cannot face the Martials head on, lest their blades break. But there is an efficiency to the killing that freezes my blood. I wonder if I will ever get used to it.

A small form appears out of the shadows, weapon glinting. The intricate tattoos that mark her as a *Zaldara*, the head of her Tribe, are concealed by long, dark sleeves. I hiss at Afya Ara-Nur so she knows where I am.

"Took you long enough." She glances around, black and red braids swinging. "Where in the ten hells is Elias? Can he disappear now too?"

Elias finally told Afya of the Waiting Place, of his death in Kauf Prison, of his resurrection and his agreement with Shaeva. That day, the Tribeswoman cursed him roundly for a fool before finding me. *Forget him now, Laia*, she had said. *It's damned stupid to fall for a once-dead ghost-talker, I don't care how pretty he is.*

"Elias didn't come."

Afya swears in Sadhese and moves toward the wagons. She explains softly to the prisoners that they must follow her men, that they must make no noise.

Shouts and the high twang of a bow echo from the village, fifty yards from where I stand. I leave Afya behind and sprint toward the houses where, in a darkened alley outside the village inn, Afya's fighters dance away from a half dozen Empire soldiers, including the legionnaire in command. Tribal arrows and darts fly, deft counters to the Martials' deadly blades. I dash into the fray, slamming the hilt of my dagger into an aux's temple. I needn't have bothered. The soldiers go down quickly.

Too quickly.

There must be more men nearby—a hidden force. Or a Mask lurking, unseen.

"Laia." I jump at my name. Darin's golden skin is dark with mud to hide his presence. A hood covers the unruly, honey-colored hair that has finally grown in. Looking at him, no one would ever know he'd survived six months in Kauf Prison. But within his mind, my brother battles demons still. It is those demons that have kept him from making Serric steel.

He's here now, I tell myself sternly. *Fighting. Helping. The weapons will come when he's ready.*

"Mamie isn't here," he says, turning when I tap his shoulder, voice haggard with disuse. "I found her foster son, Shan. He said the soldiers took her from her wagon when the caravan stopped for the night."

"She must be in the village," I say. "Get the prisoners out of here. I'll find her."

"The village shouldn't be empty," Darin says. "This doesn't feel right. You go. I'll look for Mamie."

"One of you bleeding needs to find her." Afya appears behind us. "Because I'm not going to do it, and we have to get the prisoners hidden."

"If something goes wrong," I say, "I can use my invisibility to slip away. I'll meet you back at the camp as soon as I can."

My brother raises his eyebrows, considering my words in his quiet way. When he chooses to be, he is as immovable as the mountains—just like our mother was.

"I go where you go, sis. Elias would agree. He knows—"

"If you are so chummy with Elias," I hiss, "then tell him that the next time he commits to helping with a raid, he needs to follow through."

Darin's mouth curves in a brief, crooked smile. Mother's smile. "Laia, I know you're angry at him, but he—"

"Skies save me from the men in my life and all the things they think they know. Get out of here. Afya needs you. The prisoners need you. Go."

Before he protests, I dart into the village. It is no more than a hundred cottages with thatched roofs that sag beneath the snow, and narrow, dim streets. The wind wails through neatly tended gardens, and I nearly trip over a broom abandoned in a lane. The villagers left this place recently, I sense, and with haste.

I tread carefully, wary of what might lurk in the shadows. The stories whispered in taverns and around Tribal campfires haunt me: wraiths tearing out the throats of Mariner sailors. Scholar families found in burned-out encampments in the Free Lands. Wights—tiny winged menaces—destroying wagons and tormenting livestock.

All of it, I'm certain, is the foul handiwork of the creature that called itself Keenan.

The Nightbringer.

I pause to peek through the front window of a darkened cottage. In the stygian night, I can see nothing. As I move to the next house, my guilt circles in the ocean of my mind, scenting my weakness. *You gave the Nightbringer the armlet*, it hisses. *You fell prey to his manipulation. He is a step closer to destroying the Scholars. When he finds the rest of the Star, he'll set the jinn free. Then what, Laia?*

But it could take the Nightbringer years to find the next piece of the Star, I reason to myself. And there might be more than one piece left. There might be dozens.

A flicker of light ahead. I tear my thoughts from the Nightbringer and move toward a cottage along the north edge of the village. Its door stands ajar. A lamp burns within. The door is propped wide enough that I can slip through without disturbing it. Anyone planning an ambush would see nothing.

Once inside, it takes a moment for my vision to adjust. When it does, I stifle a cry. Mamie Rila sits tied to a chair, a gaunt shadow of her former self. Her dark skin hangs loosely on her frame, and her thick, curly hair has been shaved off.

I almost go to her. But some old instinct stops me, crying out from deep within my mind.

A boot thumps behind me. Startled, I whirl, and a floorboard creaks beneath my feet. I catch a telltale flash of liquid silver—*Mask!*—just as a hand locks around my mouth and my arms are wrenched behind my back.

III: Elias

No matter how often I sneak out of the Waiting Place, it never gets easier. As I approach the western tree line, a flash of white nearby causes my stomach to plunge. A spirit. I bite back a curse and hold still. If it spies me lurking so far from where I'm supposed to be, the entire bleeding Forest of Dusk will know what I'm up to. Ghosts, it turns out, love to gossip.

The delay chafes. I'm already late—Laia was expecting me more than an hour ago, and this isn't a raid she'll skip just because I'm not around.

Almost there. I lope through a fresh layer of snow to the border of the Waiting Place, which glimmers ahead. To a layperson, it's invisible. But to me and Shaeva, the glowing wall is as obvious as if it were made of stone. Though I can pass through it easily, it keeps the spirits in and curious humans out. Shaeva has spent months lecturing me about the importance of that wall.

She will be vexed with me. This isn't the first time I've disappeared on her when I'm supposed to be training as Soul Catcher. Though she is a jinn, Shaeva has little skill in dealing with dissembling students. I, on the other hand, spent fourteen years concocting ways to skip out on Blackcliff's Centurions. Getting caught at Blackcliff meant a whipping from my mother, the Commandant. Shaeva usually just glowers at me.

"Perhaps I too should institute whippings." Shaeva's voice cuts through the air like a scim, and I nearly jump out of my skin. "Would you then appear when you are supposed to, Elias, instead of shirking your responsibilities to play hero?"

"Shaeva! I was just . . . ah, are you . . . steaming?" Vapor rises in thick plumes from the jinn woman.

"*Someone*" — she glares at me — "forgot to hang up the washing. I was out of shirts."

And since she is a jinn, her unnaturally high body heat will dry her washed laundry . . . after an hour or two of unpleasant dampness, I'm sure. No wonder she looks like she wants to kick me in the face.

Shaeva tugs at my arm, her ever-present jinn warmth driving away the cold that has seeped into my bones. Moments later, we are miles from the border. My head spins from the magic she uses to move us so swiftly through the Forest.

At the sight of the glowing red jinn grove, I groan. I *hate* this place. The jinn might be locked in the trees, but they still have power within this small space, and they use it to get into my head whenever I enter.

Shaeva rolls her eyes, as if dealing with a particularly irritating younger sibling. The Soul Catcher flicks her hand, and when I pull my arm away, I find I cannot walk more than a few feet. She's put up some sort of ward. She must finally be losing her patience with me if she's resorting to imprisonment.

I try to keep my temper — and fail. "That's a nasty trick."

"And one you could disarm easily if you stayed still long enough for me to teach you how." She nods to the jinn grove, where spirits wind through the trees. "The ghost of a child needs soothing, Elias. Go. Let me see what you have learned these past weeks."

"I shouldn't be here." I give the ward a violent if ineffectual shove. "Laia and Darin and Mamie need me."

Shaeva leans into the hollow of a tree and glances up at the snippets of star and sky visible through the bare branches. "An hour until midnight. The raid must be under way. Laia will be in danger. Darin and Afya too. Enter the grove and help this ghost move on. If you do, I will drop the ward and you can leave. Or your friends can keep waiting."

"You're grumpier than usual," I say. "Did you skip breakfast?"

"Stop stalling."

I mutter a curse and mentally arm myself against the jinn, imagining a barrier around my mind that they cannot penetrate with their evil whispers. With each step into the grove, I sense them watching. Listening.

A moment later, laughter echoes in my head. It is layered—voice upon voice, mockery upon mockery. The jinn.

You cannot help the ghosts, fool mortal. And you cannot help Laia of Serra. She shall die a slow, painful death.

The jinns' malice spears through my carefully constructed defenses. The creatures plumb my darkest thoughts, parading images of a dead, broken Laia before me until I cannot tell where the jinn grove ends and their twisted visions begin.

I close my eyes. *Not real.* I open them to find Helene slain at the base of the nearest tree. Darin lies beside her. Beyond him, Mamie Rila. Shan, my foster brother. I am reminded of the battlefield of death from the First Trial so long ago—and yet this is worse because I thought I left violence and suffering behind me.

I recall Shaeva's lessons. *In the grove, the jinn have the power to control your mind. To exploit your weaknesses.* I try to shake the jinn away, but they hold fast, their whispers snaking into me. At my side, Shaeva stiffens.

Hail, traitor. They slip into formal speech when they speak to the Soul Catcher. *Thy doom is upon thee. The air reeks of it.*

Shaeva's jaw tightens, and immediately I wish for a weapon to shut them up. She has enough on her mind without them taunting her.

But the Soul Catcher simply lifts a hand to the nearest jinn tree. Though I cannot see her deploy the magic of the Waiting Place, she must have, because the jinn fall silent.

"You need to try harder." She turns on me. "The jinn want you to dwell on petty concerns."

"The fates of Laia and Darin and Mamie aren't petty."

"Their lives are nothing against the sweep of time," Shaeva says. "I will not be here forever, Elias. You must learn to pass the ghosts through more swiftly. There are too many." At my mulish expression, she sighs. "Tell me, what do you do when a ghost refuses to leave the Waiting Place until their loved ones die?"

"Ah . . . well . . ."

Shaeva groans, the look on her face reminding me of Helene's expression when I didn't show up to class on time.

"What about when you have hundreds of ghosts screaming to be heard all at once?" Shaeva says. "What do you do with a spirit who did horrific things in life but who feels no remorse? Do you know why there are so few ghosts from the Tribes? Do you know what will happen if you do not move the ghosts fast enough?"

"Now that you mention it," I say, my curiosity piqued, "what *will* happen if—"

"If you do not pass the ghosts through, it will mean your failure as Soul Catcher and the end of the human world as you understand it. Hope to the skies that you never see that day."

She sits down heavily, sinking her head into her hands, and after a moment, I drop beside her, my chest lurching unpleasantly at her distress. This is not like when the Centurions were angry with me. I didn't bleeding care what they thought. But I *want* to do well for Shaeva. We have spent months together, she and I—carrying out the duties of Soul Catcher mostly, but also debating Martial military history, bickering good-naturedly about chores, and sharing notes on hunting and combat. I think of her as a wiser, *much* older sister. I don't want to disappoint her.

"Let go of the human world, Elias. Until you do, you cannot draw upon the magic of the Waiting Place."

"I windwalk all the time." Shaeva has taught me the trick of speeding through the trees in the blink of an eye, though she is faster than I.

"Windwalking is physical magic, simple to master." Shaeva sighs. "When you took your vow, the magic of the Waiting Place entered your blood. *Mauth* entered your blood."

Mauth. I suppress a shudder. The name is still strange on my lips. I did not know that the magic even had a name when it first spoke to me through Shaeva, months ago, demanding my vow as Soul Catcher.

"Mauth is the source of all the world's fey power, Elias. The jinn, the efrits, the ghuls. Even your friend Helene's healing. He is the source of *your* power as Soul Catcher."

He. As if the magic is alive.

"*He* will aid you in passing on the ghosts if you let him. Mauth's true power is here"—the Soul Catcher gently taps my heart, then my temple— "and here. But until you forge a soul-deep bond with the magic, you cannot be a true Soul Catcher."

"Easy for you to say. You're jinn. The magic is part of you. It doesn't come easily to me. Instead it yanks at me if I stray too far from the trees, like I'm a wayward hound. And if I touch Laia, bleeding hells—" The pain is excruciating enough that thinking of it makes me grimace.

See, traitor, how foolish it was to trust this mortal bit of flesh with the souls of the dead?

At the intrusion of her jinn kin, Shaeva slams a shock wave of magic into their grove that is so powerful even I feel it.

"Hundreds of ghosts wait to pass, and more come every day." Sweat rolls down Shaeva's temple, as if she's fighting a battle I cannot see. "I am much disturbed." She speaks softly and glances into the trees behind her. "I fear the Nightbringer works against us, stealthily and with malice. But I cannot fathom his plan, and it worries me."

"Of course he works against us. He wants to set the trapped jinn free."

"No. I sense a dark intent," Shaeva says. "If harm should befall me before your training is complete . . ." She takes a deep breath and collects herself.

"I can do this, Shaeva," I say to her. "I swear it to you. But I told Laia I'd help her tonight. Mamie might be dead. Laia might be dead. I don't know, because I'm not there."

Skies, how to explain it to her? She's been away from humanity for so long that she can't possibly understand. Does she comprehend love? On the days when she teases me about talking in my sleep, or tells strange, funny tales because she knows I ache for Laia, it seems as if she does. But now . . .

"Mamie Rila gave up her life for mine, and by some miracle she still lives," I say. "Don't make me welcome her here. Don't make me welcome Laia."

"Loving them will only hurt you," Shaeva says. "In the end, they will fade. You will endure. Every time you bid farewell to yet another part of your old life, a piece of you will die."

"You think I don't know that?" Every moment stolen with Laia is the in-furiating evidence of that fact. The few kisses we've had, cut short because of

Mauth's oppressive disapproval. The chasm opening between us as the truth of my vow sinks in. Every time I see her she seems further away, as if I peer at her through a spyglass.

"Fool boy." Shaeva's voice is soft with empathy. Her black eyes lose focus, and I feel the ward drop. "I will find the ghost and pass him on. Go. And do not be careless with your life. Full-grown jinn are nearly impossible to kill, except by other jinn. When you join with Mauth, you too will become resilient to attack, and time will cease to affect you. But until then, be wary. If you die again, I cannot bring you back. And"—she kicks at the ground self-consciously—"I've grown used to you."

"I won't die." I grip her shoulder. "And I promise I'll do the dishes for the next month."

She snorts her disbelief, but by then, I am moving, windwalking through the trees so rapidly I can feel the branches cutting my face. A half hour later, I hurtle past Shaeva's and my cottage, through the borders of the Waiting Place, and into the Empire. The moment I'm clear of the trees, storm winds buffet me and my windwalking slows, the magic weakening as I leave the Forest behind.

I feel a pull at my core tugging me back. Mauth, demanding my return. The pull is almost painful, but I grit my teeth and continue on. *Pain is a choice. Succumb to it and fail. Or defy it and triumph.* Keris Veturia's training, drilled into my very bones.

By the time I arrive outside the village where I was to meet Laia, midnight is long past and moonlight pushes meekly through the snow clouds. *Please let the raid have gone smoothly. Please let Mamie be all right.*

But the instant I enter the village, I know something is off. The caravan is empty, the wagon doors creaking in the storm. A thin layer of snow has already settled on the bodies of the soldiers guarding the caravans. Among them, I find no Mask. No Tribal casualties. The village is silent when it should be in an uproar.

Trap.

I know it instantly, as sure as I'd know my own mother's face. Is this Keris's work? Did she learn about Laia's raids?

I pull my hood up, draw on a scarf, and drop into a crouch, observing the tracks in the snow. They are faint—brushed away. But I catch sight of a familiar boot print: Laia's.

These tracks aren't here out of carelessness. I was meant to know that Laia went into the village. And that she didn't come out. Which means the trap wasn't set for her.

It was set for me.

IV: The Blood Shrike

"Curse you!" I keep an iron grip around Laia of Serra, but she resists me with all her strength. She refuses to drop her invisibility, and I feel as if I'm grappling with an angry, camouflaged fish. I curse myself for not knocking her out the moment I grabbed her.

She lands a nasty kick to my ankle before elbowing me in the gut. My hold on her weakens, and she's out of my hands. I lunge toward the sound of her boot scraping the floor, savagely satisfied at the huff of her breath leaving her lungs as I tackle her. Finally, she flickers into being, and before she can play her little disappearing trick again, I twist her hands back and truss her tighter than a festival-day goat. Still panting, I shove her into a chair.

She looks at the other occupant of the cabin—Mamie Rila, bound and barely conscious—and snarls through her gag. She kicks out like a mule, her boot connecting beneath my knee. I grimace at the pain. *Don't backhand her, Shrike.*

Even as she fights, a fey part of my mind trills at the life within her. She has healed. She is strong. The fact should irk me.

But the magic I used on Laia binds us together, a tie that runs deeper than I'd like. I feel relief at her vigor, as if I'd learned that my little sister Livia is healthy.

Which she won't be for much longer, if this plan doesn't work. Fear lances through me, followed by a harsh stab of memory. The throne room. Emperor Marcus. My mother's throat: cut. My sister Hannah's throat: cut. My father's throat: cut. All because of me.

I will not see Livia die too. I *need* to carry out Marcus's orders and bring down Commandant Keris Veturia. If I don't return to Antium from this mission with something I can use against her, Marcus will take his rage out on his empress—Livia. He has done so before.

But the Commandant appears unassailable. The low-class Plebeians and Mercator traders support her because she quelled the Scholar revolution. The most powerful families in the Empire, the Illustrians, fear her and Gens Veturia. She's too wily to allow an assassin close, and even if I did take her out, her allies would rise up in revolt.

Which means I must first weaken her status among the Gens. I must show them that she is still human.

And to do that, I need Elias Veturius. The son who is supposed to be dead, who Keris *claimed* was dead, but who is, I recently learned, very much alive. Presenting him as evidence of Keris's failure is the first step toward convincing her allies that she's not as strong as she appears.

"The more you fight me," I say to Laia, "the tighter your bonds will get." I yank on the ropes. When she winces, I feel an unpleasant twinge deep within. A side effect of healing her?

It will destroy you if you're not careful. The Nightbringer's words about my healing magic echo in my mind. Is this what he meant? That the ties to those I healed are unbreakable?

I cannot dwell on it now. Captain Avitas Harper and Captain Dex Atrius enter the cottage we've requisitioned. Harper gives me a nod, but Dex's attention flits to Mamie, his jaw tight.

"Dex," I say. "It's time."

He doesn't look away from Mamie. Unsurprising. Months ago, when we were hunting down Elias, Dex interrogated Mamie and other members of Tribe Saif on my orders. His guilt has plagued him since.

"Atrius!" I snap. Dex's head jerks up. "Get into position."

He shakes himself and disappears. Harper waits patiently for orders, unruffled by Laia's muffled curses and Mamie's moans of pain.

"Check the perimeter," I tell him. "Make sure none of the villagers wandered back." I didn't spend weeks setting up this ambush so a curious Plebe could ruin it.

As Laia of Serra follows Harper's progress out the door, I pull out a dirk and pare my nails. The girl's dark clothes fit her closely, hugging those irritating curves in a way that makes me conscious of every awkwardly jutting bone in my body. I've taken her pack, along with a well-worn dagger I recognize with a jolt. It's Elias's. His grandfather Quin gave it to him as a sixteenth year-fall gift.

And Elias, apparently, gave it to Laia.

She hisses against the gag as her gaze darts between me and Mamie. Her defiance reminds me of Hannah. I wonder briefly if, in another life, the Scholar and I could have been friends.

"If you promise not to scream," I tell her, "I'll take off your gag."

She considers before nodding once. The moment I pull off the gag, she lashes out.

"What have you done to her?" Her seat thumps as she strains toward a now unconscious Mamie Rila. "She needs medicine. What kind of monster—"

The crack that echoes through the cottage when I slap her into silence surprises even me. As does the nausea that almost doubles me over. *What the skies?* I grab the table for support but straighten before Laia can see.

She juts out her chin as she lifts her head. Blood drips from her nose. Surprise fills those golden, catlike eyes, followed by a healthy dose of fear. *About time.*

"Watch your tone." I keep my voice low and flat. "Or the gag goes back in."

"What do you want from me?"

"Just your company."

Her eyes narrow, and she finally notices the manacles attached to a chair in the corner.

"I'm working alone," she says. "Do with me what you wish."

"You're a gnat." I go back to paring my nails, stifling a smile when I see how the words irritate her. "At best, a mosquito. Don't presume to tell me what to do. The only reason you haven't been crushed by the Empire is that I haven't allowed it."

Lies, of course. She's raided six caravans in two months, freeing hundreds of prisoners in the process. Skies know how long she'd have continued if I hadn't received the note.

It arrived two weeks ago. I didn't recognize the handwriting, and whoever— or whatever—delivered it avoided detection by an entire bleeding garrison of Masks.

THE RAIDS. IT IS THE GIRL.

I've kept the raids quiet. We already have trouble with the Tribes, who are enraged at the Martial legions deployed in their desert. In the west, the Karkaun Barbarians have conquered the Wildmen clans and now heckle our outposts near Tiborum. Meanwhile, a Karkaun warlock by the name of Grímarr has rallied his clans, and they lurk in the south, raiding our port cities.

Marcus has only recently secured the loyalty of the Illustrian Gens. If they learn that a Scholar rebel roams the countryside wreaking havoc, they'll grow restive. If they learn it's the same girl Marcus was supposed to have killed in the Fourth Trial, they'll smell blood in the water.

Another Illustrian coup is the last thing I need. Especially now that Livia's fate is tied to Marcus's.

Once I got the note, connecting Laia to the raids was easy enough. The reports out of Kauf Prison matched the reports about the raids. *A girl who appears one moment, disappears the next. A Scholar risen from the dead, wreaking vengeance on the Empire.*

It was not a ghost, but a girl. A girl and one uniquely talented accomplice.

We stare at each other, she and I. Laia of Serra is all passion. Feeling. Everything she thinks is written on her face. I wonder if she understands what duty even is.

"If I'm a gnat," she says, "then why—" Understanding flashes across her face. "You're not here for me. But if you're using me as bait—"

"Then it will work effectively. I know my quarry well, Laia of Serra. He'll be here in less than a quarter hour. If I'm wrong . . ." I twirl my dirk on my fingertip. Laia pales.

"He died." She seems to believe her own lie. "In Kauf Prison. He's not coming."

"Oh, he'll come." Skies, I hate her as I say it. He will come for her. He always will. As he never will for me.

I banish the thought—*weakness, Shrike*—and kneel in front of her, knife in hand, running it along the *K* the Commandant carved into her. The scar is old now. She might see it as a flaw against that glowing skin. But it makes her look stronger. Resilient. And I hate her for that too.

But not for much longer. For I cannot let Laia of Serra walk free. Not when bringing Marcus her head could buy his favor—and thus more life for my little sister.

I think briefly of the Cook and her interest in Laia. The Commandant's former slave will be angry when she learns the girl is dead. But the old woman disappeared months ago. She might be dead herself.

Laia must see murder in my eyes, because her face goes ashen and she shies back. Nausea lashes through me again. My vision flashes white, and I lean into the wooden armrest of her chair, the knife tipping forward, into the skin over her heart—

"Enough, Helene."

His voice is as harsh as one of the Commandant's lashes. He's come in through the back door, as I suspected he would. *Helene.* Of course he'd use my name.

I think of my father. *You are all that holds back the darkness.* I think of Livia, covering up the bruises on her throat with layer upon layer of powder so the court does not think her weak. I turn.

"Elias Veturius." My blood goes cold when I see that, despite the fact that I set the ambush, he has managed to surprise me. For instead of coming alone, Elias has taken Dex prisoner, binding his arms and holding a knife to his throat. Dex's masked face is frozen in a grimace of rage. *Dex, you idiot.* I glare at him in silent rebuke. I wonder if he even tried to fight back.

"Kill Dex if you wish," I say. "If he was fool enough to get caught, I won't miss him."

The torchlight reflects briefly in Elias's face. He looks at Mamie—at her broken body and sagging form—and his eyes sharpen in rage. My throat goes dry at the depth of his emotion as he shifts his attention back to me. I see a hundred thoughts written in the set of his jaw, in his shoulders, in the way he holds his weapon. I know his language—I've spoken it since the age of six. *Stand firm, Shrike.*

"Dex is your ally," he says. "You're short on those these days, I hear. I think you'll miss him very much. Release Laia."

I am reminded of the Third Trial. Of Demetrius's death by his hand. Leander's. Elias has changed. There's a darkness to him, one that wasn't there before.

You and me both, old friend.

I haul Laia up from the chair and slam her against the wall, putting my knife to her throat. This time, I am prepared for the wave of sick, and I grit my teeth as it washes over me.

"The difference between us, Veturius," I say, "is that I don't care if my *ally* dies. Drop your weapons. You'll see manacles in the corner. Put them on. Sit down. Shut up. If you do, Mamie lives and I agree not to pursue your band of caravan-raiding criminals or the prisoners they freed. Refuse, and I will hunt them down and kill them myself."

"I—I thought you were decent," Laia whispers. "Not good but . . ." She glances down at my blade and then at Mamie. "But not this."

That's because you're a fool. Elias wavers, and I dig the knife in deeper.

The door opens behind me. Harper, daggers drawn, brings a wave of cold with him. Elias ignores him, his attention fixed on me.

"Let Laia go too," he says. "And you have a deal."

"Elias," Laia gasps. "No—the Waiting—" I hiss at her, and she falls silent. I don't have time for this. The longer I waver, the more likely Elias is to think of a way to escape. I made sure he'd know Laia entered the village; I should have expected him to catch Dex. *You idiot, Shrike. You underestimated him.*

Laia tries to speak, but I dig my blade into her throat, purposefully drawing blood. She trembles, her breaths shallow. My head pounds. The pain stokes my rage, and the part of me born from the blood of my dead parents roars, claws unsheathed.

"I know her song, Veturius," I say. Dex and Avitas won't understand my meaning. But Elias will. "I can stay here all night. All day. As long as it takes. I can make her hurt."

And heal her. I do not say it, but he sees my vicious intent. *And hurt her again, and heal her. Until you are driven mad by it.*

"Helene." Elias's rage fades, replaced by surprise. Disappointment. But he has no right to be disappointed in me. "You won't kill us."

He doesn't sound quite sure. *You used to know me,* I think. *But you don't know me anymore. I don't know me anymore.*

"There are worse things than death," I say. "Shall we learn about them together?"

His temper rises. *Tread carefully, Blood Shrike.* The Mask still lives within Elias Veturius, beneath whatever else he's become. I can push him. But I can only push him so far.

"I'll release Mamie." I offer the carrot before I brandish the stick. "A gesture of good faith. Avitas will leave her someplace your Tribal friends will find her."

It is only when Elias looks at Harper that I remember he does not know Avitas is his half brother. I consider whether the knowledge can be used against Elias but decide to hold my tongue. The secret is Harper's, not mine. I nod to him, and my second carries Mamie from the cabin.

"Let Laia go too," Elias says. "And I'll do as you ask."

"She comes with us," I say. "I know your tricks, Veturius. They won't work. You can't win this if you want her to live. Drop your weapons. Get those manacles on. I won't ask again."

Elias shoves Dex away, cutting his bonds as he does so, and then levels a punch that drops him to his knees. Dex doesn't hit back. *Fool!*

"That's for interrogating my family," Elias says. "Don't think I didn't know about it."

"Bring the horses round," I bark at Dex. He rises, dignified and straight-backed, as if there isn't blood drenching his armor. After he leaves the cottage, Elias drops his scims.

"You will let Laia down," he says. "You will not gag me. And you'll keep your bleeding distance, *Blood Shrike*."

It shouldn't hurt, him calling me by my title. After all, I am not Helene Aquilla anymore.

But when I saw him last, I was still Helene. Minutes ago, when he first saw me, he said my name.

I drop Laia, and she takes great gulps of air, color returning to her face. My hand is wet—a trickle of blood from her neck. A droplet, really. Nothing compared to the torrents that poured out of my mother, my sister, my father, as they died.

You are all that holds back the darkness.

I say the words in my mind. I remind myself why I am here. And whatever little feeling was left in me, I set to flame.

V: Laia

"Check Veturius," the Blood Shrike says to Avitas Harper when he returns without Mamie. "Make sure those manacles are secure."

The Shrike drags me to the door of the cabin, as far from Elias as she can get. The three of us in this room together feels strange and full of portent. But that feeling fades when the Shrike pushes her blade deeper into my skin.

We need to get the hells out of here. I would rather not wait around to see if the Shrike will make good on her threat to torture me. By now, Afya and Darin must be out of their minds with worry.

Dex appears at the back door. "The horses are gone, Shrike."

Enraged, the Blood Shrike looks at Elias, who shrugs. "You didn't think I'd just leave them be, did you?"

"Go find more," the Shrike says to Dex. "And bring a ghost wagon round. Harper, how long could it possibly take to make sure those bleeding chains are intact?"

Experimentally, I test my bonds, but the Shrike feels it and twists my arms savagely.

Elias sits sprawled in his chair with practiced ease, observing his former best friend. I'm not fooled by the boredom on his face. His gold-brown skin grows paler with every moment that passes, until he looks ill. The Waiting Place pulls at him—and its pull grows more insistent. I've seen it before. If he stays away too long, he will suffer.

"You're using me to get to my mother," Elias says. "She'll see it coming a mile away."

"Don't make me rethink that gag." The Shrike flushes beneath her mask. "Harper, go with Dex. I want that wagon *now*."

"What do you think Keris Veturia is doing right now?" Elias says as Harper disappears.

"You don't even live in the bleeding Empire anymore." The Blood Shrike tightens her hold on me. "So shut it."

"I don't have to live in the Empire to know how the Commandant thinks. You want her dead, right? She must know it. Which means she also knows that if you kill her, you risk civil war with her allies. So while you're out here wasting your time with me, she's back in the capital, plotting skies know what."

The Shrike frowns. She has listened to Elias's advice—and offered her own to him—her whole life. *What if he's right?* I can practically hear her thinking it. Elias catches my eye—he's looking for an opening just like I am.

"Find my grandfather," Elias says. "If you want to take her down, you need to understand how she thinks. Quin knows Keris better than anyone else alive."

"Quin's left the Empire," the Shrike says.

"If my grandfather has left the Empire," Elias says, "then cats can fly. Wherever Keris is, he'll be close by, waiting for her to make a mistake. He's not stupid enough to use one of his own estates. And he won't be alone. He has many men still loyal—"

"It doesn't matter." The Blood Shrike waves away Elias's advice. "Keris and that creature she keeps around—"

My stomach plunges. *The Nightbringer. She means the Nightbringer.*

"—are up to something," the Shrike says. "I need to destroy her before she destroys the Empire. I spent weeks hunting Quin Veturius. I don't have the time to do it again."

Elias shifts in his seat—he is preparing to make his move. The Shrike's loosened her grip on me, and I squeeze my hands together, bending, pulling, doing anything I can to wriggle out of the binding without giving it away. My slick palms grease the rope. It is not enough.

"You want to destroy her." Elias's manacles clink. Something flashes near his hands. Lock picks? How the hells did he sneak them past Avitas? "Just remember that she'll do things you're not willing to. She will find your weakness and exploit it. It's what she does best."

When Elias shifts his arm, the Shrike whips her head toward him, eyes narrowing. At that moment, Harper enters.

"Wagon's ready, Shrike," he says.

"Take her." She shoves me at Avitas. "Keep a knife at her throat." Harper pulls me close, and I ease back from his blade. If I could just distract the Shrike and Avitas for a moment, enough for Elias to attack . . .

I use a trick Elias taught me when we traveled together. I kick Avitas in the soft place between his foot and leg and then drop like a hammer from a roof.

Avitas curses, the Shrike turns, and Elias shoots from his seat, free of his manacles. He dives for his blades in less time than it takes to blink. A knife whooshes through the air above my head, and Harper ducks, dragging me with him. The Blood Shrike roars, but Elias is on her, using his bulk to bowl her over. He's got her pinned, a knife at her throat, but something glimmers at her wrist. She has a blade. Skies, she's going to stab him.

"Elias!" I shout a warning when suddenly, his body goes rigid.

A gasp bursts from his throat. The knife falls from his hand, and in a second, the Shrike has wriggled out from beneath him, lips curled in a sneer.

"Laia." Elias's eyes communicate his rage. His helplessness. And then darkness fills the room. I see the swing of long dark hair, a flash of brown skin. Depthless black eyes bore into me. Shaeva.

Then she—and Elias—disappear. The earth rumbles beneath us and the wind outside rises, sounding, for a second, like the wailing of ghosts.

The Blood Shrike leaps toward where Elias stood. She finds nothing, and a moment later, her hand is around my throat, her knifepoint at my heart. She shoves me back into a seat.

"Who the *hells*," she whispers, "was that woman?"

The door bursts open and Dex enters, scim drawn. Before he can speak, the Shrike is bellowing at him.

"Scour the village! Veturius disappeared like a bleeding wraith!"

"He's not in the village," I say. "She took him."

"*Who* took him?" I cannot speak—the knife is too close—but she doesn't let me move a muscle. "Tell me!"

"Ease up on the knife, Shrike," Avitas says. The dark-haired Mask scans the room carefully, as if Elias might reappear at any moment. "And perhaps she will."

The Blood Shrike pulls the knife back by no more than a hair. Her hand is steady, but her face beneath her mask is flushed. "Talk or die."

My words stumble over each other as I try to explain—as vaguely as I can—who Shaeva is and what Elias has become. Even as I speak the words, I realize how far-fetched they sound. The Blood Shrike says nothing, but incredulity is written in every line of her body.

When I finish, she stands, her knife loose in her hand, looking out into the night. Only a few hours until dawn. "Can you get Elias back here?" she asks quietly.

I shake my head, and she kneels before me. Her face is suddenly serene, her body relaxed. When I meet her eyes, they are distant, as if her thoughts have moved on from me.

"If the Emperor knew you lived, he'd want to interrogate you himself," she says. "Unless you're a fool, you'll agree that death would be preferable. I will make it swift."

Oh skies. My feet are free, but my hands are bound. I could wriggle my right hand free if I pulled hard enough . . .

Avitas sheaths his scim and bends behind me. I feel the brush of warm skin against my wrists and wait for them to tighten as he rebinds me.

But they do not.

Instead, the rope binding my wrists falls away. Harper breathes one word, so softly that I question whether I truly heard it.

"Go."

I cannot move. I meet the Blood Shrike's stare head on. *I will look death in the eyes.* Grief ripples across her silver features. She seems older, suddenly, than her twenty years, with the implacability of a five-body blade. All the weakness has been hammered out of her. She has seen too much blood. Too much death.

I remember when Elias told me what Marcus did to the Shrike's family. He learned it from the ghost of Hannah Aquilla, who plagued him for months before finally moving on.

As I'd listened to what happened, I'd felt sicker and sicker. I remembered another dark morning years ago. I woke up with a start that day, scared by the low, choking cries echoing through the house. I thought Pop must have brought home an animal. Some wounded creature, dying slowly and in agony.

But when I entered the main room of the house, there was Nan, rocking back and forth, Pop frantically shushing her wails, for no one could hear her mourn her daughter—my mother. No one could know. The Empire wished to crush all that the Lioness was, all that she stood for. That meant any and all connected to her.

We all went to market that day to sell Nan's jams—Pop, Darin, Nan, and I. Nan shed no tears. I only ever heard her in the dead of night, her quiet keening breaking me more than any scream could.

The Blood Shrike was also denied the right to mourn publicly. How could she? She is second-in-command of the Empire, and her family was condemned because she failed to carry out the Emperor's orders.

"I'm sorry," I whisper as she raises her dagger. I whip my fingers out—not to stop her blade, but to take her free hand. She stiffens in shock. The skin of her palm is cool, calloused. Less than a second has passed, but her surprise has kindled into anger.

The cruelest anger comes from the deepest pain. Nan used to say that. *Speak, Laia.*

"My parents were murdered too," I say. "My sister. In Kauf. I was younger, and I did not witness it. I could never mourn them. I wasn't allowed to. And no one ever spoke of them. But I think of them every day. I am sorry for you and what you lost. Truly."

For a moment, I see the girl who healed me. The girl who let Elias and me escape from Blackcliff. The girl who told me how to get into Kauf Prison.

And before that girl fades—as I know she will—I draw on my own power and disappear, rolling out of the chair, racing past Avitas and toward the door. Two steps and the Shrike is shouting, three and her dagger slices through the air after me, and then her scim.

Too late. By the time the scim drops, I am through the open door, past an unsuspecting Dex, and running for all I am worth, nothing but another shadow in the night.

VI: Elias

Shaeva plunges me into a darkness so complete that I wonder if I'm in one of the hells. She holds fast to me, though I cannot see her. We are not windwalking—it feels like we are not moving at all. And yet her body thrums with the tang of magic, and when it spills over to me, my skin burns as if I've been set alight.

Gradually, my vision brightens until I find myself hovering over an ocean. The sky above rages, thick with sallow yellow clouds. I feel Shaeva beside me, but I cannot tear my gaze from the water below, which seethes with huge forms rippling just below the surface. Evil emanates from those forms, a malevolence that I feel in the deepest parts of my soul. Terror fills me like I've never felt in all my life, not even as a child in Blackcliff.

Then the fear lifts, replaced by the weight of an ancient gaze. A voice speaks in my mind:

Night draws close, Elias Veturius. Beware.

The voice is so soft that I must strain to hear every syllable. But before I can make sense of it, the ocean is gone, the dark returns, and the voice and images fade from my memory.

»«»«

The knotted wood joists above my head and feather pillow below it tell me instantly where I am when I wake. Shaeva's cabin—my home. A log pops in the fire, and the scent of spiced korma fills the air. For a long moment, I relax into my bunk, secure in the peace one feels only when they are safe and warm beneath their own roof.

Laia! When I remember what happened, I sit up too quickly; my head aches something vicious. *Bleeding hells.*

I need to get back to the village—to Laia. I drag myself to my feet, find my scims tucked haphazardly beneath my bed, and stagger to the cottage door. Outside, a freezing wind tears through the clearing, stirring the packed snow into wild, waist-high tornadoes. The ghosts wail and cluster at the sight of me, their anguish palpable.

"Hello, little one." One of the shades drifts close, so faded I get only the barest impression of her face. "Have you seen my lovey?"

I know her. The Wisp. One of the first ghosts I met here. My voice when I speak is a rusty growl.

"I—I'm sorry—"

"Elias." Shaeva appears at the edge of the clearing, a basket of winter herbs on her wrist. The Wisp, ever shy, vanishes. "You shouldn't be up and about."

"What's wrong with me?" I demand of the Soul Catcher. "What happened?"

"You've been unconscious for a day." Shaeva ignores my obvious ire. "I reeled us here instead of windwalking. It is swifter, but more detrimental to a mortal body."

"Laia—Mamie—"

"Stop, Elias." Shaeva sits at the base of a yew tree, settling into its exposed roots and taking a deep breath. The tree almost appears to curve around her, fitting itself to her body. She pulls a handful of greens from the basket and tears the leaves violently from their stems. "You nearly got yourself killed. Is that not enough?"

"You shouldn't have grabbed me like that." I cannot hold back my anger, and she glares at me, her own temper rising. "I would have been fine. I need to get back to that village."

"You imbecile!" She casts her basket down. "The Blood Shrike had a dagger in her gauntlet. It was an inch away from your vitals. Mauth tried to pull you back, but you did not heed him. If I had not arrived, I would be shouting at your ghost right now." Her scowl is fierce. "I let you aid your friends despite my misgivings. And you squandered it."

"You can't expect me to remain in the Waiting Place and never have any human contact," I say. "I'll go mad. And Laia—I care for her, Shaeva. I can't just—"

"Ah, Elias." She rises and reaches for my hands. Though my skin is numb from the cold, I take no comfort from her warmth. She sighs, and her voice is heavy with shame. "Do you think I have never loved? I did. Once. He was beautiful. Brilliant. That love blinded me to my duties, sacred though they were. The world suffered for my love. It suffers still." She draws breath raggedly, and around us, the wails of the ghosts intensify, as if in response to her distress.

"I understand your pain. Truly. But for us, Elias, duty must reign over all else: desire, sadness, loneliness. Love cannot live here. You chose the Waiting Place, and the Waiting Place chose you. Now you must give yourself to it wholly, body and soul."

Body and soul. A chill runs up my spine as I recall something Cain said to me long ago—that one day, I'd have a chance at freedom. *True freedom—of body and of soul.* Did he envision this, I wonder? Did he set me on the path to freedom knowing that one day it would be wrenched from me? Was this always my destiny?

"I need some time. A day," I say. If I'm to be chained to this place for eternity, then I at least owe Laia and Mamie a goodbye—though I've no idea what I'll say.

Shaeva pauses. "I'll give you a few hours," she finally says. "After that, no more distractions. You have much to learn, Elias. And I do not know how much time I have to teach you. The moment you took the vow to become Soul Catcher, my power began to fade."

"I know." I nudge her with my boot, smiling in an attempt to dispel the tension between us. "Every time you don't feel like doing the dishes, you remind me." I mimic her sober voice. *"Elias, my power fades . . . so make sure you sweep the front steps, and bring in firewood, and—"*

She chuckles. "As if you even know how to swee—sweep—"

Her smile vanishes. Frantic lines form around her mouth, and her hands clench and unclench, like she's desperate for weapons she doesn't possess.

The snow around us slows its swirling. The wind goes soft, as if cowed, and then ceases completely. The shadows in the trees deepen, so black they seem like a portal to another world.

"Shaeva? What the hells is happening?"

The Soul Catcher shudders, riven with dread. "Go inside the cabin, Elias."

"Whatever's going on, we face it tog—"

She digs her fingers into my shoulders. "There is so much you do not yet know, and if you fail, the world will fall. This is but the beginning. Remember: Sleep in the cottage. They cannot hurt you there. And seek the Tribes, Elias. Long have they been my allies. Ask about the stories of the dea—" Her voice chokes off as her back arches.

"Bleeding hells! Shaeva—"

"*The moon sets on the archer and the shield maiden!*" Her voice changes, multiplies. It is a child's voice and an old woman's layered over her own, as if all the versions that Shaeva was and ever could be are speaking at once.

"*The executioner has arisen. The traitor walks free. Beware! The Reaper approaches, flames in his wake, and he shall set this world alight. And so shall the great wrong be set right.*"

She flings her hand up to the sky, to constellations hidden behind thick snow clouds.

"Shaeva." I shake her shoulders insistently. *Get her inside!* The cottage always soothes her. It's her only sanctuary in this skies-forsaken place. But when I try to pick her up, she throws me off. "Shaeva, don't be so damned stubborn—"

"Remember all that I say before the end," she whispers. "That is why he has come. That is what he wants from me. Swear it."

"I—I swear—"

She lifts her hands to my face. For once, her fingers are cold. "Soon you will learn the cost of your vow, my brother. I hope you do not think too ill of me."

She falls to her knees, knocking over the basket of herbs. The green and yellow leaves spill out, the bright color incongruous against the ashen snow. The clearing is quiet. Even the ghosts have gone silent.

That can't be right. The thickest concentration of ghosts is always around the cabin. But the spirits are gone. Every last one.

In the Forest to the west, where moments ago the shadows were only shadows, something stirs. The darkness moves, twisting as if in agony, until it writhes into a hooded figure cloaked in robes of purest night. From beneath the cowl, two tiny suns stare out at me.

I have never seen him before. I have only heard him described. But I know him. Bleeding, burning hells, I know him.

The Nightbringer.

VII: The Blood Shrike

A row of severed heads greets Dex, Avitas, and me as we pass beneath Antium's iron-studded main gate. Scholars, mostly, but I spot Martials too. The streets are lined with dirty piles of slush, and a blanket of clouds lies thick over the city, depositing more snow.

I ride past the grisly display, and Harper follows, but Dex stares at the heads, hands tight on his reins. His silence is unnerving. The interrogation of Tribe Saif still haunts him.

"Get to the barracks, Dex," I say. "I want reports on all active missions on my desk by midnight." My attention falls on two women loitering outside a nearby guard post. Courtesans. "And go distract yourself after. Get your mind off the raid."

"I do not frequent brothels," Dex says quietly as he follows my gaze to the women. "Even if I did, it's not that easy for me, Shrike. And you know it."

I shoot Avitas Harper a glare. *Go away*. When he's out of earshot I turn to Dex. "Madam Heera's in Mandias Square. The House of Forgetting. Heera is discreet. She treats her women—and men—well." At Dex's hesitation, I lose my patience. "You're letting your guilt eat at you, and it cost us in the village," I say. That raid was meant to get us something to use against Keris. We failed. Marcus won't be pleased. And it's my sister who will suffer that displeasure.

"When I am dispirited," I go on, "I visit Heera's. It helps. Go or don't. Doesn't matter to me. But stop being woeful and useless. I don't have the patience for it."

Dex leaves, and Harper nudges his horse over. "You frequent Heera's?" There's something more than mere curiosity in his voice.

"Reading lips again?"

"Only yours, Shrike." Harper's green eyes drop to my mouth so quickly I almost miss it. "Forgive my question. I assumed you had volunteers to meet your . . . needs. The previous Shrike's second-in-command did sometimes procure courtesans for him, if you need me to—"

My cheeks grow warm at the image *that* conveys. "Stop talking, Harper," I say. "While you're behind."

We gallop ahead toward the palace, its pearlescent sheen a bare-faced lie that hides the oppressiveness within. The outer gates are bustling at this hour, Illustrian courtiers and Mercator hangers-on all jockeying to get into the throne room to obtain the Emperor's favor.

"An attack on Marinn would go a long way in—"

"—fleet is already engaged—"

"—Veturia will crush them—"

I suppress a sigh at the never-ending machinations of the Paters. It drove my father to distraction, the way they schemed. When they see me, they fall silent. I take grim pleasure in their discomfort.

Harper and I cut through the courtiers quickly. The men in their long, fur-edged cloaks back away from the slush kicked up by my mount. The women, sparkling in court finery, watch surreptitiously. No one meets my gaze.

Swine. Not one of them offered a word of remembrance in honor of my family after Marcus executed them. Not even privately.

My mother, father, and sister died as traitors, and nothing can change that. Marcus wanted me to feel shame, but I do not. My father gave his life trying to save the Empire, and one day that fact will be known. But now it is as if my family never existed. As if their lives were mere hallucinations.

The only people who have dared to mention my parents to me are Livia, a Scholar hag I haven't seen in weeks, and a Scholar girl whose head should be in a sack at my waist right now.

I hear the buzz of voices in the throne room long before I see its double doors. As I enter, every soldier salutes. They've learned, by now, what happens to those who don't.

Marcus sits rigid on his throne, big hands fisted on the armrests, masked face emotionless. His blood-red cape pools onto the floor, reflecting luridly off his silver-and-copper armor. The weapons at his side are razor-sharp, to the chagrin of the older Illustrian Paters, who appear soft beside their emperor.

The Commandant is not here. But Livia is, her face as impassive as a Mask's as she perches on her own throne beside Marcus. I hate that she is forced to sit here, but still, relief rushes through me; at least she's alive. She is resplendent in a lavender gown heavy with gold embroidery.

My sister's back is straight, her face powdered to hide the bruise on her cheek. Her ladies-in-waiting—yellow-eyed cousins of Marcus—cluster a few feet away. They are Plebeians, plucked from their village by my sister as a gesture of goodwill toward Marcus and his family. And I suspect that, like me, they find court insufferable.

Marcus fixes his attention on me, despite the obviously distressed Mariner ambassador standing before him. As I approach, the Emperor's shoulders twitch.

"You don't need to warn me, damn you," he mutters. The ambassador furrows his brow, and I realize that Marcus isn't responding to the man. He's talking to himself. At the Mariner's confusion, the Emperor beckons him near.

"Tell your doddering king that he needn't cower," Marcus says. "The Empire is not interested in a war with Marinn. If he needs a token of our goodwill, have him provide me a list of his enemies. I'll send him their heads as a gift." The ambassador pales and backs away, and Marcus gestures me forward.

I do not acknowledge Livia. Let the court think we are not close. She has enough to deal with without half of these vultures trying to take advantage of her relationship with me.

"Emperor." I kneel and bow my head. Though I've been doing so for months now, it hasn't gotten any easier. Beside me, Harper does the same.

"Clear the room," Marcus growls. When the Illustrians do not move quickly enough, he flings a dagger at the nearest one.

Guards usher the Illustrians away, and the lot of them are unable to get out fast enough. Marcus smiles at the sight, his harsh chuckle jarring against the fear that pervades the room.

Livia rises and gathers the folds of her dress gracefully. *Faster, sister*, I think to myself. *Get out of here.* But before she steps down from her throne, Marcus grabs her wrist. "You stay." He forces her into her seat. My sister's gaze meets mine for an infinitesimal moment. I sense no fear, only warning. Avitas steps back, a silent witness.

Marcus pulls a roll of parchment from his armor and flings it at me. The crest flashes in the air as it flies to my hand, and I recognize the *K* with crossed swords beneath it. The Commandant's seal.

"Go on," he says. "Read it." Beside him, Livia watches, wariness in her body, though she's learned to train it from her face.

> My Lord Emperor,
>
> The Karkaun warlock Grimarr has intensified the raids
> on Navium. We need more men. The Paters of Navium are in

agreement; their seals are below. A half legion should be sufficient.

Duty first, unto death,

General Keris Veturia

"She has an entire legion down there," I say. "She should be able to put down a paltry Barbarian rebellion with five thousand men."

"And yet"—Marcus yanks another parchment from within his armor, and another, flinging them all at me—"from Paters Equitius, Tatius, Argus, Modius, Vissellius—the list goes on," he says. "All requesting aid. Their proxies here in Antium have been hounding me since Keris's message came in. Three hundred civilians are dead, and those Barbarian dogs have a fleet approaching the port. Whoever this Grímarr is, he's trying to take the damn city."

"But surely Keris can—"

"She's *up* to something, you dim bitch." Marcus's roar echoes through the room, and in two steps, his face is inches from mine. Harper tenses behind me, and Livia half rises from her throne. I give my head the slightest shake. *I can handle him, little sister.*

Marcus stabs his fingers into my skull. "Get it through your thick head. If you'd taken care of her like I ordered, this wouldn't be happening. *Shut it, damn you.*"

He whirls, but Livia hasn't spoken. His gaze is fixed on the middle distance between himself and my sister, and I recall, uneasily, Livia's suspicion that Marcus sees the ghost of his twin, Zak, murdered months ago during the Trials.

Before I can think on it, Marcus steps so close my mask ripples. His eyes look as though they might pop from his head.

"You didn't ask for assassination, my lord." I ease away very slowly. "You asked for destruction, and destruction takes time."

"I asked"—he leashes his rage, his sudden calm more chilling than his anger—"for competence. You've had three months. She should have worms crawling out of her eye sockets by now. Instead, she's stronger than ever, while the Empire grows weaker. So tell me, Blood Shrike: What are you going to do about her?"

"I have information." I put every bit of conviction I possess into my voice, my body. I am certain. I will bring her down. "Enough to destroy her."

"What information?"

I can't tell him what Elias revealed about Quin. It's not useful enough, and even if it was, Marcus would question me further. If he learns I had Laia and Elias in my grasp and lost them, he'll break my sister in half. "The walls have ears, my lord," I say. "Not all are friendly."

Marcus considers me. Then he turns, drags my sister to her feet, and shoves her into the side of her own throne, wrenching her arm behind her back.

Her stillness is that of a woman who has quickly grown used to violence and who will do what she must to survive it. I clench my hands around my weapons, and Livvy catches my eyes. Her terror—not for herself, but for me—checks my temper. *Remember that the more anger you show, the more he'll make her suffer.*

Even as I force myself to be logical, I hate that I am. I hate myself for not lopping off those hands that have hurt her, not cutting out that tongue that has called her foul names. I hate that I cannot hand her a blade so she can do it herself.

Marcus tilts his head. "Your sister plays oud so well," he says. "She's entertained many of my guests, charmed them even, with the beauty of her musicianship. But I'm sure she can find other ways to entertain them." He leans close to Livia's ear, and her gaze drifts faraway, her mouth hard. "Do you sing, my love? I'm certain you have a beautiful voice." Slowly, deliberately, he draws back one of her fingers. Further, further, further . . . This cannot be borne. I step forward and feel a viselike grip on my arm.

"You'll make it worse," Avitas murmurs in my ear.

Livia's finger cracks. She gasps but makes no other sound.

"That," Marcus says, "is for your failure." He grabs another of Livia's fingers, bending it back so carefully that I know he is taking joy from each second of it. Sweat beads on her forehead, and her face is white as bone.

When her finger finally breaks, she whimpers and bites her lip.

"My brave bird." Marcus smiles at her, and I want to rip his throat out. "You know I like it better when you scream." When he turns back to me, his smile is gone. "And that is a reminder of what's to come if you fail me again."

Marcus flings my sister onto her throne. Her head knocks against the rough stone. She shudders and cradles one hand, but her hatred blazes out at Marcus before she tamps it down, her face composed once more.

"You will go to Navium, Shrike," Marcus says. "You will learn what the Bitch of Blackcliff is planning. You will destroy her, piece by piece. And you will do it quickly. I want her head on a spear by the Grain Moon, and I want the Empire begging for it to happen. Five months. That's enough time even for you, is it not? You will update me through the drums every three days. And"—he glances at Livia—"if I'm not satisfied with your progress, I'll keep breaking your little sister's bones until she's nothing but jagged edges."

VIII: Laia

For hours, I run, cloaking myself from a maddening number of Martial patrols, holding my invisibility until my head throbs and my legs tremble from cold and exhaustion. My mind spins with worry for Elias, for Darin, for Afya. Even if they are safe, what in the skies will we do now that the Empire has caught on to the raids? The Martials will flood the countryside with soldiers. We cannot continue. The risk is too great.

Never mind. Just get to the camp. And hope to the skies that Darin got there too.

At midnight a day after the raid, I finally spot the tall, naked oak that shelters our tent, its branches grousing in the wind. Horses nicker, and a familiar figure paces beneath the tree. *Darin!* I nearly sob in relief. My strength has left me, and I find I cannot call out. I simply drop into visibility.

When I do, darkness flashes across my vision. I see a shadowy room, a hunched figure. A moment later, the vision is gone, and I stumble toward the camp. Darin spies me and runs, pulling me into a hug. Afya bursts from the round fur tent my brother and I use as shelter, anger and relief mingling on her face.

"You're a bleeding idiot, girl!"

"Laia, what happened?"

"Did you find Mamie? Are the prisoners safe? Did Elias—"

Afya holds up a hand. "Mamie's with a healer from Tribe Nur," the *Zaldara* says. "My people will get the prisoners to the Tribal lands. I meant to join them, but . . ."

She glances at Darin, and I understand. She did not wish to leave him alone. She did not know if I'd return. I tell them swiftly of the Blood Shrike's ambush and Elias's disappearance.

"Did you see Elias?" *Please let him be all right.* "Did he come out of the Forest?"

Afya shudders as she looks over her shoulder to the towering wall of trees that marks the western border of the Waiting Place. Darin only shakes his head.

I glower at the trees, wishing I had the power to burn a path through to the jinn's cabin. *Why did you snatch him away, Shaeva? Why do you torment him so?*

"Come inside." Darin tugs me into the tent and tucks a woolen blanket from his sleeping roll around my shoulders. "You'll catch your death."

Afya pulls away the fur covering the hole at the top of the tent and stirs the ashes of our small cook fire until her brown face is lit bronze. Long minutes later, I'm shoveling down the potato-and-squash stew Darin has made. It's overcooked, with so much red pepper in it that I nearly choke—Darin was always hopeless in the kitchen.

"Our raiding days are over," Afya says. "But if you wish to keep fighting the Empire, then come with me. Join Tribe Nur." The Tribeswoman pauses, considering. "Permanently."

My brother and I exchange a glance. Tribespeople only accept new family members through marriage or the adoption of children. To be invited to join a Tribe is no small thing—and by the *Zaldara*, no less.

I reach for Afya's hand, stunned at her generosity, but she waves me off.

"You're practically family anyway," Afya says. "And you know me, girl. I want something in return." She turns to my brother. "Many died to save you, Darin of Serra. The time has come for you to begin forging Serric steel.

I can procure you materials. Skies know the Tribes need as much help as we can get."

My brother flexes his hand as he always does when the phantom pains of his missing fingers plague him. His face goes pale, his lips thin. The demons within awaken.

I want so desperately for Darin to speak, to accept Afya's offer. It might be the only chance we have to continue fighting the Empire. But when I turn to him, he is leaving the tent, muttering about needing air.

"What news from your spies?" I say quickly to Afya, hoping to shift her attention from my brother. "The Martials have not drawn down their forces?"

"They sent another legion into the Tribal desert from Atella's Gap," Afya says. "They've arrested hundreds around Nur on false charges: graft and transporting contraband and skies know what else. Rumor is that they're planning to send the prisoners to Empire cities to be sold as slaves."

"The Tribes are protected," I say. "The treaty with Emperor Taius has held for five centuries."

"Emperor Marcus doesn't care a fig about that treaty." Afya frowns. "That's not the worst of it. In Sadh, a legionnaire killed the *Kehanni* of Tribe Alli."

I cannot hide my slack-jawed shock. *Kehannis* are the keepers of Tribal stories and history, second in rank only to the *Zaldars*. Killing one is a declaration of war.

"Tribe Alli attacked the closest Martial garrison in retaliation," Afya says. "It's what the Empire wanted. The commanding Mask came down like a hammer out of the hells, and now all of Tribe Alli is either dead or in prison. Tribe Siyyad and Tribe Fozi have sworn vengeance on the Empire. Their *Zaldars* ordered attacks on Empire villages—nearly a hundred Martials dead at last count, and not just soldiers."

She gives me a significant look. If the Tribes turn on Martial innocents—children, civilians, the elderly—the Empire will hit back hard.

"They're provoking us." Afya peers out at the sky to gauge the time. "Weakening us. We need that steel, Laia. Think on my offer." She pulls on her cloak to leave, pausing at the flap of the tent. "But think quickly. A strangeness taints the air. I can feel it in my bones. It's not just the Martials I fear."

Afya's warning plagues me all night. Not long before dawn, I give up on sleep and slip outside the tent to where my brother sits watch.

The ghosts of the Waiting Place are restive—angered, no doubt, by our presence. Their anguished cries join with the howling wind out of the north, an icy, hair-raising chorus. I pull my blanket close as I drop next to my brother.

We sit in silence, watching the treetops of the Waiting Place brighten from black to blue as the eastern sky pales. After a time, Darin speaks.

"You want to know why I won't make the weapons."

"You don't have to tell me if you don't wish to."

My brother bunches his fists and opens them, a habit he's had since we were little. The middle and ring fingers of his left, dominant hand are sheared off.

"The materials are easy enough to get," he says. The wails of the ghosts intensify, and he raises his voice.

"It's the making that's complicated. The mixture of the metals, the heat of the flame, how the steel is folded, when the edge is cooled, the way the blade is polished. I remember most of it, but . . ." He squints, as if trying to see something just out of sight. "I've forgotten so much. In Kauf Prison, in the death cells, whole weeks disappeared. I can't remember Father's face anymore, or Nan's." I can barely hear him over the ghosts. "And what if your friend Izzi died for nothing? What if Afya's family died for nothing?

What if Elias swore himself to an eternity as Soul Catcher for nothing? What if I make the steel and it breaks?"

I could tell him that would never happen. But Darin always knows when I'm lying. I take my brother's left hand. It is calloused. Strong.

"There's only one way we can find out, Darin," I say. "But we won't do it until—"

I'm interrupted by a particularly shrill cry from the Forest. The tops of the trees ripple, and the earth groans. Slips of white gather amid the trunks closest to us, their cries peaking.

"What's gotten into them?" Darin winces at the sound. Usually, ignoring the ghosts is easy enough for us. But right now, even I want to clap my hands over my ears.

Which is when I realize that the ghosts' cries are not without meaning. There are words buried beneath their pain. One word, specifically.

Laia. Laia. Laia.

My brother hears it too. He reaches for his scim, but his voice is calm, like it used to be before Kauf. "Remember what Elias said. You can't trust them. They're howling to rattle us."

"Listen to them," I whisper. "*Listen,* Darin."

Your fault, Laia. The ghosts press up against the unseen border of the Waiting Place, their forms blending into one another to form a thick, choking mist. *He's close now.*

"Who?" I move toward the trees, ignoring my brother's protests. I've never entered the Forest without Elias by my side. I do not know if I can. "Do you speak of Elias? Is he all right?"

Death approaches. Because of you.

My dagger is suddenly slippery in my grasp. "Explain yourselves!" I call out.

My feet carry me close enough to the tree line that I can see the path Elias takes when he meets us here. I've never been to Elias and Shaeva's cabin, but he's told me that it sits at the end of this trail, no more than a league beyond the tree line. Our camp is here because of that path—it's the fastest way for Elias to reach us.

"There's something wrong in there," I say to Darin. "Something's happened—"

"It's just ghosts being ghosts, Laia," Darin says. "They want to lure you in and drive you crazy."

"But you and I have never been driven mad by the ghosts, have we?" At that, my brother falls silent. Neither of us knows why the Waiting Place doesn't set us on edge as badly as it does others, like the Tribes or Martials, all of whom give it a wide berth.

"Have you ever seen so many spirits this close to the border, Darin?" The ghosts appear to multiply by the second. "It cannot be just to torment me. Something has happened to Elias. Something is *wrong*." I feel a pull that I cannot explain, a compulsion to move toward the Forest of Dusk.

I hurry to the tent and gather my things. "You don't have to come with me."

Darin's already grabbing his pack. "Where you go, I go," he says. "But that's a big forest. He could be anywhere in there."

"He's not far." That strange instinct pulls at me, a hook in my belly. "I am certain of it." When we reach the trees, I expect resistance. But all I find are ghosts packed so densely that I can barely see through them.

He's here. He's come. Because of you. Because of what you did.

I force myself to ignore the spirits and follow the scanty trail. After a time, the ghosts thin out. When I look back, a palpable fear ripples through their ranks.

Darin and I exchange a glance. *What in the skies would a ghost fear?*

With every step, it is harder to breathe. This is not my first time in the Waiting Place. When Darin and I began the caravan raids a few months ago, Elias windwalked us across from Marinn. The Forest was never welcoming— but nor was it so oppressive.

Fear lashes at me, and I move faster. The trees are smaller here, and through the open patches, a clearing appears, along with the sloped gray roof of a cottage.

Darin grabs my arm, his finger on his lips, and pulls me to the ground. We inch forward with painstaking care. Ahead of us, a woman pleads. Another voice curses in a familiar baritone. Relief pours through me. *Elias.*

The relief is short-lived. The woman's voice goes quiet. The trees shudder violently, and a blur of dark hair and brown skin shoots into view. Shaeva. She locks her fingers into my shoulder and drags me to my feet.

"Your answers lie in Adisa." I wince and try to squirm away, but she holds me with a jinn's strength. "With the Beekeeper. But beware, for he is cloaked in lies and shadow, like you. Find him at your peril, child, for you will lose much, even as you save us all—"

Her body is jerked away, dragged as if by an invisible hand back to the clearing. My heart thunders. *Oh no, skies no—*

"Laia of Serra." I would recognize that ophidian hiss anywhere. It is the sea awakening and the earth shuddering away from itself. "Always appearing where you are not wanted."

Darin cries a warning, but I stride forward into the clearing, caution overcome by rage. Elias's armored form is pinned against a tree, every muscle straining against invisible bonds. He thrashes, an animal in a trap, fists clenched as the whole of his body leans toward the center of the clearing.

Shaeva kneels, black hair brushing the ground, skin waxy. Her face is unlined, but the devastation emanating from her feels ancient.

The Nightbringer, cloaked in darkness, stands above her. The sickle blade in his shadow hand glows, as if made of poison-dipped diamonds. He holds it with light fingers, but his body tenses—he means to use it.

A snarl erupts from my throat. I must do something. I must stop him. But I find I can no longer move. The magic that ensnares Elias has gripped Darin and me too.

"Nightbringer," Shaeva whispers. "Forgive my wrong. I was young, I—"

Her voice fades to a choke. The Nightbringer, silent, brushes his fingers across Shaeva's forehead like a father giving his benediction.

Then he stabs her through the heart.

Shaeva's body seizes once, her arms windmilling, her body jerking up, as if yearning toward the blade, and her mouth opens. I expect a shriek, a scream. Instead, words pour out.

One piece remains, and beware the Reaper at the Gates!
The sparrows will drown, and none will know it.
The past shall burn, and none will slow it.
The Dead will rise, and none can survive.
The Child will be bathed in blood but alive.
The Pearl will crack, the cold will enter.
The Butcher will break, and none will hold her.
The Ghost will fall, her flesh will wither.
By the Grain Moon, the King will have his answer.
By the Grain Moon, the forgotten will find their master.

Shaeva's chin falls. Her lashes flutter like a butterfly's wings, and the blade embedded in her chest drips blood that is as red as mine. Her face goes slack.

Then her body bursts into flame, a flash of blinding fire that fizzles into ashes after only seconds.

"No!" Elias shouts, two streaks of wet on either side of his face.

Do not make the Nightbringer angry, Elias, I want to scream. *Do not get yourself killed.*

A cloud of cinders swirls about the Nightbringer—all that is left of Shaeva. He looks up for the first time at Elias, cocks his head, and advances, dripping sickle in hand.

Distantly, I remember Elias telling me what he learned from the Soul Catcher: that the Star protects those who have touched it. The Nightbringer cannot kill Elias. But he can hurt him, and by the skies, I will not have anyone else I care about hurt.

I hurl myself forward—and bounce back. The Nightbringer ignores me, comfortable in his power. *You will not hurt Elias. You will not.* Some feral darkness rises within me and takes control of my body. I felt it once before, months ago when I fought the Nightbringer outside Kauf Prison. An animal cry explodes from my lips. This time when I push ahead, I get through. Darin is a half step behind, and the Nightbringer flicks his wrist. My brother freezes. But the jinn's magic has no effect on me. I leap between the Nightbringer and Elias, dagger out.

"Don't you dare touch him," I say.

The Nightbringer's sun eyes flare as he looks first at me, then at Elias, reading what is between us. I think of how he betrayed me. *Monster!* How close is he to setting the jinn free? Shaeva's prophecy answered the question moments ago: one piece of the Star left. Does the Nightbringer know where it is? What did Shaeva's death gain him?

But as he observes me, I remember the love that roiled within him, and the hate as well. I remember the vicious war waged between the two and the desolation left in their wake.

The Nightbringer's shoulder ripples as if he is unsettled. Can he read my thoughts? He shifts his attention over my shoulder to Elias.

"Elias Veturius." The jinn leans over me, and I cringe back, pressing against Elias's chest, caught between the two of them: my friend's pounding heart and despair at Shaeva's death, and the Nightbringer's eldritch wrath, fueled by a millennium of cruelty and suffering.

The jinn doesn't bother looking at me before he speaks. "She tasted sweet, boy," he says. "Like dew and a clear dawn."

Behind me, Elias stills and takes a steadying breath. He meets the Night-bringer's fiery stare, his face paling in shock at what he sees there. Then he growls, a sound that seems to rise out of the very earth. Shadows twist up like vines of ink beneath his skin. Every muscle in his shoulders, his chest, his arms strains until he is tearing free of his invisible bonds. He raises his hands, a shock wave bursting from his skin, knocking me on my back.

The Nightbringer sways before righting himself. "Ah," he observes. "The pup has a bite. All the better." I cannot see his face within that hood. But I hear the smile in his voice. He rises up as wind floods the clearing. "There is no joy in destroying a weak foe."

He turns his attention east, toward something far out of sight. Whispers hiss on the air, as if he's communicating with someone. Then the wind snatches at him and, as in the forest outside Kauf, he disappears. But this time, instead of silence to mark his passing, the ghosts who fled to the borders of the Waiting Place pour into the clearing, swarming me.

You, Laia, this is because of you!

Shaeva is dead—

Elias is condemned—

The jinn a breath from victory—

Because of me.

There are so many. The truth of their words breaks over me like a net of chains. I try to stand against it, but I cannot, for the spirits do not lie.

One piece remains. The Nightbringer must find only one more piece of the Star before he is able to free his kin. He is close now. Close enough that I can no longer deny it. Close enough that I must act.

The ghosts tornado around me, so angry I fear they will tear off my skin. But Elias cuts through them and lifts me to my feet.

Darin is beside me, grabbing my pack from where it has fallen, glaring at the ghosts as they ease back into the trees, barely restrained.

Before I even say the words, my brother nods. He heard what Shaeva said. He knows what we must do.

"We're going to Adisa." I say it anyway. "To stop him. To finish this."

IX: Elias

The full burden of the Waiting Place descends like a boulder dropping onto my back. The Forest is part of me, and I can feel the borders, the ghosts, the trees. It's as if a living map of the place has been imprinted on my mind.

Shaeva's absence is at the heart of that burden. I gaze at the fallen basket of herbs that she'll never add to the korma that she'll never eat in the house she'll never step foot in again.

"Elias—the ghosts—" Laia draws close. The usually mournful spirits have transformed into violent shades. I need Mauth's magic to silence them. I need to bond with him, the way Shaeva wanted me to.

But when I grasp at Mauth with my will, I feel only a trace of the magic before it fades.

"Elias?" Despite the shrieking ghosts, Laia takes my hand, her lips drawn down in concern. "I'm so sorry about Shaeva. Is she really—"

I nod. She's gone.

"It was so fast." Somehow, I am comforted by the fact that someone is as stunned as I am. "Are you—will you be—" She shakes her head. "Of course you're not all right—skies, how could you be?"

A groan from Darin pulls our attention away from each other. The ghosts circle him, darting close and whispering skies know what. *Bleeding hells.* I need to get Laia and Darin out of here.

"If you want to get to Adisa," I say, "the fastest way is through the Forest. You'll lose months going around."

"Right." Laia pauses and furrows her brow. "But, Elias—"

If we speak more of Shaeva, I think something inside me will break. She was here, and now she's gone, and nothing can change that. The permanence of death will always feel like a betrayal. But raging against it when my friends are in danger is the act of a fool. I must move. I must make sure Shaeva didn't die for nothing.

Laia is still speaking when I take Darin's hand and begin to windwalk. She goes quiet as the Forest fades past us. She squeezes my hand, and I know that she understands my silence.

I cannot travel with Shaeva's swiftness, but we reach one of the bridges over the River Dusk after only a quarter hour, and seconds later, we're beyond it. I angle northeast, and as we move through the trees, Laia peeks at me from beneath the wing of hair that has fallen over her eye. I want to speak to her. *Damn the Nightbringer,* I want to say. *I don't care what he said. I only care that you are all right.*

"We'll be there soon," I begin, before another voice speaks, a hateful chorus that is instantly recognizable.

You will fail, usurper.

The jinn. But their grove is miles away. How are they projecting their voices this far?

Filth. Your world will fall. Our king has already thwarted you. This is just the beginning.

"Piss off," I snarl. I think of the whispers I heard just before the Nightbringer disappeared. He was giving these fiery monsters orders, no doubt. The jinn laugh.

Our kind are powerful, mortal. You cannot replace a jinn. You cannot hope to succeed as Soul Catcher.

I ignore them, hoping they'll shut the hells up. Did they ever do this to

Shaeva? Were they always bellowing in her head, and she just never told me?

My chest aches when I think of the Soul Catcher—and of so many others. Tristas. Demetrius. Leander. The Blood Shrike. My grandfather. Are all those who get close to me fated to suffer?

Darin shivers, gritting his teeth against the onslaught of the ghosts. Laia's skin is gray, though she walks on without a word of complaint.

In the end, they will fade. You will endure. Love cannot live here.

Laia's hand is cool and small in mine. Her pulse flutters against my fingers, a tenuous reminder of her mortality. Even if she survives to be an old woman, her years are nothing against the life of a Soul Catcher. She will die and I will abide, becoming less and less human as time passes.

"There." Laia points ahead. The trees thin, and through them I spot the cottage where Darin recovered from his injuries at Kauf, months ago now.

When we reach the tree line, I release the siblings. Darin grabs me and pulls me into a rough hug. "I don't know how to thank you—" he begins, but I stop him.

"Stay alive," I say. "That'll be thanks enough. I'll have enough problems here without your ghost showing up." Darin offers a flash of a smile before glancing at his sister and prudently heading for the cottage.

Laia twists her hands together, not looking at me. Her hair has come free from its braid as it always does, in fat, unruly curls. I reach for one, unable to help myself.

"I . . . have something for you." I rummage around in a pocket and pull out a piece of wood. It is unfinished, the carvings on it rough. "You reach for your old armlet sometimes." I feel ridiculous all of a sudden. Why would

I give her this hideous thing? It looks like a six-year-old made it. "It's not finished. But . . . ah . . . I thought—"

"It's perfect." Her fingers brush mine as she takes it. That touch. *Ten hells.* I steady my breath and crush the desire that thrums in my veins. She slides the armlet on, and seeing her in that familiar pose, one hand resting on the cuff—it feels right. "Thank you."

"Watch your back in Adisa." I turn to practicalities. They are easier to speak of than this feeling in my chest, like my heart is being carved out of me and lit on fire. "The Mariners will know your face, and if they know what Darin can do—"

I catch her smile and realize that, like a fool, I'm telling her things she already knows.

"I thought we would have more time," she says. "I thought we'd find a way out for you. That Shaeva would release you from your vow or . . ."

She looks like I feel: broken. I need to let her go. *Fight the Nightbringer,* I should say. *Win. Find joy. Remember me.* For why should she come back here? Her future is in the world of the living.

Say it, Elias, my logic screams. *Make it easier for both of you. Don't be pathetic.*

"Laia, you should—"

"I don't want to let you go. Not yet." She traces my jaw with a light hand, her fingers lingering on my mouth. She wants me—I can see it, feel it—and it makes me desire her even more desperately. "Not so soon."

"Neither do I." I pull her into my arms, reveling in the warmth of her body against mine, the curve of her hip beneath my hand. She tucks her head beneath my chin and I breathe her in.

Mauth tugs at me, harsh and sudden. Against my will, I sway back toward the Forest.

No. *No.* Ghosts be damned. Mauth be damned. Waiting Place be damned.

I grab her hand and pull her toward me, and as if she was waiting for it, she closes her eyes and rises up on her toes. Her hands tangle in my hair, drawing me tightly toward her. Her lips are soft and lush, and when she presses every curve into me, I nearly lose my feet. I hear nothing but Laia, see nothing but Laia, feel nothing but Laia.

My mind races forward to me laying her down on the Forest floor, spending hours exploring every inch of her body. For a moment I see what we could have had: Laia and her books and patients, and me and a school that taught more than death and duty. A little one with gold eyes and glowing brown skin. The white in Laia's hair one day, and the way her eyes will mellow and deepen and grow wiser.

"You are cruel, Elias," she whispers against my mouth. "To give a girl all she desires only to tear it away."

"This isn't the end for us, Laia of Serra." I cannot give up what we could have. I don't care what bleeding vow I made. "Do you hear me? This is not our end."

"You've never been a liar." She dashes her hands against the wetness in her eyes. "Don't start now."

Her back is straight as she walks away, and when she reaches the cottage, Darin, waiting outside, rises. She goes past him quickly, and he follows.

I watch her until she is just a shadow on the horizon. *Turn around*, I think. *Just once. Turn around.*

She doesn't. And perhaps it's just as well.

X: The Blood Shrike

I spend the rest of the day in the Black Guard barracks, reading through spy reports. Most are mundane: a prisoner transfer that could guarantee the loyalty of a Mercator house; an investigation into the death of two Illustrian Paters.

I pay closest attention to the reports out of Tiborum. With the approach of spring, the Karkaun clans are expected to come pouring out of the mountains, raiding and reaving.

But my spies say the Karkauns are quiet. Perhaps their leader, this Grímarr, committed too many forces to the attack on Navium. Perhaps Tiborum is uncommonly lucky.

Or perhaps those blue-faced bastards are up to something.

I request reports from all the northern garrisons. By the time the midnight bells ring, I am exhausted and my desk is only half-clear. But I stop anyway, forgoing a meal despite the rumbling in my belly, and pulling on my boots and a cloak. Sleep will not come. Not when the crack of Livia's bones still rings through my head. Not when I'm wondering what ambush the Commandant will have waiting for me in Navium.

The hallway outside my quarters is silent and dark. Most of the Black Guard should be asleep, but there's always at least a half dozen men on watch. I don't want to be followed—I suspect the Commandant has spies among my men. I head for the armory, where a hidden passage leads into the heart of the city.

"Shrike." The whisper is soft, but I jump anyway, cursing at the sight of the green eyes shining like a cat's from across the hall.

"Avitas," I hiss. "Why are you lurking out here?"

"Don't take the armory tunnel," he says. "Pater Sissellius has a man watching the route. I'll have him taken care of, but there wasn't time tonight."

"Are you spying on me?"

"You're predictable, Shrike. Any time Marcus hurts her, you take a walk. Captain Dex reminded me that it's against regulations for the Shrike to be unaccompanied, so here I am."

I know Harper is simply carrying out his duties. I have been irresponsible, wandering the city at night without any guards. Still, I'm vexed. Harper serenely ignores my discontent and nods to the laundry closet. There must be another passageway there.

Once we're inside the narrow space, my armor clanks against his, and I grimace, hoping no one hears us. Skies know what they would say at finding us pressed together in a dark closet.

My face heats thinking of it. Thank the skies for my mask. "Where's the bleeding entrance?"

"It's just—" He reaches around me and up, rummaging through uniforms. I lean back, catching a V-shaped glimpse of the smooth brown skin at his throat. His scent is light—barely there—but warm, like cinnamon and cedar. I take a deeper sniff, glancing up at him as I do.

To find him staring at me, eyebrows raised.

"You smell . . . not unpleasant," I say stiffly. "I was simply noticing."

"Of course, Shrike." His mouth quirks a little. Is that a bleeding *smile*?

"Shall we?" As if sensing my annoyance, Harper pushes open a section of the closet behind me and moves through quickly. We do not speak again as we wend our way through the secret passageways of the Black Guard barracks and out into the chill spring night.

Harper drops back when we are aboveground, and I soon forget he is near. Hood pulled low, I ghost through Antium's lower level, through the crowded Scholar sector, past inns and bustling taprooms, barracks and Plebeian-heavy neighborhoods. The guards at the upper gate do not see me as I pass into the city's second tier—a trick I play to keep my edge.

I find myself toying with my father's ring as I walk, the ring of Gens Aquilla. Sometimes, when I look at it, I still see the blood that coated it, the blood that spattered my face and armor when Marcus cut Father's throat.

Don't think about that. I spin it round, trying to take comfort from its presence. *Give me the wisdom of all the Aquillas*, I find myself thinking. *Help me defeat my foe.*

I soon reach my destination, a wooded park outside the Hall of Records. At this hour, I expected the hall to be dark, but a dozen lamps are lit, and the archivists are still hard at work. The long, pillared building is spectacular for its size and simplicity, but I take comfort from it because of what is within: records of lineages, births, deaths, dispatches, treaties, trade agreements, and laws.

If the Emperor is the heart of the Empire and the people are its life-blood, then the Hall of Records is its memory. No matter how hopeless I feel, coming here reminds me of all the Martials have built in the five hundred years since the Empire was founded.

"All Empires fall, Blood Shrike."

When Cain steps from the shadows, I reach for my blade. I have thought many times about what I would do if I saw the Augur again. Always, I saw myself remaining calm. Silent. I would hold myself aloof from him. I would give him nothing of my mind.

My intentions vanish at the sight of his accursed face. The passion with which I want to break his frail neck astounds me. I didn't know I could have this much hate in me. Hannah's pleading fills my ears—*Helly, I'm sorry*—and my mother's calm words as she knelt for her death. *Strength, my girl.* My father's ring cuts into my palm.

But as I draw the blade, my arm freezes—and drops, forced to my side by the Augur. The lack of control is enraging and unsettling.

"Such anger," he murmurs.

"You destroyed my life. You could have saved them. You—you *monster.*"

"What of you, Blood Shrike? Are you not a monster?" Cain's hood is low, but I can still make out the inquisitive gleam of his gaze.

"You're different," I spit. "You're like them. The Commandant, or Marcus, or the Nightbringer—"

"Ah, but the Nightbringer is no monster, child, though he may do monstrous things. He is cloven by sorrow and thus locked in a righteous battle to amend a grievous wrong. Much like you. I think you are more similar than you know. You could learn much from the Nightbringer, if he deigned to teach you."

"I don't bleeding want anything to do with any of you," I hiss. "You *are* a monster, even if you—"

"But you are a paragon of perfection?" Cain tilts his head, appearing genuinely curious. "You live and breathe and eat and sleep on the backs of those less fortunate. Your entire existence is due to the oppression of those you view to be lesser. But why you, Blood Shrike? Why did fate see fit to make you the oppressor instead of the oppressed? What is the meaning of your life?"

"The Empire." I shouldn't answer. I should ignore him. But a lifetime of reverence dies hard. "That is the meaning of my life."

"Perhaps." Cain shrugs, a strangely human gesture. "I did not, in truth, come here to argue philosophy with you. I came with a message."

He pulls an envelope from his robes. At the sight of the seal—a bird winging over a shining city—I snatch it from him. *Livia.*

As I open it, I keep one eye on the Augur.

> *Come to me, sister. I need you.*
> *Yours always,*
> *Livia*

"When did she send this?" I scan the message quickly. "And why did she send it with you? She could have—"

"She asked, and I acquiesced. Anyone else would have been followed. And that would not have aligned with my interests. Or hers." Cain touches my masked brow gently. "Fare thee well, Blood Shrike. I will see you once more, before your end."

He steps back and vanishes, and Harper appears out of the dark, jaw clenched. Apparently, he likes the Augurs as much as I do.

"You can keep them out of your head," he says. "The Nightbringer too. I can show you how, if you like."

"Fine," I say, already making for the palace. "On the way to Navium."

We soon reach the balcony of Livvy's apartments, and I do not spot a single soldier. Avitas is stationed below, and I'm reminding myself to yell at Faris, who captains Livvy's personal guard, when the air shifts. I'm not alone.

"Peace, Shrike." Faris Candelan steps out of the arched doorway that leads into Livvy's quarters, his hands up, short blond hair a mess. "She's waiting for you."

"You should have bleeding told her it was stupid to summon me."

"I don't tell the Empress what to do," Faris says. "I just try to make sure no one hurts her while she's doing it." Something about how he says it makes the hair on my neck rise, and in two steps, I have a dagger at his throat.

"Watch it with her, Faris," I say. "You flirt like your life depends on it, but if Marcus suspects she is disloyal he will kill her, and the Illustrian Paters will believe he had every right to do it."

"Don't worry about me," Faris says. "I've got a lovely Mercator girl waiting for me in the Weaver's district. Most spectacular hips I've ever seen. Would have been there by now"—he glares at me until I release him—"but some-one needed to be on duty."

"Two people," I say. "Who's your backup?"

A figure steps into the light from the shadows beside the door: a thrice-broken nose, deep brown skin, and blue eyes that always sparkle, even beneath the silver mask.

"Rallius? Ten hells, is that you?"

Silvio Rallius salutes before flashing a grin that made knees weak at Illustrian parties across Serra for nearly all of my teenage years—including my knees, before I learned better. Elias and I hero-worshipped him, though he is only two years older. He was one of the few upperclassman who wasn't a monster to the younger students.

"Blood Shrike." He salutes. "My scim is yours."

"Words as pretty as that smile." I don't return his, and he realizes then that he's dealing with the Blood Shrike and not a young cadet from Blackcliff. "Make them true. Protect her, or your life is forfeit."

I slip past them both and into Livvy's bedroom. As my eyes adjust, the floorboards near a tapestry creak. Cloth whispers as the contours of the room come into focus. Livia's bed is empty; on her side table, a cup of tea—wildwood, from the scent of it—sits untouched.

Livia pokes her head out from behind the tapestry and motions me forward. I can barely make her out, which means any spies within the walls can't see her either.

"You should have drunk the tea." I am careful of her wounded hand. "It must hurt."

Her clothes rustle, and a soft click sounds. Stale air and the smell of wet stone wash over me. A hallway stretches before us. We step in, and she closes the door, finally speaking.

"An empress who bears her pain with fortitude is an empress who gains respect," she says. "My women have spread the rumor that I scorned the tea. That I bear the pain without fear. But bleeding hells, it hurts."

The moment she says it, a familiar compulsion comes over me: the need to heal her, to sing her better.

"I can—I can help you," I say. Bleeding skies, how will I explain it to her? "I—"

"We don't have time, sister," she whispers. "Come. This passage connects my rooms to his. I've used it before. But be silent. He cannot catch us."

We pad down the hallway toward a tiny crack of light. The muttering begins when we're halfway down. The light is a spy hole, big enough to admit sound but too small to see through very clearly. I glimpse Marcus, bare of armor, stalking back and forth across his cavernous quarters.

"You have to stop doing this when I'm in the throne room." He digs his hands into his hair. "Do you want to have died just so I can get hurled off the throne for being insane?"

Silence. Then: "I won't *bleeding* touch her! I can't help that her sister's gagging for it—"

I nearly choke, and Livvy grips me. "I had my reasons," she whispers.

"I will do what I must to keep this empire," Marcus growls, and for the first time I see . . . something. A pale shadow, like a face glimpsed in a mirror underwater. A second later, it's gone, and I shake myself. A trick of the light, perhaps. "If that means breaking a few fingers to keep your precious Blood Shrike in line, so be it. I *wanted* to break her arm—"

"Ten hells," I breathe to Livia. "He's barking. He's gone mad."

"He *thinks* what he's seeing is real." Livia shakes her head. "Maybe it is. It doesn't matter. He cannot remain on the throne. At best, he's taking orders from a ghost. At worst, he's hallucinating."

"We have to support him," I say. "The Augurs named him Emperor. If he's deposed or killed, we risk civil war. Or the Commandant swooping in and naming herself Empress."

"Do we?" Livvy takes my hand with her good one and places it on her stomach. She doesn't speak. She doesn't have to.

"Oh. You—that's why you and he—oh—" Blackcliff prepared me for many things. It did not prepare me for my sister's pregnancy by the man who slit the throats of our parents and sister.

"This is our answer, Shrike."

"His heir," I whisper.

"A regency."

Bleeding skies. If Marcus disappears after the child is born, Livia and Gens Aquilla would run the Empire until the child came of age. We could train the boy up to be a true and just statesman. The Illustrian Gens would accept it because the heir would be from a highborn house. The Plebeians would accept it because he is Marcus's son and thus represents them too. But . . .

"How do you know it's a boy?"

She turns her eyes—my eyes—our mother's eyes—to me, and I have never seen anyone look so sure of anything in my life. "It's a boy, Blood Shrike," she says. "You must trust me. He already quickens. By the Grain Moon, if all is well, he will be here."

I shiver. The Grain Moon again.

"When the Commandant finds out, she'll come after you. I have to—"

"Kill her." Livia takes the words from my mouth. "Before she finds out."

When I ask Livia if Marcus knows of the pregnancy, she shakes her head. "I confirmed it only today. And I wanted to tell you first."

"Tell him, Livvy." I forget her title. "He wants an heir. Perhaps he won't—" I gesture to her hand. "But no one else. Hide it as best you can—"

She puts a finger to my lips. Marcus's muttering has stopped.

"Go, Shrike," Livvy breathes.

Mother! Father! Hannah! Suddenly I cannot breathe. He won't take Livvy too. I'll die before I let it happen. "I'll fight him—"

My sister digs her fingers into my shoulder. The pain focuses me. "You'll fight him." She shoves me toward her room. "He'll die because he's no match for your anger. And in the frenzy to replace him, our enemies will have us both killed because we would have made it easy for them to do so. We *must* live. For him." She touches her stomach. "For Father and Mother and Hannah. For the Empire. Go."

She shoves me out the door, just as light floods the passageway. I race through her room, past Faris and Rallius, flipping over the balcony to the rope tied below, cursing myself as Marcus shouts, as he lands the first blow, as the crack of another of my sister's bones echoes in my ears.

PART II

INFERNO

XI: Laia

FOUR WEEKS LATER

Darin and I jostle through the sea of Scholar refugees on the rutted dirt road into Adisa, two more tired bodies and dirty faces amid the hundreds seeking sanctuary in Marinn's shining capital city.

Silence hangs like a fog over the refugees as they plod onward. Most of these Scholars were turned away from the other Mariner cities. All have seen homes lost, family and friends tortured or murdered, raped or imprisoned.

The Martials wield their weapons of war with merciless efficiency. They want to break the Scholars. And if I don't stop the Nightbringer—if I don't find this "Beekeeper" in Adisa—they will.

Shaeva's prophecy haunts me. Darin and I discuss it obsessively, trying to make sense of each line. Bits of it—the sparrows, the Butcher—dredge up old memories, scraps of thoughts that I cannot quite grasp hold of.

"We'll figure it out." Darin glances over, reading the furrow in my brow. "We have bigger problems."

Our shadow. The man appeared three days ago, trailing us as we left a small village. Or at least, that is when we first noticed him. Since then, he's remained far enough away that we cannot get a good look at him, but close enough that my blade feels fused to my palm. Every time I don my invisibility in the hopes of getting closer to him, he disappears.

"Still there." Darin chances a look behind us. "Lurking like a bleeding wraith."

The circles beneath my brother's eyes make his irises look almost black. His cheekbones jut out, as they did when I first rescued him from Kauf. Since our shadow appeared, Darin has slept little. But even before that, nightmares of Kauf and the Warden plagued him. Sometimes I wish the Warden back to life, just so I could kill him myself. Strange how monsters can reach from beyond the grave, as potent in death as they were in life.

"We'll lose him at the city gates." I try to sound convincing. "And lie low when we get in. Find a cheap inn to stay at where no one will look at us twice. And then," I add, "we can ask around for the Beekeeper."

Under the guise of adjusting my hood, I glance back quickly at our shadow. He's close now, and beneath the scarf that hides his face, his red, sickle mouth curves into a smile. A weapon flashes in his hand.

I spin back around. We wind down from the foothills, and Adisa's gold-flecked wall comes into view, a marvel of white granite that glows orange under the fading, blood-streaked sky. Along the eastern wall, a mass of gray tents blooms out for nearly a mile: the Scholar refugee camp. In the bay to the north, sea ice floats in fat chunks, its briny smell slicing through the dirt and grime of the road.

Clouds sit low on the horizon, and an estival wind blows in from the south, scattering them. As they part, a near-collective gasp ripples through the travelers. For in the center of Adisa, a spire of stone and glass soars into the sky, pinioning the heavens. It twists like the horn of some mythical creature, impossibly balanced and glowing white. I have only ever heard it described, but the descriptions do it no justice. The Great Library of Adisa.

An unwelcome memory surfaces. Red hair, brown eyes, and a mouth that lied, lied, lied. Keenan—the Nightbringer—telling me that he too wanted to see the Great Library.

She tasted sweet, boy. Like dew and a clear dawn. My skin crawls thinking of the filth he spat in the Waiting Place.

"Look." I nod to the throngs gathered outside the city gates, pushing to enter before they close at nightfall. "We can lose him there. Especially if I disappear."

When we are closer to the city, I drop in front of Darin, as if adjusting a bootlace. Then I pull on my invisibility.

"I'm right next to you," I whisper when I stand, and Darin nods, weaving quickly now through the crowd, using his sharp elbows to muscle forward. The closer we get to the gate, the slower it goes. Finally, as the sun dips into the west, we stand before the massive wooden entrance, carved with whales and eels, octopuses and mermaids. Beyond, a cobbled street curves up and disappears into a warren of brightly painted buildings, lamps winking in their windows. I think of my mother, who came to Adisa when she was only a few years older than me. Did it look the same? Did she share the awe I feel now?

"Your guarantor, sir?"

One of the dozens of Mariner guards fixes his attention on Darin, and despite the seething crowds, he is coolly polite. Darin shakes his head in confusion. "My guarantor?"

"Who are you staying with in the city? What family or guild?"

"We're staying at an inn," Darin says. "We can pay—"

"Gold can be stolen. I require names: the inn where you plan to procure rooms and your guarantor, who can vouch for your quality. Once you provide names, you will wait in a holding area while your information is verified, after which you may enter Adisa."

Darin looks uncertain. We do not know anyone in Adisa. Since leaving Elias, we have tried several times to get in touch with Araj, the Skiritae leader who escaped Kauf with us, but have heard nothing back from him.

Darin nods at the soldier's explanation, as if we have any idea what we will do instead. "And if I don't have a guarantor?"

"You'll find the entrance to the Scholar refugee camp east of here." The soldier, who until now had kept his attention on the pressing crowd behind us, finally looks at Darin. The man's eyes narrow.

"Say—"

"Time to go," I hiss to my brother, and he mumbles something to the soldier before quickly shoving back into the crowd.

"He can't have known my face," Darin says. "I've never met him before."

"Maybe all Scholars look alike to him," I say, but the explanation rings hollow to me. More than once, we turn to see if the soldier follows. I slow down only when I spot him at the gate, speaking with another group of Scholars. Our shadow also appears to have lost us, and we head east, making our way to one of a dozen long lines that lead into the refugee camp.

Nan told me stories of what Mother did when she led the northern Resistance here in Adisa, more than twenty-five years ago. The Mariner King Irmand worked with her to protect the Scholars. To give them work and homes and a permanent place in Mariner society.

Things have clearly gone to pot since then.

Even from outside the boundaries of the camp, its gloom is pervasive. Bands of children wander through the tents ahead, most far too young to be left unaccompanied. A few dogs slink through the muddy roadways, occasionally sniffing at the open sewers.

Why is it always us? All of these people—so many children—hunted and abused and tormented. Families stolen, lives shattered. They come all this way to be rejected yet again, sent outside the city walls to sleep in flimsy tents, to fight over paltry scraps of food, to starve and freeze and suffer more.

And we are expected to be thankful. To be happy. So many are—I know it. Happy to be safe. To be alive. But it's not enough—not to me.

As we get closer to the entrance, the camp comes into clearer view. White parchment flutters from the cloth walls. I squint at it, but it's not until we're nearing the front of the line that I finally make out what's on it.

My own face. Darin's. Staring out sullenly beneath damning words:

BY PERSONAL DECREE

OF KING IRMAND OF MARINN

WANTED:
LAIA AND DARIN OF SERRA

FOR: INCITEMENT OF REBELLION, AGITATION,

AND CONSPIRING AGAINST THE CROWN

REWARD: 10,000 MARKS

It looks like the posters from the Commandant's office at Blackcliff. Like the one from Nur, when the Blood Shrike was hunting Elias and me and offering a massive reward.

"What in the skies," I whisper, "did we do to King Irmand to offend him so? Could the Martials be behind it?"

"They don't bleeding know we're here!"

"They have spies, just like everyone else," I say. "Look back, like you see someone you recognize, and then walk—"

A commotion at the back of the line ripples toward us as a squad of

Mariner troops marches toward the camp from Adisa. Darin hunches down, taking refuge deeper in his hood. Shouts ring out ahead of us, and light flares sharply, followed quickly by a plume of black smoke. Fire. The shouts quickly turn to cries of rage and fear.

My mind seizes; my thoughts go to Serra, to the night the soldiers took Darin. The pounding at our door and the silver of the Mask's face. Nan's and Pop's blood on the floor and Darin screaming at me. *Laia! Run!*

Voices around me rise in terror. Scholars in the camp flee. Groups of children cluster, making themselves small, hoping they are not noticed. Blue-and-gold-clad Mariner soldiers weave through the tents, tearing them apart as they search for something.

No—someone.

The Scholars around us scatter, running every which way, driven by a fear that's been hammered into our bones. *Always us!* Our dignity shredded, our families annihilated, our children torn from their parents. Our blood soaking the dirt. What sin was so great that Scholars must pay, with every generation, with the only thing we have left: our lives?

Darin, calm just a moment ago, is motionless beside me, looking as terror-stricken as I feel. I grab his hand. I cannot fall apart now—not when he needs me to hold it together.

"Let's go." I pull him away, but there are soldiers herding those in the lines back toward the camp. Close by, I spy a dark space between two refugee tents. "Quick, Darin—"

A voice cries out behind us. "They're not here!" A Scholar woman who is naught but skin and bones tries to shake off a Mariner soldier. "I've told you—"

"We know you're sheltering them." The Mariner who speaks is taller than me by a few inches, her scaled silver armor tight against the powerful muscles of her shoulders. Her chiseled brown face lacks the cruelty of a Mask, but she is nearly as intimidating. She tears a poster off the side of one of the tents where it's been pinned. "Turn over Laia and Darin of Serra, and we will leave you be. Otherwise we *will* raze this camp and scatter its refugees to the four winds. We are generous, true. That does not make us fools."

Beyond the soldier, dozens of Scholar children are being herded toward a makeshift holding pen. A cloud of embers explodes into the sky as, behind them, two more tents go up in flames. I shudder at the way the fire growls and vaunts, as if it is celebrating the screams rising from my people.

"It's the prophecy," Darin whispers. "Do you remember? *The sparrows will drown, and none will know it.* The Scholars must be the sparrows, Laia. The Mariners have always been called the sea people. They are the flood."

"We cannot let it happen." I make myself say the words. "They're suffering because of us. This is the only home they have. And we're taking it away from them."

Darin immediately understands my intent. He shakes his head, taking a step back, movements jerky and panicked. "No," he says. "We can't. How are we supposed to find the Beekeeper if we're in prison? Or dead? How are we supposed to—" His voice chokes off, and he shakes his head again and again.

"I know they will lock us up." I grab him, shake him. I need to break through his terror. I need him to believe me. "But I swear to the skies that I will get us out. We cannot let the camp burn, Darin. It's *wrong*. The Mariners want us. And we're right here."

A scream erupts from behind us. A Scholar man claws at a Mariner guard, howling as she removes a child from his grasp.

"Don't hurt her," he begs. "Please—please—"

Darin watches, shuddering. "You're—you're right." He fights to get the words out, and I am relieved and proud and broken-hearted because I feel sick at the thought of watching my brother dragged back to a prison. "I'll have no one else die for me. Especially not you. I'll turn myself in. You'll be safe—"

"Not a chance," I say. "Never again. Where you go, I go."

I drop my invisibility, and vertigo nearly levels me. My sight darkens to a dank room with a light-haired woman within. I cannot see her face. *Who is she?*

When my vision clears, only a few seconds have passed. I shake the strange images away and leave the shelter of the tents.

The Mariner soldier's instinct is excellent. For though we are a good thirty feet from her, the moment we step into the light, her head swivels toward us. The plume and angled eye holes of her helmet make her look like an angry hawk, but her hand is light on her scim as she watches our approach.

"Laia and Darin of Serra." She doesn't sound surprised, and I know then that she expected to find us here—that she *knew* we had arrived in Adisa. "You are under arrest for conspiracy to commit crimes against the kingdom of Marinn. You will come with me."

XII: Elias

T hough the sun hasn't yet set, the Tribal encampment is quiet when I approach. The cook fires are doused, the horses sheltered beneath a canvas tarp. The red-and-yellow-painted wagons are sealed tight against the driving late spring rain. Wan lamplight flickers within.

I move slowly, though not out of wariness. Mauth tugs at me, and it requires all my strength to ignore that summons.

A few hundred yards west of the caravan, the Duskan Sea breaks against the rocky shore, its roar nearly drowning out the mournful cries of white-headed gulls above. But my Mask's instincts are as sharp as ever, and I sense the approach of the *Kehanni* of Tribe Nasur long before she appears—along with the six Nasur Tribesmen guarding her.

"Elias Veturius." The *Kehanni's* silver dreadlocks hang to her waist, and I can clearly make out the elaborate storyteller's tattoos on her dark brown skin. "You are late."

"I am sorry, *Kehanni*." I don't bother giving her an excuse. *Kehannis* are as skilled at trapping lies as they are at telling stories. "I beg your forgiveness."

"Bah." She sniffs. "You begged to meet with me too. I do not know why I consented. Martials took my brother's son a week ago, after they raided our grain stores. My respect for Mamie Rila is all that keeps me from gutting you like a pig, boy."

I'd like to see you try. "Have you heard from Mamie?"

"She is well-hidden and recovering from the horrors your ilk inflicted upon her. If you think I will tell you where she is, you are a bigger fool than I suspected. Come."

She jerks her head toward the caravan, and I follow. I understand her rage. The Martials' war on the Tribes is evident in every burned-out wagon littering the countryside, every ululating wail rising from Tribal villages as families mourn those taken.

The *Kehanni* moves quickly, and as I trail her, Mauth's pull grows stronger, a physical wrench that makes me want to sprint back to the Waiting Place, three leagues distant. A sense of wrongness steals over me, as if I've forgotten something important. But I can't tell if it is my own instinct prickling or if Mauth is manipulating my mind. More than once in the past few weeks, I've felt someone—or something—flitting at the edges of the Waiting Place, entering and then leaving, as if trying to gauge a reaction. Every time I've felt it, I've windwalked to the border. And every time, I've found nothing.

The rain has, at least, silenced the jinn. Those fiery bastards hate it. But the ghosts are troubled, forced to remain in the Waiting Place longer than they should because I cannot pass them through fast enough. Shaeva's warning haunts me.

If you do not pass the ghosts through, it will mean your failure as Soul Catcher and the end of the human world as you understand it.

Mauth pulls at me again, but I make myself ignore it. The *Kehanni* and I weave our way through the wagons of the caravan until we reach one that sits apart from the rest, its black draping in sharp contrast to the elaborate decorations of the other wagons.

It is the home of a *Fakir*—the Tribesperson who prepares bodies for burial.

I wipe the rain from my face as the *Kehanni* knocks on the wooden back door. "With respect," I say, "I need to speak to *you*—"

"I keep the stories of the living. The *Fakira* keeps the stories of the dead."

The back door of the wagon opens almost immediately to reveal a girl of perhaps sixteen. At the sight of me, her eyes widen and she pulls at her halo of red-brown curls. She chews on her lip, freckles stark against skin that is lighter than Mamie's but darker than mine. Deep blue tattoos wind up her arms, geometric patterns that make me think of skulls.

Something about the uncertainty of her posture reminds me of Laia, and a pang of longing flashes through me. I realize that I've frozen at the door, and the *Kehanni* shoves me into the wagon, which is lit brightly by multi-colored Tribal lamps. A shelf along the back is filled with jars of fluid, and there is a faint smell of something astringent.

"This," the *Kehanni* says from the door once I'm inside, "is Aubarit, our new *Fakira*. She is . . . learning." The *Kehanni* curls her lip slightly. No wonder the *Kehanni* agreed to help me. She's simply foisting me onto a girl who will likely be no help at all. "She will deal with you."

The door slams, leaving Aubarit and me staring at each other for an awkward moment.

"You're young," I blurt out as I sit. "Our Saif *Fakir* was older than the hills."

"Fear not, *bhai*." Aubarit uses the honorific for *brother*, and her shaking voice reflects her anxiety. I immediately feel guilty for bringing up her age. "I have been trained in the Mysteries. You come from the Forest, Elias Veturius. From the domain of the *Bani al-Mauth*. Does she send you to aid us?"

Did she just say Mauth? "How do you know that name, Mauth? Do you mean Shaeva?"

"Astagha!" Aubarit squeaks the oath against the evil eye. "We do not use her name, *bhai*! The *Bani al-Mauth* is holy. The Chosen of Death. The Soul Catcher. The Guardian at the Gates. The sacred Mystery of her existence is known only to the *Fakirs* and their apprentices. I would not have even spoken of it, only you came from the Jaga al-Mauth." *Place of Mauth.*

"Shaev . . . ah, the *Bani al-Mauth*." I suddenly find it hard to speak. "She's . . . dead. I'm her replacement. She was training me when—"

Aubarit drops so fast, I think her heart has failed.

"*Banu al-Mauth*, forgive me." I note the alteration of the title to reflect a male instead of a female—which is when I realize that she has not had some sort of fainting fit. She is kneeling. "I did not know."

"No need for that." I pull her to her feet, embarrassed at her awe. "I'm struggling to pass the ghosts on," I say. "I need to use the magic at the heart of the Waiting Place, but I don't know how. The ghosts are building up. Every day there are more."

Aubarit blanches, and her knuckles pale as she clasps her hands together. "This—this cannot be, *Banu al-Mauth*. You *must* pass them on. If you do not—"

"What happens?" I lean forward. "You spoke of Mysteries—how did you learn them? Are they written down? Scrolls? Books?"

The *Fakira* taps her head. "To write down the Mysteries is to rob them of their power. Only the *Fakirs* and *Fakiras* learn them, for we are with the dead as they leave the world of the living. We wash them and commune with their spirits so they move easily through the Jaga al-Mauth and to the other side. The Soul Catcher does not see them—she—you—are not meant to."

Have you ever wondered why there are so few ghosts from the Tribes? Shaeva's words.

"Do your Mysteries say anything of the Waiting Place's magic?"

"No, *Banu al-Mauth*," Aubarit says. "Though . . ." Her voice drops and takes on the cadence of a long-memorized chant. "*If thou seekest the truth in the trees, the Forest will show thee its sly memory.*"

"A memory?" I frown—Shaeva said nothing of this. "The trees have seen much, no doubt. But the magic I have doesn't allow me to speak with them."

Aubarit shakes her head. "The Mysteries are rarely literal. Forest *could* mean the trees—or it could be referring to something else entirely."

Metaphorical talking trees won't help me. "What of the *Bani al-Mauth?*" I ask. "Did you ever meet her? Did she speak to you of the magic or how she did her work?"

"I met her once, when Grandfather chose me as his apprentice. She gave me her benediction. I thought . . . I thought she sent you to help us."

"Help you?" I say sharply. "With the Martials?"

"No, with—" She swallows back the words. "Do not concern yourself with such trifles, *Banu al-Mauth*. You must move the spirits, and to do that you must remove yourself from the world, not waste your time helping strangers."

"Tell me what's going on," I say. "I can decide whether it concerns me or not."

Aubarit wrings her hands in indecision, but when I chuff expectantly, she speaks, her voice low. "Our *Fakirs* and *Fakiras*," she says, "they're dying. A few were killed in Martial attacks. But others . . ." She shakes her head. "My grandfather was found in a pond just a few feet deep. His lungs were filled with water—but he knew how to swim."

"His heart might have failed."

"He was strong as a bull and not yet in his sixth decade. That's only part of it, *Banu al-Mauth*. I struggled to reach his spirit. You must understand, I have been training as a *Fakira* since I could speak. I have never fought to commune with a spirit. This time, it felt as if something was blocking me. When I succeeded, Grandfather's ghost was deeply troubled—it would not speak to me. Something is *wrong*. I've not heard from the other *Fakirs*—

everyone is so concerned with the Martials. But this—this is bigger than that. And I do not know what to do."

A sharp tug nearly pulls me to my feet. I sense impatience on the other end. Perhaps Mauth doesn't wish me to learn this information. Perhaps the magic *wants* me to remain ignorant.

"Get word out to your *Fakirs*," I say. "Their wagons should no longer be set apart from the rest of the caravan, by order of the *Banu al-Mauth*, who has expressed concern for their safety. And tell them to have their wagons repainted to match the others in the Tribe. It will make it more difficult for your enemies to find you—" I stop short. The pull at my core is strong enough that I feel like I might be sick. But I press on, because no one else is going to help Aubarit or the *Fakirs*.

"Ask the other *Fakirs* if they are also finding it hard to commune with the spirits," I say. "And find out if it's ever happened before."

"The other *Fakirs* don't listen to me."

"You are new to your power." I need to go, but I cannot just leave her here, doubting herself, doubting her worth. "But that doesn't mean you don't have it. Think of the way your *Kehanni* wears her strength, like it's her own skin. That's who you must be. For your people."

Mauth pulls me yet again, forcefully enough that, against my will, I stand. "I have to return to the Waiting Place," I say. "If you need me, come to the border of the Forest. I'll know you're there. But do *not* try to enter."

Moments later, I'm back out in the heavy rain. Lightning cracks over the Waiting Place, and I feel it hit within my domain: north, near the cabin, and closer, near the river. The awareness feels innate, like knowing I've gotten a cut or bite.

As I windwalk home, I turn Aubarit's words over in my head. Shaeva never told me the *Fakirs* were so deeply connected to her work. She never mentioned that they knew of her existence, let alone that they had built an entire mythology around her. All I knew about the *Fakirs* was what most Tribespeople know about them—that they handle the dead and that they are to be revered, albeit with more fear than one would revere a *Zaldar* or a *Kehanni*.

Maybe if I'd bleeding paid attention, I'd have noticed a connection. The Tribes have always been deeply wary of the Forest. Afya hates being near it, and Tribe Saif never came within fifty leagues of it when I was a child.

As I near the Waiting Place, Mauth's pull, which by now should have weakened, gets stronger. Does he simply want me to come back? Does he want something more?

The border is finally before me, and the moment I pass through, I am blasted by the howls of the ghosts. Their rage has peaked—transformed into something violent and deranged. How in the ten hells did they get so riled up in the hour that I was gone?

They press close to the border with a strange, single-minded focus. At first, I think that they are all pushing at something close to the wall. A dead animal? A dead body?

But as I shove past them, shuddering at the chills rippling through my body, I realize that they aren't pressing at something near the wall. They are pushing at the wall itself.

They are trying to get out.

XIII: The Blood Shrike

The southern sky is stained black with smoke when the riverboat finally begins the approach to Navium. The rain that has drenched us for the past two weeks lingers on the horizon, taunting us, refusing to provide any relief. The Empire's greatest port city burns, and my people burn with it.

Avitas joins me on the wide prow while Dex barks orders at the captain to move faster. Thunder echoes—Navium's drums issuing coded orders with a frenzy one only ever hears during an attack.

Harper's silver face is tight, his mouth drawn down in what is almost a frown. He's spent hours on the road teaching me to close my mind against intrusion, which meant a great deal of time staring into each other's faces. I've gotten to know his well. Whatever news he's about to deliver, it's bad.

"Grímarr and his forces attacked at dawn three weeks ago," he says. "Our spies say the Karkauns have been hit by a famine in the south. Tens of thousands dead. They've been raiding the southern coast for months now, but we had outdated information on the fleet they'd amassed. They showed up with more than three hundred ships and struck the merchant harbor first. Of the two hundred fifty merchant vessels at port, two hundred forty-three were destroyed."

That's a blow the Mercator Gens won't soon forget. "Countermeasures?"

"Admiral Lenidas took the fleet out twice. The first time, we took down three Barbarian craft before a squall forced us back to port. The second time, Grímarr pressed the attack and drove us back."

"Grímarr drove back Admiral Lenidas?" Whoever this skies-forsaken

Karkaun is, he's no fool. Lenidas has commanded the Empire's navy for the past thirty years. He designed Navium's military port, the Island: a watchtower with an enormous body of water surrounding it, and a circular, protected port beyond, which houses men, ships, and supplies. He has fought the Barbarians for decades from the Island.

"According to the report, Grímarr countered every trick Lenidas threw at him. After that, the Karkauns choked off the port. The city is effectively under siege. And the death toll is up to a thousand in the Southwest Quarter. That's where Grímarr is hitting the hardest."

The Southwest Quarter is almost entirely Plebeian—dockworkers, sailors, fishermen, coopers, blacksmiths, and their families.

"Keris Veturia is orchestrating an operation to rout the next Barbarian attack."

"Keris shouldn't be orchestrating anything without Lenidas to temper her," I say. "Where is he?"

"After his second failure, she executed him," Avitas says, and from his long pause, I know he's as disturbed at the news as I am. "For gross dereliction of duty. Two days ago."

"That old man lived and breathed duty." I am numb. Lenidas trained me personally for six months when I was a Fiver, just before I got my mask. He was one of the few southern Paters my father trusted. "He fought the Karkauns for fifty years. Knew more about them than anyone alive."

"Officially, the Commandant felt that he had lost too many men in the attacks and ignored too many of her warnings."

"And unofficially she wanted to take control." Damn her to the hells. "Why did the Illustrian Paters allow it? She's not a deity. They could have stopped her."

"You know how Lenidas was, Shrike," Avitas says. "He didn't take bribes, and he didn't let the Paters tell him what to do. He treated Illustrians and Mercators and Plebeians alike. The way they saw it, he let the merchant harbor burn."

"And now Keris is in command of Navium."

"She's summoned us," Avitas says. "We've been informed that an escort will bring us to her. She is at the Island."

Hag. She is already attempting to wrest control from me before I've even entered the city. I meant to go to the Island first. But now if I do, I will appear the supplicant, seeking approval from my betters.

"Curse her summons."

A commotion at the docks catches my attention. The chuffing screams of horses split the air, and I spot the black-and-red armor of a Black Guard. The soldier curses as he attempts to keep hold of the beasts, but they buck and jerk away from him.

Then, as suddenly as they began to panic, the beasts calm, dropping their heads, as if drugged. Every man on the dock steps back.

A figure in black comes into view.

"Bleeding hells," Avitas murmurs from beside me.

The Nightbringer's eerie, bright eyes fix on me. But I am not surprised. I expected Keris to keep that jinn monster close. She knows I'm trying to kill her. She knows that if she can use her supernatural pet to get into my head, I'll never succeed.

I think back to the hours spent with Avitas, learning to shield my mind. Hours listening to his calm voice explain how to imagine my innermost thoughts as gems locked in a chest, hidden in a shipwreck at the bottom of a forgotten sea. Harper doesn't know about Livia's pregnancy. I spoke of it to no one. But he knows the Empire's future depends on destroying the Commandant. He was an exacting instructor.

But he could not test my skill. I hope to the skies that my preparation was enough. If Keris learns Livvy is pregnant, she'll have assassins descending within days.

But as we dock, my thoughts are scattered. *Pull yourself together, Shrike. Livvy's life depends on it. The Empire depends on it.*

When I step onto the gangplank, I do not look into the Nightbringer's eyes. I made that mistake once before, months ago, when I met him back in Serra. Now I know that his eyes showed my future. I saw the deaths of my family that day. I didn't understand it at the time—I assumed my own fear had gotten the best of me.

"Welcome, Blood Shrike." I cannot hide my shudder at the way the Nightbringer's voice scrapes against my ear. He beckons me closer. *I am Mater of Gens Aquilla. I am a Mask. I am a Black Guard. I am the Blood Shrike, right hand to the Emperor of the Martials.* I order my body to remain still while I stare him down with all the power of my rank.

My body betrays me.

The sounds of the river docks fade. No water slapping against the hulls of ships. No stevedores calling out to each other. No masts creaking, and no distant boom of sails or roar of the sea. The silence that cloaks the jinn is complete, an aura that nothing can penetrate. Everything falls away as I close the distance between us.

Maintain control, Shrike. Give him nothing.

"Ah," the Nightbringer says quietly, when I stand before him. "Felicitations, Blood Shrike. I see you are to be an aunt."

XIV: Laia

The Mariner prison is spare, cold, and eerily silent. As I pace my poorly lit cell, I place a hand against the stone wall. It is so thick that I could scream and scream and Darin, across the hall from me, might never know.

He must be going mad. I imagine him clenching and unclenching his fists, boots scraping against the floor, wondering when we will escape. *If we will escape.* This place might not be Kauf, but it is still a prison. And my brother's demons will not let him forget it.

Which means I must stay levelheaded for the both of us and find a way out of here.

The night creeps by, dawn breaks, and it's not until the late afternoon that the lock on my door clanks and three figures backlit by lamplight step into my cell. I recognize one as the captain who arrested us and a second as one of her soldiers. But it is the third woman, tall and heavily cloaked, who catches my attention.

Because she is surrounded by ghuls.

They gather like hungry crows at her feet, hissing and pawing at her. I know, instantly, that she cannot see them.

"Bring in the brother, Captain Eleiba." The woman's Serran is husky and musical. She could be a *Kehanni* with a voice like that. She looks to be around Afya's age or perhaps a bit older, with light brown skin and thick, straight black hair pulled up in a knot. Her back is poker straight, and she walks gracefully, as if balancing a book on her head. "Sit, child," she says, and though her voice is pleasant enough, an underlying malice raises my hackles. Are the ghuls influencing her? I did not know they had such power.

They feed off sorrow and sadness and the stink of blood. Spiro Teluman spoke those words to me long ago. What sorrow plagues this woman?

Darin soon joins me, slowing when he enters, eyes wide. He sees the ghuls too. When he takes a seat on my cot beside me, I reach for his hand and squeeze. *They cannot hold us. I will not let them.*

The woman observes me for a long moment before smiling. "You," she says to me, "look nothing like the Lioness. And you"—she glances at Darin—"are her spitting image. Clever of her to keep you hidden. I expect it's why you're still alive."

The ghuls slither up the woman's cloak, hissing into her ear. Her lips curve into a sneer. "But then, my father tells me that Mirra always enjoyed her little secrets. I wonder, are you like her in other ways? Looking always to fight instead of fix, to break instead of build, to—"

"You shut it about my mother." My face grows hot. "How *dare* you—"

"You will please address Crown Princess Nikla of Marinn as *Princess* or *Your Highness*," Eleiba says. "And you will speak with respect for one of her station."

This woman, infested with ghuls who are influencing her mind, will one day rule Marinn? I want to frighten the fey creatures away from her, but I cannot manage it without looking as if I'm attacking her. Mariners are less skeptical than Scholars when it comes to the fey, but something tells me she still won't believe me if I tell her what I see.

"Don't bother, Eleiba." Nikla snorts. "I should have known she'd have the same lack of subtlety the Lioness did. Now, girl, let us discuss why you are here."

"Please." I speak through gritted teeth, knowing that my life is in Nikla's hands. "My brother and I are here to—"

"Make Serric steel weaponry," Nikla says. "Supply the Scholar refugees flooding the city. Instigate an uprising. Challenge the Mariners, despite all we have done for your people since the Empire uprooted them hundreds of years ago."

I am so flabbergasted that I almost cannot speak. "No," I sputter. "No, Princess, you have it wrong. We're not here to make weaponry, we—"

Do I tell her of the Nightbringer? Of Shaeva? I think of the stories of fey violence whispered along the road, stories I've been hearing for months. The ghuls may tell her that I lie. But I must warn her. "A threat approaches, Princess. A *great* threat. You have no doubt heard the tales of Mariner ships sinking in calm seas, of children disappearing in the dead of night."

Beside Nikla, Eleiba stiffens, her eyes jerking toward mine, filled with recognition. *She knows!* But Nikla holds up a hand. The ghuls chuckle nastily, slitted red eyes fixed on me.

"You sent your allies ahead of you to spread such lies among the Scholar population," she says. "Tales of monsters out of legend. Yes, your little friends did your work well."

Araj. *The Skiritae.* I sigh. Elias warned me that the Skiritae leader would spread word of my exploits far and wide. I hadn't given it much thought.

"They seeded your reputation among the newly arrived Scholars, a downtrodden and easily manipulated population. And then you arrived with your brother, your mother's legacy, and promises of Serric steel, safety, and security. All insurgents tell the same tale, girl. It just changes a bit with the telling."

"We don't want trouble." My trepidation rises, but I channel my grandfather, Pop, thinking of the time he delivered twins and I panicked. It was my first delivery, and with a few words, his serenity soothed me until my hands no longer shook. "We just want to—"

"Don't patronize me. My people have done *everything* for yours." Nikla paces the small cell, the ghuls following her like a pack of loyal dogs. "We have taken them into our city and integrated them into the fabric of Mariner culture. But our generosity is not without limits. Here in Marinn, we are not sadists, like the Martials. But we do not take kindly to rabble-rousers. Know that if you do not cooperate with me, I will have Captain Eleiba put you both on the next ship down to the Tribal lands—as we did your friends."

Oh hells. So that's what happened to Araj and Tas and the rest of the Skiritae. Skies, I hope they are all right.

"The Tribal lands are crawling with Martials." I try to temper my anger, but the more this woman talks, the more I want to scream. "If you send us there, we'll be killed or enslaved."

"Indeed." Nikla tilts her head, and the lamplight makes her eyes as red as the ghuls'. Did the Nightbringer set the ghuls on her? Is she another of his human allies, like the Warden or the Commandant?

"I have an offer for you, Darin of Serra," Nikla goes on. "If you've any sense, you'll see that it's more than fair. You wish to make Serric steel. Very well. Make Serric steel—for the Mariner army. We will provide you what you need, as well as accommodations for you and your sister—"

"No." Darin's gaze is fixed to the floor, and he shakes his head. "I won't do it."

Won't, I note. Not *can't*. A spark of hope flares within. Does my brother remember how to make the steel after all? Did something on the road from the Forest of Dusk to Adisa shake loose, allowing him to recall that which Spiro had taught him?

"Consider—"

"I won't do it." Darin stands, towering over Nikla by half a foot. Eleiba steps in front of the princess, but Darin speaks quietly, hands open at his sides. "I won't arm another group of people so that my own can live at their mercy."

"Please let us go." I kick out at the ghuls, scattering them for a moment before they congeal around Nikla again. "We don't mean you any harm, and you have greater things to worry about than two Scholars who want to stay out of trouble. The Empire has turned on the Tribes, and it might turn on Marinn too."

"The Martials have a treaty with Marinn."

"They had a treaty with the Tribes too," I say. "And yet hundreds have been killed or captured in the Tribal desert. This new emperor—you do not know him, Princess. He's . . . different. He's not someone you can work with. He's—"

"Don't talk politics to me, little girl." She doesn't see the ghul that clings to the side of her face, its mouth split in an odious smile. The sight of it nauseates me. "I was a force to be reckoned with in my father's court well before you were born." She turns to Darin. "My offer stands. Make weapons for my army, or take your chances in the Tribal lands. You have until dawn tomorrow to decide."

«««

D arin and I don't bother discussing Nikla's offer. I know there is no chance in the hells that he would accept. The ghuls have their hooks in her—which likely means the Nightbringer has a hand in Mariner politics. The last thing the Scholars need is another group lording it over us because we do not have the weapons for a fair fight.

"You said *won't*." I considered long and hard before bringing up Darin's seemingly offhand comment. My brother paces the cell, antsy as a penned horse. "When Nikla asked you to make the weapons, you didn't say you *can't* do it. You said you *won't*."

"Slip of the tongue." Darin stops his pacing, his back to me, and though it stings to admit it, he's lying. Do I push him or let it go?

You've been letting it go, Laia. Letting it go means Izzi died for nothing. It means Elias was imprisoned for nothing. It means Afya's cousin died for nothing.

I try a different tack. "Do you think Spiro—"

"Could we not talk about Spiro, or weaponry, or forging?" Darin sits down beside me, shoulders slumped, as if the walls of the cell are making him smaller. He clenches and unclenches his fists. "How the hells are we going to get out of here?"

"An excellent question," a soft voice says from the door. I jump—seconds ago, it was sealed shut. "One that I might have a solution to, if you care to hear it."

A young, dark-skinned Scholar man leans against the doorframe, in full view of the guards. Except, I realize, there are no guards to see him. They have disappeared.

The man is handsome, with black hair that's half pulled up and the rangy body of a swordsman. His forearms are tattooed, though in the darkness, I cannot make out the symbols. He tosses a key up and down like a ball. There is an insouciance to him that irritates me. The glint of his eyes and his wily smile are instantly familiar.

"I know you." I take a step back, wishing I had my dagger with me. "You're our shadow."

The man drops into a mocking bow, and I am immediately distrustful. Darin bristles.

"I am Musa of Adisa," the man says. "Son of Ziad and Azmath of Adisa. Grandson of Mehr and Saira of Adisa. I am also the only friend you have in this city."

"You said you have a solution to our problem." Trusting this man would be stupid, but Darin and I need to get the hells out of here. All Nikla's talk about putting us on a ship sounded like rubbish. She will not let a man who knows the secret of Serric steel simply walk away.

"I'll get you two out of here—for a price."

Naturally. "What price?"

"You"—he looks at Darin—"will make weapons for the Scholars. And you"—he turns to me—"will help me resurrect the northern Scholar's Resistance."

In the long silence that follows his proclamation, I want to laugh. If our circumstances were less dire, I would have. "No thank you. I've had enough of the bleeding Resistance—and those who support it."

"I expected you to say as much," Musa says. "After the way Mazen and Keenan betrayed you." He offers a grim smile as my fists curl, and I stare at him in shock. *How does he know?*

"Apologies," he says. "Not Keenan. *The Nightbringer.* In any case, your mistrust is understandable. But you need to stop the jinn lord, no? Which means you need out of here."

Darin and I gape at him. I get my voice back first. "How do you know about the—"

"I watch. I listen." Musa taps his foot and glances down the hall. His shoulders stiffen. Voices rise and fall from beyond the door to the cellblock, sharp and hurried. "Decide," he says. "We're nearly out of time."

"No." Darin speaks for us both, and I frown. It's unlike him. "You should leave. Unless you want to get thrown in here with us."

"I'd heard you were stubborn." Musa sighs. "Listen to logic, at least. Even if you do find your way out of here, how will you find the Beekeeper while the Mariners hunt you? Especially if he doesn't want to be found?"

"How did—" I stop myself from asking. He's already told me. He watches. He listens. "You know the Beekeeper."

"I swear I'll take you to him." Musa cuts his hand, blood dripping on the floor, and I raise my eyebrows. A blood oath is no small thing. "After I get you out of here. *If* you agree to my terms. But we need to move. *Now.*"

"Darin." I grab my brother's arm and drag him to a corner of the cell. "If he can take us to the Beekeeper, we'll save weeks of time."

"I don't trust him," Darin says. "You know I want to get out of here as much as you do. More. But I won't make a promise I can't keep, and neither should you. Why does he want you to help him with the Resistance? What's in it for him? Why not do it himself?"

"I don't trust him either," I say. "But he's offering us a way out." I consider my brother. I consider his lie earlier. And though I don't want to hurt him, I know that if we ever want to get out of here, I have to.

"Pardon me," Musa says. "But we really need to—"

"Shut it," I snap at him before turning back to Darin. "You lied to me," I say. "About the weapons. No"—I raise my hand at his protest—"I'm not angry. But I don't think you understand what you're doing. You're *choosing* not to make the weapons. It's a selfish choice. Our people need you, Darin.

And that should matter more than your desires or your pain. You saw what's happening out there to the Scholars," I say. "It's not going to stop. Even if I defeat the Nightbringer, we'll always be lesser unless we can stand up for ourselves. We *need* Serric steel."

"Laia, I want to make it, I do—"

"Then *try*," I say. "That's all I'm asking. Try. For Izzi. For Afya, who has lost a half dozen of her Tribe trying to help us. For"—my voice cracks—"for Elias. For the life he gave up for you."

Darin's blue eyes widen in surprise and hurt. His demons rise, demanding his attention. But somewhere beneath the fear, he is still the Lioness's son, and this time, the quiet courage he has had all our lives wins out.

"Where you go, sis," he says, "I go. I'll try."

In seconds, Musa—who has been shamelessly eavesdropping—gestures us into the hall. The moment Darin is out, he grabs Musa by the neck and shoves him against the wall. I hear a sound like an animal chittering, but it goes silent after Musa makes a strange slashing motion with his hand. A *ghul?*

"If you hurt my sister," Darin says quietly, "if you betray her, or abuse her trust or cause her pain, I swear to the skies I will kill you."

Musa chokes out an answer, and as Darin lets him down, keys clang in the door down the hall. Seconds later, it flies open and Eleiba enters, scim drawn.

"Musa!" she snarls. "I should have *bleeding* known. You are under arrest."

"Well, now you've done it." Musa rubs his neck where Darin grabbed him, mild irritation on his fine features. "We could have been away by now if not for your brotherly posturing." With that, he whispers something, and Eleiba falls back, cursing, as if something we cannot see attacks her.

Musa looks between Darin and me with arched brows. "Any other threats? Discussions you wish to waste my time with? None? Good. Then let's get the bleeding hells out of here."

« « «

D awn approaches by the time Musa, Darin, and I emerge from a tailor's shop and out into Adisa. My head spins from the strange, interconnected series of tunnels, passageways, and alleys Musa took to get us here. But we are out. We are free.

"Not bad timing," Musa says. "If we hurry, we can get to a safe house before—"

"Wait." I grab him by the shoulder. "We're not going anywhere with you." Beside me, Darin nods vehemently. "Not until you tell us who you are. Why did Captain Eleiba know you? What in the skies attacked her? I heard a noise. It sounded like a ghul. Since Princess Nikla was crawling with them, you understand why I am concerned."

Musa easily extricates himself from my grip, straightening his shirt, which I notice is quite finely made, for a Scholar.

"She wasn't always like that," he says. "Nik—the princess, I mean. But that doesn't matter now. Dawn isn't far away. We really don't have time—"

"Stop making excuses," I snarl. "And start explaining."

Musa groans in irritation. "If I answer *one* question," he says, "will you stop being so annoying and let me get you to a safe house?"

I consider, glancing at Darin, who gives me a noncommittal shrug. Now that Musa's gotten us out, I only need one bit of information from him. Once I get it, I can become invisible and knock him out, and Darin and I can disappear.

"Fine," I say. "Who's the Beekeeper, and how can I find him?"

"Ah, Laia of Serra." His white teeth shine like those of a smug horse. He offers me his arm, and under the brightening sky, I finally get a closer look at his tattoos—dozens of them, big and small, all clustered around a hive.

Bees.

"It's me, of course," Musa says. "Don't tell me you hadn't guessed."

XV: Elias

For days, I cajole and threaten and lure the ghosts away from the border wall. Skies only know what will happen if they break out. They grow more frenzied by the hour, it seems, until I can barely hear myself think over their accursed caterwauling.

A fortnight after I've left Aubarit—and with no sense of how to move the ghosts any quicker or how to help the *Fakira*—I retire to Shaeva's cottage for the night, desperately grateful for this, my only sanctuary. The ghosts paw at me as I enter, wild as an Isle South typhoon.

She shouldn't have—

My husband, is he here, tell me—

Have you seen my lovey—

Usually, I feel guilty when I close the cottage door on the ghosts. Not today. I'm too exhausted, too angered by my failure, too disgusted by the relief I feel at the sudden, complete silence within Shaeva's home.

Sleep in the cottage. They cannot hurt you there.

Somehow, Shaeva magicked the cottage to insulate it from the ghosts and jinn. That bit of sorcery didn't die with her. She knew I would need a place where I could collect my thoughts, and I am grateful for it.

But my thankfulness doesn't last long. After I've cleaned up and cooked a paltry meal that Shaeva would have scoffed at, I can't bring myself to sleep. I pace in a circle, guilt gnawing at my gut. The Soul Catcher's boots still sit by her bed. The arrows she was fletching lie untouched on her worktable. These small tokens from her life used to bring me comfort, especially in the days just after she died. Like the cottage itself, they reminded me that she believed I could be Soul Catcher.

But tonight, her memory plagues me. *Why did you not listen to me, Elias? Why did you not learn?* Skies, she would be so disappointed.

I kick at the door violently—a stupid decision, as now my foot aches. I wonder if my entire life will be a series of moments in which I realize I'm an idiot long after I can actually do anything about it. Will I ever feel like I know what I'm doing? Or will I be an old man, tottering about, flummoxed by whatever recent foolishness I've committed?

Don't be pathetic. Strangely, Keris Veturia's taut voice rises in my mind. *You know the question: How do you move the ghosts faster? Now find the answer. Think.*

I consider Aubarit's words. *You must move the spirits, and to do that you must remove yourself from the world.* A variation on Shaeva's advice. But I *have* removed myself from the world. I said farewell to Laia and Darin. I kept away all others who approached the Forest. I burgle my supplies quietly from villages instead of buying them from another human, the way I yearn to.

The Forest will show thee its sly memory. Were the Mysteries referring to Mauth? Or was there something more to the statement? *Forest could be referring to something else entirely*, Aubarit had said. The ghosts, perhaps? But they don't spend enough time in the Waiting Place to know anything.

Though, now that I think of it, not all of the spirits move on swiftly.

The Wisp. I grab my scims—more out of habit than because I actually need them—and head out. Just before entering the cottage, I heard her voice. But she's not here now.

Damn you, Elias, think. The Wisp used to avoid Shaeva. When the ghost speaks at all, it's to me, and it's always about her "lovey." And, unlike the other shades, she likes water. She often lurks near a spring just south of the cottage.

The path to it is well-worn; when I moved into the cottage, Shaeva lost no time in passing all water-fetching chores to me. *What's the point of having muscles*, she'd teased, *if you can't carry things for others?*

I catch a glint of white as I draw closer and soon find the Wisp at the edge of the spring, staring down into it.

She turns her face toward me and flits backward—she's in no mood to talk. But I can't afford to let her get away.

"You're looking for your lovey, right?"

The Wisp stops and appears before me so suddenly that I rock back on my heels.

"You know where she is?" Her thin voice is painfully happy, and guilt twists in my gut.

"Ah, not exactly," I say. "But perhaps you could help me? And I could help you?"

The Wisp tilts her head, considering.

"I'm trying to learn about the magic of the Waiting Place," I say before she disappears again. "About Mauth. You've been here a long time. Can you tell me anything about the Forest having a . . . a memory?"

"Where is my lovey?"

I curse. I should've known better than to think a ghost—and one who refuses to move on—could help me.

"I'm sorry," I say. "I'll look for your lovey." I turn back for the cottage. Perhaps I need sleep. Perhaps I'll have a better idea in the morning. Or I could go back to Aubarit and see if she remembers anything else. Or find another *Fakira* . . .

"The memory is in the pain."

I spin so fast it's a miracle my head doesn't fly off. "What—what did you say?"

"The memory is in the pain." The Wisp circles me, and I spin as she does. I'm not letting her out of my sight. "The memory is where the greatest hurt lies, the greatest anger."

"What in ten hells do you mean, 'the greatest hurt'?"

"A hurt like mine. The memory is in the pain, little one. In *their* pain. They burn with it, for they have lived with it much longer than I."

Their pain.

"The jinn?" My stomach sinks. "You're speaking of the jinn."

But the Wisp is gone now, calling out to her lovey. I try to follow her, but I can't keep up. Other ghosts, drawn by my voice, cluster near, flooding me with their suffering. I windwalk away from them, though I know it's wrong to ignore their misery. Eventually, they'll find me again and I'll be forced to try to pass some on, simply so I don't lose my mind at their badgering. But before they do, I need to sort this out. The longer I wait, the more the ghosts will amass.

Think quickly, Elias! Could the jinn help me? They've been imprisoned here for a thousand years, but they were free once, and they possessed the most powerful magic in the land. They are fey. Born of magic, like the efrits, the wraiths, the ghuls. Now that the idea is in my head, I've latched on to it like a dog to a bone. The jinn *must* have some deeper knowledge of the magic.

And I need to figure out a way to get it from them.

XVI: The Blood Shrike

"The Paters of Navium," the Nightbringer says as we leave the docks, "wish to greet you."

I barely hear him. He knows Livia is pregnant. He will share that information with the Commandant. My sister will confront attackers and assassins likely within days, and I am not there to keep her safe.

Harper falls back, speaking urgently to the Black Guard who brought us our horses. Now that he knows of the pregnancy he'll be sending orders to Faris and Rallius to triple the guard around Livia.

"The Paters are at the Island?" I ask the Nightbringer.

"Indeed, Shrike."

For now, I must put my faith in Livia's bodyguards. My more immediate issue is the Commandant. She's already taken the upper hand by sending the Nightbringer to throw me off my guard. She wants me weak.

But I will not give her that satisfaction. She wants to order me to the Island? Fine. I need to take control of this sinking ship anyway. If the Paters are nearby, all the better. They can bear witness as I wrench Keris's power from her.

As we ride through the streets, the full devastation of the Karkaun attack is apparent in every collapsed building, every burn-scarred street.

The ground shudders, and the unmistakable whistle of a stone ripping out of a ballista splits the air. As we get closer to the Island, the Nightbringer is forced to change course, leading us near the embattled Southwest Quarter of Navium.

Screams and shouts fill the air, penetrating over the roar of fire. I pull up a bandanna to block out the choking smells of singed flesh and stone.

A group of Plebeians hurries past, most carrying nothing but children and the clothes on their backs. I watch a woman with a hood pulled low. Her face and body are hidden by a cloak, her hands stained a deep gold. The color is so unusual that I nudge my horse forward to get a closer look.

A fire brigade gallops by, buckets of seawater splashing everywhere. When they are past, the woman is gone. Soldiers lead families from the swiftly spreading chaos. Cries for aid seem to come from all sides. A child with blood streaming down her face stands in the middle of an alley, bewildered and silent, no guardian in sight. She's no more than four, and without thinking, I turn my horse toward her.

"Shrike, no!" Avitas reappears and kicks his mount in front of mine. "One of the men will take care of her. We have to get to the Island."

I make myself turn away, ignoring the pull that has come over me to go to the child, to heal her. It is so strong that I have to grab the pommel of my saddle, lacing my fingers under it to keep myself from dismounting.

The Nightbringer watches me from the back of a cloud-white stallion. I sense no malice, only curiosity.

"You are not like her," he observes. "The Commandant is not a woman of the people."

"I thought you'd appreciate that about her, being that you are not a man of the people yourself."

"I am not a man of *your* people," the Nightbringer says. "But I do wonder at Keris. You humans give your loyalty so willingly for just a little hope."

"And you think we are fools because of it?" I shake my head. "Hope is stronger than fear. It is stronger than hate."

"Precisely, Blood Shrike. Keris could use it as a weapon. But she does not. To her folly."

He makes a poor ally, I think to myself, *or a dissatisfied one, to criticize her so openly.*

"I'm not her ally, Blood Shrike." The Nightbringer cocks his head, and I sense his amusement. "I am her master."

A half hour later, Navium's key-shaped double harbor comes into view. The rectangular merchant harbor, which opens into the sea, has been decimated. The channel is littered with charred masts and soggy, torn sails. The huge, rusted sea chains that protect the harbor gleam with moss and barnacles, but at least they are up. Why the hells *weren't* they up when Grímarr attacked? Where were the guards on the watchtowers? Why weren't we able to halt the assault?

At its northern end, the merchant harbor widens into an inner harbor made of two rings. The Island is the center ring, connected to the mainland by a bridge. A crenellated tower dominates the Island. From its top, one can see up and down the coast for miles. The outer ring of the harbor is a covered, circular dock with hundreds of slipways for the Martial fleet. Its scale is mind-boggling.

Dex swears as we get closer. "The ships are docked, Shrike," he says. "We're just letting them pummel us."

Though the earlier report from Harper said as much, I don't believe it until I see the ships myself, bobbing quietly in their slips. My hands curl into fists as I think of the destruction I just witnessed.

When we finally reach the bridge that leads to the Island, I stop short. For hanging from a rope over the wall is Admiral Lenidas, a fat crow perched atop his twisted body. I bite my lip to keep from retching. His broken limbs and lash-marred skin tell the tale of a slow, painful death.

I take the stairs up to the watchtower two at a time. Dex and Harper run to catch up, the latter clearing his throat just before we enter the command room.

"Shrike." He leans close, his distress evident. "She's penned a play," he says. "I can feel it. Don't act the part she's written for you."

I nod shortly—did he think I didn't know that?—and enter the tower. The Veturius men guarding it immediately salute. The Commandant barks out orders to the runners to take to the drum towers, ignoring me entirely. The top brass of Navium, along with a dozen of its Paters, are gathered around a map on a massive table. As one, they turn.

"Nephew." I recognize Janus Atrius—Dex's uncle and the Pater of Gens Atria. He nods a quick greeting at his nephew before saluting me. I cannot read his features, but he glances askance at Keris before speaking—a look I am not meant to miss, I think. "Shrike, have you been briefed?"

"Half of the Southwest Quarter is on fire," I say. "That's all the briefing I need. Why are we not fighting back? Night won't fall for hours. We need to use the light that remains."

Janus and a few of the other Paters mutter their agreement. But the rest shake their heads, a few raising their voices in dispute. Admiral Argus and Vice Admiral Vissellius exchange a look of disgust that I make note of. I won't find an ally in either of them.

"Blood Shrike." The Commandant has finished with the runners, and her cool voice silences the room. Despite the hatred that rises in me at her patronizing tone, I admire the way she wields her power. Though the men in this room are lords of their own Gens, not a single one will defy her. "We expected you days ago. I—we"—she glances at the Paters and navy officers—"are yours to command."

This woman trained all expression from my face, but it is difficult not to show my surprise. As Blood Shrike, I am a superior officer, and the Emperor sent me to take command of Navium's defense. But I did not expect the Commandant to give it up so easily. I did not expect her to give it up at all.

Harper gives me a warning look. *Don't act the part she's written for you.*

"Keris." I hide my wariness. "Why do we not have boats in the water?"

"The weather is treacherous, Shrike. For the past few weeks storms have moved in swiftly." She walks to the tall windows that look south. From here, I can see the whole coast, along with the distant masts of a massive Karkaun fleet. "That cloud bank"—she nods to it—"has been there for three days. The last time we took the fleet out, the weather was similar."

"Lenidas knew sea weather better than anyone."

"Lenidas ignored the orders of a superior officer simply because she commands an army instead of a navy." Admiral Argus leads one of the more powerful Mercator Gens, and his rage at his lost ships is clear. "General Veturia ordered him not to take out the fleet, and he didn't listen. We all"—he gives the room a glower—"supported Lenidas's execution."

"Not all," Janus Atrius says stiffly.

"Lenidas is not the point," I say. The old man is dead, and while he didn't deserve to die in disgrace, this is not a battle I can win. "Keris, have you been in the Southwest Quarter since the attack began?"

Argus pushes forward, planting himself in front of me like a squat, belligerent toad. "The Commandant has—"

Beside me, Dex half draws a scim. "Interrupt me one more time, Argus," I say, "and I'll have Captain Atrius make me a necklace of your entrails."

The Paters fall silent, and I let them consider the threat before I speak.

"Paters," I say, "I won't launch the fleet without your approval. But consider our losses. More than a thousand killed already and dozens dying by the hour. I've seen children with their limbs blasted off, women trapped beneath rubble dying slowly. Grímarr the Karkaun is a vicious foe. Will we let him take our city?"

"Most of the city is safe," Vissellius argues. "It is only the Southwest Quarter that has—"

"Just because they're not Mercators or Illustrians doesn't make their lives any less valuable. We have to do *something*."

Keris holds up a hand to silence her allies. "The watchtower ballistae—"

"Are too far from the ships to do any real damage," I cut her off. "What in the skies was your plan? To sit here and just let them destroy us?"

"Our plan was to allow them to believe they could storm the city," the Commandant says. "When they made the mistake of landing their troops, we would wipe them out. We would launch an attack on their ships"—she points this out on the map—"from a nearby cove, where we would move the fleet at night. We would stop the Karkaun ground forces while still capturing their ships, which would replace those the Mercators lost in the attack on the harbor."

The bleeding weather has nothing to do with this after all. She wants the Barbarian ships. She wants them so she can get Navium's Paters in her pocket—all the better to secure their support when she tries to take down Marcus again.

"And you were planning to do this when, exactly?"

"We expected three more weeks of siege. We've been choking off their supplies. Grímarr and his men will run out of food eventually."

"Once they finish with the Southwest Quarter," I say, "they'll move to the Southeast. You're willing to allow dozens of neighborhoods—thousands of homes—to be besieged for nearly a month. There are more than a hundred thousand people living—"

"We are evacuating the southern parts of the city, Shrike."

"Not fast enough." I consider. We must protect Navium, of course. But I smell a trap. Harper taps a thumb on his scim hilt. He senses it too.

And yet I cannot let Grímarr murder my people at will. "Admiral Argus, how long to prepare the fleet?"

"We could launch by second bell, but the weather—"

"We will engage the Karkauns at sea," I say, and though I promised I'd get the Paters' permission, I have no time for it. Not when every minute brings more Martial deaths. "And we will do it now."

"I'm with you, Shrike." Janus Atrius steps forward, as do a half dozen other Paters and officers. Most, however, are clearly opposed.

"Consider," Keris says, "that the fleet is our only defense, Shrike. If a storm comes in—"

"You and I both know," I say quietly, "that this has nothing to do with the weather."

I glance at Dex, who nods, and Harper, who watches the Commandant fixedly. His expression is unreadable. *Don't act the part she's written for you.*

In the end, I might be playing into her hands. But I'll just have to concoct a way out of whatever trap she's laid for me. These are the lives of my people, and come what may, I cannot leave them to die.

"Admiral Argus." My tone brooks no disapproval, and though his eyes are rebellious, one look from me quells it. "Launch the fleet."

«««

After an hour, the men are mustered, and the laborious process of dropping the sea chains begins. After two hours, the fleet sails from the circular war port and into the merchant harbor. After three, our men are locked in combat with the Karkauns.

But after four hours, the sky, thick with clouds and rain, deepens from a threatening gray to an eerie dark purple, and I know we are in trouble. Lightning cracks across the water, striking mast after mast. Flames leap high, distant bursts of light that tell me the battle is turning—and not in our favor.

The storm comes suddenly, roiling toward Navium from the south as if whipped forth by a wrathful wind. By the time it hits, it is far too late to turn the fleet back.

"Admiral Argus has sailed these seas for two decades," Dex says quietly as the storm intensifies. "He might be Keris's dog, but he'll bring the fleet home. He'll have no wish to die."

I should have gone with them. But the Commandant and Harper and Dex all protested—the one thing the three of them agreed on.

I seek out Keris, who speaks quietly with one of the drum-tower runners.

"No reports yet, Shrike," she says. "The drum towers cannot hear anything over the storm. We must wait."

The runner steps away, and we are, for a moment, alone.

"Who is this Grímarr?" I ask her. "Why do we know nothing about him?"

"He's a zealot, a warlock priest who worships the dead. He believes it is his spiritual duty to convert all those who are unenlightened. That includes the Martials."

"By killing us."

"Apparently," Keris says softly. "He's a relatively young man, a dozen or so years older than you. His father traded furs, so Grímarr traveled the

Empire extensively as a boy—to learn our ways, no doubt. He returned to his people a decade ago, just as a famine hit. The clans were starving, weak—and malleable." The Commandant shrugs. "So he molded them."

I'm surprised at the depth of her knowledge, and she must see it on my face. "What is the first rule of war, Blood Shrike?"

Know your enemy. I don't even have to say it.

I look out at the storm and shudder. The gale feels fey. Wild. Thinking of what will happen if our fleet succumbs makes my stomach churn. We sent out nearly every vessel, holding back only a dozen ships. Night approaches, and still we have no word.

We cannot lose the fleet. We are the Empire. The Martials. Argus's men are trained for this. They've seen storms far worse.

I cycle through every scrap of hope I can claw from the recesses of my mind. But as the minutes pass, the distant flashes of battle continue unabated. And those flashes that are closer to Navium—those that belong to our fleet—grow fewer and fewer.

"We should put up the sea chains, Shrike," the Commandant finally says. The Paters agree with a dozen angry *ayes*.

"Our fleet is still out there."

"If the fleet survives, we will know in the morning and we can lower the chains. But if they do not, then we keep the Karkauns from penetrating to the heart of Navium."

I nod my assent, and the order is given. The night drags on. Does the storm carry the shrieking taunts of Karkaun warlocks? Or is that just the wind? *Hope is stronger than fear. It is stronger than hate.* I said those words to the Nightbringer, and as night deepens to an impenetrable blackness, I hold on to them. No matter what dawn brings, I will not give up hope.

Soon, the sky pales. The clouds thin and roll back. The city is swept clean and sparkling, the red and gray roofs gleaming in the wan sunlight. The sea is as smooth as glass.

And, except for the mass of Karkaun ships bobbing well off the coast, it is empty.

The Martial fleet is gone.

Impossible.

"You did not listen." The Pater who speaks is the head of Gens Serica, a wealthy family of silk merchants who have long been established in the south. My father considered him a friend. The man is pale; his hands shake. There is no venom to his words, because he is in shock. "And the fleet—the city—"

"I did warn you, Blood Shrike." As Keris speaks, the hairs on the back of my neck rise. Her gaze is cold, but the spot of triumph she's buried deep within shows itself. *What the skies?*

We just lost the entire bleeding fleet. Thousands of men. Even the Commandant couldn't have anything to rejoice in the death of her own people.

Unless that was her plan this entire time.

Which, I now realize, it must have been. In one swoop, she has undermined my authority, destroyed my reputation, and guaranteed that the Paters will turn to her for guidance. And all it cost her was the entire bleeding fleet. The plan is repugnant—evil—and because of that, I did not even consider it. But I should have.

Know your enemy.

Bleeding skies. I should have realized she would never hand over power so easily.

And yet she couldn't have known the storm was coming. None of us could have, not with the sky so clear and the threatening cloud bank so distant.

Suddenly—and far too late for it to be any use—I remember the Nightbringer. After delivering me to the Island, he disappeared. I thought nothing more of him. But what of his power? Can he create storms? Would he?

And if so, would the Commandant have requested it of him? She could have proved my incompetence in a thousand ways. Losing the entire fleet seems excessive. Even with me out of the way, how will she defend Navium with no navy?

No, something else is going on. Some other game. But what is it?

I look to Dex, who shakes his head, stricken. I cannot bring myself to look at Harper.

"I will go to the beach to see if anything can be salvaged from the wrecks," the Commandant says. "If I have your leave, Shrike."

"Go."

The Paters file out of the room, no doubt to take the news to the rest of their Gens. Keris trails them. At the door, she stops. Turns. She is the Commandant again, and I the ignorant student. Her eyes are exultant—and predatory. The exact opposite of what they should be, considering our loss.

Keris smiles, a smirk from a murderess sharpening her blades for the kill. "Welcome to Navium, Blood Shrike."

XVII: Laia

The night is deep when we arrive at Musa's safe house, a forge that squats in Adisa's central shipyard, just beyond the Scholar refugee camp. At this hour, the shipyard is empty, its silent streets eerily shadowed by the skeletons of half-built vessels.

Musa does not even glance over his shoulder as he unlocks the forge's back door, but I am uneasy, unable to shake the sense that someone— something—watches us.

Within a few hours, that feeling is gone, and the yard thunders with the shouts of builders, the pounding of hammers, and the protesting creak of wood as it is bowed and nailed into place. From my room, on the forge's upper level, I peer down into a courtyard where a gray-haired Scholar woman stokes an already roaring fire. The cacophony surrounding this place is perfect for clandestine weapon-making. And Musa said he'd get Darin whatever supplies he needs. Which means my brother *must* make weapons. He is out of excuses.

I, on the other hand, might still find a way out of the bargain Musa insisted on. *You will help me resurrect the northern Scholar's Resistance.* Why has Musa not done it already? He has resources. And there must be hundreds of Scholars who would join up—especially after the Empire's genocide.

Something else is going on—something he's not telling me.

After a much-needed bath, I make my way downstairs, clad in a wool dress of deep red and soft new boots that are only a little big. The ping of steel on steel echoes in the courtyard, and two women laugh over the din. Though the courtyard houses the forge, the building I'm in has the personal touches of a house—thick rugs, a shawl thrown over a bureau, and cheerful Tribal lanterns. At the foot of the stairs, a long, wide hall leads to a drawing room. The door is ajar, and Musa's voice carries through.

"—very knowledgeable and can assist you," Musa says. "When can you start?"

A long pause. "Now. But it will take me a bit to get the formula right. There is much I don't remember." Darin sounds stronger than he has in weeks. Rest and a bath must have done him good.

"Then I'll introduce you to the smiths here. They make pots, pans, horseshoes—enough household items to justify the amount of ore and coal we'll need."

Someone clears her throat loudly behind me. The sounds of smithing have stopped, I realize, and I turn to find the silver-haired, brown-skinned Scholar woman from the courtyard. She wears a burn-scarred leather smock, and her face is wide and pretty. Beside her, a young woman who is clearly her daughter watches me with dark green eyes that sparkle in curiosity.

"Laia of Serra," the older woman says. "I am Smith Zella, and this is my daughter, Taure. It is an honor to meet the heir of the Lioness." Zella clasps my hands between her own. "Do not believe the lies the Mariners spread about your mother, child," she says. "They are threatened by you. They wish to hurt you."

"What lies?"

"We've heard all about what you did in the Empire." Taure speaks up breathlessly, and the admiration in her tone alarms me.

"It was luck, mostly. You—you mentioned my mother—"

"Not luck." Musa strolls out of the drawing room, Darin in tow. "Laia clearly has her mother's courage—and her father's sense of strategy. Zella, show Darin where he'll be making weapons, and get him what he needs. Laia, come inside, if you please. Lunch awaits."

The two smiths leave with my brother, Taure with one last reverent glance over her shoulder, and I fidget as Musa waves me into the drawing room.

"What skies-forsaken stories did you tell them about me?" I hiss at him.

"I said nothing." He piles a plate with fruit, bread, and butter and hands it to me. "Your reputation precedes you. The fact that you nobly sacrificed yourself for the good of the refugee camp helped."

My skin tingles warningly at the smugness on his face. Why, exactly, would he look so pleased about it?

"Did you plan for Darin and me to be captured?"

"I had to test you somehow, and I knew I could spring you from prison. I made sure Captain Eleiba knew you were coming into the city. Anonymously, of course. I knew if you were the leader I hoped you were, you'd never let your people suffer while you cowered. And if you weren't, I'd have dragged you out of hiding and turned you over myself."

I narrow my eyes at him. "What do you mean, 'leader'?"

"It's just a word, Laia. It won't bite. In any case, I was right—"

"How dare you make those poor people suffer! They lost their homes, their belongings. The Mariners ripped that camp apart!"

"Calm down." Musa rolls his eyes. "No one died. The Mariners are too civilized for such tactics. Captain Eleiba and I have our . . . differences. But she's an honorable woman. She has already replaced their tents. By now she will know it was me who gave up your whereabouts, of course. She'll be hopping mad about it too. But I can deal with her later. First we—"

"We?"

"First"—Musa clears his throat pointedly—"*you* need to eat. You're irritable. I don't like talking to irritable people."

How can he take all of this so lightly? I take a step toward him, my hands curling into fists, temper rising.

Almost immediately, a force shoves me back. It feels like a hundred sets of tiny hands. I try to squirm away, but the hands hold me tight. On instinct, I try to disappear, and I even flicker out of sight for a moment. But to my shock, Musa grabs my arm, unaffected by my magic, and I flicker back into view.

"I have my own magic, Laia of Serra," he says, and the mirth has left his face. "Yours doesn't work on me. I know what Shaeva said—you discussed it with your brother on your way here. *Your answers lie in Adisa. With the Bee-keeper. But beware, for he is cloaked in lies and shadow, like you.* The magic is my lie, Laia, as it is yours. I can be your ally, or I can be your enemy. But either way, I will hold you to your promise to help resurrect the Resistance."

He releases me, and I scramble away, straightening my dress, trying not to show how much his revelation has rattled me.

"It just seems as if this is a game to you," I whisper. "I don't have time to help you with the Resistance. I need to stop the Nightbringer. Shaeva told me to look for the Beekeeper. Here you are. But I thought—"

"You thought I would be a wise old man ready to tell you exactly what you must do to stop the jinn? Life is rarely so simple, Laia. But be assured that this is no game. It is the survival of our people. If you work with me, you can succeed in your mission to bring down the Nightbringer while also helping the Scholars. For instance, if we work with the king of Marinn—"

I snort. "You mean the king who has a price on my head?" I say. "The one who ordered men and women and children who have seen genocide to be put in camps outside the city instead of treated like humans? That king?"

I push my plate away, frustrated now, food half-eaten. "How can you help me? Why would Shaeva send me to you?"

"Because I can get you what you need." Musa tips his seat back. "It's my specialty. So tell me: What *do* you need?"

"I need . . ." *To be a mind reader. To have fey powers beyond disappearing. To be a Mask.*

"I need eyes on the Nightbringer," I say. "And on his allies. The prophecy said he needed only one more piece to complete the Star. I need to know if he has found it or if he's close. I need to know if he's . . . cozying up to anyone. Gaining their trust. Their . . . their love. But . . ." Saying the words aloud makes me feel hopeless. "How am I supposed to accomplish that?"

"I have it on good authority that he's in Navium now and has been for the past month."

"How did you—"

"Don't make me say it again, Laia of Serra. What do I do?"

"You watch." My relief is so keen that I'm not even irritated at Musa's arrogance. "You listen. How fast can you get me information on the jinn?"

Musa strokes his chin "Let's see. It took me a week to learn that you'd broken Elias out of Blackcliff's dungeons. Six days to learn that you'd set off a riot in Nur. Five to learn what Elias Veturius whispered in your ear the night he abandoned you in the Tribal desert for Kauf Prison. Two to learn that the Warden—"

"Wait," I choke out. The room suddenly feels warm. I have tried not to think of Elias. But he haunts my thoughts, a ghost who is always on my mind and always out of reach. "Just wait. Go . . . go back. What did Elias whisper in my ear the night he left me for Kauf?"

"It was good." Musa gazes off musingly. "Very dramatic. Might use it myself on some lucky girl one day."

Skies, he is insufferable. "Do you know if Elias is all right?" I tap my fingers on the polished table, trying to check my impatience. "Do you know—"

"My spies don't enter the Forest of Dusk," Musa says. "Too afraid. Forget about your pretty Martial. I can get the information you need."

"I also need to know how to stop the Nightbringer," I say. "How to fight him. And that's the kind of thing I can find only in books. Can you get me into the Great Library? There must be *something* there about the history of the jinn, about how the Scholars beat them before."

"Ah." Musa spears a slice of apple and pops it into his mouth, then shakes his head. "That could take some time, as I'm banned from it. I'd suggest you sneak into the library, but King Irmand has contracted Jaduna to ward off any fey creatures trying to do exactly that."

Jaduna. I shudder. Nan told stories of the hot-tempered magic-wielders said to live in the poisoned lands west of the Empire. I'd prefer not to find out if the tales are true.

Musa nods. "Exactly," he says. "They sniff out magic like sharks sniff out blood. Trust me, you wouldn't want to cross one of them."

"But—"

"Fret not. We'll think of something else. And in the meantime, you can start carrying out your part of our deal."

"Listen." I try to sound reasonable. I don't think Musa will be willing to listen to this argument more than once. "You must see that I have no idea how—"

"You're not getting out of this," he says. "Stop trying. I do not expect you to recruit a hundred fighters tomorrow," he says. "Or next week. Or even next month. First you have to be someone worth listening to, someone worth following. For that to happen, the Scholars in Adisa and in the camps need to know who you are and what you've done. And that means that for now, all I need from you is a story."

"A—a story?"

"Yes. Your story. Get yourself a cup of tea, Laia. I think we'll be here a while."

«‹«

I spend my days with Darin, pumping bellows and shoveling mounds of coal into a furnace, trying to make sure that the spray of sparks that explodes with every strike of his hammer doesn't burn down the forge. We battle across the courtyard to test his blades, most of which break. But he keeps at it, and every day he spends at the forge makes him stronger, more like his old self. It is as if lifting the hammer has reminded him of the man he was before Kauf—and the man he wants to be now.

I, meanwhile, have no purpose at all other than to wait.

"No sneaking around outside the forge." Musa's said it a dozen times. "The Jaduna I spoke of report to the king. If they see you, you'll find yourself back in prison, and I don't fancy having to rescue you again."

If Musa has information for me, he doesn't share it. Nor do we have any news from the outside world. With every day that goes by, I am more mistrustful. Does the Scholar man truly intend to help me? Or are his promises to aid me a ploy to get Darin to make weapons?

A week flies past. Then another. The Grain Moon is a mere eight weeks away, and I am spending my time testing blades that keep breaking. One morning, while Musa is out, I sneak into his quarters, hoping to find something—anything—about his past, the Resistance, or his information network. But all I discover is that he has a taste for candied almonds, which I find tucked away in drawers, beneath the bed, and most bizarrely, in a set of old boots.

On most evenings, Musa introduces me to other Scholars he knows and trusts. Some are refugees, like me, but many are Adisan Scholars. Every time, I have to tell my story again. Every time, Musa refuses to explain his plan for resurrecting the Resistance.

What were you thinking, Shaeva? Why did you send me to this man?

News finally arrives in the form of a scroll that appears in Musa's hand one day, in the middle of dinner. Darin and Zella are deep in conversation, Taure is telling me the story of a girl she's fallen for in the camps, and I'm staring daggers at Musa, who is placidly stuffing his face as if the fate of the world doesn't hinge on his ability to get me information.

My fixed glare is the only reason I even see the scroll appear. One second, it's not there, the next, he's unrolling it.

"The Nightbringer," he says, "is in Navium with the Commandant, the Paters of the city, the Blood Shrike, and her men. He hasn't left there in weeks. There is some infighting between the Commandant and the Blood Shrike, apparently—"

I groan. "That doesn't help me at *all*. I need to know whom he's seeing. Whom he's talking to—"

"Apparently, he's spent a great deal of time in his chambers, recovering from sinking the Martial fleet," Musa says. "Must take a lot of energy, murdering a few thousand souls and sending their vessels to the bottom of the sea."

"I need more," I say. "He has to be doing *something* beyond sitting in his quarters. Are there any fey creatures around him? Are they getting stronger? How fare the Tribes?"

But Musa has nothing more to offer—not yet, anyway.

Which means I have to take matters into my own hands. I *need* to get out into the city. Jaduna or not, I need to at least learn what's happening elsewhere in the Empire. After dinner, as Darin, Taure, and Zella discuss the different clays used for cooling a blade, I yawn and excuse myself. Musa has long since retired, and I pause outside his room. Snores rumble within. Moments later, I am invisible and cutting my way west, toward Adisa's central markets.

Though I was only in the refugee camp for moments, the difference between it and the Mariner city is stark. The camp was dingy tents and sucking mud. Adisa's cobbled streets are lined with houses of azure and violet, more alive at night than during the day. The camp was full of young Scholars with jutting collarbones and swollen bellies. Here, I don't see a single starving child.

What kind of king would allow this? Is there no space in this massive city for the Scholar souls freezing beyond its gates?

Maybe it's not the king. Maybe it's his ghul-infested daughter. The creatures flit through the market too, a seething blight lurking on the fringes of the crowds.

In the city's center, brightly dressed Mariners haggle and joke and trade. Silk kites sail like ships overhead, and I stop to ogle clay vessels with entire books painted on their sides. An Ankanese seer from the far south rasps out fortunes, and a kohl-eyed Jaduna watches him, the gold coins strung across her forehead catching the light. Recalling Musa's warning, I head away from the woman.

All around me, Mariners walk the streets with a surety I fear I will never possess. The freedom of this place, the ease of it—it feels like none of it is for me or my people. All this belongs to others, to those who do not abide at the crossroads of uncertainty and despair. It belongs to people so used to living free that they cannot imagine a world in which they are not.

"—do you expect? The Tribes won't lie down and take it like the Scholars. They won't allow their people to be enslaved."

Two Mariner cooks argue loudly over the pop of frying pastries, and I inch closer.

"I understand their anger," one of them says. "But to target innocent villagers—"

Someone jostles me, and I just manage to hold on to my invisibility. The crowds here are too thick, so I leave them behind, not stopping until I spot a group of children gathered in a doorway.

"—she burned Blackcliff to a crisp *and* killed a Mask—"

A few are Adisan Scholars, full-cheeked and finely dressed. Others are Mariners. All cluster around wanted signs featuring me, Darin, and—I'm surprised to see—Musa.

"—I heard she stabbed Kauf's warden in the face—"

"—I think she'll save us from the wraiths—"

All I need from you is a story, Musa had said. It is strange to hear that story now, altered into something else entirely.

"—Uncle Musa says she's got magic, like the Lioness—"

"—My da says Uncle Musa is a liar. He says the Lioness was a fool and a murderess—"

"—My ama says the Lioness killed children—"

My heart twists. I know their words shouldn't bother me. They are only children. But I want to show myself anyway. *She was funny and clever*, I want to say. *She could shoot a sparrow on a branch from a hundred paces. She only ever wanted true freedom for us—for you. She only ever wanted better.*

Another child appears in the alley. "*Kehanni! Kehanni!*" she yells. The children race away to a nearby courtyard where a deep voice rises and trembles and swoops—a *Kehanni* spinning a tale. I follow them, to find the yard bursting with an audience collectively holding its breath.

The *Kehanni* has silver hair and a face that has seen a thousand tales. She wears a heavily embroidered, calf-length dress over wide, mirror-hemmed pants that catch the lamplight. Her voice is throaty, and though I should move on, I find an empty spot against a wall to listen.

"The ghuls surrounded the child, drawn by his sadness." She speaks Serran, and her accent is heavy. "And though he wished to help his ailing sister, the fey creatures whispered poison into his ears, until his heart became as twisted as the roots of an old jinn tree."

As the *Kehanni* sings her story, I realize there is truth within this tale—a history of sorts. Hadn't I just witnessed exactly what she described, only with Princess Nikla?

The *Kehannis'* stories, I realize, have as much history in them as any book in the Great Library. More, perhaps, for there is no skepticism in the old tales that might occlude the truth. The more I consider it, the more excited I get. Elias learned to destroy efrits from a song Mamie Rila sang him. What if the stories could help me understand the Nightbringer? What if they could tell me how to stop him? My excitement has me moving away from the wall, toward the *Kehanni*. Finally, I have a chance to learn something useful about the jinn.

Laia . . .

The whisper brushes against my ear and I jump, jostling the man next to me, who yelps, looking about for whoever bumped him.

Quick as I can, I weave my way through the still-rapt audience and out of the courtyard. Something is watching me. I feel it. And whatever it is, I don't want it making trouble among those listening to the *Kehanni*.

I shove back through the crowded market, looking over my shoulder repeatedly. Black scraps of shadow flit just out of my vision. Ghuls? Or something worse? I speed my gait, exiting the market and entering a quiet side street. I look back once more.

The past shall burn, and none will slow it.

I recognize the whisper, the way it grates like rotted claws across my mind. *Nightbringer!* I am too frightened even to cry out. All I can do is stand there, useless.

I spin, trying to pick him out of the shadows.

"Show yourself." My voice is barely above a whisper. "Show yourself, you monster."

You dare to judge me, Laia of Serra? How can you, when you know not the darkness that lives within your own heart?

"I'm not afraid of you."

The words are a lie, and he chuckles in response. I blink—an instant of darkness, nothing at all—and when I open my eyes, I sense I am alone again. The Nightbringer is gone.

By the time I return to the forge, my body trembles. The place is dark—everyone has turned in. But I don't drop my invisibility until I'm alone in my room.

The moment I do, my vision goes black. I am standing in a room—a cell, I realize. I can just make out a woman in the darkness. She is singing.

A star she came

Into my home

And lit it bright with glo-ry

The song floats all around me, though the words grow muffled. A strange sound splits the song, like the branch of a tree breaking. When I open my eyes, the vision is gone, as is the singing. The house is quiet, other than Darin murmuring in his sleep from next door.

What in the skies was that?

Is it the magic affecting me? Or the Nightbringer? Is this him—is he toying with my mind? I sit up quickly, glancing about my darkened room. Elias's armlet is warm in my hand. I imagine his voice. *The shadows are just shadows, Laia. The Nightbringer can't hurt you.*

But he can. He has. He'll do so again.

I retreat to my bed, refusing to release the armlet, trying to keep Elias's soothing baritone in my mind. But I keep seeing the Nightbringer's face. Hearing his voice. And sleep does not come.

XVIII: Elias

The jinn know I'm coming. The moment I reach their grove, I'm unnerved by an expectant sort of quiet. A waiting. Strange, how silence can speak as loudly as a scream. Yes, they know I'm here. And they know I want something.

Hail, mortal. My skin crawls at the choral voice of the jinn. *Come to beg forgiveness for your existence?*

"I've come to ask for help."

The jinns' laughter knifes at my ears. "I do not wish to trouble you." It irks, but humility might serve me well. I certainly can't brazen my way through this. "I know you suffer. I know what was done to you long ago is the heart of your suffering. And I've been imprisoned too."

You think the horrors of your puny human prison can begin to approach our torment?

Skies, why did I say that? Stupid. "I just . . . I don't wish pain like that on anyone."

A long silence. And then: *You are like her.*

"Like Shaeva?" I say. "But the magic bonded with her, and it won't bond with me—"

Like your mother. Keris. The jinn sense my dismay and laugh. *You think not? Perhaps you do not know her as well as you think you do. Or perhaps, mortal, you do not know yourself.*

"I'm not a heartless, murdering—"

The magic of the Soul Catcher will never be yours. You are too deeply linked to those you love. Too open to pain. Your kind is weak. Even Keris Veturia could not release her mortal attachments.

"The only thing my mother is attached to is power."

I sense that in their arboreal prison, the jinn are smug. *How little you know, boy. Your mother's story lives in your blood. Her past. Her memory. It is there. We could show you.*

The silk in their voices reminds me of the time a Senior Skull tried to tell fourteen-year-old me to come to his room so he could show me a new blade his father gave him.

You wish to know her better. Deep in your heart, the jinn say. *Do not lie to us, Elias Veturius, for when you are in our grove, your subterfuge is for naught. We see all.*

Something rough slithers past my ankles. Vines rise up out of the earth like giant, bark-encrusted snakes. They twist up around my legs, locking me into place. I try to draw my scims, but the vines bind the weapons to my back and coil around my shoulders, holding me fast.

"Stop this. Sto—"

The jinn shove their way into my mind, probing and turning and examining it, bringing their fire to places that were never meant to see the light.

I push back at them, but to no avail. I am trapped in my own head, in my memories. I see myself as a babe again, looking up into the silver face of a woman whose long blonde hair is darkened with sweat. The Commandant's hands are bloody, her face flushed. Her body trembles, but when she touches my face, her fingers are gentle.

"You look like him," she whispers. She doesn't look angry, though I always thought she would. Instead, she appears perplexed, almost bewildered.

Then I'm watching myself as a young boy of four, wandering through Camp Saif, a thick jacket buttoned up to my chin against the chill winter night.

While the other Tribal children have clustered around Mamie Rila to hear a terrifying tale about the King of No Name, I watch as young Elias walks to the rocky desert beyond the circle of wagons. The galaxy is a pale cloud across the onyx sky, the night bright enough for me to pick my way forward. From the west, a rhythmic thump draws close. A horse materializes on a nearby ridge.

A woman dismounts, her gleaming armor flashing beneath heavy Tribal robes. A dozen blades glint from her chest and back. The wind whips at the hard, dry earth around her. In the glowing starlight, her blonde hair is the same silver as her face.

This didn't happen, I think wildly. *I don't remember it. She left me. She never came back.*

Keris Veturia drops to one knee but remains a few feet away, as if she doesn't want to scare me. She appears so young—I can scarcely fathom it is her.

"What is your name?" At last, I recognize something about her—that hard voice, as cold and unfeeling as the land beneath our feet.

"Ilyaas."

"Ilyaas." The Commandant draws my name out, as if searching for its meaning. "Go back to the caravan, Ilyaas. Dark creatures walk the desert at night."

I don't hear my response, because I am now in a room outfitted with nothing but a cot, a desk, and a wide fireplace. The arched windows and thick walls, along with the scent of salt, tell me I'm in Navium. Summer has come swiftly to the south, and heavy, warm air pours through the window. Despite that, a fire burns in the grate.

Keris is older—older than she was when I last saw her months ago, just before she poisoned me. She lifts up her undershirt and examines what looks to be a bruise, though it is difficult to tell, since her skin is silver. I remember then that she stole the Blood Shrike's shirt of living metal, long ago. It has fused to her body as closely as her mask has fused to her face.

Her *ALWAYS VICTO* tattoo is clearly visible beneath the silver of the shirt, except now it says *ALWAYS VICTORI*.

As she feels out the bruise, I notice a strange object in the room, all the more unusual against the simplicity of the quarters. It's a crude clay sculpture of a mother holding a child. The Commandant studiously ignores it.

She drops her shirt and puts her armor back on. As she stares into the mottled mirror, her gaze shifts to the statue. She watches it in the reflection, wary, as if it might come to life. Then she turns on her heel, snatches it up, and tosses it, almost casually, into the hearth fire. She calls through the closed door. Moments later, a slave enters.

The Commandant nods at the burning sculpture. "You found it," she says. "Did you speak to anyone of it?" At the man's denial, the Commandant nods and beckons him closer.

Don't do it, I want to tell him. *Flee.*

My mother's hands blur as she breaks his neck. I wonder if he even felt it.

"Let's keep it that way," she says to his slumped body, "shall we?"

I blink, and I am back in the jinn grove. No vines drag me down to the Forest floor, and dawn paints the grove red and orange. Hours have passed.

The jinn still scuttle through my mind. I fight back, shoving them out, pushing into *their* consciousness. Their surprise is palpable, and their guard drops for a moment. I feel their rage, their shock, a shared, deep pain—and a swiftly suppressed panic. A furtiveness.

Then I am cast out.

"You're hiding something," I gasp. "You—"

Look to your borders, Elias Veturius, the jinn snarl. *See what we have wrought.*

An attack. I feel it as clearly as I'd feel an attack on my own body. But this assault doesn't come from outside the Forest. It comes from within.

Go and see the horror of ghosts who break free of the Waiting Place. See your people ravaged. You cannot change it. You cannot stop it.

I curse, hearing the Augur's words from so long ago thrown back in my face. I windwalk to the southern border with a speed that would rival Shaeva's. When I arrive, thousands of ghosts cluster in one spot, pushing against the border with single-minded violence, almost feral with the desire to escape.

I reach for Mauth, for the magic, but I might as well be grasping at air. The ghosts part as I make my way through them, their shrieking disappointment reverberating in my bones.

The border appears whole, but spirits might still have escaped. I run my hands over the glowing gold wall, trying to find any weaknesses.

Far in the distance, the red and blue of Tribe Nasur's wagons gleam in the morning light, the smoke of cook fires fading into a stormy sky. To my surprise, the encampment has grown—and moved closer to the Forest. I recognize the green-and-gold-draped wagons curved in a circle not far from the shore of the Duskan Sea. Tribe Nur—Afya's tribe—has joined Aubarit's.

Why is Afya here? With the Martials so belligerent, the Tribes shouldn't congregate in one place. Afya's savvy enough to know that.

"*Banu al-Mauth?*"

Aubarit appears from a dip in the land just ahead.

"*Fakira.*" I step out of the Forest, my pulse still thundering in warning, though I sense nothing out of the ordinary. "Now isn't really a good—"

"Elias *bleeding* Veturius!" I know the small woman who shoves past Aubarit by the fire in her eyes, for in every other way, she is unrecognizable. Her face is lined, and the kerchief that hides her usually impeccable braids cannot mask their disarray. Purple shadows nest beneath her eyes and I smell the sharp tang of sweat. "What the hells is going on?"

"*Zaldara!*" Aubarit looks scandalized. "You will address him as the *Banu*—"

"Do not call him that! His name is Elias Veturius. He is a foolish man, just like any *other* foolish man, and I suspect he is the reason Tribe Nur's ghosts are *stuck*—"

"Afya, slow down," I say. "What in ten hells—" My voice chokes off as Mauth tugs violently at me, almost pulling me off my feet. I sense the urgency behind the summons and whip around. Floating on the breeze just a few yards away, a face materializes.

It's contorted, angry, and moving swiftly toward the Tribal encampments. Another follows it, called to the distant caravan like vultures drawn to carrion.

Some of the ghosts escaped. Before I arrived, they got out.

Perhaps they will only drift about, wailing and pining for life. They have no bodies. They can't actually do anything.

I've barely even formed the thought when, with chilling suddenness, a flock of birds lifts from the trees near the caravans, cawing in alarm.

"Elias—" Afya speaks, but I jerk my hand up. For a moment, all is quiet. And then, the screaming begins.

XIX: The Blood Shrike

Blood Shrike,

    Summer is in full bloom in Antium, and it grows difficult to hide from the heat. The Emperor rejoices in the change of seasons, though he is much troubled by the concerns of the crown.

    The seasonal storms are as bad as the heat and no one at court is unaffected. I offer aid where I can, but it is challenging.

    I am thankful every day for the Plebeians. Their support of both the Emperor and myself is a comfort during this trying time.

Loyal to the end,

Empress Livia Aquilla Farrar

Someone opened Livia's letter long before it got to me. My sister's attempts to code her thoughts, while clever, are useless. By now, the Commandant will know that she is well into her pregnancy. The Nightbringer will have told her.

As for the rest of the letter, Keris will have deciphered that as well: that Livia can't hide the pregnancy for much longer; that the Emperor grows more unstable; that my sister keeps the wolves at bay; that Plebeian support is all that allows Marcus to remain on the throne.

That I must defeat the Commandant soon, if I want Livia and her child to survive.

I read the letter while wandering Navium's southern beach, which is littered with the wreckage of the fleet. Tattered sails, moss-covered masts, weathered scraps of wood. All are proof of my failure to protect the city.

As I kneel to run my hands over a piece of ocean-smoothed hull, Dex appears behind me.

"Pater Tatius will not see you, Shrike."

"What's the excuse this time?"

"He's visiting a sick aunt." Dex sighs. He looks as exhausted as I feel. "He's been talking to Pater Equitius."

Indeed. The Pater of Gens Equitia just gave us the same excuse two days ago. And though I suspected Tatius might, like all the other Paters, try to avoid me, I'd hoped for better.

"There aren't any Paters left to approach," Dex says as we turn away from the beach and up to the Black Guard barracks. "Argus and Vissellius are dead, and their heirs blame you. The rest are too angry about the fleet. Tatius lost a quarter of his Gens in the storm."

"This isn't just about the fleet," I say. "If it were, they would lecture me, demand that I grovel and apologize." These are, after all, Martial Paters. They love talking down to women as much as they love their money. "Either they're afraid of the Commandant or she's offering them something that I cannot—something they cannot refuse."

"Money?" Dex says. "More ships?"

"She doesn't have ships," I say. "Even if we miraculously took over Grímarr's fleet, we would only just have enough ships to replace the navy. And she's wealthy, but not wealthy enough to pay off all of those Paters."

There's more to this. But how the hells do I find out what it is if none of the Paters will talk to me?

As we wind up toward the city, the scarred, still-burning Southwest Quarter comes into view. Grímarr has attacked twice more in the two weeks since I arrived. Without a fleet, we've had no choice but to hunker down and hope that the fires from their missiles do not spread.

During both attacks, the Paters and Keris froze me out of the decision-making, with Keris smoothly and quietly ignoring my orders *for the greater good*. Only Janus Atrius backs me, and his lone voice is nothing against the unity of Keris's allies.

I want to start lopping off heads. But Keris is looking for an excuse to take me down—either by jailing me or killing me. If I start killing Paters, she'll have it.

No, I have to be more cunning. I click my horse forward. I can do nothing about Grímarr's attacks. But I can weaken Keris—*if* I can get information on her.

"We'll have a day or two of quiet while Grímarr figures out the Karkauns' next move," I tell Dex. "There are a few files on the Paters in my desk. All their dirty little secrets. Start cornering them discreetly. See if you can get them to talk."

Dex leaves me, and when I return to the barracks, I find Avitas waiting, shoulders stiff with disapproval.

"You should not be traveling the city alone, Shrike," Avitas says. "Regulation states—"

"I can't waste you or Dex on escorting me everywhere," I say. "Did you find it?"

He nods me inside my quarters.

"There are at least two hundred estates in the mountains beyond the city." He rolls out a map on my desk, and the houses are all marked. "Nearly all of them are affiliated with Gens that are allied with Keris. Three are abandoned."

I consider what Elias said of Quin's whereabouts. *Wherever Keris is, he'll be close by, waiting for her to make a mistake. He's not stupid enough to use one of his own estates. And he won't be alone.*

One of the abandoned houses is at the bottom of a valley—no water source and no forest around it for soldiers to hide in. The other is too small to house more than a dozen or so men.

But the third . . .

"This one." I tap it. "Built into a hill. Defensible. Nearby stream. Easy tunneling for a quick escape. And look"—I point to the other side of the hills—"towns remote enough that he could send men there for supplies and he wouldn't attract much notice."

We set off immediately, two Black Guards trailing to make sure any spies are dispatched. By noon, we are deep within the mountains east of Navium.

"Shrike," Harper says when we are clear of the city. "You should know that the Commandant had a late-night visitor."

"The Nightbringer?"

Avitas shakes his head. "Three break-ins of her quarters at the Island over the course of the last two weeks. During the first, my spy reported that a window was left open. During the second, an item was left on Keris's bed. A sculpture."

"A sculpture?"

"A mother holding a child. The Commandant destroyed it and killed the slave who discovered it. During the third visit, another sculpture was left. My contact pulled this one from the ashes of the fire."

He reaches into a saddlebag and offers me a rough sculpture of yellow clay, blackened on one side. It is of a crudely made woman, her head bowed.

Her hand reaches down with strange plaintiveness to a child who reaches back. They do not touch, though they sit on the same base.

The figures have thumb indents for eyes and lumps for noses. But their mouths are open. It looks as if they are screaming. I shove the sculpture back at Avitas, disturbed.

"No one's seen the intruder." Avitas tucks the object away. "Other than what my spy saw, the Commandant has hidden the break-ins well."

There are plenty of people who could get into the Commandant's quarters unseen. But for her to then not catch them after they'd been there once—that indicates a level of skill I've known only one person to have. A woman I haven't seen in months. The Cook.

I mull it over as we travel higher into the mountains, but it doesn't make sense. If Cook can sneak into the Commandant's quarters, why not just kill her? Why leave her peculiar statues?

Hours later, after winding through switchbacking mountain trails, we arrive at the foot of a sweeping, old-growth forest. Navium glitters to the west, a cluster of lights and still-smoldering fires with the black snake of the Rei winding through it.

We abandon the horses beside a creek, and I draw a dagger as we make for the tree line. If Quin is out there, he won't take kindly to Emperor Marcus's Blood Shrike showing up unannounced.

Harper unhooks his bow, and we slip cautiously into the woods. Crickets chirp, frogs sing—the wild sounds of a summer countryside. And though it is dark, there's moon enough for me to see that no one has trod these woods for months, maybe years.

With every step, my hopes diminish further. I'm to send a report to Marcus tomorrow. What the bleeding hells am I going to say if Quin *isn't* out here?

Harper curses, the sound sharp and unexpected, and I hear a hissing *snick*. It's followed by a muffled grunt. A phalanx of axes swings down from the trees.

Harper only just dives out of the way, and I have never been happier to see an ally nearly have his head sliced off.

We spend the next two hours avoiding carefully laid booby traps, each one more intricate and well-hidden than the next.

"What a bleeding lunatic." Harper cuts a trip wire that drops a net laced with razor-sharp shards of glass. "He's not even trying to catch anyone. He just wants them dead."

"He's not a lunatic." I drop my voice. The moon is high. It's past midnight. "He's thorough." Glass gleams through the trees—a distant window.

Something in the air shifts, and the night creatures go quiet. I know, as sure as I know my own name, that Harper and I are no longer alone in this forest.

"Let's get this over with." I sheathe my blade, hoping to the skies that I'm not talking to a pack of highway bandits or some crazed hermit.

Silence. A moment during which I'm certain I'm wrong.

Then the whisper of footsteps behind us, all around us. Far ahead, a powerful silver-faced figure emerges from behind a tree, his thick white hair half-hidden by a hood. He doesn't look any different than he did months ago, when I first snuck him out of Serra.

Two dozen men surround us, their uniforms impeccable, Gens Veturia colors worn proudly. When I step forward, their backs snap straight and, as one, they salute.

"Blood Shrike." Quin Veturius salutes last. "About damned time."

«««

Quin orders Harper to stay with his men, then leads me through the crumbling house built into the mountain and into a series of caverns. It's no wonder Keris hasn't found the old man. These tunnels are so extensive it would take months to explore all of them.

"I expected you weeks ago," Quin says as we walk. "Why haven't you assassinated Keris yet?"

"She's not an easy woman to kill, General," I say. "Especially when Marcus can't afford for it to look like an assassination." We trek upward until we emerge onto a small, flat plateau, walled in on four sides but open to the sky. It is home to a hidden garden, wild with the beauty of a place once lovingly cared for but left alone for too long.

"I have something for you." I pull Elias's mask from my pocket. "Elias gave it to me before he left Blackcliff. I thought you'd want it."

Quin's hand hovers over the mask before he takes it. "It was a nightmare to get that boy to keep it on," he says. "I thought he would lose the damned thing one day."

The old man turns the mask over in his hand, and the metal ripples like water. "They become part of us, you know. It is only when they join with us that we become our truest selves. My father used to say that after the joining, a mask held a soldier's identity—and that without it, a bit of his soul was stripped away, never to be recovered."

"And what do you say, General?"

"We are what we put into the mask. Elias put little into it, and so it offered little in return." I expect him to ask me about his grandson, but he simply pockets the mask. "Tell me of your foe, Blood Shrike."

As I relate the attack on Navium, the loss of the fleet, even the presence of the statue, Quin is silent. We walk to a pond in the garden, bordered by paint-chipped stones.

"She's up to something, General," I say. "I need your help to figure out what it could be. To figure *her* out."

"Keris learned to walk here, before I moved her and her mother to Serra." He nods to a barely visible path that leads to a pergola dripping with ivy. "She was nine months old. Tiny little thing. Skies, Karinna was so proud. She loved that girl to bits."

He raises his eyebrows at the look on my face. "You thought my dear late wife was the monster from whom Keris learned? Quite the opposite. Karinna wouldn't let anyone touch a hair on that girl's head. We had dozens of slaves, but Karinna insisted on doing everything herself: feeding her, changing her, playing with her. They adored each other."

The idea of a sunny-haired baby Keris is so far from what she is now that I can't conjure the image. I force myself to hold back the dozens of questions in my head. Quin's voice is slow—almost halting—and I wonder if he's spoken to anyone about this.

"I wasn't there for them early on," he says. "I was already a lieutenant general when Karinna and I married. The Karkauns were pushing hard in the west, and the Emperor couldn't spare me."

He sounds . . . not sad, but almost wistful. "And then Karinna died. The Emperor didn't give me leave, so it was a year before I returned home. By then Keris had stopped speaking. I spent a month with her, and then it was back to the battlefield. When she was chosen for Blackcliff, I was certain she'd die in the first week. She was so soft. So much like her mother."

"But she didn't die," I say. I try not to tap my foot in impatience. I wonder when he's going to get to the point.

"She's a Veturia," Quin says. "We're hard to kill. Skies know what she dealt with at Blackcliff. She didn't have your luck in friends, girl. Her fellow students made her life hell. I tried to train her, like I trained Elias, but she wanted nothing to do with me. Blackcliff warped her. Just after she graduated, she allied with the Nightbringer. He is the closest thing she has to a friend."

"He's not her friend. He's her master," I murmur, remembering the jinn's words. "What of Elias's father?"

"Whoever he was, she cared for him." We are past the pond now. Beyond the edge of the plateau, low, rolling hills ease into the flats of the Tribal desert, blue with the approach of dawn. "After Elias was chosen, she was unnerved, worried she would lose her commission. I'd never seen emotion like that in her before then, or since. She said she let the child live because his father would have wanted it."

So Keris loved Arius Harper? His file was scant, but the Commandant always hated Elias so much, I assumed his father had forced himself on her.

"Did you know Arius Harper, General?"

"He was a Plebeian." Quin gives me a curious look, mystified by the sudden change in topic. "A Combat Centurion at Blackcliff who was reprimanded repeatedly for showing mercy to the students—kindness, even."

"How did he die?"

"He was murdered by a group of Masks the day after they graduated—Keris's fellow Senior Skulls. A vicious killing—more than a dozen of them beat him to death. Illustrian, all of them. Their fathers covered it up well enough that even I didn't know of it when it first happened."

Why would a group of Masks murder a Centurion? Did Keris know? Did she ask them to do it? But Quin said she didn't have allies at Blackcliff—that the other students tormented her. And if she didn't have Arius killed—if she truly loved him—then why does she hate Elias so much?

"You think Arius Harper is the father?" Quin catches on. "So Captain Harper is—"

"Elias's half brother." I curse under my breath. "But none of that matters. Her past, her history—none of it explains what she's doing in Navium," I say. "She gave up the fleet just to wrest power from me. Why?"

"My grandson always told me you were smart, girl." Quin scowls at me. "Was he wrong? Don't just look at her actions. Look at *her*. What does she want? Why? Look at her past, her history. How has it altered her mind? The Nightbringer is her master, you say. What does *he* want? Will she get it for him? What could she be doing for the Paters that they would agree to let that swine Grímarr wreak havoc in the poor parts of the city? Use that head of yours. If you think my daughter cares about the fate of a port city far from the seat of power, you are sorely mistaken."

"But she's been ordered to—"

"Keris doesn't care about orders. She cares about one thing: power. You love the Empire, Blood Shrike. So you believe that because Keris was also raised as a Mask, she must be loyal to it too. She is not. She is loyal only to herself. Understand that, and perhaps you'll best her. Fail, and she'll have your guts for supper before the week is out."

XX: Laia

The moment the sky pales, I throw on my dress and slip downstairs. If I move swiftly enough, I might still catch the Tribal caravan I saw last night—and the *Kehanni* too.

But Zella awaits me at the door, fidgeting in apology.

"Musa asked that you remain here," she says. "For your own safety, Laia. Princess Nikla has Jaduna patrolling the city for you. Apparently, one of them caught wind that you were here last night." She wrings her hands. "He says not to use your magic, as you'll just lead the Jaduna here, and get us all thrown in prison. His words," she adds quickly. "Not mine."

"What do you know about him, Zella?" I ask quickly, before she walks away. "What is he doing out there? Why hasn't he started the Resistance himself?"

"I'm just a smith, Laia. And an old family friend of his. If you have questions, you'll have to ask him."

I curse and slink out to the courtyard, where I assist Darin as he polishes a stack of scims against a set of smooth gray stones.

"I heard him, Darin," I say after relating my run-in with the Nightbringer. "Gloating right beside me. Then he was gone. Which means he could be anywhere. He might even have the last piece of the Star."

I want so much to conquer the self-doubt rising in me. To quash it and simply believe that I can stop the jinn. Fear does not rule me as it once did. But some days it stalks me with the ire of a jilted lover.

My brother slides a scim across one of the stones. "If the Nightbringer did have the last piece of the Star," he says, "we'd know. You give him too much credit, Laia, and you don't give yourself enough. He fears you. He fears what you'll learn. What you'll do with that knowledge."

"He shouldn't fear me."

"He damned well should." Darin runs a cloth across the scim he's polished and hands it to me before reaching for his first Serric steel blade, the one I carried across the Empire after Spiro Teluman gave it to me.

"It makes no sense for him to be afraid," I say. "I gave him the armlet. I let him kill Shaeva. Why the hells should he be afraid of me?"

My voice rises, and on the other side of the courtyard, Taure and Zella exchange a glance before making themselves scarce.

"Because you can stop him, and he knows it." Darin tightens the brace he has fashioned for his left hand. He uses it in place of his two missing fingers, to steady his hammers, and I almost never see him without it. This time, he clips in his scim hilt instead of a hammer. "Why else would he kill Shaeva or ally himself with the Commandant? Why ensure the Waiting Place is in disarray? Why sow so much chaos if he's not afraid of failing? And"—Darin pulls me up—"why else would he turn up the very moment you realized you might get answers from the *Kehanni*?"

That fact escaped me, and it makes me even more eager to speak to the Tribeswoman. When the skies is Musa going to be back?

"Spiro would kill me if he saw how little artistry that has." Darin nods to my blade. "But if they're true Serric steel, we can celebrate that, at least. Come on. Maybe this is the batch that won't break."

Sparks fly as Darin's scim and mine crash against each other. The last set of blades we tried didn't break until well into our battle, so I settle in for an arduous contest. After a few minutes, the rough simplicity of the blade has raised blisters on my palms. It is so different from the fine dagger Elias gave me. But it holds.

Zella and Taure emerge from the house, watching with growing excitement when, even after I press the attack, the blades remain whole.

Darin assails me, and I let my ferocity loose, pouring my frustration into every blow. Finally, my brother calls a halt, unable to suppress a grin. He takes the blade from me.

"It has no heart." He hefts it, and his eyes sparkle as they haven't in months. "No soul. But it will do. On to the next."

Zella and Taure join us as we spar across the courtyard, as one after the other, the blades finally hold true. I do not notice Musa until he steps from the house to applaud jauntily.

"Beautiful," he says. "I had full faith that you—"

I grab Musa by the arm and drag him toward the front door, ignoring his curses of protest. "I need to see a *Kehanni*, and I've been waiting hours for you to return."

"The Tribes left Adisa to fight the Martials in the desert," Musa says. "They're not holding back, either." With a chill, I remember Afya speaking of the attacks on Martial villagers.

"Well, they can't be far outside the city," I say. "I just saw a *Kehanni* telling stories near Adisa's main market. Silver hair, purple-and-white wagons."

"Tribe Sulud," Musa says. "I know the *Kehanni* you speak of. She won't just tell you what you want to know, Laia. She'll want payment."

"Fine, we'll pay her. Whatever she wants—"

"It's not that simple." Musa pulls his arm from my grip. "She's not a street hawker selling cheap trinkets. She tells stories on her terms. Traditional gifts for such exchanges are items we don't have access to: bolts of silk, chests of gold, stores of food."

I examine him up and down, from the silver-buckled boots to the soft leather breeches to the shirt made of finely spun cotton. "Don't tell me you're not wealthy. Taure said your father used to harvest half the honey in Marinn."

"I have some clothes. A bit of gold," he says. "But the Mariners seized my wealth and my property and my hives and inheritance when—" He shakes his head. "Anyway, they took it, and now my means are limited."

Zella and Taure exchange a glance at that, and I remind myself to find them later. I need answers about Musa's past, and it's clear he won't give them to me. My brother still clutches one of the new scims. Sunlight glances off the blade, hitting me in the face.

"I know what to offer her," I say. "Something she'll want. Something she can't refuse."

Musa follows my gaze to the Serric steel blade. I expect him to tell me the Scholars need the blades more or that we don't have enough. Instead, he raises his eyebrows.

"You know what the Tribes are doing in the south," he says. "They're showing no mercy to any Martial—whether soldier or civilian."

I flush. "Do you have information for me on the Nightbringer?" Musa, of course, shakes his head. "Then this is the best chance we have to learn something—if Darin agrees to part with the blades, of course."

Darin offers a resigned sigh. "You need to stop the Nightbringer," he says. "You need information to do it. I'm certain she'll take the blades. But, Laia—"

I cross my arms, waiting for his criticism.

"Mother made exchanges like this," he says. "Exchanges that she perhaps didn't want to make. She did it for the good of her people. It's why she was the Lioness. Why she was able to lead the Resistance. But in the end, it added up. It cost her. And it cost us."

"Mother did what she had to," I say. "It was for us, Darin, even if it didn't feel like it. Skies, I wish I had half her courage, half her strength. I'm not—this isn't easy. I don't want innocents hurt. But I need *something* on the Nightbringer. I think Mother would agree."

"You don't—" Something flickers in Darin's face—pain, perhaps, or anger, emotions he tries to keep as deeply buried as a Mask would. "You have your own strength," he finally says. "It doesn't have to be the same as the Lioness's."

"Well, this time it does." I harden myself, because if I don't, then I'm back to figuring out what the hells I can take the *Kehanni* when what I should be doing is getting to her as fast as possible. Beside me, Musa shakes his head, and I turn on him, temper rising.

"You wanted me to be a Resistance leader," I say. "Here's a lesson I learned from the last Resistance fighter I knew. To lead, you have to do ugly things. We leave in an hour. Come along or stay. It doesn't matter to me."

I do not wait for Musa's answer as I walk away. But I feel his surprise, and Darin's. I feel their disappointment. And I wish it did not bother me so much.

XXI: Elias

The screams echoing from the Tribal encampment are distinctly human, and they grow louder by the moment. I sprint toward them, Aubarit and Afya following, the latter demanding that I explain what's happening.

"Get to shelter." I cut off the *Zaldara*'s tirade. "I'll answer your questions later—just *hide*."

Dozens of people flee the Nur caravan, and as I approach it, I draw my scims. The closest screams come from a bright green wagon covered in mirrors. I know it well. It belongs to Afya's little brother, Gibran.

The back of the wagon bursts open, and the handsome young Tribesman emerges. He grabs a man from within the wagon and tosses him like a rag doll.

"Uncle Tash!" Afya gasps and runs past me, toward her brother. "Gib, *no!*"

Her brother turns to look at her, and the Tribeswoman slowly backs away, her face frozen in terror. Gibran's eyes are pure white. He's possessed. The escaped ghost has taken over his body.

Because I didn't pass them through fast enough. Because there are too many, and they have no place to go but back into the world of the living.

Gibran lunges for Afya. Though she is a dozen feet away, he reaches her in one leap and lifts her up by her throat. The small woman kicks out at him, her face purpling. Before I can get to him, Gibran throws her too.

My Mask's instinct kicks in, and I drop into a stalking crouch. If I can knock the Tribesman unconscious, perhaps something in Aubarit's Mysteries will tell me how to exorcise the ghost.

But a ghost-possessed Tribesman is no ordinary foe. The way he threw Afya makes it clear that the spirit within him has physical powers far beyond what Gibran himself possesses.

My skin prickles. He's seen me. I duck behind a wagon. He knows I'm coming, but I don't have to make it easy for him.

In the distance, a group of men and women snatch up children and race for the river, Aubarit screaming at them to move faster. I scan the riverbank for Afya, but she has disappeared.

When I turn back to Gibran, he's gone. *Idiot, Elias. Never turn your back on a foe.* I sheathe my scims—I don't want to hurt him.

Too late, I hear a whoosh in the air—*attack!* Gibran is on my back, and I lurch to my knees beneath his unnatural weight. His arm, thin but muscled from months of battling Martials, comes around my throat, and he has the strength of five men. He babbles in my ear, his voice a fey growl.

"They razed it, burned it, corn silk and blood and flour—"

I know I can die as Soul Catcher. But by the skies, I won't die by the hand of a ghost-possessed Tribesman choking the life out of me while gibbering in my ear.

I claw at Gibran's arm, unnerved by his strength. Suddenly, a metallic *thunk* reverberates, and his hold loosens. Gasping and grabbing my throat, I back away from him to see Afya holding a cast-iron pan. She retreats from Gibran, who, though momentarily weakened, is getting to his feet.

"Run!" I bellow at Afya, leaping upon Gibran's back. "To the river! Run!" She whirls as Gibran goes down. He's impossible to keep in one place. I land a blow on his head. A second. A third. Skies, I'm going to have to kill him if I want the ghost out of him. *I can't kill him. He's just a boy. He doesn't deserve this.*

"Damn you!" It is half snarl, half cry. Gibran makes Afya laugh like no one else. He loves with his whole heart—his family and his friends and his many lovers. And he's young—too young for such a horrific fate. "Get out of him," I bellow. "Get out! Get—" On my fifth blow, Gibran finally loses consciousness. The ghost oozes out of him, slumped, as if exhausted, and disappears. Back to the Waiting Place, I hope.

"Gib!" Afya returns from where she's retreated, dropping the pan. "Did it kill him? What the hells happened? Where did that thing come from?"

"It escaped the Waiting Place." If Gibran dies, it will be me who killed him by failing to pass the ghosts on. *Don't die, Gibran. Please don't die.* "Are there others?"

Afya shakes her head, but I can't be sure until I check the whole camp myself. I'm certain I saw more than one ghost escape.

"How did they escape?" Afya asks. "What happened?"

"I failed." I look into my friend's eyes. I make myself do it, because it's true and she deserves to know. I think she will be angry, but she just grabs my shoulder and squeezes.

"I have to figure out if there are any more." I shake her off. Her understanding is a gift I don't deserve. "Keep everyone near the river—inside it, if they're able. Ghosts hate water."

"Help me get him up," Afya says, and when I've slung Gibran's arm around her neck, she drags him away. But she has only gone a few dozen yards when she freezes. Her body goes stiff, like a bow string yanked taut, then slack as wet dough. Gibran falls to the ground, and she takes a deep, wolflike sniff of the air. She turns toward me, eyes white as snow.

No.

Afya moves at me with impossible speed. The contrast between the familiarity of her face and form and the violence of her actions raises a chill along my spine. She has her frying pan in her hand, and I know that if she hits me with that thing, Soul Catcher or not, I'm going to have one hell of a headache. She swings it at me clumsily, and I catch her wrist, squeezing hard enough to make a normal woman drop the pan.

But she only growls at me, a guttural moan that chills my blood.

Think, Elias, think. Battle can't have been the only thing you learned at Blackcliff.

A little girl, hiding until now, rushes past us trying to escape. Like an animal sensing weaker prey, Afya rips away from me and bounds after the girl. The child pumps her small legs, but she isn't fast enough. When Afya leaps upon her, the girl's neck cracks, and the thing that has possessed my friend grunts triumphantly. I howl in rage.

Deep in the Forest, the jinn laugh. I ignore them, drawing on the Mask deep within, refusing to allow myself to get distracted.

No human could hear the jinn, but the spirit within Afya stops and tilts its head, listening. I use her inattention to send a throwing knife straight at her face. The hilt hits her square in the forehead. Her eyes roll back, and she thuds to the dirt. For the moment, I push my concern for Afya aside and step over her prone body, scanning the area around me for more ghosts.

And suddenly, I feel a flicker of magic within me. The little magic I received when vowing myself as Soul Catcher responds to something greater. Thin tendrils of darkness coil like smoke out of the Waiting Place toward me. *Mauth!*

For a moment, Mauth's magic fills me. The ghost that oozes out of Afya is no match for this power, and I wrap the magic around the spirit to bind it and then fling it back to the Waiting Place. I spot the last ghost a hundred yards away, lurking inside the body of a young woman attacking her family. I whip the magic out like a shepherd's crook and hook the ghost. It howls in rage, but I yank it out of the girl's body and send it flying back to the Forest.

Skies, the power—the ease of it. It's like I was born to it. I want to crow, I am so happy. Finally—*finally*—the magic has come to me.

Afya moans, and I drop beside her. Already, a goose egg rises on her head, but she's not seriously hurt, not like Gibran. I reach for her, thinking to carry her to her Tribe, but the moment I do so, the power that suffused me dissipates.

"What—no—" I grasp for it with my hands, but it leaves me, dark tendrils disappearing back into the Forest. I feel strangely desolate, as if my own strength has left me. The only trace of the magic is a tug from Mauth—that dark insistence that's always there when I leave the Waiting Place.

"*Banu al-Mauth?*"

Aubarit appears behind me, her hand at her mouth when she sees Afya. "The *Zaldara*—her brother—"

"I'm sorry, *Fakira*," I say. "It was my fault the ghosts escaped."

Another tug at my gut from Mauth. This one stops me in my tracks. It feels different from before. Not impatient—urgent.

Jinn laughter fills my ears, and the sound is edged in vengeance and flame. *Do you smell anything, Elias Veturius? Smoke, perhaps?*

What are they up to? The jinn cannot escape their imprisonment in the grove—that, at least, I can be sure of. The magic of the Star has locked them there, and their only power is their voice. Voices can be ignored.

And voices can be used. Come home, Elias. See what awaits.

Home. *Home.*

Shaeva's cabin. My sanctuary. My safety. *Sleep in the cottage. They cannot hurt you there.*

I fly to the trees without an explanation to Aubarit. The second I'm through the border I sense interlopers—many of them, far to the north. It's the same presence I felt for weeks lurking around the edges of the Forest. In the brief time that they are in the Forest, I see them in my mind's eye. Larger than ghuls or wights, but smaller than wraiths. *Efrits.*

The jinn must have warned them, for they flee the Waiting Place. Even if I windwalk, they are too far away—I will never catch them.

Long before I reach the clearing, I know. Before I smell the smoke, see the dying flames, before I walk past the spot Shaeva died and the place where I was named Soul Catcher, I know.

Still, I do not believe until the glowing embers of Shaeva's cabin are burning through my boots. The efrits did not just set it alight; they broke the beams and razed the garden. They destroyed it—and the magic it was made with. My sanctuary—my home—is gone, and I will never get it back.

And all the while, the jinn laugh.

XXII: The Blood Shrike

Grímarr and his men attack the next night at sundown, just after Avitas and I return to Navium. Having destroyed much of the Southwest Quarter, they aim now for the Southeast. The bombardment is swift and merciless, and by the time the sun has faded, the Quarter is hotter than a pyre. Drums echo from all corners of the city, ordering evacuations. The ballistae on the watchtowers sing, and the Commandant has troops amassing near the beaches in case of a land invasion, but other than that, we do not counter the Karkauns.

I know the Commandant will have me blocked from entering the Island. She'll have a phalanx of guards around it. The very thought of it enrages me. *You could fight her. You could enlist the Black Guard and lay a trail of bloody havoc.*

But skies know that if Grímarr takes the city, Navium will need every soldier it can get.

I make for the Southeast Quarter with Harper, Dex, Janus Atrius, and a handful of other Black Guards at my back. The shouts and screams of men and women bring my attention back to what is before me: utter devastation. High buildings have been reduced to rubble and ash, as terrified Plebeians try desperately to escape the Quarter. Many are injured, and though there are some soldiers giving the evacuees orders, no one appears to know where the hells the Plebeians are supposed to go.

Hope is stronger than fear. It is stronger than hate. The sentiment rings through my head. Then Livia's words: *I am thankful every day for the*

Plebeians. Their support of both the Emperor and myself is a comfort during this trying time.

And Quin's: *She cares about one thing: power.* How can I take it away from her?

A tenuous plan forms in my head. "Dex, open the Black Guard barracks. Get out the word that the Plebeians should take shelter there. Gens Aquilla has a manor north of here. It's a half hour walk, at most. Order the caretaker to clear out the lower levels of the house and provide food, drink, and a place to sleep. We'll be using it as an infirmary."

"Gens Atria has a house close to the Aquilla manor." Dex looks to his uncle, who nods.

"I'll give the order to have it opened," Janus says.

"Take the men." I gesture to the other Black Guards. "Get physicians to both manors. Find medical supplies from the outer districts. And make sure every single person, physician or patient, knows that they are there by order of the Blood Shrike."

After Dex and Janus leave with the men, I turn to Harper.

"Get me information on the assets of every Pater who was at the Island the day we arrived," I say. "Every ship. Every last scrap of lace or drop of rum or whatever the hells they trade in. I want to know how those Paters make their money. And get eyes in the homes of Admiral Argus and Vice Admiral Vissellius. Argus's wife was spotted at the dressmaker's spending obscene amounts of money two nights ago. I want to know why she wasn't in mourning with the rest of the family."

While Dex immediately took to horse, Harper merely shifts on his saddle. What in the bleeding skies is wrong with him?

"Did you not hear me? *Go*."

"You must have a guard with you at all times, Blood Shrike," Avitas says. "Not because you are incapable, but because the Blood Shrike must show her strength. There is strength in numbers."

"There is strength in winning," I say. "To win, I need men I trust to carry out my orders." Avitas's jaw tenses, and he wheels his horse away.

By midnight, the bombardment has stopped. The Black Guard barracks are full of those who have escaped the Southeast Quarter, and Manor Aquilla and Manor Atria are bursting with the injured.

As I walk among the ill at Manor Aquilla, my body is drawn toward those suffering the most. The need to heal is overpowering. Dozens of songs fill my head at the sight of so much pain.

"They're Plebeians." Dex, who has rejoined me, shakes his head. "Every last one."

"Blood Shrike." A white-smocked man appears, his sharp-featured face paling at the sight of me. "I am Lieutenant Silvius. Sit, please—"

"I'm fine." The winter in my voice has him standing taller. "Tell me what you require, Lieutenant."

"Medicines, teas, bandages, spirits," Silvius says. "And more hands."

"Dex," I say, "help the lieutenant. I'll deal with them." I nod to an angry crowd gathering outside the infirmary.

When I emerge, the crowd goes silent, their respect for the Blood Shrike so deeply ingrained that even in the face of their suffering, they hold their tongues—all but one woman, who shoves through until she's inches from my face.

"My baby boy is in there," she whispers. "I don't know if he's alive, if he's hurting or—"

"Your families are being cared for," I say. "But you must let the physicians work."

"Why aren't we fighting back?" An aux soldier limps forward, uniform ripped, forehead leaking blood. "My entire family, they—" He shakes his head. "Why aren't we fighting?"

"I don't know," I say. "But we *will* stop the Barbarians. They won't set foot on Navium's shores. I vow it, by blood and by bone." The tenor of the crowd shifts—a weight has been lifted.

As the throng dissipates, I feel the tug of my healing again. *Hope is stronger than fear.* What if I was able to give these people a greater measure of hope?

A quick glance tells me that Lieutenant Silvius is deep in conversation with Dex. I slip across the back courtyard to the children's wing. The nurse nods a greeting but leaves me be.

While her attention is elsewhere, I cross the room and drop beside a dark-haired child. His eyelashes curl the way mine never will, his cheeks round and ashen. I take his small, cold hand in mine and search out his song.

Sails like birds on the sea, the laugh of his father, watching for dolphins on the water—

It is pure, a shaft of sunlight falling onto a glittering ocean. I do not hum his song aloud. Instead, I sing it in my head, as I did long ago, for Cook. One bar, two, three, until weakness fills me. When I open my eyes, his face has lost its unnatural gray hue, and I move on. With each child, I do just enough to ease their pain and bring them back from the edge.

My body grows fatigued, but there are dozens of injured left. One by one, I sing them well, until I can hardly walk. I need to leave. I need to rest.

But then a whimper breaks the quiet—a little boy in the back of the infirmary, dark-haired and gray-eyed. The wound on his chest weeps into his bandage. I stumble the few steps to his bed. He is awake.

"I'm afraid," he whispers.

"The pain will soon be gone."

"No," he says. "Of them."

It takes me a moment to understand. "The Karkauns."

"They'll come back. They'll kill us."

I look around. A wooden tray sits nearby, thick enough to prove my point.

"See, lad, if I open my hand and try to break this wood"—I smack the tray—"nothing happens. But if I make a fist . . ." I punch through the wood easily, startling the nurse.

"We are Martials, child. We are the fist. Our enemies are the wood. And we shall break them."

After I find his song and he falls into slumber, I head for the door. When I emerge into the courtyard, I'm stunned to see that dawn is only an hour or two away. The infirmary is much quieter now. On the other side of the yard, Dex stands with Silvius, his head bent thoughtfully as the physician speaks. Remembering Harper's comment about strength in numbers, and concerned at the depth of my fatigue, I almost call out to my friend.

But I stop myself. There is a charge in the air between Dex and Silvius that makes me smile, the first time I've felt anything other than rage or exhaustion all day.

I head for the courtyard gate without Dex. It's a short enough walk to the barracks.

My senses are dulled as I walk, my legs growing weaker. A platoon of soldiers patrols nearby, saluting when I pass, and I am barely able to acknowledge them. I wish then that I'd asked Dex to accompany me. I hope to the skies there's no Karkaun assault. Right now, I couldn't fight off a fly.

Exhausted as I am, the part of me that raged and screamed at my own impotence in the face of Grímarr's attacks has quieted. I will sleep tonight. Maybe I'll even dream.

A step behind me.

Dex? No. The street is empty. I squint, trying to see into the darkness. A furtive scrape ahead of me this time—someone trying to remain unobserved.

My senses prickle. I didn't spend a decade and a half at Blackcliff only to get accosted by some idiot a few blocks from my own barracks.

I draw my scim and summon my Shrike's voice. "You'd be a fool to try it," I say. "But by all means, entertain me."

When the first dart comes flying out of the dark, I whip it out of the air by force of habit. I spent hundreds of hours deflecting missiles as a Yearling. A knife follows the dart.

"Show yourself!" I snarl. A shadow moves to my right, and I fling a throwing knife at it. The figure thuds to the ground only a dozen yards from me, clutching at his neck.

I make for him, aiming to unhood him. *Filthy, traitorous coward—*

But my legs will not move. Pain explodes along my side, sudden and white-hot. I look down. There's blood everywhere.

From the infirmary? No. It's my blood.

Walk, Shrike. Move. Get out of here.

But I cannot. I have no strength at all. I drop to my knees, able to do nothing more than watch as my life drains out of me.

XXIII: Laia

When Musa and I set out from Adisa, the sun blazes high, burning away the morning mist that has rolled in off the sea. But we do not clear the walls until early evening, as the guards are carefully watching all who leave as well as all who enter.

Musa's disguise—that of an old man with a piebald donkey—is frighteningly effective, and the guards don't look at him twice. Still, he waits until it is completely dark before bagging his tattersall cloak and raggedy wig. In a copse of trees, he pulls the Serric steel scims from a high pile of sticks on the donkey's back and sends the creature off with a slap to the rump.

"My sources tell me Tribe Sulud left late last night, which means we'll find their camp in one of the coastal villages to the south," Musa says. I nod a response, peering over my shoulder. The shadows of the night billow and contract. Though summer is in full bloom, I shiver and move swiftly across the marshy grasses.

"Will you stop looking back like that?" Musa says, immune as ever to my magic. "You're making me nervous."

"I just wish we could go faster," I say. "I feel strange. Like there's something back there." The Nightbringer disappeared so swiftly last night that I questioned whether he was even in Adisa. But since then, I haven't been able to shake the sense that something watches me.

"I have mounts hidden down the road. Once we get to them, we can move more quickly." Musa laughs at my obvious impatience. "What, you don't want to pass the time in conversation with me?" he says. "I'm hurt."

"I just want to get to the *Kehanni*," I mumble, though this is not the only reason I chafe at the delay. Musa regards me thoughtfully, and I lengthen my stride. He doesn't believe that I should offer to supply weapons to the Tribes, even if it means gaining information on the Nightbringer. Not when those weapons might be used to kill innocent Martial civilians in the south.

But he doesn't stop me, though he easily could with that eerie magic of his. Instead, he accompanies me, his distaste palpable.

His disappointment gnaws at me. It is part of the reason I do not speak to him. I do not want his judgment. But there's more to my silence.

Speaking to him would mean learning about him. Understanding him. Maybe befriending him. I know what it is to travel with someone, to break bread and laugh and grow close to them.

And though perhaps it's foolish, that frightens me. Because I also know the pain of losing friends. Family. *Mother. Father. Lis. Nan. Pop. Izzi. Elias.* Too many lost. Too much pain.

I shake off my invisibility. "It's not as if you'll actually answer any of my questions. Anyway, I *do* want to talk to you, it's just—"

Dizziness sweeps over me. I recognize the feeling. *No, not now, not when I need to get to the* Kehanni. Though inside I scream with frustration, I cannot stop the vision: the dank room, the shape of a woman. Her hair is light. Her face is in shadow. And that voice again, so familiar.

A star she came
Into my home
And lit it bright with glo-ry
Her laughter like
A gilded song
A raincloud sparrow's sto-ry.

I want to get closer. I want to see the face. I know the voice—I have heard it before. I search my memories. *Who is she?* A soft crack sounds. The singing stops.

"Oi!" I wake to Musa smacking my face, and I shove him away.

"What the *hells*, Musa?"

"You're the one who collapsed like some sort of swooning theater hero-ine," he says crossly. "I've been trying to wake you for an hour. Does that happen every time you use your invisibility? Rather inconvenient."

"Just the past few times." I get to my feet. My head aches, but I cannot tell if it is from falling or from Musa's slap. "It never used to happen," I say. "And the blackouts are getting longer."

"The more you use the magic, the more it takes from you. At least, that's what I've seen." Musa offers me his canteen and chivvies me forward. This time, he peers over his shoulder.

"What?" I say. "Did you see something back there? Is—"

"It's after dark. Highwaymen aren't unheard of this far from the city. Best if we reach the horses. You were complaining that I never answer questions. Ask, and I'll try not to disappoint you."

I know he's distracting me, but my curiosity is piqued. I have not spoken with anyone about my magic. I wanted to talk to Darin, but didn't want to burden him. The only one who might understand is the Blood Shrike, with her powers of healing. I scowl at the thought of having a discussion with her about it. "How does your magic take from you?"

Musa is quiet for a long time as we walk, the night growing deeper around us. The stars are a streak of silver light above, illuminating the road almost as well as a full moon.

"The magic makes me seek control when there is none to be found," he says. "It is the magic of manipulation—of speaking—of getting lesser creatures to bend to my will. It's why I was so good with my father's bees. But when I rely too much on it, it makes me into my worst self. A tyrant."

"These creatures you can manipulate," I say. "Do they include ghuls?"

"I'd not sully my mind by communicating with those little brutes."

A chitter comes from somewhere near Musa's feet, and I spot a flash of iridescence, like torchlight on water. It disappears, and Musa lifts his hands, which I could have sworn were empty a moment ago. Now he holds a scroll.

"For you," he says.

I snatch the scroll from him, reading through it quickly before dropping my arm in disgust. "This doesn't tell me anything."

"It tells you that the Blood Shrike was injured." He looks down at the parchment. "And that the Paters have turned against her. Her survival is quite miraculous. Interesting. I wonder—"

"I don't *care* about the bleeding Blood Shrike or Martial politics," I hiss. "I need to know whom else the Nightbringer is spending his time with."

"You sound like an ex-lover." Musa lifts his eyebrows, and I realize he must know about me and Keenan. About what happened between us. Embarrassment floods me. I wish now that I *hadn't* opened up to him.

"Ah, Laia-*aapan.*" He uses the Mariner honorific for *little sister* and jostles me with an arm. "We've all made mistakes in love. Me most of all."

Love. I sigh. Love is joy coupled with misery, elation bound to despair. It is a fire that beckons me gently and then burns when I get too close. I *hate* love. I yearn for it. And it drives me mad.

In any case, it is not something I want to discuss with anyone, least of all Musa.

"Among the Paters," I say, "is there anyone with whom the Nightbringer has spent more time?"

Another crooning chitter. "My friend here says he will find out."

I catch a glimpse of shimmering, iridescent wings, and shiver with sudden knowledge.

"Musa," I whisper, "is that a bleeding wight?" Wights are fey, like wraiths, but smaller, swifter, and craftier. Stories say they are tricksters who enjoy luring humans to their deaths.

"My little spies. Swift as the wind. Obsessed with candied almonds—which you might have noticed when you poked around my room." He gives me an arch look and I flush, embarrassed. "And they're actually very sweet creatures, once you get to know them."

"Wights"—I raise my eyebrows—"are sweet?"

"I wouldn't cross one, no. But they're very loyal. More loyal than most humans, anyway."

And strangely, it is that comment, delivered almost defensively, that finally makes me less suspicious of Musa. I do not trust him—not yet. But, I realize, I like him. I did not know how much I missed having someone to talk to. With Darin, the simplest conversation sometimes feels like dancing on butterflies' wings.

"What of my end of the bargain?" I ask. "You're spreading my story and making me out to be some sort of . . . hero—"

"Leader, actually."

I *knew* a deal with him wouldn't be as simple as recruiting Resistance fighters. "You want me to *lead* the Resistance?"

"If I'd told you that in the prison cell, you'd have rejected my offer."

"Because I have no wish to lead anyone. Look at what happened to my mother. To Mazen." Musa's calm only incenses me further. "Why don't you do it yourself? Why me?"

"I'm a Scholar of Adisa," Musa says. "My family has lived here for more than two hundred years. The refugees don't need me to speak for them. They need someone who understands their pain to plead their case before King Irmand."

I glance at him, alarmed. "Is this what you meant when you said you wanted to work with the king? Have you forgotten that he wants to imprison Darin and me—*and* you?"

"That's Nikla's doing." Musa shrugs off my protests. "I doubt she told her father she had you and Darin in her clutches. He's old. Ailing. She's used his weakness to push the Scholars out of Adisa and into the camps. To strip land and titles from Adisan Scholars. But the princess doesn't rule yet. While the king lives, there's hope that he'll listen to reason. Especially from the daughter of the Lioness, who he considered a friend."

He catches sight of my face in the dark and chuckles. "Don't look so worried," he says. "You won't go in unprepared. We'll have one chance to plead our case before the king. The future of our people depends on how successful we are. We need support from the refugees *and* Adisan Scholars before then. It's why I've had you meet with so many of my friends. If we have enough Scholars at our backs, King Irmand will have to listen to us."

But gathering so many will take time—time I do not have. Guilt stabs through me. Musa has spent weeks building me up. But the moment I learn how to stop the Nightbringer, I'll have to depart Adisa. And where does that leave him?

Alive, to fight, I tell myself firmly, *instead of dead in a jinn-fueled apocalypse.*

Shortly after we reach the horses, a summer storm rolls in from the ocean, drenching us in minutes. Still wary, I insist that we ride through the night.

Musa's wights report Tribe Sulud's location, and we finally draw to a halt outside a coastal village just as the fishing trawlers drift out to sea. The sodden fields around the village are thick with farmhands harvesting summer crops. Tribe Sulud's wagons sit near the docks, a stone's throw from the village's only inn, where Musa takes rooms.

I hope the *Kehanni* knows something about the Nightbringer. The approach of the Grain Moon, seven weeks away, looms over me like an executioner's ax. *Please.* I cast my wish to the stars, hoping the universe is listening. *Please let me learn something useful.*

Musa insists we clean up—*She won't let us in her wagon if we smell of horse and sweat.* By the time we emerge from the inn, a group of Tribesmen awaits us. They greet Musa as an old friend and me with a formal politeness. Without fanfare, we are led to the largest of the wagons, painted with purple fish and yellow flowers, white herons and crystalline rivers. Pendants of tarnished silver hang from the wagon's back, and when the door swings open, they jangle merrily.

The *Kehanni* wears a simple robe instead of the finery of the other night, but her bearing is no less noble. The bracelets on her arms jingle, hiding the heavy, faded tattoos on her arms.

"Musa of Adisa," she greets him. "Still getting yourself into trouble you can't get out of?"

"Always, *Kehanni*."

"Ah." She watches him shrewdly. "So you have finally seen her for what she is."

An old pain flashes in Musa's eyes, and I know that they are not speaking of me. "I have hope for her yet."

"Do not wait for her, child. Sometimes those we love are lost to us, as surely as if Death himself had claimed them. All we can do is mourn the divergence of their path. If you try to walk it, you too will fall into darkness."

Musa opens his mouth as if to respond, but the *Kehanni* turns to me. "You bring questions, Laia of Serra. Do you bring payment?"

"I have Serric steel weapons," I say. "Six blades, freshly forged."

The *Kehanni* sniffs and summons one of her kinsmen. Musa catches my eye, and though he says nothing, I find myself fidgeting. I think of what Darin said. *You have your own strength. It doesn't have to be the same as the Lioness's.*

"Wait." I place my hands on the weapons just as the *Kehanni* is handing them to the Tribesman. "Please," I say. "Use them in defense. Use them to fight the soldiers. But not . . . not those who are innocent. Please."

The Tribesman looks at the *Kehanni* questioningly. She murmurs something to him in Sadhese, and he steps out.

"Laia of Serra, you would tell a Tribeswoman how to defend herself?"

"No." I twine my fingers together. "I would ask that these blades, which are a gift, not be used to shed the blood of innocents."

"Hmph," the *Kehanni* says. Then she leans over to the front of her wagon and offers me a small wooden bowl of salt. I breathe a sigh of relief and put a pinch on my tongue, the custom Afya taught me. We are under her Tribe's protection now. None who belong to it may harm us.

"Your gift is accepted, Laia of Serra. How may I aid you?"

"I heard you spinning the old tales in Adisa. Can you tell me of the jinn? Do they have any weaknesses? Is there a way to . . ." *Kill them*, I nearly say, but the word is so cold. "Hurt them?"

"During the Fey-Scholar War, your ancestors murdered the jinn with steel and salt and summer rain fresh from the heavens. But you ask the wrong question, Laia of Serra. I know of you. I know you do not seek to destroy the jinn. You seek to destroy the Nightbringer. And he is something else altogether."

"Can it be done? Can he be killed?"

The *Kehanni* leans back in a pile of soft pillows and considers. The slide of her fingers against the wagon's lacquered wood sounds like sand hissing through an hourglass.

"He is the first of his kind," she says. "Rain will turn to steam on his skin, and steel to molten metal. As for salt, he will simply laugh to see it used against him, for he has inured himself to its effects. No, the Nightbringer cannot be killed. Not by a human, anyway. But he can be stopped."

"How?"

Rain thuds on the wooden roof of the wagon, and I'm reminded suddenly of the drums of the Empire, the way their tattoo echoed down into my bones, leaving me jittery.

"Come back tonight," the *Kehanni* says. "When the moon is high. And I will tell you."

Musa sighs. "*Kehanni*, with respect—"

"Tonight."

I shake my head. "But we—"

"Our stories are not bones left on the road for any hungry animal that happens along." The *Kehanni*'s voice rises, and I flinch back. "Our stories have purpose. Souls. Our stories breathe, Laia of Serra. The stories we tell have power, of course. But the stories that go untold have just as much power, if not more. I will sing you such a story—a story that was long untold. The story of a name and its meaning. Of how that name matters more than any other single word in existence. But I must prepare myself, for such stories are dragons drawn from a deep well in a dark place. Does one summon a dragon? No. One may only invite it and hope it emerges. So. Tonight."

The *Kehanni* refuses to say anything more, and soon Musa and I retreat to the inn, exhausted. He disappears into his room with a half-hearted wave.

The Tribeswoman said the Nightbringer can be stopped. Will she tell me how? I shiver in anticipation. What sort of story will she sing tonight?

A story that was long untold. The story of a name and its meaning. I open the door to my room, still wondering. But at the threshold, I freeze.

Because there is someone inside.

XXIV: Elias

Without the cottage to protect me, my mind is vulnerable to the jinn. But though I try to stay awake, I am, in the end, only human.

Since becoming Soul Catcher I have not dreamed. I only realize it now, when I open my eyes and find myself in a dark alley on an empty street. A flag flaps in the wind—black with crossed hammers. Marcus's sigil. I taste salt in the summer air, overlaid by something bitter. Blood. Smoke. Burnt stone.

Whispers ride the air, and I recognize the sibilant tones of the jinn. Is this one of their illusions? Is it real?

A whimper breaks the silence. A hooded figure slumps on the ground behind me. I watch for a moment before moving toward the figure. I'm wary as a pale hand emerges from a cloak, clenched tightly around a blade. But when I see the face beneath the hood, my caution disappears.

It's the Blood Shrike. Blood blooms from her hunched body, staining the cobblestones around her, merciless and inexorable.

"I'm sorry . . ." the Blood Shrike whispers when she sees me. "For what I did to Mamie. The Empire—" She coughs, and I crouch beside her, a hand on her back. She feels warm. Alive.

"Who did this to you?" Some part of me knows this is a dream, but that part fades and I'm simply in it, living it, as if it's real. The Shrike's face is drawn and white, her teeth chattering though the night is clear and warm. When I run my hands over her arms, trying to find her injury, she shudders, lifting back her cloak to show a wound in her belly. It looks bad.

Very bad.

It's a dream. Just a dream. Still, fear stabs through me. I was angry at her when I last met her, but seeing her like this transfers my rage to whoever did this to her. Plans fall into place. *Where is the nearest infirmary? Get her there. No—the barracks. Which barracks?*

But I can't do any of that, for this is a dream.

"Are you here to welcome me to—what did she call it—the Waiting Place?"

"You're not dead," I say. "And you're not going to die. Do you hear me?" A powerful memory hits me—the first Trial, Marcus attacking her, the Shrike's too-light body against mine as I carried her down the mountain.

"You're going to live. You're going to find whoever did this to you. You're going to make them pay. Get up. Get to safety." Urgency grips me. I *must* say these words to her. I feel that knowledge in my bones. Her pupils dilate; her body straightens.

"You are Blood Shrike of the Empire," I say. "And you are meant to survive. Get *up*."

When she finds my eyes, her own are glassy. I catch my breath, for they are so real—the shape, the emotions, the color of them, like the violet heart of a quiet sea. The way her face changes beneath her mask, the stiffness of her jaw as she grits her teeth.

But then she fades, as does the city. Silence descends. Darkness. When I open my eyes again, I expect to be back in the Waiting Place. But this time, I'm in a room I've never seen. The smooth wood floor is swept clean and strewn with mirrored cushions. There is a faint, familiar fragrance in the air, and my heart thuds faster, my body recognizing the scent before my mind does.

The door opens and Laia enters. Her dark hair has fallen loose from her braid, and she chews on her lip as she always does when she's deep in thought. The faint glow of a torch seeps in from the hallway behind her, lighting her face a soft gold-brown. Purple half-moons shadow her eyes.

The ocean thunders distantly, the creak of fishing boats a strange counter-melody to that roar.

I step toward her, gripped by a soul-deep longing for her to be real. I want to hear her speak my name. I want to dip my hands into the cool shade of her hair, to take solace in her gaze.

She freezes when she sees me, her mouth falling into an O. "You—you're here. How—"

"It's a dream," I say. "I'm in the Waiting Place. I fell asleep."

"A dream?" She shakes her head. "No, Elias. You're real. I was *just* down-stairs talking to Musa—"

Who the bleeding hells is Musa?

"Jealous?" She laughs, and immediately I want to hear her laugh again. "Now I know this isn't a dream. Dream Elias would know that he never needs to be jealous."

"I'm not—" I consider. "Never mind. I am jealous. Tell me he's old, at least? Or grouchy? Or maybe a bit stupid?"

"He's young. And handsome. And smart."

I snort. "He's probably rubbish in be—" Laia smacks me on the arm. "Battle," I say quickly. "I was going to say *battle.*"

"He doesn't hold a candle to you." Laia shakes her head. "I must be more exhausted than I thought—but I—I could have sworn I was awake. I feel awake. Did you windwalk here? How could you, if you were sleeping?"

"I wish it weren't a dream," I say. "I do. But it has to be, otherwise I couldn't—"

I reach out my hand, and for a moment it hovers near hers. I take it, for once not dreading the interference of the ghosts, and she squeezes. Her palm fits perfectly against mine, and I lift her hand and brush my lips across her fingers.

"I couldn't do this." I speak softly. "The ghosts—the Waiting Place—they wouldn't let me."

"Then tell me, dream Elias," she murmurs. "What did you say to me? The night you left me in the Tribal desert. The night you left me the note. What did you say?"

"I said—" I shake my head. Mamie Rila used to say that dreams are the bits of ourselves we can't face in the day, coming to visit at night. If I had never left Laia that night . . . if Keenan had never gotten the chance to betray her . . . if I'd not been caught by the Warden . . . if I'd never vowed to stay in the Waiting Place . . .

Then I wouldn't be stuck there. For eternity.

This dream version of Laia questions me because I question myself. Part of me knows I should pay attention to those questions. That they are a weakness I should crush.

But most of me just wants to revel in the fact that I am seeing Laia and I wasn't sure I ever would again.

"I miss you." She pushes back a curl, and I can't take my eyes off the skin of her wrist, disappearing into a bell-shaped sleeve, or the hollow in her neck, or the shape of her legs, long and perfectly curved in riding breeches. *It's a dream, Elias,* I remind myself sternly, trying to ignore how badly I want to feel those legs wrapped around me. *Of course her legs look incredible and perfect and I wish we could—*

When she puts her hand to my face, I savor the whorls in her fingertips, the gentle scrape of her nails. I look down into her eyes, golden and endless and full of all the desire I feel. I don't want this to disappear. I don't want to wake up to ghosts howling and jinn plotting.

I unravel her braid. She takes my other hand and puts it on her hip, and I trace the curve with a light touch that makes her close her eyes.

"Why is it like this?" she asks. "Why must we be apart? I miss what we should have been, Elias. Is that possible —"

Her hand drops to my chest, to the shredded remains of my shirt, torn in the battle with the ghosts.

"What the skies happened to you?" She looks me over with a healer's concern. "And why do you smell like smoke?"

Self-examination again. Her questions are my own subconscious, holding me accountable for my mistakes.

"Efrits burned down Shaeva's — my — house. Part of a jinn trick to torment me."

"No." She pales. "Why? The Nightbringer?"

"Perhaps. He must have sent the efrits, and the jinn in the grove told them when it was safe to enter the Forest." I shake my head. "I'm nothing like Shaeva, Laia. I'm not getting the ghosts through fast enough. Three of them escaped and did terrible things. I can't control the jinn. And I can't stop the ghosts' suffering."

"It is my fault." Laia slumps. "If I hadn't trusted him — given him the armlet — he wouldn't have gone after her. Shaeva should never have died."

It's such a *Laia* thing to say that I stare at her, perplexed. This is a dream, is it not? And the Blood Shrike . . . I hope that was a dream.

I expect Laia to say something I would think. Instead, she continues to berate herself. "I ask myself *every* day why I did not see him for what he was —"

"No." I brush away the tears from her black eyelashes. "Don't blame yourself." My voice is low, scratchy—why have I forgotten how to talk? "Please, it's not—"

She lifts her face, and my desire for her pools low and sudden. I can't stop myself from pulling her body to mine. She gasps softly and rises. Her lips against mine are urgent. She doesn't know when she'll kiss me again. The same frantic need courses through me.

My mind shouts at me that this is too real. But no ghosts trouble us. I want her. She wants me. And we have wanted each other for so long.

She pulls away from the kiss, and I'm certain I will wake up, that this skies-given time with her, devoid of ghosts railing at us or Mauth pulling at me, is about to end. But she only shoves away the remnants of my shirt before running her nails gently across my skin, sighing with pleasure or want or both.

I can't bear her lips away from mine, so I dip down again, but on my way I'm distracted by her shoulder. I find myself kissing it, then nipping at her neck, a primal part of me deeply satisfied by the moan I elicit from her, by the way her body relaxes into mine.

As her breath heaves, more ragged with every kiss on her throat, I feel her twine her leg around mine—yes—and I drop my hands to lift her up. The bed is too far, but there's a wall, and when I pin her against it, she rakes her hand across my back, murmuring, "Yes, Elias, yes," until I am shaking with need.

"The things," I whisper in her ear, "that I want to do to you . . ."

"Tell me." Her tongue flicks across my ear, and I forget to breathe. "Show me."

When she wraps her legs around my waist, when I feel the heat of her against me, it undoes me, and I flip her onto her back on the bed and drop down over her. She draws circles on my chest and then moves her hand lower . . . lower. I curse in Sadhese and capture her wrist.

"Me first," I say, tracing the indent of her stomach and, spurred on by her sighs, dropping my hand further, moving in time with her body until she arches her back, her arms trembling against my neck. As we both start to rid ourselves of clothes, our eyes meet.

She smiles at me, a sweet smile, unsure and hopeful and bemused. I know that smile. I think about it all the time.

But it is not a smile a dream could ever re-create. And this feeling within me—my desire. Hers. They are also not emotions a dream could ever simulate.

Could this be real? Could I have windwalked here somehow?

Who bleeding cares? You're here now.

But I hear something—whispers—the same whispers I heard when I was with the Blood Shrike. The jinn.

A warning flares down my spine. This isn't a dream. Laia is here, in this inn. I am here. And if I'm here, then it's the jinn who have done it. How the bleeding hells did they move me? How did they know where Laia was? And *why* have they brought me here?

I pull my hands away to sit up, and she growls in disappointment. "You're right," I say. "I—I am here. This is real. But it shouldn't be."

"Elias." She laughs again. "It has to be a dream, or we couldn't do this. But it is the best dream." She reaches for me again, pulling me down. "You're exactly like *you*. Now where were—"

She pauses, and it's as if the world has frozen. Nothing moves, not even the shadows. A moment later, the world unfreezes and Laia shudders, as if a chill has entered her very blood.

Or her mind. For when she looks at me, she is no longer Laia. Her eyes are pure white, and I jump away from her as she shoves me, her strength unnatural. *A ghost?* My mind screams. *Skies, is she possessed?*

"Go back!" Her voice has completely changed, and I recognize it as the voice that spoke out of Shaeva when I took my vow to become Soul Catcher. The voice that spoke to me in that strange in-between place when Shaeva stole me away from the raid. Mauth's voice.

Laia's whole body shifts, changing into shadow, her features faded, her body unfamiliar.

"Where is she?" I demand. "What did you do with her?"

"Go back. The jinn deceive you. They use your weakness against you. *Go back.*"

Mauth—in Laia's shadow form—swings at me, as if trying to beat me toward the Waiting Place. I'm thrown backward by the blow.

"Stop this." I lift my hands. "Who brought me here? Was it you? Was it the jinn?"

"The jinn, you fool," says Mauth—for I won't allow myself to think of him as Laia, no matter what form he takes. "They siphon the power that you do not use. They strengthen themselves. They distract you with the lures of the human world. The more you feel, the more you fail. The more you fail, the stronger they become."

"How—how are you talking to me?" I say. "Are you possessing her? Are you hurting her?"

"Her fate is not your concern." Mauth shoves me, but I plant my feet. "Her life is not your concern."

"If you've hurt her—"

"She will not remember this—any of this," Mauth says. "Go back. Surrender to me. Forget your past. Forget your humanity. You must, do you see? Do you understand?"

"I cannot!" I say. "It's part of me. But I need the magic—"

"The magic will allow you to pass the ghosts through with nary a thought. It will allow you to quell the jinn. But you must leave your old self behind. You are Elias Veturius no more. You are the Soul Catcher. You are mine. I know what your heart desires. It can never be."

I try desperately to push those wishes away. So stupid. So small. A house and a bed and a garden and laughter and a future.

"Forget your dreams." Mauth's anger mounts. "Forget your heart. There is only your vow to serve me. Love cannot live here. Seek out the jinn. Find their secrets. Then you will understand."

"I'll never understand," I say. "I'll never let go of what I fought so hard to keep."

"You must, Elias. Otherwise all is lost."

Mauth spins out of Laia, a teeming cyclone of cindered shadows, and she collapses in a heap. I take one step toward her before Mauth yanks me into darkness. Seconds or minutes or hours later, I slam into the singed earth outside Shaeva's cabin. Warm summer rain falls in sheets, drenching me within seconds.

Bleeding, burning hells, it was real. I was with Laia in Marinn—and she won't even remember it. I was with the Blood Shrike in Navium. Did she survive her wound? I should have helped her. Gotten her to the barracks.

Just thinking of them ignites Mauth's wrath. I double over, hissing at the fire that tears through me.

Seek out the jinn. Find their secrets. Mauth's order rings through my head. But I sought the jinns' help once before. They used it to bedevil me so the spirits could escape.

The Commandant's words float through my mind. *There is success. And there is failure. The land in between is for those too weak to live.*

I need to get to the magic. And to do that, Mauth, at least, thinks I need the jinn. But this time, I won't go to those creatures as Elias Veturius. I won't even go to them as the Soul Catcher.

I'll go to them as Mask Veturius, dread Martial, soldier of the Empire. I'll go to them as the estranged, murderous son of the Bitch of Blackcliff, as the monster who killed his friends and assassinated the Empire's enemies as a child and who watched stonily as Yearlings were whipped to death before his eyes.

This time, I will not ask the jinn for help.

I will take it.

XXV: The Blood Shrike

You are Blood Shrike of the Empire. And you are meant to survive.
Who spoke the words? I try to grasp at the memory. Someone was here, on this dark street with me. A friend . . .

But when I open my eyes and pull myself to my knees, I am alone, left with nothing but the echo of those words.

My knees shake as I try to pull myself to my feet. But no matter how deeply I breathe, I can't get any bleeding air. *Because you're losing all your blood, Shrike.*

I rip off my cloak and tie it around my stomach, groaning at the pain of it. *Now* is when I need a damned patrol to pass, but of course the Commandant, who no doubt planned this, would make sure there was none.

But there might be more assassins. I have to get up. Get to the Black Guard barracks.

Why? a voice whispers. *The darkness waits with open arms. Your family waits.*

Mother. Father. I need to remember something about them. I fist my hands and feel something cold, round. I look down—a ring. A bird in flight.

You are all that holds back the darkness. Someone said those words to me. But no—those words do not matter. Not against the pain that slams through me, waves and waves of it.

You are all that holds back the darkness. The memory burns in my mind. I put a hand to my eyes, and my mask ripples. The cool metal lends me strength as nothing else can, snapping me out of my torpor.

My father spoke those words to me. *Livia! The baby! The regency!* My family lives. The Empire lives. And I must protect both.

I crawl forward, teeth gritted, enraged at the tears streaming unchecked down my face at the astounding pain of my wound. *Break it down.* How many steps to the barracks? It's a quarter mile from here at least. Five hundred strides at most. Five hundred strides is nothing.

What about when you get there? What if someone sees you? Will you let your men see you weak? What if someone spots you on the way? The assassin can't possibly be alone.

Then I will fight his accomplices too. And I will live. Because if I do not, all is lost.

I look down at my father's ring and force myself forward, taking strength from it. I am a Mask. I am an Aquilla. I am the Blood Shrike. Pain is nothing.

I reach the wall of a nearby house and drag myself to my feet. The houses are darkened at this time of night, and though I might find aid at one of them, I might also find enemies. The Commandant is nothing if not thorough. If she sent an assassin, then she'd pay off the street where he was meant to kill me, to make sure no one helped.

Move, Shrike. I make it down the street before my legs begin feeling strange. Cold. I slow down, hoping to catch my breath. And then suddenly, I'm not moving anymore. I'm on my knees. Bleeding hells. I know this feeling. Weakness. Uselessness. Helplessness. I've felt it before, after Marcus stabbed me during the First Trial.

Elias saved me then. Because he was—is—my friend. How could I ever see him as anything else after what we have been through? If I am sorry for anything now, before the end, it is that I hunted him. That I hurt his family. That I hurt *him.*

Will I see him now? In the Waiting Place? Will he welcome me? What folly that he is chained to that place—what folly when this world needs his light.

"You deserved better," I whisper.

"Shrike!" The scrape of boots has me baring my teeth and brandishing my dagger. But I recognize the black hair and gold skin, and though I'm confused, I'm not really surprised, because he is my best friend, after all, and he'd never let me just die.

"You—you came—"

"Shrike, listen to me, stay awake. Stay with me." But no—it's not Elias. The voice doesn't offer the slow, deep warmth of summer. It's cool and harsh—all wrong. It's winter. Like me. Then there's another voice, also familiar. Dex. "There's a physician in the Aquilla house—"

"Get him," the cool voice says. "Help me with her armor first—she'll be easier to carry. Careful with her stomach."

I know the first voice now. Avitas Harper. Strange, quiet Harper. Thoughtful and watching and filled with an emptiness that calls to me.

He works quickly to unbuckle my armor, and I stifle a moan when it comes off. Dex's handsome, dark face, strained in the half-light, clarifies. A good soldier. A true friend. But he's always in pain. Always alone. Hiding.

"It's not fair," I whisper to him. "You should love whom you wish. How the Empire would treat you if they knew, it's not—"

Dex's face pales, and he glances quickly at Avitas. "Save your strength, Shrike," he says. Then he's gone, and a muscled arm comes around my waist. Harper pulls my hand across his shoulders, and we take a step—another—but I am staggering. I've lost too much blood.

"Pick me up, you idiot," I gasp. A moment later I am weightless, and I sigh.

"You're going to be fine, Hel—Shrike." A crack in Harper's voice. Emotion? Fear?

"Don't let anyone see me," I whisper. "This—this is undig—dignified."

A bark of laughter. "Only you would think that while your guts are leaking out onto the damned pavement. Hold on, Blood Shrike. The barracks aren't far."

He makes for the front entrance, and I shake my head emphatically. "Take me through the back. The Plebeians we're sheltering can't see me like this—"

"We don't have a choice. The fastest way to the infirmary is through the front door—"

"No!" I thrash and shove Harper's chest. He doesn't so much as twitch. "They cannot see me like this! You know what she'll do. She'll use it against me. The Paters already think I'm weak."

"Captain Avitas Harper." Harper freezes at the voice, deep and ancient and brooking no argument. "Bring her this way."

"You get the bleeding hells away from us." Harper backs away two steps, but the Nightbringer holds out his hands.

"I could kill you both with a thought, child," he says softly. "If you wish for her to live, bring her."

Harper hesitates for a moment and then follows. I want to protest, but my mouth is unable to form words. His body is taut as a wire pulled tight, heart thudding swift like a river current. But his masked face is serene. Some part of me relaxes. My sight darkens. *Ah, sleep . . .*

"Stay with me, Shrike." Harper speaks sharply, and I groan in protest. "Keep your eyes open. You don't have to speak. All you have to do is stay awake."

I force myself to focus on the swirling robes of the Nightbringer. He whispers, but I cannot make out the words. A brick wall that rose before us disappears. *Magic!* Moments later, the barracks come into view. The guards stationed outside look up, hands on their scims. But the Nightbringer speaks again, and they turn away as if they haven't seen us.

"Set her down, Captain." We enter my quarters, and the Nightbringer gestures to my bed. "And then leave."

Harper settles me onto the bed slowly. Still, I grimace, another wave of pain washing over me at the strain on my wound. When he backs away, I feel cold.

"I will not leave her." He straightens and looks the Nightbringer in the face without flinching.

The Nightbringer considers. "Very well. Get out of the way."

The jinn sits beside me on the bed. He throws back my shirt, and I catch a glimpse of his hand beneath the sleeve of his robe. It is shadowy and twisted, with an eerie glow beneath the darkness that makes me think of banked embers. I think of a day long ago in Serra, the first time I met him. I remember how he sang—just one note—and the bruises on my face healed.

"Why are you helping me?"

"I cannot help you," the Nightbringer says. "You can, however, help yourself."

"Can't—can't heal myself."

"Your healing power allows you to recover more quickly than a normal human," he says. Distantly, I realize that Avitas is hearing all of this. That maybe I should have had him leave the room. But I am too weak to care. "How else could you still live, child, after losing so much blood? Consider the wound, and then find your song. Do it. Now."

The words are not a request but an order.

I hum tunelessly, fighting the pain, searching for my song. I close my eyes, and I am a girl again, comforting Hannah when she came into my bed at night, terrified of monsters. Mother would find us huddling together and sing us to sleep. Sometimes in the deep night at Blackcliff, thinking of her song brought me peace. But when I sing now, nothing happens.

Why would it? My song is not one of peace. It is one of failure and pain. My song is one of battle and blood, death and power. It is not the song of Helene Aquilla. It is the song of the Blood Shrike. And I cannot find it. I cannot wrap my mind around it.

This is it then. Cut down on the street like a drunk civvie who couldn't tell a blade from a bottle.

The Nightbringer sings two notes. *Rage*, I think. *Love.* A raw, cold world lives in that short song—my world. Me.

I sing the two notes back to him. Two notes become four, four become fourteen. *Rage for my enemies*, I think. *Love for my people. This* is my song.

But it hurts, bleeding hells, it hurts. The Nightbringer takes my hand. "Pour the pain into me, child," he says. "Turn it away from yourself."

His words unleash a flood. Even as the burden of my wound transfers to him, he does not flinch. He does not move at all, his cloaked form a statue as he accepts it. My skin stitches itself back together, burning with an ache that makes me cry out.

A blade hisses as it leaves its sheath. "What the bleeding hells did you do to her?"

The Nightbringer turns to Avitas and gestures. Immediately, Harper drops the scim as if burned.

"Look." The jinn moves, nodding down to my wound, which is now nothing but a star-shaped scar. It weeps blood, but it will not kill me.

Harper's low oath tells me that I will soon have a great deal of explaining to do. But I can worry about that later. My body is exhausted, but when the Nightbringer releases me, I make myself sit up.

"Wait," I whisper. "Will you tell her of this?" He knows of whom I speak.

"Why would I tell her? So that she can attempt to kill you again? I am not her servant, Blood Shrike. She is mine. She attacked you against my orders. I have no patience for defiance, thus I have thwarted her."

"I don't understand. Why would you help me? What do you want from me?"

"I am not helping you, Blood Shrike." He stands and gathers his robes. "I am helping myself."

«»«»«»

When I wake, night has fallen, and the rafters shudder with reverberations of catapult projectiles. The Barbarians must have recommenced their bombardment of Navium.

I am alone in my room, but my armor is hung neatly from the wall. A curse slips through my lips as I rise. My wound has gone from deadly to irritatingly painful. *Stop whinging. Get your armor on.* I limp to the wall, every joint as stiff as an old woman's in deep winter. I hope a few minutes on my feet will warm up my body enough that I can at least ride.

"Off to get yourself killed again so soon?" The familiar rasp is so unexpected that I don't believe I'm hearing it at first. "Your mother would be appalled."

Cook perches in the window as usual, and even with the hood, even though I've seen her scars before, the violence of her mangled face is jarring enough that I look away. Her cloak is ripped, her shock of white hair a bird's nest. The yellow stains on her fingers tell me immediately who has been leaving clay statues in the Commandant's quarters.

"I heard you got stabbed." The Cooks drops into the room. "Thought I'd come yell at you for allowing it to happen." She shakes her head. "You're a fool. You should know better than to walk alone at night within a hundred miles of the Bitch of Blackcliff."

"And leave you to kill her?" I snort. "Hasn't worked out well for you, has it? All you've done is left a few disturbing statues in her quarters."

Cook grins, an eerie thing. "I'm not trying to kill her." She does not elaborate. Her gaze drops to my stomach. "You haven't thanked me for murdering the other assassins who were coming for you. Or for telling Harper to stop squinting at reports so he could drag your carcass to safety."

"Thank you," I say.

"I trust you know that sun-eyed bastard wants something from you?"

I don't waste time asking how she knows the Nightbringer healed me. "I don't trust him," I tell her. "I'm not a fool."

"Then why did you let him help you? He's planning a war, did you know? And he's likely got a part in it for you. You just don't know what it is yet."

"A war." I sit up. "The war with the Karkauns?"

Cook hisses, snatches a candle off a table near the door, and throws it at my head. "Not that war, stupid! *The* war. The one that's been brewing since the day my idiot people decided it would be wise to attack and destroy the jinn. *That's* what this is all about, girl. That's what the Commandant is up to. It's not just the Karkauns she wants to defeat."

"Explain yourself," I say. "What are you—"

"Get out of here," she says. "Get far away from the Commandant. She's set on taking you down, and she'll have her way. Go to your sister. Keep her safe. Keep that emperor of yours in check. And when the war *does* come, be ready for it."

"I *must* take down the Commandant first," I say. "This war you speak of—" A step sounds in the hallway beyond the door. Cook leaps into the window, one hand coiled around the frame. I notice something strange about that hand. The skin is smooth—not young like mine, but not the skin of a white-haired granny either.

Those dark blue eyes pin me. "You want to take down the Bitch of Black-cliff? You want to destroy her? You have to become her first. And you don't have it in you, girl."

XXVI: Laia

I am fuzzy-headed and confused when I pull on my boots. I've slept all day—such strange dreams I had. Wonderful, and yet—

"Laia!" Musa's voice is a low hiss at the door. "Bleeding hells, are you all right? Laia!"

The door bursts open before I can get a word out, and Musa takes two steps in and grabs my shoulders, as if to make sure I am real.

"Get your things." He scans the windows and beneath the bed. "We need to get the hells out of here."

"What's happened?" I say. My thoughts immediately go to the Nightbringer. To his minions. "Is it—is he—"

"Wraiths." Musa's face has paled to the color of an unpolished scim. "They attacked Tribe Sulud, and they might be coming for us."

Oh no. *No.* "The *Kehanni*—"

"I don't know if she's alive," he says. "And we can't risk finding out. Come on."

We race down the back stairs of the inn and out to the stables as silently as possible. It is late enough that most of the village is in bed, and waking anyone would only bring about questions—and a delay.

"The wraiths killed everyone silently," Musa says. "I wouldn't have known anything was wrong if the wights hadn't woken me up."

I pause as I throw a saddle onto my horse. "We should find out if there are any survivors."

Musa swings up onto his mount. "If we go into that camp, skies know what we'll find."

"I've faced a wraith before." I finish with my horse. "There were nearly fifty Tribespeople in that camp, Musa. If even one of them is alive—"

Musa shakes his head. "Most of them left early. Only a few wagons stayed with the *Kehanni* to keep watch over her until she was ready to leave. And she stayed because—"

"Because of us," I say. "Which is why we owe it to her to make sure neither she nor any of her kinsmen needs help."

He groans in protest but follows me as I leave the stables and head for the camp. I expect it to be silent, but the steady drizzle of rain pings off the wagon roofs, making it difficult for us to hear our own footsteps.

The first body is sprawled at the entrance to the encampment. It is *wrong*, broken in a dozen different ways. A lump rises in my throat. I recognize the man—one of the Tribesmen who welcomed us. Three more of his family members lie a few yards from him. I know instantly that they too are dead.

But we do not see the *Kehanni*. A quiet chitter near Musa's ear tells me that the wights have noticed her absence too. Musa nods to the *Kehanni*'s wagon. When I make for it, Musa puts an arm in front of me.

"*Aapan*." The strain on his face matches the foreboding in my heart. "Maybe I should go first. In case."

"I saw the inside of Kauf Prison, Musa." I slip past him. "It can't be any worse."

The back door opens silently, and I find the *Kehanni* crumpled against the far wall. She looks so much smaller than she did just hours ago, an old woman whose last story was stolen from her. The wraiths did not cut her—in fact, I do not see a single open wound. But the odd angles of her limbs tell me exactly how she died. I clap my hand against my mouth to hold back my sick. Skies, she must have been in so much pain.

A moan comes from her, and both Musa and I jump.

"Oh bleeding hells." I am by her side in two steps. "Musa, go to the horses. Look in the right saddlebag—"

"No." The *Kehanni's* sunken eyes gleam with faint, failing light. "Listen." Musa and I both fall silent. We can barely hear her over the rain.

"Seek out the Augurs' words," she whispers. "Prophecy. The Great Library—"

"Augurs?" I don't understand. "What do the Augurs have to do with the Nightbringer? Are they allies?"

"Of a kind," the *Kehanni* whispers. "Of a kind."

Her eyelids droop. She's gone. From the wagon door, a loud, panicked chitter sounds.

"Let's go," Musa hisses. "The wraiths are circling back. They know we're here."

With the panic of the wights spurring us, we race through the rain at a pace that drives the horses into a frothing sweat. *I'm sorry, I'm sorry.* I think the words over and over, but I don't know to whom I speak. My horse, for making it suffer? The *Kehanni*, for asking her a question that killed her? The Tribesmen who died trying to protect her?

"The Augurs' prophecies," Musa says when we finally slow our horses for a rest. "The only place we'll find them is the Great Library. She—she was trying to tell us. But it's impossible to get in."

"Nothing is impossible." Elias's words come back to me. "We'll get in. We must. But first we have to make it back."

Again, we push through the night, but this time, Musa needs no urging. I spend half the ride looking over my shoulder and the other half plotting ways to get into the Great Library. The skies clear, but the roads are still treacherous with mud. The wights remain near us, their wings occasionally flashing in the dark, their presence offering a strange comfort.

When the walls of Adisa come into view in the deepest hour of the night, I want to sob in relief. Until the hazy glow of flame materializes.

"The refugee camp." Musa urges his horse on. "They're burning the tents."

"What the hells happened?"

But Musa has no answer. The camp is in such chaos when we reach it that the Mariners, frantically evacuating the Scholars, do not notice two more faces amid the hundreds running through the narrow, ash-filled lanes. Musa disappears to speak to one of the Mariners before finding me again.

"I don't think the Mariners did this," Musa shouts over the roar of the flames. "Otherwise why would they be helping? And how could the fire have spread so quickly? One of the soldiers I spoke with said they caught wind of it only an hour ago."

We plunge into the smoke-choked streets, tearing open tents, pulling out those who are sleeping, who remained unaware, shooing children to the outskirts of the camp. We do whatever we can, however we can, with the frantic anguish of those who know that nothing will be enough. Screams rise around us from those who are trapped. From those who cannot find their family members. From those who have found their family members injured or dead.

Always us. My eyes burn from smoke; my face is wet. *Always my people.*

Musa and I go back again and again, carrying out those who cannot walk themselves, pulling to safety as many Scholars as we can. A Mariner soldier hands us water to drink, to give to the survivors. I freeze when she looks up. It is Captain Eleiba, her eyes red-rimmed, hands trembling. She meets my gaze but only shakes her head and turns back to her own tasks.

You'll be all right. All is well. You'll be fine. I speak nonsense to those who are burned, who cough blood from all the smoke. *Of course we'll find your mother. Your daughter. Your grandson. Your sister.* Lies. So many lies. I hate myself for telling them. But the truth is crueler.

Hundreds are still trapped in the camp when I notice something strange through the smoke and haze. A red glow rises from the city of Adisa. My throat is parched, burned from inhaling so much smoke, but suddenly it goes even more dry. Has the fire from the camp spread? But no—it couldn't have. Not over the massive city wall.

I back away from the refugee camp, hoping I can see better from outside it. Dread spreads slowly through my body. The same feeling I've had when something terrible has happened and I wake up having forgotten. And then I remember.

Cries rise up all around me, like ill spirits let loose. I am not the only one who has noticed the glow from Adisa.

"Musa." The Scholar man lurches back toward the camp, desperate to save even one more person. "Look—"

I pull him around to face the city. A warm wind off the ocean parts the fug of smoke over the camp for a moment. That's when we see it.

To call the fire enormous would be like calling the Commandant unkind. It is immense, an inferno that transforms the sky into a lurid nightmare. The thick cloud of smoke is illuminated by the flames, impossibly high, as if shooting from the depths of the earth to the very heavens.

"Laia." Musa's voice is weak. "It's—it's—"

But he doesn't have to say it. I knew as soon as I saw the height of the flames. No other building in Adisa is so tall.

The Great Library. The Great Library is on fire.

XXVII: Elias

For two weeks, I plot how I'll seize the truth from the jinn. The mercantile in a nearby village provides most of what I need. The rest depends on the weather, which finally cooperates when an early summer storm sweeps in from the east, drenching the entirety of the Waiting Place.

I don't mind the rain. I catch a dozen buckets' worth of it. By the time I transport them to the jinn grove, the deluge has dulled the unholy glow of the trees to an ocherous red.

Once in the grove, I smile, waiting for the jinn to begin tormenting me. *Come on, you devils. Watch me. Listen to my thoughts. Squirm over what's coming.*

When I am past the first row of trees, the canopy grows tangled. All is silent, but the air thickens, weighing me down, as if I'm walking through water in full Martial armor. It is an effort to remove the bag of salt I have stowed away. But as I make rings of salt around the trees, the jinn stir, snarling softly from within their prisons.

I take out an ax—its steel edge freshly sharpened—and give it a few test swings. Then I dip it in the bucket of rainwater and sink it six inches into the closest jinn tree. The shriek that arises from the grove is both hair-raising and horribly satisfying.

"You're keeping secrets," I say. "I want to know them. Tell me, and I'll stop."

You fool. Cut open the trees and we will simply burst forth.

"Lies." I slip into the voice of a Mask, as if I were interrogating a prisoner. "If your freedom was that simple, you'd have gotten your efrit friends to break you out long ago."

I dip the ax in the rainwater again and, on inspiration, scoop up some of the salt to rub on it. At my second strike, the jinn scream so loudly that the ghosts clustered nearby streak away. When I lift the ax for a third time, the jinn speak.

Stop. Please. Come closer.

"If you're tricking me—"

If you want our secrets, you must take them. Come closer.

I move deeper into the grove, the ax clutched tightly. Mud slimes my boots.

Closer.

Every step grows more difficult, but I drag myself forward until I can't move at all.

How does it feel to be trapped, Soul Catcher?

Quite suddenly, I cannot speak or see or feel anything beyond the steady thud of my heart. I fight against the darkness, the silence. I cast myself against the walls of this prison like a moth caught in a jar. In my panic, I reach for Mauth. But the magic doesn't respond.

How does it feel to be chained?

"What the hells," I rasp, "are you doing to me?"

Look, Elias Veturius. You wanted our secrets. They are before you.

Suddenly, I am free of their grasp. The trees ahead thin out as the land curves to a rise. I stagger toward it and find myself looking down a slope at a shallow valley nestled in a bend of the fast-rushing River Dusk.

And in that valley are dozens—no, hundreds of stone structures. It's a city I've never seen. A city Shaeva never mentioned. A city that has never made itself known to me on the strange internal map I have of the Waiting Place. It looks—and feels in my mind—like empty space.

"What is this place?" I ask.

A bird sails down into the valley through the thick sheets of rain, some small, squirming creature caught in its claws. The treetops sway in the wind, heaving like a restless sea.

Home. The jinn speak without rancor, for once. *This is home.*

Mauth nudges me forward, and I make my way through tall, soaked summer grasses down into the city, dagger at the ready.

It is unlike any city I've ever seen, the streets curved in concentric half circles around a building on the banks of the River Dusk. The streets, the buildings—everything is made of the same strange black stone. The color is so pure that I reach out more than once to touch it, awestruck by its depth.

I soon sheathe my dagger. I've been in enough graveyards to know what they feel like. There isn't a soul in the place. There aren't even ghosts.

Though I want to explore every single street, I'm drawn to the large building on the riverbank. It's bigger than the Emperor's palace in Antium and a hundred times more beautiful. Stone blocks sit upon one another with such perfect symmetry that I know no human cut them.

I see no columns or domes or ornate patterns. The structures in the Empire or Marinn or the Tribal deserts reflect their people. Those cities laugh and cry and shout and snarl. This city is one note, the purest note ever sung, held until my heart wants to break at the sound.

A low set of stairs leads to the main building. At my touch, the two massive doors at the top of the stairs open as easily as if their hinges were oiled this morning. Within, three dozen blue-fire torches sputter to life.

Which is when I realize that the walls, which appeared to be a deep black stone, are something else entirely. They reflect the flame like water reflects sunlight, transforming the entire room to a gentle sapphire blue. Though the massive windows are open to the elements, the thunder of the storm outside is muted to a murmur.

I cannot make heads or tails of what this place is. Its size makes me think it was used for gatherings. Yet there is only one low bench in the center of the room.

Mauth tugs me up a staircase, through a series of antechambers, and into another room with a huge window. It is filled with the scents of the river and the rain. Torches paint the room white.

I lift my hand to touch the wall. When I do, it comes alive, filled with misty images. I yank my hand back, and the images fade.

Gingerly, I touch it again. At first, I cannot understand the pictures. Animals play. Leaves dance on the wind. Tree hollows transform into kindly faces. The images remind me of Mamie Rila—of what her voice is like when she sings a tale. Which is when I understand: These are children's stories. Children lived here. But not human children.

Home, the jinn said. Jinn children.

I make my way, room by room, to the top of the building, stopping in a high rotunda that overlooks the city and the river.

When I touch the walls, images appear again. This time, though, they are of the city itself. Strips of orange and yellow and green silk flutter in the windows. Jewel-like flowers grow in overflowing boxes. The trill and hum of voices tell of a happier time.

People clad in smoky black robes walk the city. One woman has dark skin and tight curls, like Dex's. Another has pale skin and fine hair, like the Blood Shrike's. Some are scim-thin, and others are heavier, like Mamie was before the Empire got its hands on her. Each, in their own way, walks with a grace that I only ever saw in Shaeva.

But they do not walk alone. All are surrounded by ghosts.

I spot a man with auburn hair and a face so beautiful I can't even be irritated by it. He is surrounded by ghost children, love suffusing every bit of him as he speaks with them.

I can't hear what he says, but I can understand his intent. He offers the ghosts love. Not judgment or anger or questions. One by one, the spirits drift into the river at ease. At peace.

Is this, then, the secret of what Shaeva did? I've only to offer the spirits love and they'll move on? It can't be. It's antithetical to everything she said about quelling my emotions.

The ghosts here are calm, far more serene than they were when Shaeva lived. I do not sense the frantic pain that suffuses the Waiting Place as I know it. There are also far fewer of them. Little groups of them follow the black-robed figures obediently.

Instead of a lone Soul Catcher, there are dozens. No, hundreds.

Other figures drift from the buildings, human in form but made of deep black-and-red flame, glorious and free. Here and there I spot children switching from human to flame and back with the rapidity of a hummingbird's wings.

When the Soul Catchers and their ghosts pass, the jinn move aside, inclining their heads. The children watch from afar, mouths agog. They whisper, and their body language reminds me of how Martial children act when a Mask passes by. Fear. Awe. Envy.

And yet the Soul Catchers are not isolated. They speak to each other. One woman smiles when a flame child comes running toward her, transforming into a human just before the jinn scoops him up. They have *family*. Partners. Children.

An image of Laia and me in a house, making a life together, flashes through my mind. Could it be possible?

The city ripples. A frisson of sorts, a portent made manifest in the shiver in the air. The jinn turn to the rim of their valley, where a row of flags fly, green with a purple quill and an open book: the sigil of the Scholar Empire, before it fell.

The images come swiftly. A young human king arrives with his retinue. The auburn-haired jinn welcomes him, a brown-skinned jinn woman at his side and two flame children fidgeting behind them. The jinn wears a crown with discomfort, as if he's not used to it.

I finally recognize him. The hair is different, as is the build, but something about his manner is familiar. This is the King of No Name. The Nightbringer.

Flanking the king and his queen are two flame-formed jinn bodyguards armed with black-diamond sickles. Despite their nonhuman physiques, I recognize the one who stands by the children. Shaeva. She watches the visiting Scholar king with fascination. He notices.

The images speed up. The Scholar king wheedles, then cajoles, then demands the secrets of the jinn. The Nightbringer rejects him, but the Scholar king refuses to give up.

Shaeva meets the Scholar in his guest quarters. Over weeks, he befriends her. Laughs with her. Listens to her, scheming even as she falls desperately in love with him.

A sense of foreboding grows, thick as mud. The Nightbringer haunts the streets of his own city when everyone's sleeping, sensing a threat. When his wife speaks to him, he smiles. When his children play with him, he laughs. Their fears are quelled. His only grow.

Shaeva finds the Scholar king in a clearing beyond the city. His manner reminds me of someone, but the knowledge wavers at the edges of my mind before slipping away. Shaeva and the Scholar argue. He calms her anger. Makes promises. Even at the distance of a thousand years, I know he'll break those promises.

Three moons rise and set. Then the Scholars attack, tearing into the Forest of Dusk with steel and fire.

The jinn cast them back easily, but with bewilderment—they do not understand this. They know the humans want their power. *But why, when we keep the balance? Why, when we take the spirits of your dead and move them on so that you are not haunted by them?*

Ghosts fill the city. But the jinn must fight, so there are not enough Soul Catchers to move the spirits on. Forced to wait and suffer, the spirits cry out, their wails an eerily prescient dirge. The jinn king meets with the efrit lords as the Scholars press the attack. His flame children are sent far away with hundreds of others, howling tearful goodbyes to their parents.

The images follow the children into the Forest.

Oh no. No. I want to pull my hand from the wall, to stop the images. Danger closes in on the little ones. The crack of a twig, a shadow flitting among the trees. And all the while these waist-high flame children scurry through the Forest. They are unknowing, illuminating the trunks and leaves and grasses with brilliance, some deep fey magic that lends beauty to all that they touch. Their whispers sound like bells, and they move like cheery, brave little campfires on a freezing night.

A sudden silence descends. *You're walking into an ambush! Protect them, you fools!* I want to scream at the guards. Humans pour from the trees, armed with swords gleaming with summer rain.

The flame children cluster together, terrified. As they join, their fire burns brighter.

And then their flames go out.

I don't want to see anymore. I know the tale. Shaeva gave the Scholar king the Star. He and his coven of magic-users locked away the jinn.

Do you see now, Elias Veturius? the jinn ask.

"We destroyed you," I say.

You destroyed yourselves. For a thousand years you've had only one Soul Catcher. Shaeva, at least, was jinn. Her magic was innate. Still, the ghosts built up—you saw her struggle. But you have no magic. How can a talentless mortal do that which a jinn could not? The ghosts press against the borders like rainwater presses against a dam. And you will never move the ghosts swiftly enough to stop the dam from bursting. You will fail.

For once, the jinn play no tricks. They do not need to. The truth in their words is terrifying enough.

XXVIII: The Blood Shrike

Night is thick on Navium when I jerk out of sleep.

"The beach." I don't realize I've spoken the words aloud until I hear the creak of armor. Avitas, keeping watch in a chair near my door, shudders awake, scim in hand.

"Some guard you make." I snort. "You were fast asleep."

"My apologies, Shrike," he says stiffly. "I have no excuse—"

I roll my eyes. "That was a joke." I swing my legs out of the bed and search around for my breeches. Avitas reddens and faces the wall, drumming his fingers on his dagger's hilt.

"Don't tell me you've not seen a naked soldier before, Captain."

A long pause, then a chuckle, low and husky. It makes me feel . . . strange. Like he's about to tell me a secret. Like I would lean in closer to hear it. "Not one like you, Blood Shrike."

Now my skin feels hot, and I open my mouth, trying to think of a retort. Nothing. Skies, I'm relieved he can't see me over here, red as a tomato and gaping like a fish. *Don't act the fool, Shrike.* I lace my pants, throw on a tunic, and grab my armor, pushing away my embarrassment. At Blackcliff, I saw Dex, Faris, Elias—all of my friends—stripped down to absolutely nothing, and I didn't bat an eyelid. I'm not about to humiliate myself with blushes over this.

"I have to get to the beach." I yank on my bracers, wincing at the twinge in my stomach. "I have to see if . . ." I don't want to say it or even think it, in case I'm utterly deluded.

"Would you care to explain that first?" Harper nods to my stomach. *Right.* He saw me heal myself. He heard what the Nightbringer said.

"I would not."

"Silvius—the physician—came to check on you at Dex's request. I didn't let him in. Told him Dex exaggerated the seriousness of your wound. And he mentioned that a group of children in the Aquilla infirmary saw miraculous improvement in a very short span of time." Harper pauses, and when I say nothing, he sighs in exasperation. "I'm your second, Shrike, but I don't know your secrets. And so I cannot protect you when others try to ferret them out."

"I don't need protection."

"You are second-in-command of the Empire," he says. "If you didn't need protection, it would be because no one saw you as a threat. Needing protection is not a weakness. Refusing to trust your allies *is*." Harper's voice rarely rises above the familiar monotone of a Mask. Now it cracks like a whip, and I gaze at him in surprise.

Shut it, and get out. I don't have time for this. I only just stop myself from saying it. Because he's not wrong.

"You'll want to sit down for this," I say. When I finish telling him of the magic—the efrit, healing Elias and then Laia, and all that came after—he looks thoughtful. I expect him to ask questions, to delve deeper, to push for more.

"No one will know of it," he says. "Until you're ready. Now—you mentioned the beach."

I am surprised that he moved on so quickly. But I am thankful too. "I heard a story when I was young," I say. "About the Nightbringer—a jinn whose people were imprisoned by the Scholars. Who has lived for a thousand years fueled by the desire to wreak vengeance on them."

"And this is relevant because . . ."

"What if there is a war coming? Not the war with the Karkauns, but a bigger war." I can't explain the feeling I got when Cook spoke of it. A shiver on my skin. Her words had the weight of truth to them. I think back to what Quin said of the Nightbringer. *What does he want? Will she get it for him? What could she be doing for the Paters that they would agree to let that swine Grímarr wreak havoc in the poor parts of the city?*

"You heard the Nightbringer. The Commandant isn't an ally or a compatriot. She's his servant. If he wants a war with the Scholars, then she's the one who will help him carry it out. She's destroyed the Scholars within the Empire. Now she looks to those who have escaped."

"To Marinn." Harper shakes his head. "She'd need a fleet to take on the Mariners. Their navy is unparalleled."

"Exactly." I curse in pain as I pull on my armor, and Avitas is at my side in a second, buckling it with careful fingers. "Though I wonder—Keris wouldn't help the Nightbringer out of loyalty. You heard Quin. She's loyal only to herself. So what's he offering her in return?"

"The Empire," Harper says. "The throne. Though if that were the case, why did he save your life?"

I shake my head. I do not know. "I need to get to the beach," I say. "I'll explain later. Get me those reports on the Paters and their holdings. Tell the Plebeians about the infirmaries and the shelters. Open more—seek the help of our allies. Requisition houses if you must. Make sure the flag of the Shrike and the flag of the Emperor fly wherever the Plebeians are offered shelter. If I'm right, we're going to need Plebeian support soon."

I find a dark cloak, tuck my hair under a scarf, and slip out the door, every sense heightened. I feel the pull of the Plebeians who lie injured in the courtyard of the Black Guard barracks, but I force myself to ignore them. Tonight, I must work a different sort of magic.

Though I take the tunnels into the city, eventually I ascend into Navium's streets. The Commandant has patrols out everywhere, watching for Karkauns attempting to penetrate the city. Though the beach is only two miles from the Black Guard barracks, it takes me nearly three hours to get there—and even then, I double back twice to make sure I wasn't followed.

When I close in on the beach, I spy the guards immediately. Most lurk along the low, rugged cliffs that run down to the wide swath of sand. But many patrol the beach itself.

Ostensibly, the soldiers are here to ensure that Grímarr doesn't land his men on the beaches without anyone knowing. But if that were the only reason, there wouldn't be so many of them. No, there's another reason they're here. The Commandant is taking no chances. She must know that I recovered.

I slip from the shadow of a bungalow and scurry toward a shed barely taller than I am. Once ensconced, I check my kerchief, slather my mask with mud from a tin I've brought with me, and bolt for the corner of a tackle shop that lies even closer to the beach.

I edge nearer until finally, I am close enough to realize that there is no way to get down to that beach without someone noticing. Not without back-up, anyway. *Bleeding, burning skies.*

I wish suddenly for Elias. Impossible jobs with low likelihood of success are Elias's forte. Somehow, he always pulled them off, no matter the cost—and usually with a cheeky comment. It was both inspiring and irritating.

But Elias isn't here. And I can't risk getting caught. Frustrated, I back away—which is when a shadow appears beside me. My scim is half-drawn when a hand clamps over my mouth. I bite it and elbow my attacker, who hisses in pain but, like me, remains silent, lest the Commandant's men hear. *Cedar. Cinnamon.*

"Harper?" I hiss.

"Bleeding hells, Shrike," he gasps. "You've sharp elbows."

"You *idiot*." Skies, I wish I didn't have to whisper. I wish I could turn the full force of my rage against him. "What the hells are you doing here? I gave you orders—"

"I passed Dex your orders." Harper at least looks somewhat apologetic, but that does little to soften my anger. "This is a two-Mask job, Shrike. Shall we get to it before we're discovered?"

Curse him, he is aggravating. More so because he's right. Again. I elbow him a second time, knowing it's childish but delighting in his pained *oof*.

"Go distract those fools." I nod to the nearest cluster of guards. "And make it good. If you're here, you might as well not muck it up."

He disappears, and not an hour later, I am flitting away from the beach, having seen what I needed to see. Harper meets me at our prearranged spot, only slightly worse for wear after tricking the soldiers into thinking that a Karkaun raiding party had turned up nearby.

"Well?" he asks.

I shake my head. I don't know whether to be thrilled or horrified.

"Get me a horse," I say. "I've a cove I need to visit. And figure out a way to get in touch with Quin." I look back at the beach, still littered with the remnants of destroyed ships. "If this is as bad as I think it is, we're going to need all the help we can get."

«««

More than a week after I nearly died in Navium's streets and a month after I arrived in the city, Grímarr launches his final assault.

It comes at midnight. Karkaun sails bob perilously close to shore, and drums from the eastern watchtower convey the worst: Grímarr is preparing to launch small craft to ferry his ground forces to Navium. He is sick of waiting. Sick of having his supply lines cut off by Keris. Sick of being starved out. He wants the city.

Navium's catapults are a blur of fire and stone, a paltry defense against the hundreds of ships shooting flaming projectiles into the city. From the Island, the Commandant issues orders to the 2,500 men waiting in the ruins of the Southeast Quarter, where the Karkauns are expected to land. They are, Dex tells me, mostly auxes. Plebeians. Good men, many of whom will die if my plan doesn't work.

Dex finds me in the courtyard of the Black Guard barracks, where the Plebeians who have taken shelter grow increasingly agitated. Many have family members who will face off with Grímarr and his hordes today. All have been forced to flee their homes. With every minute that passes, the chances that they'll have anything to return to grow less likely.

"We're ready, Shrike," Dex says.

At my order, two dozen men—men who have done nothing but follow orders—will die. Runners, drum-tower guards, the drummers themselves. If we want to beat Grímarr, we must beat the Commandant—and that means cutting her lines of communication. We can take no chances. After the drums are silenced, we will have minutes—if that—to enact our plan. Everything must go right.

You want to destroy her? You have to become her first.

I give Dex the order and he disappears, a group of twenty men going with him. Moments later, Avitas arrives with a scroll. I hold it up—the mark of Keris Veturia, a *K*, is clearly visible to the Plebeians closest to me. The news spreads quickly. Keris Veturia, commander of the city, the woman who has allowed the Plebeian sectors of Navium to burn, has sent the Blood Shrike and the Black Guard a message.

I send a silent thank-you to Cook, wherever she is. She got me that seal, risking herself in the process, delivering it to me with a terse warning: *Whatever you have planned, it better be good. Because when she hits back, it will be hard, in the place you least expect it, in the place where it will hurt the most.*

I open the missive—which is empty—pretend to read it, and crush it, casting it into the closest fire, as if in a rage.

The Plebeians watch, resentment simmering. *Almost there. Almost.* They are dry tinder ready to burst into flames. I have spent a week preparing them, slipping them stories of the Commandant feasting with Navium's Paters while the Plebeians starve. From there, the rumors bloom: Keris Veturia wants the Karkaun ships to create a personal merchant fleet. The Paters will allow the merciless warlock Grímarr to ransack the Southeast Quarter if the Illustrian and Mercator districts are saved. Lies all, but each has enough truth to be plausible—and wrath-inducing.

"I will not accept this." I speak loudly enough for the room to hear. My rage is an act, but I quickly stoke it into reality. All I have to do is recall Keris's crimes: She gave up thousands of lives just to get her hands on those ships for the Nightbringer's war. She persuaded a passel of weak-minded Paters to put their greed ahead of their people. She is a traitor, and this is the first step to taking her down.

"Shrike." Avitas takes a step back, playing his part with impressive skill. "Orders are orders."

"Not this time," I say. "She cannot just sit there in that tower—a tower she *stole* from the finest admiral this city ever knew—and expect that we won't challenge her."

"We don't have the men—"

"If you go to challenge Keris Veturia"—a Black Guard ally planted amid the crowd and dressed in Plebeian clothing speaks up—"then I will go with you. I have grievances of my own."

"And I." Two more men stand, both allies of Gens Aquilla and Gens Atria. I look to the rest of the Plebeians. *Come on. Come on.*

"And I." The woman who speaks is not one of mine, and when she stands, her hands on a cudgel, she is not alone. A younger woman beside her, who looks to be a sister, stands with her. Then a man behind her.

"And I!" More chime in, urged on by those around them, until all are on their feet. It is a replica of the riot Mamie Rila planned—except this time, the rioters are at *my* back.

As I turn to leave, I note that Avitas has disappeared. He will bring the aux soldiers whom he turned to our cause, as well as Plebeians from the other shelters we've opened.

We spill into the streets, heading for the Island, and when Harper finds me with his people, I have a mob at my back. Avitas marches by my side, a torch in one hand, his scim in the other. For once, his face is angry instead of calm. Harper is Plebeian, but like all Masks, he keeps his emotions close. I never once thought to ask him how he felt about what was happening in the Plebeian quarters.

"Eyes ahead, Shrike." He glances at me, and I'm unnerved that he seems to know what I'm thinking. "Whatever you're feeling guilty about, you can deal with it later."

When we finally reach the bridge to the Island, the city guards, alerted to our approach, close ranks. As I march up to them, an aux bursts through the crowd, exactly on time.

"The Karkauns have attacked the drum towers," he says breathlessly to the captain of the city guard, a Plebeian himself. "They've killed the drummers and the guards. There's no way for the Commandant to communicate with the men."

"The city *will* fall if you do not move," I say to the guard captain. "Let me past and be remembered as a hero. Or continue to defend her and die a coward."

"No need for dramatics, Blood Shrike."

Across the bridge, the large wooden doors that lead to the Island tower are open. The Commandant emerges, backed by a dozen Paters. Her cold voice shakes, the slightest tremor of rage. Behind her, the Paters take in the scims and torches and angry faces arrayed before them. Silently, the guards stand aside, and we cross the bridge.

"Shrike," the Commandant says. "You do not understand the delicate workings of—"

"We're dying out here!" an angry voice calls out. "While you dine on roast fowl and fresh fruit in a tower that doesn't belong to you."

I hide a smirk. One of the Paters had a shipment of fruit delivered to the Island three days ago. I ensured that news of that delivery got back to the Plebeians.

"General Veturia!" A runner arrives from the Southeast Quarter, and this time it's not one of mine. "The Karkauns have made landfall. The warlock Grímarr leads the charge, and his men are pouring into the Quarter. There—there are reports of pyres being built. A group of Martials who were caught refused to swear fealty to Grímarr and were thrown on the pyre. Our troops need orders, sir."

Keris hesitates. It's just one moment. One instant of weakness. *You want to destroy her? You have to become her first.*

"I am taking control of this military operation." I shove past her, past the Paters, and motion Avitas and the aux soldiers who have moved to the front of the crowd to follow. "You have been relieved of duty, Keris Veturia. You are welcome to observe, as are the Paters." *Let this work. Please.*

I head up the winding stairs, Avitas and the auxes at my back. When we reach the Island's command level, Avitas lights a blue-fire torch and we keep moving, up to the roof. All our hopes lie in that torch. It seems so small now, insignificant in the great dark night.

He waves it thrice. We wait.

And wait.

Bleeding skies. We can't have gotten the timing right on every part of this plan only for it to go wrong now.

"Shrike!" Harper points to the western sea, where, from behind a craggy hook of land, a forest of masts emerges.

The Martial fleet.

Gasps echo from the Plebeians who I ensured followed us up to the top of the tower. To a man, the Paters appear either ill or terrified.

As for the Commandant—in the years I have known her, I've never seen her shocked or even mildly surprised. Now, her face and knuckles go so white she could be a corpse.

"The fleet didn't sink that night," I hiss at her. "It sailed away. And you had your jinn master stir up old shipwrecks to wash to shore so that our people would believe the Martial fleet had gone under and that I was to blame. I went to the beach, Keris, got past all your guard dogs. The masts, the sails, all the detritus that washed up—they were from ships that must have been under the sea for decades."

"Why would I hide the fleet? That's preposterous."

"Because you need those ships for the Nightbringer's war with Marinn and the Scholars," I snap at her. "So you thought you'd wait out the Karkauns. Let a few thousand Plebeians die. Let that bastard Grímarr attack on land. Decimate his forces. Steal his ships. Suddenly, you'd have a fleet twice the size of the Mariners'."

"Admiral Argus and Vice Admiral Vissellius will *never* follow your orders."

"So you admit that they're alive?" I almost laugh. "I'd wondered why their Gens mourned while their wives didn't appear upset at all."

Navium's drum towers suddenly begin thundering orders, my own drummers sending messages in place of those Dex and his men killed. A squad of runners appears from the base of the watchtower; they had only been awaiting my signal. I relay orders to the men in the Southwest Quarter, who by now must be facing pitched battles with the Karkaun invaders.

The Commandant, I notice, edges toward the stairs. Almost immediately, she is flanked by my men, who halt her retreat. I want her to watch. I want her to witness her plan unravel.

Avitas holds out one last torch, and I take it first to the southern part of the tower, near the sea, and then north, toward the war harbor.

The heavy clank of channel chains dropping is audible even from here. From the war harbor, the last of the fleet—those two dozen ships we didn't send out—emerges.

None of the hundreds of Plebeians watching from the bridge below could mistake the flags flying upon the masts: two crossed swords on a field of black. The original flag of Gens Veturia, before Keris added her foul *K* to it.

Nor could anyone mistake the identity of the proud, white-haired figure standing at the helm of the lead vessel.

"Admiral Argus and Vice Admiral Vissellius are dead," I say to Keris. "The fleet now answers to Admiral Quin Veturius. Veturia men—true Veturia men—man the fleet, along with volunteers from Gens Atria."

I know the moment that Keris Veturia understands what I've done. The moment when she realizes that her father, whom she had thought to be in hiding, has arrived. The moment that she realizes I have bested her. Sweat beads on her brow, and she clenches and unclenches her fists. The neck of her uniform is open, unbuttoned in agitation. I spot her tattoo: *ALW*—

When she catches me looking, her lips go thin and she yanks up the collar.

"It did not have to be this way, Blood Shrike." The Commandant's voice is soft, as it always is when she is at her most dangerous. "Remember that, before the end. If you'd just gotten out of the way, you could have saved so many. But now . . ." She shrugs. "Now I will have to resort to harsher measures."

A chill ripples across my shoulders, but I force myself to shake it off and turn to the Black Guards, all from allied Gens. "Get her to the interrogation cells." I do not watch them take her away. Instead, I turn to the Paters.

"What did she offer you?" I say. "A market for your goods? For your weapons, Pater Tatius? And your grain, Pater Modius? For your horses, Pater Equitius, and your lumber, Pater Lignius? War creates such opportunity for greedy, cowardly swindlers, does it not?"

"Shrike." Avitas translates a drum message. "Grímarr turns his forces back. He's seen the attack on the ships. He goes to defend his fleet."

"It won't do any good." I speak only to the Paters. "The southern seas will run red with the blood of the Karkauns tonight," I say. "And when the people of Navium tell this story, they will speak your names the same way they speak of the Karkauns: with disgust and scorn. Unless you swear your fealty to Emperor Marcus Farrar and your loyalty to me in his place. Unless you get your men and yourselves onto those ships"—I nod to the vessels emerging from the war harbor—"and fight the enemy yourselves."

It doesn't take long. Dex remains at the Island to oversee the battle and get the Plebeians back to safety. Avitas and I take the last ship out at my insistence. My blood rises, hungry for a fight, raring to have my revenge on those Barbarian bastards, to pay them back for weeks of bombardment. I will find Grímarr. I will make him hurt.

"Shrike." Avitas, who disappeared belowdecks, returns holding a gleaming war hammer.

"I found this at the Aquilla manor," he says, "when I was checking through the supplies. Look."

The black metal is emblazoned with four words I know well. *Loyal to the end.*

The hammer fits in my hand as if I was born for it, neither too heavy nor too light. One end has a sharp hook to use for quick kills, and the blunt end is perfect for bashing heads.

Before the end of the night, the hammer sees both. When the sky finally pales, only a dozen Barbarian ships remain, and they all make a swift retreat south, with Quin Veturius in hot pursuit. Though I hunted him, Grímarr the warlock priest eluded me. I caught a single glimpse of him, tall and pale and deadly. He still lives—but not for long, I think.

The shouts of the men of our fleet fill me with fierce joy. We won. *We won*. The Karkauns are gone. Quin will destroy those who remain. The Plebeians backed me. And the Commandant is imprisoned. The full extent of her treachery will soon be revealed.

I arrive back at the Black Guard barracks, armor bloodied, war hammer slung across my back. The Plebeians within give way, a cheer rising at the sight of me, Harper, and my men.

"Blood SHRIKE. Blood SHRIKE."

The chants propel me up the stairs to my quarters, where a missive waits, sealed with Emperor Marcus's sigil. I already know what it is: a pardon for Quin Veturius, reinstatement as Pater of his Gens, and a new posting for him—as Navium's fleet admiral. I requested it days ago, via secret drum message. Marcus, after much convincing from Livia, granted it.

"Blood SHRIKE. Blood SHRIKE."

Someone knocks on my door, and Avitas opens it to an ashen-faced Dex. My body turns to lead at his expression.

"Shrike." His voice is choked. "A drum message just came in from Antium. You're to leave all unfinished matters and return immediately to the capital. The Empress—your sister—has been poisoned."

XXIX: Laia

The past shall burn, and none will slow it.

The Nightbringer told me what was coming. He might as well have screamed his plans into my face. And I was too much of a fool to see it.

"No—Laia—stop!" I barely hear the voice over the roar of flames in the refugee camp. I push through the crowds of gobsmacked Mariners and Scholars, up toward the city. I could still make it to the library. I could still find the book on the Augurs. Only the upper levels of the library burn. Perhaps the lower levels have survived—

"What the *hells* are you doing?" Musa spins me around, face streaked with ashes and tears. "The Mariners have left the refugee camp. They're heading to the library to try to save it. The Scholars need help, Laia!"

"Get Darin!" I shout. "And Zella and Taure. I *must* get to the library, Musa."

"*Aapan*, there are still Scholars who—"

"When will you understand? The Resistance doesn't matter. The *only* thing that matters is stopping him. Because if we don't, he sets the jinn free, and everyone dies—including all those we've saved."

His answer is lost in the panic all around us. I turn and run, throwing on my invisibility and cutting through the Mariners pushing past the front gate. Hundreds of Adisa's residents pour into the streets, many watching the library burn, stunned, others hoping to help. Fire brigade wagons scream through the streets, and soldiers unroll great snakelike hoses to pump water in from the sea.

I fly past all of them, thanking the skies for my invisibility. By the time I reach the Great Library itself, blue-robed librarians stream from the front entrances, carrying books and scrolls and artifacts, pushing carts filled with priceless tomes. Many try to return, but the blaze spreads, and their country-men hold them back.

But there is no one to stop me, and I squeeze past the bottleneck of Mariners who are escaping through the front doors. The lower levels of the library are a sort of controlled chaos. A Mariner man stands atop a desk, bellowing orders at a small army of men and women. They obey as quickly and efficiently as if he were a Mask threatening whippings.

I gaze up. Even the first level of this place is absolutely massive, a laby-rinth with a dozen hallways branching every which way. What are the chances that a book on Augur prophecies would be on this floor?

Think, Laia! The Mariners have been entrusted with the world's know-ledge for centuries because they're careful and organized. Which means there must be a map around here somewhere. I find it carved into a plaque on the wall beside the head librarian. The library has more than twenty levels and so many types of books that my head spins. But just when I begin to despair, I spot *Martial History—level 3.*

The stairs are emptier than the lower level—the librarians are not stupid enough to go to the upper floors. As I pass the second level, smoke fills the stairwell and flames crackle distantly. But the path is clear, and it isn't until I get to the third floor that I understand the extent of the fire.

This level is half-engulfed. But though the smoke is thick and the fire hungry, the shelves to my right are untouched. I pull my shirt over my face, my eyes already streaming, and hurry toward them, grabbing a book off the nearest shelf. *Ankanese Seers and the Lie of Foresight.* I move to the next shelf, which has a thousand books about the Southern Lands, and then to the next, which is all about the Tribes. *Scholar History. Scholar Conquest. Lacertian Martials.*

I'm getting closer. But so is the fire. When I glance over my shoulder, I can no longer see the stairwell. The flames move faster than they should, and faces twist within them. *Wind efrits!* They use their power to fan the flames hotter, faster—to spread them. I crouch low. Invisible though I might be, I do not know if they can see through my magic, like ghuls can. If they spot me, I am done for.

The dull gilt of another book catches my eye because of its title: *Always Victorious: The Life and Conquests of General Quin Veturius.*

Elias's grandfather. I glance up and can just make out the plaque: *Martial History*. I scan the titles quickly. Everything on this shelf appears to be about generals and emperors, and I snarl in frustration. Would that Musa and I had gotten back to the city faster! Even one hour would have made all the difference. Even ten minutes.

I'm close. So close.

"You there!"

A red-gowned woman appears behind me, deep scarlet tattoos winding up her arms. The silver and gold coins woven into her brown hair and strung across her forehead glow orange. My invisibility obviously doesn't work on her, because her pale, kohl-rimmed eyes fix on me. A Jaduna.

"You are Laia of Serra." Her eyes widen in surprise when she gets a closer look at me, and I take a step back. She must have seen my face on the proclamations that Princess Nikla plastered all over Adisa.

"Leave here, girl. Quickly—the stairs are still clear."

"I have to find a book on the Augurs, on their prophecies—"

"You won't be alive to read it if you stay." She grabs my arm, and her touch immediately cools my skin. *Magic!* I notice then that the air around her is chilly and clear of smoke. The fire doesn't trouble her, despite the fact that I can barely breathe.

"Please." I gasp for air and sink lower as the smoke thickens. "Help me. I *need* those prophecies. The Nightbringer—"

The Jaduna does not appear to be listening. She yanks me forcibly toward the stairs, but I dig my heels in.

"Stop!" I try to wrench my arm away. "The Nightbringer wants to set the jinn free."

I babble, desperate for her aid. But she pulls me on, employing her magic, dragging me to safety with inexorable force.

"We Jaduna have no quarrel with the jinn," she says. "Or the *Meherya*. His plans do not concern us."

"Everyone believes that nothing concerns them until the monsters are knocking on their doors!" She winces at my shriek, but I do not care. "Until they are burning down *your* homes and destroying *your* lives and killing *your* families!"

"My responsibility is the Great Library, and that means getting you—and anyone else who is in danger—out."

"Who the skies do you think is to blame for burning this place down? Isn't *that* your responsibility?" As I say it, the smoke parts and something white barrels toward us with a precision that suggests a malicious consciousness. *Efrit!*

"Watch out!" I tackle the Jaduna onto her back, cringing as the wind efrit passes so close that the skin on my neck stings. The Jaduna rolls out from under me, tracking the efrit with cold fury. She crooks her fingers, rises and streaks toward the creature like a comet, her gown turning ice-white as she cuts through the flames and disappears. Immediately, I turn back to the shelf, but I cannot see it through the smoke. Gagging, I drop all the way to my hands and knees and crawl forward.

Laia. Is the whisper in my head? Or is it real? Someone in a dark robe kneels before me, peering down with bright eyes. It's not really the Nightbringer. If it were, I wouldn't be able to hold my invisibility. It's a projection of some sort, or ghuls playing tricks on me. But that does not lessen my disgust—or my fear.

You'll die here, choking on smoke, the Nightbringer says. *Dead like your family. Dead for no reason at all, beyond your own foolishness. I did warn you . . .*

"Laia!"

The image of the Nightbringer dissipates. The voice calling me is familiar—and real. Darin. What the *hells* is he doing here? Immediately, I spin about, scrabbling toward his voice as he calls my name again. I find him at the top of the stairs, half of which are now engulfed in flame. *Bleeding fool!*

I dare not drop my invisibility for fear of blacking out again, but when I am close, I call out and grab his arm.

"I'm here! Go, Darin, go back! I have to find something!"

But my brother latches on to me and drags me down the stairs. "We *both* have to go!" he shouts. "The second level is gone!"

"I have to—"

"You have to *live* if you want to stop him!" Darin's eyes blaze. He uses all his force, and the third level is now a wall of fire behind me.

We barrel down the stairs, weaving through blazing hunks of fallen masonry and an inferno of burning embers. I flinch as they land on my brother's bare arms, but he ignores them, pulling me down, down, down. A huge beam groans, and Darin only just lunges out of the way as it lands on the stairs with a thunderous crash. We are forced to go back up a few steps, and I inhale a lungful of smoke. My chest burns with pain, and I double over, unable to stop coughing.

"Put your arm around me, Laia," Darin shouts. "I can't see you!"

Skies, I cannot breathe—I cannot think. *Do not drop the invisibility. Darin might not be able to carry you out of here. Do. Not. Drop. It.*

We reach the second level, and the stairs are engulfed. Oh bleeding hells. I am a fool. I should never have come here. If I hadn't, Darin would never have followed. Now we will both die. Mother would be so ashamed of me, so angry at my recklessness. *I'm sorry, Mother. I'm sorry, Father. Oh skies, I'm so sorry.* This is how Elias died. At least I'll see him again in the Waiting Place. At least I will be able to bid him farewell.

Darin sees something I do not: a way through. He drags me forward, and I scream. The heat on my legs is too much.

And then we are past the worst of the flames. My brother carries me now, lifting me from my waist as my feet scrape against the ground. We burst through the burning front doors and into the night. Everything is a blur. I catch an impression of scaffolds and buckets and pumps and people, so many people.

Blackness engulfs me, and when I open my eyes again, I am propped up against the wall of a side street with Darin crouched in front of me, covered in ash and burns and sobbing in relief.

"You are so *stupid*, Laia!" He shoves me. I must be visible again, for he hugs me, shoves me again, and hugs me a second time. "You're the only one I have. The only one left! Did you even *consider* that before running into a burning building?"

"I'm sorry." My voice is hoarse, barely audible. "I thought . . . I hoped . . ." Skies, the book. I did not find the book. As the full impact of my failure washes over me, I feel sick. "The—the library?"

"It is gone, girl." Darin and I both turn as a figure materializes out of the darkness. The Jaduna's beautiful red dress is scorched now, but she still exudes a physical chilliness, winter encased in skin. Her kohl-rimmed eyes fix on me. "The efrits have done their work well."

Darin stands slowly, reaching for his scim. I drag myself to my feet beside him, leaning against the wall as dizziness makes the world tilt. The Jaduna will no doubt arrest us now. And there's no way we can outrun her. Which means somehow, I have to find the strength to fight her.

The Jaduna does not approach. She merely observes me for a moment.

"You saved my life," she says. "The efrit would have killed me. I owe you a debt."

"Please do not arrest us," I say. "Leave us be—that will be repayment enough."

I expect a retort, but she only watches me with that inscrutable gaze. "You are young to stand so deeply in the shadow." She sniffs at me. "You are like him—your friend. The one they call Musa. I have seen him in the city, whispering his stories, using the sway in his voice to create a legend. Both of you—tainted by darkness. You must come to my home, to Kotama, in the east. My people can help you."

I shake my head. "I cannot go east. Not when the Nightbringer is still a threat."

The woman shakes her head, bemused. "The *Meherya?*"

"You said that before," I say. "I do not know what it means."

"It is his name, Laia of Serra. His first, truest name. It defines all he has done and all he will do. His strength is in his name, and his weakness. But"—she shrugs—"that is old magic. The Nightbringer's vengeance has long been foretold. You would be wise to leave here, Laia of Serra, and go to Kotama—"

"I do not care about Kotama." I lose my temper, forgetting that I am speaking to a woman who can probably kill in a dozen ways with a twist of her hand. "I have to stop him."

"Why?" She shakes her head. "If you stop him, do you not know what will happen? The consequence, the devastation—"

"I do not know how I will stop him now, in any case."

The wind rises, and screams echo from the street beyond—the fire is in danger of spreading to the city. The Jaduna frowns and looks over her shoulder before snapping her fingers. Something small and rectangular appears in her hands. "Perhaps this will help."

She tosses it to me. It is a thick, heavy book with silver letters embossed on the side. *A History of Seers and Prophets in the Martial Empire* by Fifius Antonius Tullius.

"That," the Jaduna says, "is sufficient repayment of a debt. Remember my offer. If you come to Kotama, ask for D'arju. She is the finest teacher in the Bay of Tears. She will help you control the darkness, lest it grow beyond your ken."

The Jaduna disappears. I open the book to find a gilded image of a man in a dark robe. His face is hidden, but his hands are bleached of color and his red eyes look out from his shadowed cowl. An Augur.

Darin and I exchange a glance and then hurry away from the place before the Jaduna changes her mind.

«««

Two hours later, my brother and I tear through Adisa's streets. I hope to the skies Musa is back at the forge, because I have no time to hunt him down in the refugee camp. Not now. Not after what I've just read.

To my relief, the forge is lit when I go tearing in, and Musa sits in the main room, Zella tending to a burn on his arm. He opens his mouth, but I do not let him speak.

"The Shrike survived an assassination attempt," I say. "Do you know how? When it happened? What the circumstances were?"

"Sit down, at least—"

"I need to know *now*, Musa!"

He grumbles and disappears into his room. I hear him rifling around and then returning with a stack of scrolls. I grab for one, but he smacks my hand. "These ones are in code." Long minutes pass as he reads one after another. "Ah—here. She was stabbed by one of Keris's minions," he says. "One of her men transported her to the barracks. The Nightbringer was seen leaving her quarters, and two nights later she was back to issuing orders."

I flip the book about the Augurs open to a page I've marked. "Read," I say.

"*The blood of the father and the blood of the son are harbingers of darkness,*" Musa reads. "*The King shall light the Butcher's path, and when the Butcher bows to the deepest love of all, night approaches. Only the Ghost may stand against the onslaught. Should the Lioness's heir claim the Butcher's pride, it will evanesce, and the blood of seven generations shall pass from the earth before the King may seek vengeance again.* Curse the Augurs, this makes *no* sense."

"It does," I say, "if you know that the shrike is a type of bird known for impaling its prey on thorns before it consumes it. I read it in a book once. People call it the 'butcher bird.' That's where the name *Blood Shrike* comes from."

"This prophecy can't be talking about her," Musa says. "What about the other prophecy? *The Butcher will break, and none will hold her.*"

"Maybe that part hasn't happened yet," Darin offers. "We're looking for a piece of the Star, right? Do those reports say anything about the Blood Shrike wearing jewelry? Or is there a weapon she always has near her?"

"She has—" Musa rifles through the scrolls again before cocking his head and listening. One of his wights chitters swiftly. "A ring? Yes—she has the ring of the Blood Shrike, received in the fall of last year, when she assumed the office. And she has the ring of Gens Aquilla."

"When," I ask, "did she get that ring?"

"I don't bleeding—" He cocks his head again. "Her father gave it to her," Musa says. "Before he died. The day he died."

The blood of the father. It must have gotten on the ring when he died. And of course it would be her pride because it's a symbol of her family.

"And the Nightbringer?" I say. "He's been in Navium all this time?"

I know the answer before Musa nods. "Do you see now, Musa?" I twist the armlet Elias gave me around my arm. "The Nightbringer stayed in Navium because his target was there the whole time. He never had to leave. She has it—the Blood Shrike has the last piece of the Star."

XXX: Elias

B anu al-Mauth.

As I wander the city of the jinn, a voice calls out, penetrating distantly, a hair-thin fishing line cast into an endless ocean. But I know who it is. Aubarit Ara-Nasur. The *Fakira*. I told her that if she needed me, she should come to the edge of the Forest and call me.

But I can't go to her. Not with all that I now know. For I understand, finally, why Mauth forbids his Soul Catchers their humanity. Humanity means emotions. Emotions mean instability. Mauth's entire purpose is to bridge the world of the living and the dead. Instability threatens that.

The knowledge brings me a strange sort of peace. I don't know how I will release my humanity. I don't know if I can. But at least I know why I should.

Mauth stirs. The magic rises up from the earth in a dark mist, fusing into a tenuous vine. I reach for it. The magic is limited, as if Mauth doesn't trust me enough to give me more.

I leave the city of jinn and am immediately confronted by a cloud of ghosts so thick I can barely see through them.

Banu al-Mauth. *Help us.*

The plea in Aubarit's voice is audible, even from here. She sounds terrified. *Sorry, Aubarit. I'm sorry. But I can't.*

"Little one." I startle at the ghost who has materialized before me. The Wisp. She circles in great agitation.

"You must come," she whispers. "Your people fade. Your family. They need you the way my lovey needed me. Go to them. Go."

"My . . . family?" My mind goes to the Commandant, the Martials.

"Your true family. The desert singers," the Wisp says. "Their pain is great. They suffer."

I can't go to them, not now. I *must* pass the ghosts through or they'll keep building up, the jinn will keep stealing magic, and I'll be stuck dealing with an even bigger problem than I already have.

Banu al-Mauth. *Help us. Please.*

But if the Tribes are in danger, I must at least try to see why. Perhaps some small act of mine can help them and I can still return to the Forest quickly and continue with my task.

I try not to pay attention to the way the earth cracks behind me, the way the ghosts scream and the trees moan. When I reach the southern border, I bolster the wall with my physical magic to make sure no ghosts follow me and make for the distant glimmer of Tribal wagons.

Once I'm out of the Waiting Place, I hear a familiar tattoo: Martial drums. The closest garrison is miles away, but the echo is ominous, even from here. Though the drumbeats are too far away for me to translate, a lifetime of Martial training tells me that whatever is happening, it's not good. And that it concerns the Tribes.

When I reach the camp, it has exploded in size. Where before there were only Tribe Nasur and Tribe Saif, there are now more than a thousand wagons. It looks like a *majilees*, a meeting of the Tribes, called only in the most dire of circumstances.

Which puts thousands upon thousands of Tribespeople in one place. If I were a Martial general attempting to put down any hint of insurgency and take slaves, this would be the perfect place to do it.

Children scatter at my approach, hiding under carts. The stench is awful—sickly sweet—and I spot the carcasses of two horses left to rot in the sun, a cloud of flies buzzing above them.

Did the Martials already attack? But no, if they'd been through here, they would have taken the children as slaves.

To the north, I spot a circle of heart-stoppingly familiar wagons. Tribe Saif. My family.

I approach the wagons slowly, wary of what I'll find. When I'm only a few yards away, a bizarre specter materializes in front of me. It's not human—I know that right away. But it's not transparent enough to be a ghost. It appears to be something in between. At first, I don't recognize it. Then, its warped features become terrifyingly familiar. It is Uncle Akbi, the head of Tribe Saif and Mamie Rila's older brother. Uncle put me on my first pony at the age of three. The first time I returned to Tribe Saif as a Fiver, he sobbed and held me like I was his own true son.

The specter shambles toward me, and I bring up my blade. It's not a spirit. What the hells is it?

Elias Veturius, the strange half ghost of my uncle hisses in Sadhese. *She never wanted you. What would she want with a squalling, pale-eyed thing? She only took you because she feared the evil eye upon her. And what have you brought but evil and suffering, death and ruin—*

I recoil. When I was a child, I feared that Uncle Akbi thought such things. But he never said them.

Come—come and see what your failure has wrought. The specter drifts to the Saif camp, where six Tribespeople lie on cots in a row. They all appear to be dead.

Including Uncle Akbi.

"No—oh no—" I rush to him. Where in ten hells is the rest of Tribe Saif? Where is Mamie? How did this happen?

"*Banu al-Mauth!*" Aubarit appears behind me, bursting into tears at the sight of me. "I have been to the Forest a dozen times. You must help us," she wails. "The Tribes have fallen to madness. There are too many—"

"What the bleeding hells happened?"

"A fortnight ago, just after you left, another Tribe arrived. They kept coming, one after another. Some had lost their *Fakirs*, and all were struggling to move on their dead—the same struggle I had with my grandfather. And then, two days ago—"

She shakes her head. *Right when I disappeared into the Forest.* "The ghosts of the dead stopped moving on altogether. Their bodies will not die, and their *ruh*—their spirits—will not leave them. Even those with grievous injuries linger on. They—they are monstrous." The *Fakira* shudders. "They torment their families. They are driving their own kin to suicide. Your—your uncle was one of those. But you can see what has happened. Those who try to kill themselves *also* do not die."

A thin figure materializes from one of the wagons and throws herself in my arms. I wouldn't have recognized her had I not heard her voice, tired but still rich, still filled with story.

"Mamie?" She has wasted away to nothing. I want to curse and rage at the frailty of her once strong arms, the gauntness of her once beautifully rounded face. She looks as stunned to see me as I am to see her.

"Aubarit Ara-Nasur told me you dwell in the Forest, among the spirits," she says. "But I—I did not believe it."

"Mamie." Tradition demands that I mourn Uncle Akbi with her. That I share her pain. But there's no time for such things. I take her hands in mine.

They are colder than I've ever felt them. "You have to disperse the Tribes. It's dangerous having them all here in one place. Do you hear the drums?" From the mystified look on her face, I realize that she—and likely most of the rest of the camp—has not noticed the frenzy of Martial activity.

Which means the Empire is planning something even now. And the Tribes have no idea.

"Aubarit," I say. "I need to find Afya—"

"I'm here, *Banu al-Mauth*." Afya's formality stings. The Tribeswoman shuffles toward me, shoulders slumped. I want to ask her how Gibran is, but part of me is afraid to find out. "News of your arrival spread quickly."

"Get scouts out to all points other than the Forest," I say. "I think the Martials are coming. And I think they're going to hit hard. You need to be ready."

Afya shakes her head, and her old, defiant self appears. "How can we be ready when our dead won't die and we are haunted by their spirits?"

"We'll worry about that when we know what we're up against," I say quickly, though I have no idea what the answer is. "Perhaps I am wrong and the Martials are just carrying out drills."

But I'm not wrong, and Afya knows it. She moves off quickly, and her Tribesmen surround her as she begins giving orders. Gibran isn't among them.

I consider the Tribes—there are so many. And yet . . . "Aubarit, Mamie," I say. "Can you get at least some of the Tribes to head south—to scatter?"

"They will not go, Elias. Your uncle called a *majilees*. But before we could have it, three of the other Tribes' chieftains were driven mad by the spirits. Two threw themselves into the sea, and your uncle . . ." Tears fill Mamie's eyes. "Everyone is too afraid to leave. They believe there is strength in numbers."

"You must do something, *Banu al-Mauth*," Aubarit whispers. "The *ruh* of our own people are destroying us. If the Martials come, all they will have to do is round us up. We are already defeated."

I squeeze her hand. "Not yet, Aubarit. Not yet."

This is the work of the bleeding Nightbringer. He is sowing even more chaos by destroying the Tribes. Destroying my friends. Destroying Tribe Saif, my family. I know it, as surely as I know my name. I turn to the Forest, reaching out to Mauth.

Then I stop. Reaching for the magic to save the lives of people I love is exactly what Mauth *doesn't* wish me to do. *For us, Elias, duty must reign over all else. Love cannot live here.* I must curtail my emotions. My time in the jinn city taught me that. But I don't know how.

I do, however, know what it is to be a Mask. Cold. Murderous. Emotionless.

Aubarit speaks up. "*Banu*—"

"Silence." The voice is mine, but sharp and cold. I recognize it. The Mask within, the Mask I thought I'd never have to be again.

"Elias!" Mamie is affronted by my rudeness. She taught me better. But I turn my face to her—the face of Keris Veturia's son—and she takes a step back before drawing herself up. Despite all that's happening, she's still a *Kehanni*, and she will brook no disrespect, least of all from her children.

But Aubarit, perhaps sensing the storm of thoughts in my head, puts a gentle hand on Mamie's wrist, quieting her.

Duty first, unto death—Blackcliff's motto, which returns now to haunt me. *Duty first.*

I turn my mind to Mauth again, but this time, I consider. I need to stop the ghosts so that the Tribes can move them on. So that I can return to the Forest to do my duty.

I want so badly for the magic to respond. For it to communicate with me. To guide me. To tell me what I should do.

A child howls from nearby, a heartbreaking sound. I should go to him. I should see what's wrong. Instead, I ignore it. I pretend I am Shaeva, cold and unfeeling, attending my duty because that is my only concern. I pretend I am a Mask.

Far in the Forest, I feel the magic rise.

Love cannot live here. I repeat the words in my head. As I do, the magic twines out of the Forest, inching toward the Mask in me while still wary of the man. I harness that old patience the Commandant drilled into us at Blackcliff. I watch, I wait, calm as an assassin stalking a mark.

When the magic finally seeps into me, I grab on to it. Aubarit's eyes widen, for she must sense the sudden influx of power.

The paradox of the magic tears at me. I need it to save the people I care about, but I can't care about them if I want to use the magic.

Love cannot live here.

Immediately, the magic fills my sight, and that which was hidden becomes apparent. Dark shadows cluster everywhere like malignant tumors in a tortured body. Ghuls. I kick out at those close by, and they scatter but come back almost immediately. They congregate near the tents where Aubarit and the other *Fakirs* have put those who are afflicted.

Relief sweeps through me, for the solution to this is so simple that I am angry I didn't see the ghuls before.

"You need salt," I say to Aubarit and Mamie. "Those afflicted by this malady are surrounded by ghuls, who hold on to their spirits. Put salt around those who *should* be dead. The ghuls hate it. If you disperse those foul creatures, the afflicted will pass, and you should be able to commune with the spirits again."

Aubarit and Mamie disappear almost immediately to find salt and to tell the other Tribes of the antidote. As they sprinkle the salt around the afflicted, the hisses and snarls of thwarted ghuls fill the air, though I'm the only one who can hear them. I walk with the *Fakira* through the camp, the magic still with me, ensuring that the ghuls are not simply waiting for me to leave before slinking back.

I prepare to return to the Waiting Place when a distant shout stops me in my tracks. Afya pulls her horse up beside me.

"The Martials have mustered a legion," she says. "Nearly five thousand men. They're moving against us. And they're coming swiftly."

Bleeding hells. The moment I think it—the moment my worry for the Tribes rises—Mauth's magic leaves me. I feel empty without him. Weak.

"When will the Martials get here, Afya?" *Tell me they're a few days away.* Perhaps if I wish for it, it will be true. *Tell me they're still outfitting their troops, preparing weapons, readying for the assault.*

Afya's voice shakes when she answers.

"By dawn."

PART III

ANTIUM

XXXI: The Blood Shrike

Avitas Harper and I do not stop to eat. We do not stop to sleep. We drink from our canteens as we ride, halting only to change horses at a courier's station.

I can heal my sister. I can. If only I can get to her.

Three days into the journey, we reach Serra, and it is there that I finally stop, dragged bodily off my horse by Avitas, unable to fight back because of fatigue and hunger.

"Get off me!"

"You will eat." Harper is equally enraged, his pale green eyes bright as he pulls me toward the door of the Black Guard barracks. "You will rest. Or your sister has *no* hope, and neither does the Empire."

"A meal," I say. "And two hours of sleep."

"Two meals," he says. "And four hours of sleep. Take it or leave it."

"You don't have any siblings," I snarl. "Not any who know who you are, anyway. Even if you did, you didn't watch as your family—you weren't the *reason* they—"

My eyes burn. *Don't comfort me*, I scream in my head at Harper. *Don't you dare.*

Harper watches me for a moment before turning away, snapping at the guard on duty to get food and quarters ready. When he turns back, I am composed.

"Do you wish to sleep here in the barracks," Harper says, "or in your old home?"

"My sister is my home," I say. "Until I reach her, it doesn't matter where I bleeding sleep."

At some point, I fall asleep half-slumped in a chair. When I wake in the middle of the night, plagued by nightmares, I am in my quarters, a blanket tucked around me.

"Harper—" He rises out of the shadows, hesitating at the foot of my cot before kneeling beside my head. His hair is mussed, his silver face unguarded. He puts a warm hand on my shoulder and nudges me back to the pillow. For once, his eyes are transparent, filled with concern and exhaustion and something else I don't quite recognize. I expect him to lift his hand away, but he doesn't.

"Sleep now, Shrike. Just a little longer."

«««

Ten days after leaving Serra, we arrive in Antium, coated in sweat and grime from the road, our horses panting and lathered.

"She's still alive." Faris meets Avitas and me at Antium's massive iron portcullis, warned, no doubt, of our approach by the city guardsmen.

"You were supposed to protect her." I grab him by the throat, my anger lending me strength. The guards at the gate back away, and a group of Scholar slaves mortaring a nearby wall scatter. "You were supposed to keep her safe."

"Punish me, if you wish," Faris chokes out. "I deserve it. But go to her first."

I shove him away from me. "How did it happen?"

"Poison," he said. "Slow-acting. Skies only know where that monster got it from." *Keris*. This was her handiwork. It had to have been. Thank the bleeding skies she is still imprisoned in Navium.

"We usually wait six hours between when Livia's tasters test her food and when she eats it," Faris goes on. "Either Rallius or I have overseen the testers ourselves. But this time, it took more than seven hours for her tasters to drop dead. She'd only had the food in her for an hour, and we were able to purge her enough so that she didn't die immediately, but . . ."

"The child?"

"Alive, according to the midwife."

The palace is calm. Faris has, at least, kept news of the Empress's poisoning close. I expect Marcus to be nearby, but he is at court, listening to petitioners, and isn't expected back in the royal quarters for hours. A small mercy, but a welcome one.

Faris pauses outside Livia's door. "She's not what you remember, Shrike."

When I enter my sister's room, I hardly notice her ladies-in-waiting, who wear expressions of genuine mourning. It makes me hate them a little less for being so very alive while my sister hovers near death.

"Out," I tell them. "Everyone. Now. And don't bleeding say a word about this to anyone."

They file out quickly but reluctantly, looking back at my sister with sad longing. Livia always could make friends quickly—she treats everyone with such respect.

When the women have finally left, I turn to Harper. "Guard the door with your life," I say. "No one comes in. I don't care if it's the Emperor himself. Find a way to keep him out."

Avitas salutes, and the door is securely locked behind me.

Livia's room is laden with shadows, and she lies as still as death in the bed, her face bloodless. I see no wound, but I can feel the poison twisting through her body, a merciless foe eating away at her insides. Her breathing is shallow, her color poor. That she's survived this long in such a weakened state is a bleeding miracle.

"Not a miracle, Blood Shrike." A shadow steps from beside her bed, ink-cloaked and sun-eyed.

"What are you doing here?" The skies-forsaken jinn had to have known what the Commandant was doing. He might even have procured the poison for her.

"You wear your thoughts openly, like you wear your blades," the Night-bringer says. "The Commandant is not so transparent. I did not know of her plan. But I was able to hold your sister in stasis until you arrived. It is up to you now to heal her."

"Tell me why you're helping me," I demand, enraged that I have to speak to him, that I cannot immediately begin to help Livvy. "No lies. Tell me the truth. You're Keris's ally. You have been for years. This was her doing. What game are you playing?"

For a long moment, I think that he will deny being a double agent. Or that he will grow angry and lash me to bits.

When he does finally speak, it's with great care. "You have something I want, Shrike. Something whose value you do not yet realize. But in order for me to use it, it must be given in love. In trust."

"You're trying to win my love and trust? I will never grant it."

"Your love, no," he says. "I would not expect it, in any case. But your trust, yes. I want your trust. And you will give it to me. You must. One day soon, you will be tested, child. All that you cherish will burn. You will have no friends that day. No allies. No comrades in arms. On that day, your trust in me will be your only weapon. But I cannot make you trust me." He steps back to allow me access to Livia.

With one eye on the jinn, I examine her more closely. I listen to her heart. I *feel* her heart, her body, her blood with my mind. The Nightbringer did not lie about her. This poison is not one a human could survive without help.

"You waste precious time, Blood Shrike," the Nightbringer says. "Sing. I will hold her until she is ready to hold herself."

If he'd wanted to hurt me, truly hurt me, he'd have let her die. He'd have already killed me.

Livia's song flows from my lips easily. I have known her since she was a baby. I held her, cuddled her, loved her. I sing of her strength. I sing of the sweetness and humor that I know still live within her, despite the horrors she has endured. I feel her body strengthening, her blood regenerating.

But as I knit her back together, something is not right. I move down from her heart to her belly. My consciousness flinches back.

The baby.

He—and my sister is right, it is a he—sleeps now. But there is something wrong with him. His heartbeat, which instinct tells me should sound like the gentle, swift thud of a bird's wings, is too slow. His still-developing mind too sluggish. He slips away from us.

Skies, what is the child's song? I do not know him. I know nothing about him except that he is part Marcus and part Livia and that he is our only chance for a unified Empire.

"What do you want him to be?" the Nightbringer asks. At his voice, I jump, so deep in healing that I forgot he was here. "A warrior? A leader? A diplomat? His *ruh*, his spirit, is within, but it is not yet formed. If you wish him to live, then you must shape him from what is there—his blood, his family. But know that in doing so, you will be bound to him and his purpose forever. You will never be able to extricate yourself."

"He is family," I whisper. "My nephew. I wouldn't *want* to extricate myself from him."

I hum, searching for his song. Do I want him to be like me? Like Elias? Certainly not like Marcus.

I want him to be an Aquilla. And I want him to be a Martial. So I sing my sister Livia into him—her kindness and laughter. I sing him my father's conviction and prudence. My mother's thoughtfulness and intelligence. I sing him Hannah's fire.

Of his father, I sing only one thing: his strength and skill in battle—one quick word, sharp and strong and clear—Marcus if the world had not ruined him. If he had not allowed himself to be ruined.

But there is something missing. I feel it. This child will one day be Emperor. He needs something deeply rooted, something that will sustain him when nothing else will: a love of his people.

The thought appears in my head as if it's been planted there. So I sing him my own love, the love I learned in the streets of Navium, in fighting for my people, in them fighting for me. The love I learned in the infirmary, healing children and telling them not to fear.

His heart begins to beat in time again; his body strengthens. I feel him give my sister an almighty kick, and, relieved, I withdraw.

"Well done, Shrike." The Nightbringer stands. "She will sleep now, and so must you, if you do not wish for the healing to ravage your strength. Stay away from any injured people, if you can. Your power will call to you. It will demand to be heard, used, reveled in. You must resist, lest you destroy yourself."

With that, he fades away, and I look back at Livvy, sleeping peacefully, the color returned to her face. Tentatively, I reach out a hand toward her belly, drawn to the life within. I keep my hand there for a long while, my eyes filling when I feel another kick.

I am about to speak to the child when the curtains beside the bed rustle. Immediately, I scramble for the war hammer strapped across my back. The sound comes from the hallway between Marcus's room and Livvy's. My stomach sinks. I didn't even think to check that entrance. *Shrike, you fool!*

A moment later, Emperor Marcus steps out from behind the drapes there, smiling.

Maybe he didn't see me healing Livia. Maybe he doesn't know. It's been a few minutes. He couldn't have been watching that whole time. The Nightbringer would have seen him, sensed him.

But then I remember that Marcus learned to keep the Augurs out of his head *from* the Nightbringer. Perhaps he learned to keep the jinn out too.

"You've been keeping secrets, Shrike," Marcus says, his words dashing any hopes I had of keeping my magic to myself. "You know I don't like secrets."

XXXII: *Laia*

I t *had* to be the Blood Shrike. It couldn't be some soft-handed courtier or empty-headed stable boy—someone I could snitch the ring off of.

"How the skies am I supposed to get it from her?" I pace in the courtyard of the smithy. The night is deep, and Taure and Zella have returned to the refugee camp to help, as the Mariners have all but abandoned the Scholars to the elements.

"Even invisible," I say, "it will be on her finger. She is a *Mask*, for skies' sake. And if the Nightbringer is near her, I don't know if my invisibility will work. It will take me two months just to get to Navium. But the Grain Moon is less than seven weeks away."

"She's not in Navium," Musa says. "She's headed for Antium. We can send someone who is already in the city to take it. I have plenty of people."

"Or your wights," Darin says. "What if they—"

A screeching chitter disabuses us of that notion. "They won't touch any part of the Star," Musa says after listening for a moment. "Too afraid of the Nightbringer."

"In any case, read it again." I nod at the book before him. *"Only the Ghost may stand against the onslaught. Should the Lioness's heir claim the Butcher's pride, it will evanesce.* I'm my mother's heir, Musa. You chose me yourself. And I'm the Ghost. Who else do you know who can disappear?"

"If you're the Ghost," Musa says, "what's this business about you falling . . . your flesh withering? Or am I remembering this Shaeva's prophecy wrong?"

I hadn't forgotten. *The Ghost will fall, her flesh will wither.*

"It doesn't matter," I say. "Do you want to risk the fate of the world on trying to figure it out?"

"Perhaps I don't want to risk you, *aapan*," Musa says. "The refugee camp is a disaster. We have almost ten thousand homeless, another thousand injured. We need you as a voice for the Scholars. We need you as our scim and shield. And we'll need you more if the Nightbringer succeeds. If you get yourself killed, you don't do me much good."

"You knew this was the deal when you made it," I say. "You help me find the last piece of the Star and take down the Nightbringer, and when I get back, I offer myself as leader of the northern Resistance. Besides, if all goes to plan, the Nightbringer *won't* succeed."

"The Martials will still attack. Maybe not immediately, but it will happen. The Commandant has already tried to seize the Martial navy as well as the Karkaun fleet. She failed, but it's common knowledge she wanted those ships to take on the Mariners. The Free Lands need to be ready for war. And the Scholars need a strong voice to speak up for them when that day comes."

"It's not going to matter if we're all dead."

"Look at you." Musa shakes his head. "Half out the door, like you can just tear off for Antium this very instant."

"The Grain Moon is little more than six weeks away, Musa. I have no time."

"What do you propose?" Darin asks. "Laia's right—we have no time."

"Your face is known in the Empire. The Nightbringer can read your mind, and your invisibility ceases to work around him. You need people to back you in Antium," Musa says. "People who know the city and the Martials. I can, of course, provide this. We let *them* come up with a plan to get you close to the Shrike. That way, it can't be picked from your mind."

"And it can't be picked from theirs?"

"My people—well, *person*—is trained to keep out invaders. Mind like a steel trap and as quiet and clever as a wraith. However . . ."

"No *however*," I say, alarmed. "Whatever you want me to do, I'll do it when I get back."

"I've hardly asked anything of you yet, Laia."

"Something tells me you're about to make up for that," Darin murmurs.

"Indeed." Musa rises from his seat beside one of the forges, wincing as he does. "Come with me. I'll explain on the way. Though"—he looks me up and down distastefully—"you need to visit the bath first."

A sudden suspicion forms in my mind. "Where *are* we going?"

"To the palace. To speak with the king."

«««

Four hours later, I perch upon an overstuffed chair in a palace antechamber beside Musa, awaiting an audience with a man I have no wish to meet.

"This is a terrible idea," I hiss at Musa. "We have no support from the refugees or the Adisan Scholars, *no* Resistance fighters at our backs—"

"You're leaving for Antium to hunt down a jinn," Musa says. "I need you to talk to the king *before* you die."

"Just because he knew my mother doesn't mean he'll listen to me. You've lived here your whole life. You have a much better chance of persuading him to help the Scholars. Clearly he knows you; otherwise we never would have gotten this audience."

"We got this audience because he thinks he's meeting the famed daughter of his old friend. Now remember, you *must* convince him that the Scholars need aid and that there is at least a threat from the Martials," Musa says. "No need to mention the Nightbringer. Just—"

"I understand." *Since this is the tenth time you have told me,* I do not add. I take hold of the neckline of my dress—low enough to show the K the Commandant carved into me—and pull it up yet again. The gown Musa found for me is tight in the bodice and flows wide through the waist, turquoise blue silk overlaid with sea-green, gauzelike netting. The neck and hems sag with gold-threaded flowers, embroidered mirrors, and minuscule emeralds. The net deepens into a dark royal blue at the hem, which just brushes the soft fawn slippers Taure gave me. I've braided my hair into a high bun and scrubbed myself so hard my skin still smarts.

When I catch a glimpse of myself in a mirrored wall of the antechamber, I look away, thinking of Elias, wishing he could see me like this. Wishing he were beside me, dressed in his finest, instead of Musa, and that we were walking into a party or festival.

"Stop fidgeting, *aapan.*" Musa draws me from my reverie. "You'll wrinkle the dress." He wears a crisp white shirt beneath a long, fitted blue jacket with gold buttons. His hair, usually pulled back, falls past his shoulders in thick, dark waves, and he has a hood pulled low. Despite it, more than one head turned as we walked with Captain Eleiba through the halls of the palace. A few times, courtiers even tried to approach until Eleiba turned them away.

"I can't do this, Musa." My worry drives me to my feet, and I pace the antechamber. "You said we'd have one chance to convince the king to help us. That the future of our people depends on this. I'm not my mother. I'm not the right person—"

Boots clank beyond the door, and the entrance to the audience chamber opens. Captain Eleiba awaits.

"Good luck." Musa steps back. I realize that he doesn't mean to come with me.

"You *get* over here, Musa!"

"Laia of Serra," Eleiba announces in a booming voice, "daughter of Mirra and Jahan of Serra." She gives Musa a cold look. "*And* Musa of Adisa, prince consort of Her Royal Highness Nikla of Adisa."

Only after my mouth has been hanging open a few seconds do I realize how foolish I must look. Musa shakes his head.

"I'm not welcome here, Eleiba—"

"Then you shouldn't have come," the captain says. "The king awaits."

Musa remains a few paces behind me, so I cannot even glare at him properly. I enter the audience chamber, immediately awestruck by the soaring, jewel-encrusted dome above me, the mother of pearl and ebony inlaid floor, the rose quartz columns that glow with inner light. I feel, suddenly, like a peasant.

An elderly man who I assume is King Irmand waits at the north end of the room, a familiar, much younger woman at his side. Princess Nikla. The thrones they sit upon are fashioned from enormous, weathered chunks of driftwood, ornately carved with fish, dolphins, whales, and crabs.

The room is empty of anyone but the royals and their guards. Eleiba goes to stand behind the king, her anxiety evident in the tap of her finger against her thigh.

The king has the shrunken look of a once robust man who has aged suddenly. Nikla appears powerful beside her frail father, though nothing like the simply garbed woman I saw in the prison cell. Her heavily embroidered gown is similar to mine, and her dark hair is arranged in an elaborate turquoise headdress that looks, remarkably, like a wave breaking on a shore.

At the wrath in her face, my steps falter, and I search out any exits in the throne room. I wish I'd brought a weapon with me.

But the princess merely glowers. She is not, I am relieved to see, surrounded by ghuls, though a few lurk in the shadows of the throne room.

"Ah, my wayward son-in-law returns." The old man's deep voice belies his frail appearance. "I've missed your wit, boy."

"And I yours, Your Majesty." Musa's voice is sincere. He pointedly doesn't look at Eleiba.

"Laia of Serra." The crown princess ignores her husband—*husband!* "Welcome to Adisa. Long have we wished to meet you."

Long have you wished to kill me, you mean. Hag. My irritation must show on my face, because Musa gives me a warning glance before dropping into a deep bow. Reluctantly, I emulate him. The lines around Nikla's mouth tighten.

Oh skies. How can I speak to a king? I'm no one. How can I convince him of anything?

The king gestures for us to rise. "I knew your parents, Laia of Serra," he says. "You have your father's beauty. Handsome as a jinn, that one. No fire in him though. Not like the Lioness." Irmand looks at me with interest. "Well, daughter of Mirra, you have a request? In honor of your late mother, who was a friend and ally for long years, I will hear it."

Princes Nikla barely suppresses a grimace at the words *friend and ally*, and her dark eyes glint. My ire rises as I think of the things she said about my mother. As I remember what children in the city were saying about the Lioness. Nikla's stare bores into me, a challenge writ there. Behind her, something dark and furtive flits behind one of the rose quartz pillars—a ghul.

A reminder of the darkness we face, one that makes me square my shoulders and meet the king's gaze. I am not no one. I am Laia of Serra, and in this moment, I am the only voice my people have.

"The Scholars suffer needlessly, Your Majesty," I say. "And you can stop it."

I tell him of the fire in the refugee camp. Of all that the Scholars have lost. I tell him of the Empire's war on my people, the Commandant's genocide, the horrors of Kauf. And then, though Musa warned me not to, I speak of the Nightbringer. I am a *Kehanni* in this moment. And I must make them believe.

I do not dare to look at Musa until I finish the tale. His fists are clenched, knuckles white, gaze fixed on Nikla. As I told the story, my attention was on the king. I did not notice the ghuls emerging from the shadows and congregating around the princess. I did not notice them latching themselves on to her like leeches.

Musa looks as if he is watching the slow torture of someone he loves—which, I finally realize, he is.

"Help the Scholars, Your Grace," I say. "They suffer when they do not have to. And prepare your armies. Whether the Nightbringer comes or not," I say to the king, "you must—"

"I must?" The old man raises his eyebrows. "*I* must?"

"Yes," I snap. "If you want your people to survive, you *must* prepare for war."

Nikla steps toward me, hand on her weapon, before controlling herself. "Do not listen to her, Father. She is nothing. Just a little girl selling stories."

"Don't you belittle me." I step forward, and everything fades—Eleiba's hand on her weapon, the guards tensing, a murmured plea from Musa to calm down. "I am the daughter of the Lioness. I destroyed Blackcliff. I saved the life of Elias Veturius. I survived Commandant Keris Veturia. I survived the betrayals of the Resistance *and* the Nightbringer. I crossed the Empire and broke into Kauf Prison. I rescued my brother and hundreds of other Scholars. I am *not* nothing." I turn to the king now. "If you do not prepare for war, Your Grace, and the Nightbringer unleashes his jinn, we will *all* fall."

"And how do we do that, Laia of Serra, without Serric steel?" Princess Nikla says. "We know your brother still lives. Musa no doubt has him hidden away, hammering at weapons for your Resistance."

"Darin of Serra is willing to make weaponry for the Mariners," Musa cuts in smoothly, and I wonder when he talked to Darin about it. "And to teach Mariner smiths the trade. *If* an equal amount of weaponry is given to the Scholars and an equal number of Scholar smiths are taught. And *if* the Scholars who have lost their homes are given temporary quarters in the city, and employment."

"Lies," Nikla hisses. "Father, they seek to mislead you. They want only to arm their Resistance."

As much as I want to talk back, I make myself ignore Nikla. It's the king whom I must convince. "Your Majesty," I say, "it's a good offer. You won't get a better one. The Martials certainly aren't going to help you, and how else will you get Serric steel?"

The king observes me carefully now, and the sparkle of amusement in his eyes is gone. "You are bold, Laia of Serra, to tell a king what to do."

"Not bold," I say. "Just desperate and sick of seeing my people suffer."

"I hear truth in your words, girl. And yet . . ." The king looks to his daughter. Whereas without the ghuls, she looked regal, even beautiful, now she looks angry and merciless, her lips leached of color, her pupils overly bright.

The old man shakes his head. "Perhaps what you say is true," the king says. "But if we arm ourselves with Serric steel, prepare our fleets, ready our defenses, the Martials could declare war by claiming we are planning an attack."

"The Martials are in a constant state of readiness," I say. "They can't attack you just because you do the same."

I hear his age in his sigh. "Oh, child," he says. "Do you have any idea of the dance the Mariners have been forced into these past five hundred years, with the Empire snapping at our borders? Do you know how difficult that dance has grown with Scholars pouring into our country? I am old. Soon, I will die. What do I leave my daughter? Tens of thousands of refugees. The Great Library destroyed. A people divided—half wishing to help the Scholars, the other half tired from five hundred years of doing so. And I am to muster my armies? On the word of a girl who has apparently been helping to make illegal weaponry?"

"At least help the Scholars from the refugee camp," I say. "They—"

"We will replace their tents. In time. That is all we can do."

"Father," Nikla says. "I request to take this girl—and her brother, who is no doubt lurking in the city—into custody."

"No," King Irmand says, and though his words are laden with the authority of his office, I notice with a chill that his hands, spotted and shaking with palsy, give away his immense age. Soon enough, his daughter will be queen.

"If we keep them here, daughter, we give the Martials cause to question our commitment to peace. They are fugitives in the Empire, are they not?"

"Sir," I say. "*Please* listen. You were friends with my mother—you trusted her. Please, in her place, trust me now."

"It was an honor to meet a daughter of Mirra's. We had our differences, your mother and I, and I have heard wretched rumors about her over the years. But her heart was true. Of that, I am certain. In honor of our friendship, I give you and your brother two days to leave the city. Captain Eleiba will oversee your preparations and your departure. Musa"—the king shakes his head—"do not return here again."

The king reaches a hand out to the captain of his city guard. She clasps it immediately, steadying him as he stands. "See that Laia of Serra and her brother find their way to the docks, Captain. I have a kingdom to run."

XXXIII: The Blood Shrike

I cannot celebrate the fact that I have saved Livia and thus thwarted the Commandant. Marcus knows now what I can do, and though he said little after discovering me, it is only a matter of time before he uses the knowledge against me.

But worse than that is the fact that within days of arriving in Antium, I learn that Keris has managed to procure her freedom.

"The Illustrian Paters discovered a *bleeding* loophole." Marcus paces in his private study, boots crunching against the shattered remnants of a table he destroyed in a fit of rage. "It doesn't allow the head of an Illustrian Gens to be imprisoned for longer than a week without the approval of two-thirds of the *other* Illustrian Gens."

"But she's not Mater of Gens Veturia."

"She was when you threw her in jail," Marcus says. "Apparently, that's what matters."

"She let thousands die in Navium."

"Skies, you are stupid," Marcus groans. "Navium is a thousand leagues away. The Illustrians and Mercators there can do nothing to help us. They couldn't even keep her locked up. Her allies in Antium are already spreading some ridiculous story about how she wasn't to blame in Navium. Would that I could lop all their heads off." He cocks his head, muttering, "Cut off one, and a dozen more appear in their place—I know, I know—"

Bleeding skies. He's talking to his brother's ghost again. I wait for him to stop, and when he doesn't, I back away, willing him not to notice and closing the door quietly behind me. Harper waits outside, fidgeting at the mutters coming from the study.

"Keris will be here in a little more than two weeks," I say as we emerge into the noon sunshine. "And all the more dangerous for the time she spent in a cage." I glance back at the palace. "Marcus is spending more time talking to his brother's ghost, Harper. The moment Keris gets here, she'll try to take advantage of it. Get a message to Dex." My friend remained in Navium to help oversee the rebuilding of the destroyed parts of the city. "Tell him to get eyes on her. And tell him I need him back here as soon as possible."

An hour later Harper finds me pacing in my study, and we set to work. "The Plebeians are suspicious of Keris after what happened in Navium," I say. "Now we have to destroy the Illustrians' confidence in her."

"We go after her character," Avitas says. "Most of the Illustrian Paters are classist. None of her allies know Elias's father was a Plebeian. Release the information."

"It's not enough," I say. "It was years ago, and Elias is long gone. But . . ." I consider. "What about her do we *not* know? What are her secrets? That tattoo of hers—did she ever tell you anything about it when you were working with her?"

Harper shakes his head. "All I know is that it was first spotted on her nearly two decades ago, a year or so after she abandoned Elias in the Tribal desert. She was stationed in Delphinium at the time."

"I saw it back in Navium," I say. "Just a bit of it. The letters *ALW*. The ink was different. She didn't get all three letters at once. Initials, perhaps?"

"Not initials." Avitas's eyes light up. "Her Gens motto: *Always victorious.*"

Of course. "Look through the death records of Delphinium," I say. "There aren't many tattooists in the Empire. Find out if any of those who lived near Delphinium died around that time. She'd have to strip down to get that tattoo, and she'd never leave whoever did it alive."

A knock at the door jars me from my plotting. A pale-haired Plebeian corporal enters and salutes smartly.

"Corporal Favrus, sir, here to deliver the garrison reports." At the blank look on my face, he goes on. "You requested reports from all northern garrisons last month, sir."

I remember now. The Karkauns around Tiborum were too quiet, and I wanted to know if they were up to something. "Wait outside."

"I can take the report," Avitas offers. "You've a line of men waiting to give you more important information about Marcus's enemies and allies, and an appearance in the yard for some training wouldn't be a bad idea. Take your war hammer. Remind them who you are."

I almost tell him I'm too tired, but then I recall something I heard Quin Veturius tell Elias once: *When you are weak, look to the battlefield. In battle, you will find your vigor. In battle, you will find your strength.*

"I can handle intel and a bit of training," I say. "You're the only one I trust to find this out, Harper—and quickly. After Keris gets here, everything will become far more difficult."

Avitas leaves, and moments later, Favrus is gabbling to me about the Karkauns.

"They have retreated into the mountains for the most part, Shrike. There has been the occasional skirmish, but nothing unusual. Tiborum has reported nothing more than a few smaller raids on the outskirts of the city."

"Details." I'm only half listening to him as I scan a dozen other things that need my attention.

But he doesn't respond. I look up just in time to catch his fleeting look of disquiet before he describes the skirmishes in bare-bones terms: how many died, how many attacked.

"Corporal Favrus." I am used to more detailed descriptions. "Can you tell me which defense maneuvers were successful and which failed? Or which clans the Karkauns hailed from?"

"I didn't think it mattered, Shrike. The garrison commanders said the skirmishes were unimportant."

"Everything to do with our enemies is important." I hate having to turn Centurion on him, but he is a Mask and a Black Guard. He should know better. "What we do not know about the Karkauns could be our downfall. We all thought they were crouched around their fires, practicing unholy rites with their warlocks, when in fact famine and wars with the south pushed them to build up an enormous fleet that they used to lay waste to our largest port."

Favrus pales and nods sharply. "Of course, Shrike," he says. "I'll get details on those skirmishes right away."

I can tell he wants to leave, but my instinct tingles. Something strange is afoot, and I've been a Mask for too long to ignore the gnawing feeling in my gut.

As I observe the corporal, he remains stock-still, other than the sweat rolling down the side of his face. Interesting, since my office isn't particularly warm.

"Dismissed." I wave him away, pretending I haven't noticed his nervousness. I consider it as I make my way to the training yard. When I arrive, the men of the Black Guard, still wary of me, give way. I swing my war hammer and call a challenge. One of the men, an Illustrian Mask from Gens Rallia who was here long before I arrived, accepts, and I tuck the issue of Favrus at the back of my mind. Perhaps a good fight or two will rattle some answers loose.

It has been so long since I trained. I forgot the way my mind clears when all that is before me is an opponent. I forgot how good it feels to fight those who know *how* to fight. Masks, trained and true, bonded by the shared experience of surviving Blackcliff. I best the Illustrian swiftly, gratified when the men respond to my victory with a huzzah. After an hour, more of the men gather to watch the fights, and after two, I have no challengers left.

But I also do not have an answer to the question of Corporal Favrus. I am still mulling it over when a soldier named Alistar crosses the yard. He's one of Harper's friends, a Plebeian who has served here in Antium for a dozen years. A good man—and trustworthy, according to Dex.

"Alistar." The captain jogs toward me, curious. I've never singled him out before. "Do you know Corporal Favrus?"

"Of course, Blood Shrike. New to the Black Guard. He was transferred from Serra. Quiet. Keeps to himself."

"Follow him," I say. "I want to know everything about him. No detail is too small. Pay extra attention to his communications with the northern garrisons. He mentioned Karkaun skirmishes, but . . ." I shake my head, uneasy. "There's something he's not telling me."

After Alistar is dispatched, I find the old Blood Shrike's file on Corporal Favrus. I am wondering at the fact that he appears to be the most boring soldier ever to have entered the Black Guard when my door bursts open to reveal Silvio Rallius, his dark skin ashen.

"Blood Shrike, sir," he says. "Please—you need to come to the palace. The Emperor—he had some sort of fit in the throne room—started screaming at someone no one else could see. And then he left for the Empress's quarters."

Livia! I am in a frenzy by the time I reach my sister's chambers, where Faris paces outside the door, his footsteps heavy with rage.

"He's inside." His voice is choked. "Shrike, he's not fit—he—"

"Treason, Lieutenant Candelan," I snap. Skies, doesn't he know the cost of saying such things? There are other guards here who will take his words back to Marcus's enemies. There are Scholar slaves who might be in the Commandant's employ. And then where would Livia be? "All Emperors grow . . . emotional at times. You do not know the weight of the crown. You could never understand." It's rubbish, but the Emperor's Shrike must stand by his side.

At least, until I kill him.

Livia's pain hits me like a blow to the stomach the moment I enter the room. I am so *aware* of her—her suffering, her hurt. And beneath that, the steady, quick heartbeat of her child blissfully unaware of the monster who sits inches from his mother.

My sister's face is blanched, and she has one arm laid across her belly. Marcus is sprawled on a chair beside hers, trailing his hand up and down the other arm gently, like a lover would.

But I notice immediately that Livvy's arm doesn't look right. The angle is wrong. Because Marcus has broken it.

The Emperor lifts his yellow eyes to me. "Heal her, Blood Shrike," he says. "I'd like to watch you do it."

I do not waste a thought on how much I hate this man. I simply sing Livia's song quickly, unable to bear her pain any longer. Her bones knit together, clean and strong once more.

"Interesting," Marcus says in a dead voice. "Does it work on you?" he asks. "For example, if I demanded your war hammer and shattered your knees right now, would you be able to heal them?"

"No," I lie smoothly, though my insides cringe in disgust. "It doesn't work on me."

He tilts his head. "But if I shatter *her* knees, you could heal them? With your song?"

I stare at him, aghast.

"Answer the question, Shrike. Or I'll break her other arm."

"Yes," I say. "Yes, I could heal her. But she's the mother of your child—"

"She's an Illustrian whore you sold to me in exchange for your miserable life," Marcus says. "Her only use is her ability to carry my heir. As soon as he is born, I'll cast her . . . I'll—" The suddenness with which his face pales is staggering. He half roars, half screams, his fingers curled into claws. I look to the door, expecting Rallius and Faris to burst in at the sound of their Emperor in pain.

They do not. Probably because they are hoping that I'm the one causing it.

"Enough!" He speaks to neither me nor Livia. "You wanted this. You *told* me to do it. You—" Marcus grasps his head, and the moan that comes out of him is animal.

"Heal this." He grabs my hand, crushing my fingers, and puts it on his head roughly. "Heal this!"

"I—I don't—"

"Heal it, or I swear to the skies that when the time comes I'll cut my child out of her while she still lives." He grabs my left hand and slams it to the other side of his head, digging his fingers into my wrists until I hiss in pain. "*Heal me.*"

"Sit down." I have never wanted to kill someone so much. I wonder, suddenly, if my healing can be used to destroy. Can I shatter his bones with a song? Stop his heart?

Skies, I've no idea how to heal a broken man. How does one heal hallucinations? Is that all that ails him? Does he suffer from something deeper? Is it in his heart? His mind?

All I can do is seek his song. I explore his heart first, but it is strong and steady and healthy, a heart that will beat for a long time to come. I circle his mind and finally step inside. It feels like stepping into a poisoned swamp. Darkness. Pain. Rage. And a deep, abiding emptiness. I am reminded of Cook, only this darkness is different, more wounded, whereas what lived in Cook felt like nothing at all.

I try to soothe the bits of his mind that rage, but it does nothing. I catch a glimpse of something strangely familiar: a wisp of a form—yellow eyes, dark skin, dark hair, a sad face. *He could be so much more if only he did as I ask.* Zacharias?

The words are whispered on the air, but I am not sure who spoke them. Skies, what have I gotten myself into? *Help me,* I shout in my mind, though to whom, I don't know. My father, perhaps. My mother. *I don't know what to do.*

"Stop."

The word is a command, not a request, and even Marcus turns at the sound. For this is a voice that cannot be ignored, not even by the overlord of the Martial Empire.

The Nightbringer stands in the middle of the room. The windows are not open. Neither is the door. From the terrified look on Livia's face, I can tell that she too is spooked by the jinn's sudden appearance.

"She cannot heal you, Emperor," the Nightbringer says in his deep, unsettling voice. "You suffer no ailment. Your brother's ghost is real. Until you submit to its will, it will give you no peace."

"You . . ." For the first time in what feels like years, Marcus's face holds something other than malice or hatred. He looks haunted. "You *knew*. Zak said he saw the future in your eyes. Look at me—*look at me*—and tell me my end."

"I do not show you your end," the Nightbringer says. "I show you the darkest moment your future holds. Your brother saw his. You will soon face yours, Emperor. Leave the Shrike. Leave your empress. Tend to your empire, lest your brother's death be for naught."

Marcus staggers away from the Nightbringer, toward the door. He cuts me a look—enough hate in that glance that I know he isn't yet done with me—and stumbles out.

I whirl on the Nightbringer, still shaking from what I saw in Marcus's mind. The same question I asked before is on my lips: *What game are you playing?* But I do not have to speak it.

"No game, Blood Shrike," the jinn says. "The very opposite. You will see."

XXXIV: Elias

We have twelve hours until the Martials arrive. Twelve hours to prepare a few thousand Tribesmen who are in the worst fighting shape they've ever been in. Twelve hours to get the children and injured to safety.

If there were any place to run, I would ask the Tribes to get the hells away from here. But the sea lies to the east and the Forest to the north. The Martials approach from the south and west.

Mauth pulls at me, the tug getting more painful by the minute. I know I must go back to the Forest. But if I don't do something, thousands of Tribespeople will be massacred. The Waiting Place will be filled with even more ghosts. And where will that leave me?

The Tribes, it's clear, plan to stand and fight. Already, the *Zaldars* who still have their wits are readying horses and weaponry and armor. But it won't be enough. Though we outnumber the Martials, they are a superior fighting force. Ambushes in the dead of night with poisoned darts are one thing. But facing an army on a field when your men haven't slept or eaten properly in days?

"*Banu al-Mauth.*" Afya's voice is stronger than it was even an hour ago. "The salt works. We still have many dead to attend to, but the *ruh* have been released. The spirits no longer plague their families."

"But there are too many dead now." Mamie appears behind Afya, pallid and exhausted. "And they must be given burial rites."

"I spoke to the other *Zaldars*," Afya says. "We can muster a force of a thousand horse—"

"You don't need to do that," I say. "I'm going to take care of it."

The *Zaldara* looks dubious. "Using . . . your magic?"

"Not exactly." I consider. I have most of what I need, but there is one thing that will make what I must do a bit easier. "Afya, do you have any of those darts you used during the raids?"

Mamie and Afya exchange a glance, and my mother steps close enough that only I can hear her. She takes my hands.

"What are you planning, my son?"

Perhaps I should tell her. She would try to talk me out of it, I know she would. She loves me, and that love blinds her.

I extricate myself, unable to meet her eyes. "You don't want to know."

As I leave the camp, Mauth summons me with enough force that I think he will pull me to the Forest the way he did after the jinn took me to Laia.

But this is the only way.

The first time I killed, I was eleven. I saw my enemy's face for days after he was gone. I heard his voice. And then I killed again. And again. And again. Too soon, I stopped seeing their faces. I stopped wondering what their names were, or who they left behind. I killed because I was ordered to, and then, once free of Blackcliff, I killed because I had to, to stay alive.

Once, I knew exactly how many lives I had taken. Now I no longer remember. Somewhere along the way, a part of me learned how to stop caring. And that's the part of me that I must draw upon now.

As soon as I reason through it in my head, the connection between Mauth and me slackens. He offers no magic, but I am able to continue my journey without pain.

The Martial army stops to camp along the crest of a low plateau. Their tents are a dark stain against the pale desert, their cook fires like stars in the warm night. It takes a half hour of patient observation to figure out where the camp commander is and another fifteen minutes to plan my entrance— and exit. My face is known, but most of these people believe I'm dead. They will not expect to see me, and there lies my advantage.

The shadows hang thick between the tents, and I let them cradle me as I make my way through the periphery of the camp. The commander's tent is in the center, but the soldiers have erected it hastily, for instead of a clear area around it, other dwellings are staked close by. Access won't be simple— but it won't be impossible, either.

As I approach the tent, darts ready, a great part of me screams against this. *You will know victory, or you will know death.* I hear the Commandant whisper in my ear, an old memory. *There is nothing else.* It's always this way before I kill. Even when I was hunting Masks so Laia could free prisoners from ghost wagons—even then I struggled. Even then it took its toll. My foes will die, and they will take a bit of me with them.

The field of battle is my temple.

I draw close to the tent and find a fold that is hidden from anyone inside. Ever so slowly, I cut a slit. Five Masks, including the commander, sit around a table within, eating their meal and arguing about the coming battle.

They will not expect me, but they are still Masks. I will need to move swiftly, before they raise the alarm. Which means first taking them out with the darts Afya gave me.

The swordpoint is my priest.

I *must* do this. I must cut off the head of this army. Doing so will give the Tribes a chance to run. These Masks would have killed my people, my family. They would have enslaved them and beaten them and destroyed them.

The dance of death is my prayer.

But even knowing what the Masks would have done, I do not wish to kill. I do not wish to belong to this world of blood and violence and vengeance. I do not wish to be a Mask.

The killing blow is my release.

My wishes do not matter. These men must die. The Tribes must be protected. And my humanity must be left behind. I step into the tent.

And I unleash the Mask lurking within.

XXXV: The Blood Shrike

A week after Marcus's attack on Livvy, Harper finally emerges from the Hall of Records, where he has spent every waking moment since I gave him his mission.

"The record archivists were preparing for a move," he says. "Bloodline certificates and birth records and family trees all over the place. Scholar slaves were trying to clean it up, but they can't read, so it was all a jumble."

He places a stack of death certificates on my desk before collapsing into a chair across from me. "You were right. In the past twenty years, ten tattooists have died unnaturally in and around the cities where the Commandant was posted. One just recently, not far from Antium. The others lived everywhere from the Tribal lands to Delphinium. And I found something else."

He hands me a list of names. There are thirteen, all Illustrian, all from well-known Gens. I recognize two—they were found dead just recently, here in Antium. I remember reading about them weeks ago, the day Marcus ordered me to Navium. Another name also stands out.

"Daemon Cassius," I say. "Why do I know that name?"

"He was murdered last year in Serra by Scholar's Resistance fighters. It happened a few weeks before the murder of a Serran tattooist. Every one of these Illustrians was murdered shortly before the local tattooists were. Different cities. Different methods. All within the last twenty years. All Masks."

"I remember now," I say. "Cassius was at home when he was murdered. His wife found him in a locked room. Elias and I were in the middle of the Trials when it happened. I wondered how the hells a group of Scholar rebels could kill a Mask."

"Titus Rufius," Harper reads. "Killed in a hunting accident at the age of thirty-two, nine years ago. Iustin Sergius, poisoned at twenty-five, apparently by a Scholar slave who confessed to the crime sixteen years ago. Caius Sissellius was thirty-eight. He drowned on his family's own grounds, in a river he'd been swimming in since before he could walk. That was three years ago."

"Avitas, look at their ages." I examine the names carefully. "And they were Masks. Which means every one of these men graduated with her. She *knew* them."

"They all died before they should have, many in unnatural ways. So why? Why did she kill them?"

"They got in her way somehow," I say. "She was always ambitious. Maybe they were given postings she wanted, or they thwarted her somehow, or . . . oh . . . *oh.*"

I remember what Quin told me of Arius Harper: *He was murdered by a group of Masks the day after they graduated—Keris's fellow Senior Skulls. A vicious killing—more than a dozen of them beat him to death. Illustrian, all of them.*

"It wasn't because they got in her way." I relate what Quin said. "It was vengeance. They beat Arius Harper to death." I look up from the scrolls. I wonder if his father had green eyes too. "Your father."

Avitas is quiet for a long moment. "I . . . didn't know how he died."

Bleeding hells. "I'm sorry," I say quickly. "I thought—oh skies, Avitas."

"It doesn't matter." He seems to find the window of my office suddenly very interesting. "He's been gone a long time now. Why would it matter if they killed my father? The Commandant isn't the sentimental type."

I am startled by how quickly he moves on, and I consider apologizing again or telling him that if he doesn't want the nature of his father's death made public, I understand. But then I realize that what he needs is for me to move on. To be the Blood Shrike. To let it go.

"It's not sentiment," I say briskly, though I have my doubts. The Commandant did, after all, take Avitas under her wing—inasmuch as someone like her could. "It's power. She loved him. They killed him. They took her power. By murdering them, she's taking it back."

"How do we use this against her?"

"We get this information out to the Paters," I say. "They learn about the tattoo, the dead tattooists, Arius Harper, the murdered Illustrians—all of it."

"We need proof."

"We have it." I nod to the death certificates. "For anyone who cares to look. If we can get these certificates into the hands of just a few trusted Paters, the rest won't need to see them. Think of how she's handled what happened in Navium. It didn't matter that she lied. All that mattered is that people believed it."

"We should start with Pater Sissellius and Pater Rufius," Harper says. "They're her closest allies. The other Paters trust them."

For three days, Harper and I seed the rumors. And then, when I am in court listening to Marcus arguing with a Tribal envoy—

"—Illustrians from her own year! Over a *Plebeian*! Can you imagine—"

"But there's no proof—"

"Not enough to jail her, but Sissellius *saw* the death certificates. The link is obvious. You know how that man loathes idle gossip. Besides, the proof is on her body—that *vile* tattoo—"

After a few more days, I sense the change in the air. I feel the Paters distancing themselves from Keris. Some are even outright opposed to her. When she does return to Antium, she will find it a far less welcoming city than she expects.

»»»

Captain Alistar sends me a message letting me know he has information on the same day Dex returns to Antium, and I call them both to me in the training yard.

"Keris will be here within the week." Dex is fresh from the road, splattered with mud, exhausted. But he spars with me anyway, keeping his helm low so that his lips cannot be read. It's nearly impossible to hear him over the clash of weapons and grunts of men training.

"She knows you've spread the truth about the tattoo and the murders. She sent two assassins; I dispatched them before they could get here, but skies know what she'll do when she arrives. You'd best start cooking your food yourself. Farming your own grain too."

"Did she ride straight for Antium?"

"She stopped at the Roost," Dex says. "I followed her in, but her men nearly caught me. By then I thought it best to get back here. I'll check in with my spies—" Dex's gaze shifts over my shoulder, and he frowns.

At the entrance to the barracks, across the training field, a group of Black Guards crowds together. I think at first that a fight has broken out. I hurry toward them, war hammer still in hand.

One of the men calls out: "Get the bleeding physician!"

"No point, that's karka snake venom—"

They are clustered around a fellow guard who bucks as he vomits black bile onto the ground. I recognize him instantly: Captain Alistar.

"Bleeding hells." I crouch down next to him. "Get the barracks physician. Get him *now!*"

But the man could already be here and it would be too late. The black bile, the red mottling around Alistar's nose and ears. It *is* karka snake venom. He's done for.

Harper pushes through the crowd and kneels beside me. "Shrike, what—"

"Nothing—" Alistar grabs the front of my fatigues with one hand and pulls me close. His voice is little more than a death rattle. "Nothing—no attacks—nothing—Shrike—they're nowhere—"

His grip goes slack, and he slumps to the ground, dead.

Burning skies. "As you were," I say to the men. "Go on." The men scatter, except for Dex and Harper, who stare down in horror at the dead soldier.

I lean down and wrest a pile of papers from Alistar's stiff hand. I expect it to be information on Corporal Favrus. Instead I find reports from the garrisons across the north—straight from the garrison commanders.

"The Karkauns have disappeared." Harper, reading over my shoulder, sounds as mystified as I feel. "Not a single attack near Tiborum. Nothing in the deep north, not for months. Corporal Favrus lied. The Karkauns were quiet."

"The Karkauns are never quiet," I say. "This time last year, they were conquering the Wildmen clans. We stopped them in Tiborum. We stopped them in Navium. They lost their fleet. There's a bleeding famine in their southern territories, and a warlock priest whipping them into righteous fury. They should be harassing every village from here to the sea."

"Look at this, Shrike." Harper has searched Alistar's body, and he pulls out another scroll. "He must have found it in Favrus's things," Harper says. "It's in code."

"Break the code," I snap. Something is wrong—very wrong. "Find me Favrus. Alistar's death can't be a coincidence. The corporal is involved. Get messages to the northwestern garrisons. Have them send scouts to check in on the closest Karkaun clans. Find out where they are, what they are doing.

I want answers by nightfall, Harper. If those bastards are planning an assault on Tiborum, the city may fall. It might already be too late. Dex . . ."

My old friend sighs, already knowing that he's about to head back on the road.

"Head north," I say. "Check the passes around the Nevennes. They might be pushing for Delphinium. They won't have enough men to hold it, but that doesn't mean they're not stupid enough to try."

"I'll send a message through the drums as soon as I know anything, Shrike."

By nightfall, we've had word from even the most far-flung of the western garrisons. The Karkauns have completely abandoned their camps in the west. Their caves are empty, their grazing animals gone, their few fields and gardens are fallow. They can't possibly be planning an attack on Tiborum.

Which means they are gathering elsewhere. But where? And to what end?

XXXVI: Laia

M usa offers no explanation as we leave the palace, the only sign of his frustration the swift clip of his stride.

"Excuse me." I poke him in the ribs as he winds through streets unfamiliar to me. *"Your Highness—"*

"Not now," he grinds out. As much as I want to question him, we have a bigger problem, which is how the hells we're going to get rid of Captain Eleiba. The Mariner spoke briefly to the king before escorting us from the throne room and hasn't been more than a foot away from us since. When Musa enters a neighborhood where the houses are densely packed, I prepare to pull on my invisibility, expecting him to attack our chaperone. But instead, he just stops in an alley. "Well?" he says.

Eleiba clears her throat and turns to me. "His Royal Highness King Irmand thanks you for your warning, Laia, and wishes to assure you that he does not take lightly the interference of the fey creatures in his domain. He accepts Darin of Serra's offer for weapons and vows that he will provide shelter for the Scholars in the city until more permanent accommodations can be made. And he wishes you to have this." Eleiba places in my hand a silver signet ring emblazoned with a trident. "Show it to any Mariner, and they are honor bound to aid you."

Musa smiles. "I knew you'd get to him."

"But, the crown princess, she—"

"King Irmand has been ruler in Marinn for sixty years," Eleiba says. "Princess Nikla . . . was not always as she is now. The king has no other heir, and he does not wish to undermine her by disagreeing with her outright. But he knows what is best for his people."

All I can manage is a nod. "Good luck, Laia of Serra," Eleiba says quietly. "Perhaps we will meet again."

"Prepare your city." I say it before I lose my courage. Eleiba raises perfectly arched brows, and I rush on, feeling like an idiot for giving advice to a woman twenty years older and far wiser than I am. "You're the captain of the guard. You have power. Please do what you can. And if you have friends elsewhere in the Free Lands who can do the same, tell them."

When she is long gone, Musa answers my unspoken question. "Nikla and I eloped ten years ago," he says. "We were only a little older than you, but much more foolish. She had an older brother who was supposed to be king. But he died, she was named crown princess, and we grew apart."

I wince at the perfunctory nature of his recitation, a decade of history in four sentences.

"I didn't mention it before because there was no point. We've been separated for years. She took my lands, my titles, my fortune—"

"Your heart."

Musa's harsh laugh echoes off the hard stone of the buildings on either side of us.

"That too," he says. "You should change and get your things. Say goodbye to Darin. I'll meet you at the east gate with supplies and information about my contact."

He must see that I'm about to try to offer him a word of comfort, for he melts into the dark quickly. A half hour later, I've gathered my hair in a fat plait and returned the dress to Musa's quarters at the forge. Darin sits with Taure and Zella in the courtyard, stoking a low fire while the two women pack clay onto the edges of a sword.

He glances up when I appear and, spotting my packed bag, excuses himself.

"I'll be ready in an hour," he says after I tell him of my audience with the king. "Best tell Musa to make it two horses."

"The Scholars need you, Darin. And now the Mariners need you too."

Darin's shoulders stiffen. "I agreed to make weapons for the Mariners *before* I realized you'd be leaving so soon. They can wait. I won't stay behind."

"You have to," I say. "I *must* try to stop the Nightbringer. But if I fail, our people need to be able to fight. What is the point of all you suffered—all *we* suffered—if we don't even give our people a chance in battle?"

"Where you go, I go," Darin says quietly. "That was the promise we made."

"Is that promise worth more than the future of our people?"

"You sound like Mother."

"You say that like it's a bad thing."

"It *is* a bad thing. She put the Resistance—her *people*—ahead of everything: her husband, her children, herself. If you knew—"

My neck prickles. "If I knew *what*—"

He sighs. "Nothing."

"No," I say. "You've done this before. I know Mother wasn't perfect. And I heard . . . rumors when I was out in the city. But she wasn't what Princess Nikla made her out to be. She wasn't a monster."

Darin tosses his apron on an anvil and begins throwing tools in a sack, stubbornly refusing to talk about Mother. "You'll need someone to watch your back, Laia. Afya isn't there to do it and neither is Elias. Who better than your brother?"

"You heard Musa. He has someone who will help me."

"Do you know who? Has he given you a name? How do you know you can trust that person?"

"I don't, but I trust Musa."

"*Why?* You barely know him, like you barely knew Keenan—excuse me, the Nightbringer. Like you barely knew Mazen—"

"I was wrong about them." My ire rises, but I quash it; he is angry because he is scared, and I know that feeling well. "But I don't think I'm wrong about Musa. He's frustrating, and he gets on my nerves, but he's been honest. And he—we both—we have the magic, Darin. There's no one else I can even talk to about it."

"You could talk to me."

"After Kauf, I was barely able to talk to you about breakfast, let alone magic." I hate this. I *hate* fighting with him. Part of me wants to give in. Let him join me. I will be less lonely, I will feel less afraid.

Your fear doesn't matter, Laia, nor your loneliness. The Scholars' survival is what matters.

"If something happens to me," I say, "who will speak for the Scholars? Who knows the truth about the Nightbringer's plan? Who will ensure that the Mariners prepare, no matter the consequence?"

"Bleeding hells, Laia, stop." Darin never raises his voice, and I am surprised enough that I waver. "I'm coming with you. That's it."

I sigh, because I hoped it wouldn't come to this, and yet I suspected it might. My brother, stubborn as the sun. Now I know why Elias left a note all those months ago when he disappeared, instead of saying goodbye. It's not because he didn't care. It's because he cared too much.

"I'll just disappear," I say. "You won't be able to follow me."

Darin glares at me in disgusted disbelief. "You wouldn't do that."

"I would if I thought it would keep you from coming after me."

"You just expect me to be all right with this," Darin says. "To watch you leave, knowing that the only family I have left is *risking* herself *again*—"

"That's rich! What did you do, meeting with Spiro for all those months? If *anyone* should understand this, Darin, it's you." My anger takes hold now, the words pouring like poison from my mouth. *Don't say it, Laia. Don't.* But I do. I cannot stop. "The raid happened because of *you.* Nan and Pop died because of *you.* I went to Blackcliff for *you.* I got this"—I yank my collar back to reveal the Commandant's *K*—"because of you. And I traveled halfway across the bleeding world, lost one of the only true friends I've ever had, and saw the man I love get *chained* to some hellish underworld *because of you.* So don't talk to me about risking myself. Don't you bleeding *dare.*"

I didn't know how much was locked up inside me until I began shouting it. And now my rage is full-throated and throbbing, tearing out of me.

"You stay here," I snap at him. "You make weapons. And you give us a fighting chance. You *owe* that to Nan and Pop and Izzi and Elias and me. Don't think I'll bleeding forget it!"

Darin's mouth hangs open, and I stride out, slamming the forge door behind me. My anger carries me away from the shipyard and up into the city, and when I am halfway to the western gate, Musa falls into step beside me.

"Spectacular fight." He jogs to catch up with me, stealthy as a wraith. "Do you think you should apologize before you leave? You were a bit harsh."

"Is there *anything* you don't eavesdrop on?"

"I can't help it if the wights are gossips." He shrugs. "Though I was grati- fied to hear that you finally admitted how you feel about Elias out loud. You never talk about him, you know."

My face heats. "Elias is none of your business."

"As long as he doesn't stop you from keeping your promise, *aapan,*" Musa says, "I agree. I'll walk you to your horse. There are maps and supplies in the saddlebags. I marked a route straight west, through the mountains. Should get you to the Forest of Dusk in a bit more than three weeks. My contact will meet you on the other side and take you to Antium."

We come to the west gate just as a nearby belltower chimes midnight. In tune with the last bell tolling, there is a low hiss. A dagger leaving its sheath. As I reach for my own weapon, something zings past my ear.

An angry chitter erupts near me, and small hands shove at me. I drop, dragging Musa down as an arrow flies overhead. Another arrow shoots out of the darkness, but it too misses its mark, dropping in midair—courtesy of Musa's wights.

"Nikla!" Musa snarls. "Show yourself!"

The shadows shift, and the crown princess steps out of the darkness. She glares at us balefully, her face barely visible beneath the ghuls swarming all over her.

"I should have known that traitor Eleiba would let you go," she hisses. "She will pay."

More footsteps approach—Nikla's soldiers, closing in on Musa and me. Ever so slowly, Musa puts himself between me and Nikla. "Listen to reason, please. We both know—"

"Don't you speak to me!" the princess growls at Musa, and the ghuls cluck happily at her pain. "You *had* your chance."

"When I rush her," Musa whispers, barely audible, "run."

I'm just processing what he says when he's past me and heading straight for Nikla. Immediately, silver-armored bodyguards step out of the shadows and attack Musa so swiftly that he is now nothing but a blur.

I cannot just let Nikla's men take him. Skies know what they will do. But if I hurt any of these Mariners, it might turn King Irmand against us. I flip my dagger around to the hilt, but a hand grabs me and yanks me back.

"Go, little sister," Darin says, a staff in his hands. Taure, Zella, and a group of Scholars from the refugee camp are at his back. "We'll make sure no one dies. Get out of here. Save us."

"Musa—and you—if they arrest you—"

"We'll be fine," Darin says. "You were right. We have to be ready. But we don't have a chance if you don't go. Ride fast, Laia. Stop him. I'm with you, here." He taps my heart. "Go."

And like that day long ago in Serra, with my brother's voice ringing in my ears, I flee.

«««

For the first three days on the road, I hardly stop, expecting at any moment for Nikla and her men to find me. Every possible outcome plagues my mind, an ever-changing play of nightmares: The Mariners overcome Darin and Musa and Zella and Taure. The king sends soldiers to drag me back. The Scholars are left to starve—or worse, they are driven from Adisa, refugees yet again.

But four mornings after I leave, I am woken before dawn by a quiet chitter beside my ear. I so associate the sound with Musa that I expect to see him when I open my eyes. Instead, a scroll sits on my chest, with only one word printed on it.

Safe.

After that, I stop looking over my shoulder and start looking ahead. True to Eleiba's word, whenever I stop at a courier station and show the king's ring, I receive a fresh mount and supplies, no questions asked. The help couldn't come at a better time, for I am gripped by desperation. Every day brings me closer to the Grain Moon—and to the Nightbringer's victory. Every day makes it more likely that he will find a way to trick the Blood Shrike into giving him the ring, which he'll use to set his wrathful kindred free.

As I ride, I parse out the remaining bits of Shaeva's prophecy. The line about the Butcher worries me, but not as much as *the Dead will rise, and none can survive.*

The dead are Elias's domain. If they rise, does that mean they will escape the Waiting Place? What happens if they do? And what of the end of the prophecy? It makes little sense—all but *The Ghost will fall, her flesh will wither.* The meaning there is disturbingly clear: I'm going to die.

But then again, just because it's a prophecy doesn't mean it's written in stone.

I encounter many other travelers, but the king's sigil on my saddle and cloak keeps the questions at bay, and I do not invite conversation. After a week cutting through the mountains and ten days winding down into gentle, rolling farmland, the Forest of Dusk appears on the horizon, a blue line of fuzz beneath flocculent clouds. This far from the major cities there are no courier stations, and the farms and villages are far apart. But I do not feel lonely—a sense of anticipation builds.

Soon, I will be reunited with Elias.

I recall what I blurted out during my argument with Darin: *the man I love.*

I thought I loved Keenan, but that love was born out of desperation and loneliness, out of a need to see myself, my struggles, in someone else.

What I feel for Elias is different, a flame I hold close to my heart when I feel my strength flagging. Sometimes, deep in the night as I travel, I picture a future with him. But I dare not look at it too closely. How can I, when it can never be?

I wonder what he has become in the months we've been apart. Has he changed? Is he eating? Taking care of himself? Skies, I hope he has not grown a beard. I *hated* his beard.

The Forest transforms from a furred, distant line to a wall of knotted trunks that I know well. Even beneath the noontime shine of a summer sun, the Waiting Place feels ominous.

I leave my horse to graze, and as I draw near the tree line, a wind rises and the gnarled Forest canopy sways. The leaves sing in whispers, a gentle sound.

"Elias?" The silence is uncanny—no ghosts wail or cry out. Anxiety gnaws at me. What if Elias cannot pass the ghosts through? What if something has happened to him?

The stillness of the Forest makes me think of a predator stalking in tall grasses, watching its oblivious prey. But as the sun dips west, a familiar darkness rises in me, urging me toward the trees. I felt this darkness with the Nightbringer, long ago, when I sought to get answers out of him. I felt it again after Shaeva died, when I thought the jinn would hurt Elias.

It does not feel evil, this darkness. It feels like part of me.

I step into the trees, tense, blade in hand. Nothing happens. The Forest is quiet, but birds still sing, and small creatures still move through the underbrush. No ghosts approach. I move in deeper, allowing that darkness to pull me onward.

When I am far into the trees, the shadows grow thick. A voice calls out to me. No—not one voice. Many, speaking as one.

Welcome to the Waiting Place, Laia of Serra, the voices purr. *Welcome to our home, and our prison. Come closer, won't you?*

XXXVII: Elias

The Masks don't notice the darts until my first victim is facedown in his rice. They are complacent—their scouts have told them that the Tribespeople will be an easy conquest, and so they posted no guards, too confident in their own skill.

Which is formidable. But it's not enough.

The first Mask to spot me knocks the two darts I send at him out of the air and rushes me, blades appearing in his hands like magic.

But a darkness stirs within me—magic of my own. Though I am far from the Waiting Place, I have just enough physical magic to spin into a windwalk until I am behind him and I can stick him with another dart. Two of the Masks leap toward me, weapons flying, while the third—the commander—lunges for the door to raise the alarm.

I windwalk in front of him, using the infinitesimal moment of his surprise to jam a blade into his throat. *Don't think, just move, Elias.* Blood spurts all over my hands, making it exceedingly difficult not to dwell on the violence of my actions, but the other Masks approach, and this man's body makes an adequate shield, jerking as the blades of his comrades glance off his armor. I shove him at one of the remaining Masks and take on the other, ducking as he throws a punch and only just avoiding his knee as he tries to nail me in the jaw with it.

He has an open patch in his armor just above his wrist, and I grab it, stabbing him with the last of Afya's darts before he tackles me to the ground. Seconds later, his prone body is dragged off me, and the last Mask has me by the throat.

You are mortal. Shaeva reminded me of that fact before the Nightbringer murdered her. If I die here, the Waiting Place will have no guardian. The knowledge gives me the strength to knee the Mask in the groin and wrench away from him. I rip his knife from a scabbard and stab him in the chest once, twice, thrice, before drawing the blade across his throat.

The tent, which has been a whirlwind of activity, is suddenly still, other than the harsh draw of my breath. Outside, the voices of soldiers rise and fall in laughter and complaint, the din of the camp masking the ruckus of my attack.

Someone in the Martial camp will discover the Masks soon enough, so I slip out the way I came, making for the edge of the camp, where I steal a horse. By the time the first alarm sounds, I'm well away and heading west, toward the closest drum tower.

I make quick work of the legionnaires standing guard out front. One of them is mid-complaint when I shoot an arrow into his chest, and the other only realizes what is happening once he has a scim poking out of his throat. The killing comes easier now, and I'm halfway up the stairs of the tower, almost to the sleeping quarters, before a better part of me cries out: *They didn't deserve death. They didn't do anything to you.*

The final man in the tower is the head drummer, and he sits on the top floor, beside a drum as wide as he is tall, his ear trained toward another drum tower in the north. He transcribes whatever he hears on long scrolls, so engrossed in his work that he doesn't hear me. But by now, I'm far too tired to sneak. And I need him frightened. So I simply appear in the doorway, a nightmare spectacle covered in dried gore with unsheathed weapons stained with blood.

"Get up," I say calmly. "Walk to the drum."

"I—I—" He glances over the top of the tower to the door below, to the guardpost.

"They're dead." I gesture with a bloody hand, "in case you couldn't tell. Move."

He picks up his sticks, though fear makes him drop them twice.

"I'd like you to drum something out for me." I get closer and raise one of my Teluman scims. "And if you change it—even one bit—I will know."

"If I drum a false message, my commander will—he'll kill me."

"Is your commander a tall, pale-skinned Mask with a blond beard and a scar running down his chin to his neck?" At the drummer's nod, I reassure him. "He's dead. And, if you *don't* drum a false message, I'll gut you and throw you over the tower. Your choice."

The message orders the legion preparing to attack the Tribes back to a garrison forty miles from here and demands the order be carried out immediately. After the drummer is finished, I kill him. He had to have known it was coming. But still, I can't look him in the eyes as I do it.

My armor is disgusting, and I cannot bear the stench, so I shed it, steal clothes from the storeroom, and turn back to the Waiting Place. The closer I get, the more relieved I feel. The Tribes should have many hours before the Martials realize that the message they were given is false. My family will escape the Empire. And at last, I have the understanding I need to pass the ghosts through. To begin restoring the balance. It's about bleeding time.

My first clue that something is wrong—deeply wrong—comes when I approach the border wall. It should be high and gold, shimmering with power. Instead, it appears wan, almost patchy. I think to fix it, but the moment I am past the tree line, the ghosts' pain blasts into me, a barrage of memory and confusion. I make myself remember not *why* I killed all those Martials but how it felt. The way it deadened me. I push the Tribes and Mamie and Aubarit from my mind. Mauth rises now, tentative. I call to the closest ghost, who drifts forward.

"Welcome to the Waiting Place, the realm of ghosts," I say to him. "I am the Soul Catcher, and I am here to help you cross to the other side."

"I am dead?" the ghost whispers. "I thought this was a dream . . ."

The magic gives me an awareness of the ghosts that I did not have before, an insight into their lives, their needs. After a moment, I understand that this spirit needs forgiveness. But how do I offer it? How did Shaeva do so—and so quickly, with nothing but a thought?

The conundrum gives me pause, and at that exact moment, the ghosts' howling reaches a nadir. Quite suddenly I'm aware of something strange: a shift in the Forest. The land feels different. It *is* different.

After consulting the map in my head, I realize why. Someone's here— someone who shouldn't be here.

And whoever it is has found their way to the jinn grove.

XXXVIII: The Blood Shrike

I am hunched at my desk, deep in thought, when I feel a hand on my shoulder—a hand I nearly take off with the blade that jumps into my hand, until I recognize Harper's sea-green eyes.

"Don't do that again," I snarl at him, "unless you want to lose an appendage." The mess of pages on my desk tells of days spent obsessively poring over Alistar's reports. I stand, and my head spins. I might have missed a meal—or three. "What time is it?"

"Third bell before dawn, Shrike. Forgive me for disturbing you. Dex just sent a message."

"About time." It's been nearly four days since we heard anything, and I was starting to wonder if some misfortune had befallen my friend.

I hold the parchment to the lamp in Harper's hand. That is when I realize that he's shirtless and disheveled, every muscle in his body tense. His mouth is thin, and the calm that usually emanates from him is absent.

"What the hells is wrong?"

"Just read it."

> *Karkaun force of nearly fifty thousand gathering in Umbral Pass,*
> *led by Grimarr. Call up the legions. They are coming for Antium.*

"There's something else, Shrike," Avitas says. "I tried to decode the letter we found on Alistar, but she used disappearing ink. The only thing left by the time I got to it was the sign-off."

She. "Keris Veturia." Avitas nods, and I want to scream. "That traitorous bitch," I snarl. "She must have been meeting with Karkauns when she was at the Roost. Where the bleeding hells is Corporal Favrus?"

"Found him dead in his quarters. No wounds on him. Poison."

Keris had one of her assassins take him out, just like she had someone murder Captain Alistar. Knowing how badly she wants to be Empress, her intentions now are obvious: She didn't want us to know of Grímarr's approach. She wanted Emperor Marcus and me to look like fools—dangerous, incompetent fools. So what if a blood-hungry warlock lays siege to Antium? She knows that with reinforcements, we can destroy the Karkauns—though holding off a force of fifty thousand men will take its toll. Worse, she'll use the chaos created by a siege to destroy Marcus, Livia, and me. She'll beat back the Karkauns, be hailed as a hero, and get what she always wanted, what the Nightbringer has no doubt promised her: the throne.

And I cannot prove any of it. Even if I know, in my very bones, that this is her intent.

It did not have to be this way, Blood Shrike. Remember that, before the end.

"We need to tell the Emperor," I say. And somehow I need to convince him to get Livia out of the city. If Grímarr's force is coming here, there is no more dangerous a place for her. Antium will be chaos. And Keris thrives in chaos.

We are armed and locked in Emperor Marcus's war room within the hour. Runners fan out across the city, bringing in the Empire's generals, many of whom are also Paters of their Gens. A dozen maps are brought in, each laying out different sections of the terrain to the north.

"Why didn't we know about this?" asks General Crispin Rufius, the head of Gens Rufia, as he circles the room, cunning as a vulture. Marcus threw Crispin's brother over Cardium Rock months ago. I don't expect his support.

"Reports come in every day from these garrisons. If something was out of the ordinary, there are a dozen people who should have caught it."

Marcus tilts his head, as if listening to something the rest of us cannot hear. The Paters exchange a glance, and I try not to curse. Now is *not* the time for our emperor to start chatting with his dead brother. He mutters something, then nods. But when he does finally speak, he sounds perfectly calm.

"The reports were manipulated," Marcus says, "by someone who values their own interests over the Empire, no doubt." The implication is obvious, and even though I've no indication that Rufius is in any way involved in changing the reports, the rest of the men in the room look at him suspiciously. His face turns red.

"I am merely saying that this is highly irregular."

"It's done." I speak, a hand on my scim so that he remembers I lured his brother and the Paters of other allied Gens into Villa Aquilla, trapped them, and had them taken at scimpoint to Cardium Rock to die. "Now we reap the consequences. Whoever planned this wants the Empire weak. There is no greater weakness than infighting. You can continue to discuss *why* we didn't know about the Karkaun attack, or you can help us stop the bastards."

The room is silent, and Marcus, taking advantage of the moment, taps Umbral Pass, north of Antium. "Grímarr gathers his men just north of the pass," he says. "From there, it's a four-day ride to Antium on a swift horse, two weeks for an army."

For hours, we argue. Antium has six legions—thirty thousand men— guarding it. One general wants to send a legion out to stop Grímarr before he reaches the city. The captain of the city guard, my cousin Baristus Aquillus, volunteers to lead a smaller force. I pace in irritation. Every minute we don't make a decision is another minute that the Commandant gets closer to Antium, another minute that my sister's and nephew's lives are in danger from both Keris *and* the Karkauns.

As the Paters press Marcus, I expect his volatility to show. I wait for him to acknowledge the voice he hears. But for once, he appears his old self, as if the threat of war has brought back the cunning foe who plagued Elias and me during our years at Blackcliff.

By dawn, the generals have departed with new orders: to get the legions armed and ready to fight and to shore up Antium's defenses. The drums thunder ceaselessly, demanding aid from the governors of Silas and Estium. Meanwhile, Marcus calls up reserve soldiers, but he needn't have bothered. Antium's citizens are Martials through and through. Grímarr and his men savaged our port. At the news of another attack, hundreds of young men and women arrive at barracks across the city, volunteering for duty, hungry for revenge.

"My lord." I take the Emperor aside after the others leave. I wish there were a better time, but no one knows Marcus's mood from one moment to the next. And right now, he seems as sane as he's ever been. "There's the matter of your wife and heir."

Marcus's whole body goes still. He's listening to the voice that speaks to him—to Zak's ghost. I send a silent plea to the spirit to make our emperor see reason. "What of them?" he says.

"If there is a siege, this is the last place you'll want them to be. The Grain Moon is less than a month away. Livia is due then. I advise that you get her to safety, ideally in Silas or Estium."

"No."

"It's not just the siege that threatens," I say. "Keris will be here within days. She's already made one attempt on the Empress's life. She's angry. She will make another. We must thwart her *before* that happens. If she doesn't know where Livvy and your heir are, then she cannot hurt them."

"If I send my wife and unborn child out of Antium, people will think I fear those fur-wearing, woad-faced bastards." He doesn't lift his attention from the map before him, but every muscle in his body is bunched. He holds his temper by a thread. "The child should be born in Antium, in the Emperor's palace, with witnesses, so there are no questions of his parentage."

"We could do it quietly," I say, desperation creeping into my voice. I *must* secure a regency. I *must* not let any more harm come to my baby sister. I've failed enough on that score. "No one has to know she's gone. The city will be preparing for war. The Paters won't notice."

"You're suddenly very interested in the survival of my dynasty."

"Livia is the only sibling I have left," I say. "I don't want her to die. As for your dynasty, I am your Blood Shrike. I will not insult your intelligence by claiming to like you, my lord. I find you . . . difficult. But my fate and my sister's are tied to yours, and if your line fails, we both die. Please, get Livia and the child to safety." I take a deep breath. "I think it's what he would want."

I don't say Zacharias's name. Mentioning him is either brilliant or unforgivably stupid. Marcus finally looks up from the map. His jaw clenches, his fists bunch. I brace for the blow—

But then he hisses through his teeth, as if in sudden pain.

"Send her to my family," he says. "My parents are in Silas. No one is to know, especially not the Bitch of Blackcliff. If anything happens to my heir because of this, Shrike, it will be your head on a pike. After she's gone, I want you back here. You and I have something we need to do."

»«»«»

Clouds threaten on the horizon, heavy and low. I smell the storm approaching. Livvy needs to get on the road before it hits.

Faris has men positioned along the entire street, and as far as they know,
the Empress is leaving to visit an ailing aunt on the outskirts of the city. The
carriage will return with another woman dressed as Livvy by nightfall.

"Rallius and I can handle it, Shrike." Faris looks askance at the Black Guard
waiting at the end of the road—a dozen handpicked, hardened warriors.

"You are traveling with my only sister and the heir of the Empire," I say.
"I could send a legion with you and it wouldn't be enough."

"This is ridiculous," Livia says as I bundle her into the carriage. The first
raindrops begin to fall. "We will hold the city. *You* will hold the city."

"The Karkauns are coming, yes," I say. "But Keris is too. We nearly lost
you once because I wasn't wary enough of her. The *only* reason you're still
alive—"

"I know." My sister's voice is soft. She has not asked me about the healing—
about why I never healed her before. Perhaps she knows I do not wish to speak
of it.

"We cannot risk it." I harden myself. "We cannot risk the future of the
Empire. Go. Watch your back. Trust Faris and Rallius and no one else.
When it's safe again, I'll send for you."

"I *won't* go." Livia grabs my hand. "I will not leave you here."

I think of my father. His sternness. I am Mater of Gens Aquilla now, and
it is the future of the Gens—the future of my people—that I must protect.
"You will go." I pull my fingers from her grip. Thunder rumbles, closer than
I thought it would be. "You will remain hidden. And you will do it with
the grace with which you have done everything else, Empress Livia Aquilla
Farrar. Loyal to the end. Say it."

My sister bites her lip, her pale eyes glowing with anger. But then she nods, as I knew she would. "Loyal to the end," she says.

By the time the storm has broken over Antium, Livia is well away from the capital. But my relief is short-lived. *You and I have something we need to do.* I will not soon forget the abuse that Marcus inflicted on Livia. I think back to a year ago, during the Trials. To the nightmares that plagued me of Marcus as Emperor and me doing his bidding. What does he have planned for me now?

XXXIX: Laia

My blood transforms to lead at the sound of the jinn and their strange, layered voice. It throbs with cunning and rage. But beneath it flows a river of almost imperceptible sorrow, just like with the Nightbringer.

"Where is Elias?" I know they will not tell me anything of worth, but I ask anyway, hoping that some response will be better than silence.

We will tell you, they croon. *But you must come to us.*

"I'm not a fool." I rest my hand on my dagger, though doing so serves no practical purpose. "I know your king, remember? You're as slippery as he is."

No tricks, Laia, daughter of Mirra. Unlike you, we do not fear the truth, for it is the truth that shall free us from our prison. And the truth shall free you from yours. Come to us.

Elias has never trusted the jinn. I shouldn't either—I know this. But Elias is not here. Nor are the ghosts. And something is very wrong, otherwise he *would* be here. I need to get across the Forest. There is no other path to Antium—to the Blood Shrike—to the last piece of the Star.

Standing here agonizing over it isn't going to do me any good. I make my way west, following the compass in my head, moving as swiftly as I can while it is still light out. Perhaps Elias is only away for a short time. Perhaps he will return.

Or perhaps he doesn't know I'm here. Perhaps something has happened to him.

Or, the jinn whisper, *he doesn't care. He has greater things to worry about than you.* They do not say it with malice. They simply state a fact, which makes it all the more chilling.

Our king showed you, did he not? You saw it in his eyes: Elias walking away. Elias choosing duty over you. He will not help you, Laia. But we can. If you allow us, we will show you the truth.

"Why would you help me? You know why I'm here. You know what I'm trying to do."

The truth shall free us from our prison, the jinn say again. *As it will free you from yours. Let us help you.*

"Stay away from me," I say. The jinn fall silent. Do I dare hope that they will leave me be? A wind pushes at my back, ruffling my hair and pulling at my clothes. I jump, spinning, seeking the shadows for enemies. It is just wind.

But as the night drags on, I flag. And when I can walk no more, I have no choice but to stop. A broad tree trunk serves as my shelter, and I hunker against it with my daggers in hand. The Forest is strangely peaceful, and as soon as my body makes contact with the earth, the tree, I feel calmer, like I'm in a familiar place. It is not the familiarity of a well-traveled road. It is different. Older. In my very blood.

In the darkest hour of the night, sleep claims me, and, with it, dreams. I find myself flying over the Waiting Place, skimming the treetops, incensed and yet terrified. *My people. They are imprisoning my people.* All I know is that I must get to them. I must reach them, if only I can . . .

I awake to the overwhelming sense that something is wrong. The trees that surround me are not those I fell asleep beside. These trees are as wide as an Adisan avenue, and they glow an eerie red, as if on fire from within.

"Welcome to our prison, Laia of Serra."

The Nightbringer materializes from the shadows, speaking almost tenderly. He brushes his strangely glowing hands against the tree trunks as he circles them. They whisper a word at him, a word I cannot make out, but he silences them with his touch.

"You—*you* brought me here?"

"My brethren brought you. Be thankful they left you intact. They longed to tear you into a thousand pieces."

"If you could kill me, you'd have done it already," I say. "The Star protects me."

"Indeed, my love."

I recoil. "Don't you call me that. You don't know what love is."

His back was to me, but he turns now, immobilizing me with that eerily bright stare. "Ah, but I do." His bitterness curdles the very air, it is so ancient. "For I was born to love. It was my calling, my purpose. Now it is my curse. I know love better than any other creature alive. Certainly better than a girl who gives her heart to whoever happens by."

"Tell me where Elias is."

"In such a hurry, Laia. Just like your mother. Sit with my brethren a while. They have so few visitors."

"You know nothing of my mother and father. Tell me where Elias is."

My gorge rises as the Nightbringer speaks again. His voice feels too close, like he is forcing an intimacy I have not granted.

"What will you do if I do not tell you where Elias is? Leave?"

"That is exactly what I'll do," I say, but my voice is weaker than I wish it to be. My legs feel strange. Numb. Skies, I feel ill. I lean forward, and when my hands touch the earth, a jolt rolls through me. The word that comes to my mind is not the one I expect. *Home.*

"The Waiting Place sings to you. It knows you, Laia of Serra."

"Wh—why?"

The Nightbringer laughs, and it is echoed by the jinn in the grove until it feels like it is coming from all sides. "It is the source of all magic in this world. We are connected to it—through it—to each other."

There is a lie here somewhere. I can sense it. But there is truth too, and I cannot parse the fine lines between them.

"Tell me, *love*." The word sounds obscene in his mouth. "Have you had visions after using your magic?"

My blood goes cold. The woman. The cell. "You sent those visions? And you—you've been watching me."

"In truth, you shall find freedom. Let me free you, Laia of Serra."

"I don't need your truth." I want him out of my head, but he is as devious and slippery as an eel. Together with his brethren, he twists around my mind, squeezing tighter and tighter. Why did I let myself sleep? Why did I let the jinn take me? *Get up, Laia! Escape!*

"You cannot escape the truth, Laia. You deserve to know, child. It has been kept from you for far too long. Where to begin? Perhaps where you began: with your mother."

"No!"

The air before me wavers, and I do not know if the vision is real or in my head. My mother stands before me, big with child. *Me*, I realize. She paces back and forth outside a cottage as Father speaks to her. The thickly forested mountains of Marinn rise in the distance.

"We must go back, Jahan," she says. "As soon as the child is born—"

"And bring him or her with us?" My father digs his hand into the thick, unruly hair that I inherited. Laughter rings out behind him: Darin, fat-cheeked and blissfully unaware, sits with a seven-year-old Lis. My heart twists at the sight of my sister. I have not seen her face in so long. Unlike Darin, she watches everything with careful eyes, her gaze flicking back and forth between Mother and Father. She is a child whose happiness is gauged by the strange weather between her parents, sometimes sunny but more often a gale.

"We can't expose them to that kind of danger. Mirra—"

Darkness. Smell comes to me before light. Apricot orchards and hot sands. I am in Serra. My mother appears again, in leathers this time, a bow and quiver slung across her back. Her light hair is pulled back into a topknot, her stare fierce as she knocks upon a familiar weathered door. My father kneels behind her, holding me against one shoulder and Darin against the other. I am four years old. Darin is six. Father kisses our faces over and over and whispers to us, though I cannot hear his words.

When the door opens, Nan stands there, hands on her hips, so angry that I want to cry. *Don't be angry,* I want to tell her. *You will miss her later. You will regret your anger. You will wish you had welcomed her with open arms.* Nan catches sight of my father, of Darin, of me. She takes a step toward us.

Darkness. And then an eerily familiar place. A dank room. A light-haired woman within—a woman I finally recognize: my mother. And the room is not a room. It is a prison cell.

"The truth will free you from your illusions, Laia of Serra," the Nightbringer whispers. "It will free you from the burden of hope."

"I don't want it." The image of my mother won't go away. "I don't want to be free. Just tell me where Elias is," I beg, a prisoner in my own mind. "Let me go."

The Nightbringer is silent. Torchlight bobs distantly, and the door to my mother's cell opens. Mother's bruises, her wounds, her hacked hair and emaciation, are suddenly illuminated.

"Are you ready to cooperate?" The winter in that voice is unmistakable.

"I will never cooperate with you." My mother spits at the feet of Keris Veturia. The Commandant is younger but just as monstrous. A high-pitched scream stabs into my ears. The scream of a child. I know who it is. Skies, I know. Lis. My sister.

I writhe and scream myself to try to drown her out. I cannot see this. I cannot hear it. But the Nightbringer and his brethren hold me fast.

"She doesn't have your strength," Keris says to Mother. "Nor does your husband. He broke down. Begged for death. Begged for *your* death. No loyalty. He told me everything."

"He—he would never."

Keris enters the cell. "How little we know of people until we watch them break. Until we strip them down to their smallest, weakest selves. I learned that lesson long ago, Mirra of Serra. And so I will teach you. I will lay you bare. And I don't even have to touch you to do it."

Another scream, this one deeper—a man's voice.

"They ask about you," the Commandant says. "They wonder why you let them suffer. One way or another, Mirra, you will give me the names of your supporters in Serra." There is an unholy joy in Keris's eyes. "I will bleed your family until you do."

As she walks away, my mother roars at her, throwing herself against the door of her cell. Shadows move across the floor. A day passes, another. All the while, my mother listens to the sounds of Lis and Father suffering. *I* listen. She grows more crazed. She tries to break out. She tries to trick the guards. She tries to murder them. Nothing works.

The cell door opens, and the Kauf guards drag my father in. I scarcely recognize him. He is unconscious as they toss him in a corner. Lis is next, and I cannot look at what Keris has done to her. She was just a child, only twelve. *Skies, Mother, how did you stand it? How did you not go utterly mad?*

My sister shivers and curls up in the corner. Her silence, the slackness of her jaw, the emptiness in her blue eyes—they will haunt me until the day I die.

Mother takes Lis in her arms. Lis doesn't react. Their bodies sway together as Mother rocks her.

> *A star she came*
> *Into my home*
> *And lit it bright with glo-ry*

Lis closes her eyes. My mother curls around her, her hands moving toward my sister's face, caressing it. There are no tears in Mother's eyes. There is nothing at all.

> *Her laughter like*
> *A gilded song*
> *A raincloud sparrow's sto-ry*

My mother puts one of her hands on top of Lis's head, shorn now, and another on her chin.

> *And when she sleeps*
> *It's like the sun*
> *Has faded, gone so cold, see.*

A crack sounds, softer than in my visions. It is a small noise, like the breaking of a bird's wing. Lis slips lifeless to the floor, her neck broken by our mother's hand.

I think I scream. I think that sound, that shriek, is me. In this world? In some other? I cannot get out. I cannot escape this place. I cannot escape what I see.

"Mirra?" my father whispers. "Lis . . . where is . . ."

"Sleeping, my love." Mother's voice is calm, distant. She crawls to my father, pulling his head into her lap. "She's sleeping now."

"I—I tried, but I don't know how much longer—"

"Do not fear, my love. Neither of you will suffer anymore."

When she breaks my father's neck, it is louder. The quiet that follows sinks into my bones. It is the death of hope, sudden and unheralded.

Still, the Lioness does not cry.

The Commandant enters, looks between the bodies. "You're strong, Mirra," she says, and there is something like admiration in her pale eyes. "Stronger than my mother was. I would have let your child live, you know."

My mother's head jerks up. Despair suffuses every inch of her. "It wouldn't have been a life," she whispers.

"Perhaps," Keris says. "But can you be sure?"

Time shifts again. The Commandant holds coals in a gloved hand as she approaches my mother, who is tied to a table.

Far back in my mind, a memory surfaces. *Ever been tied to a table while hot coals burned into your throat?* Cook said those words to me long ago, in a kitchen at Blackcliff. Why did Cook say those words to me?

Time speeds. Mother's hair goes from blonde to pure snow white. The Commandant carves scars into her face—horrible, disfiguring scars—until it is no longer the face of my mother, no longer the face of the Lioness but instead the face of—

Ever had your face carved up with a dull knife while a Mask poured salt water into your wounds?

No. I do not believe it. Cook must have experienced the same thing as my mother. Perhaps it was the Commandant's particular way of getting rebel fighters to talk. Cook is an old woman, and my mother wouldn't be—she would still be relatively young.

But Cook never acted like an old woman, did she? She was strong. The scars are the same. The hair.

And her eyes. I never looked closely at Cook's eyes. But I remember them now: deep set and dark blue—darker still for the shadows that lurked within.

But it cannot be. *It cannot.*

"It is true, Laia," the Nightbringer says, and my very soul shudders, for I know he tells no lies. "Your mother lives. You know her. And now, you are free."

XL: Elias

How did someone get all the way to the jinn grove without me knowing? The border walls should have kept outsiders away. But not, I realize, if they're thin and weak. Ghosts push against one spot, far to the east, and I slow down. Do I shore up the wall? Move the ghosts? Their agitation is like nothing I've seen before, almost feral in its intensity.

But if there is a human in the grove, skies only know what they might be suffering at the hands of the jinn.

I head for the interloper, and Mauth pulls at me, his weight like an anvil chained to my legs. Ahead of me, ghosts attempt to block my path, a thick cloud that I can't see through.

We have her, Elias. The jinn speak, and the ghosts stop their wailing. The sudden silence is unnerving. It's as if all the Forest listens.

We have her, Elias, and we have torn her mind to shreds.

"Who?" I drag myself away from the ghosts, ignoring their cries and Mauth's pull. "Who do you have?"

Come and see, usurper.

Did they somehow capture Mamie? Or Afya? Dread grows in me like a weed, speeding my windwalking. Their machinations have already led to the suffering of Aubarit's Tribe. To Afya and Gibran being possessed by ghosts. To Mamie losing her brother, and hundreds of Tribespeople dying. The Blood Shrike is too far away for them to hurt. Of all those I love, only the Shrike and one other have been spared their predations.

But they cannot possibly have Laia. She is in Adisa, hunting for a way to stop the Nightbringer. *Faster, Elias, faster.* I battle Mauth's draw, tearing through the increasingly frenzied ghosts until I reach the jinn grove.

At first, it looks as it always does. Then I see her, crumpled on the earth. I recognize the patchy gray cloak. I gave it to her long ago, on a night when I never could have imagined how much she'd one day mean to me.

In the trees to the north, a shadow watches. *Nightbringer!* I leap for him, but he disappears, gone so fast that if not for his laugh on the wind, I'd have thought I'd imagined him.

I am at Laia's side in two steps, hardly believing she is real. The earth shudders more violently than it ever has before. Mauth is angry. But it does not matter to me. What in ten bleeding hells have the jinn done to her?

"Laia," I call to her, but when I look into her face, her gold eyes are far-away, her lips parted dully. "Laia?" I tip her head toward me. "Listen to me. Whatever the Nightbringer said to you, whatever he and his ilk are trying to convince you of, it's a trick. A *lie*—"

We do not lie. We told her the truth, and the truth has freed her. She will never hope again.

I need to get her mind out of their clutches.

How can you, usurper, when you cannot lay your hands on the magic?

"You tell me what the hells you've done to her!"

As you wish. Seconds later, my body is as rooted to the grove as Laia's is, and the jinn show me her purpose in coming through the Waiting Place. She must get to Antium, to the Blood Shrike, to the ring. She must stop the Nightbringer.

But her mission is forgotten as a fire rages in her mind, leaving her lost, wandering in a prison, forced to watch what happened to her family over and over.

We show you her story so that you can suffer with her, Elias, the jinn say. *Cry out your rage, won't you? Cry out your uselessness. The sound is so sweet.*

My scims will do nothing against this. Threats will do nothing. The jinn are in her head.

A powerful yank from Mauth nearly knocks me to my knees, so sharp that I gasp from the pain. Something is happening out in the Waiting Place. I can feel it. Something is happening to the border.

Leave her, then, Elias. Go and attend to your duty.

"I will not leave her!"

You have no choice—not if you wish the world of the living to survive.

"I will not!" My voice is raw with rage and failure. "I will not let you torment her to death, even if stopping you tears my own body to shreds. All the world can burn, but I will not simply leave her to suffer."

All things have a price, Elias Veturius. The price of saving her will haunt you for all your days. Will you pay it?

"Just let her go. Please. I—I'm sorry for your pain, your hurt. But she did not cause it. It's not her fault. Mauth, help me." Why am I begging? Why, when I know it will do no good? Only mercilessness can help me. Only abandoning my humanity. Abandoning Laia.

But I can't do it. I can't pretend that I don't love her.

"Come back to me, Laia." Her body is heavy in my arms, hair tangled, and I push it back from her face. "Forget them and their lies. That's all they are. Come back."

Yes, Elias, the jinn purr. *Pour your love into her. Pour your heart into her.*

I wish they would shut the hells up. "Come back to the world. Wherever they have taken you, whatever memory they have locked you in doesn't matter as much as you coming back. Your people need you. Your brother needs you. *I* need you."

As I speak, it's as if I can see into her thoughts. I can see the jinn clawing at her mind. They are strange, warped beings of smokeless flame that are nothing like the beautiful, graceful creatures I saw in the city. Laia tries to fight them, but she weakens.

"You are strong, Laia. And you are needed here." Her cheek feels like ice. "You have much yet to do."

Laia's eyes are glazed over, and I shudder. I hold her now. I call to her. But she will grow old and die, while I will live on. She is the blink of an eye. And I am an age.

But I can accept that. I can survive long years without her if I know that at least she *had* a chance at life. I'd give up my time with her—I would—if only she would wake.

Please. Please come back.

Her body jerks once, and for one heart-stopping moment, I think she is dead.

Then she opens her eyes, staring at me with bewilderment. *Thank the bleeding skies.* "They're gone, Laia," I say. "But we have to get you out of here." Her mind will be fragile after what the jinn just put her through. Any more pushing from the ghosts or the jinn would feel torturous.

"I can't—can't walk. Could you—"

"Put your arms around my neck," I say, and I windwalk out of the grove with Laia held close. Mauth yanks at me futilely, and the earth of the Waiting Place shakes and cracks. I reach out to the borders; the pressure is immense. The strain on them makes me break into a sweat. I need to get Laia out of here so I can corral the ghosts—get them away from the edges of the Waiting Place, lest they break free.

"Elias," Laia whispers. "Are . . . are you real? Are you a trick too?"

"No." I touch my forehead to hers. "No, love. I'm real. You're real."

"What's wrong with this place?" She shivers. "It's so full, as if it's about to burst. I can feel it."

"Just the ghosts," I say. "Nothing I can't handle." *I hope.* Flat patches of rolling grassland appear through the trees ahead: the Empire.

The border feels even weaker now than it did when I first passed through it. Many of the ghosts have followed me, and they press against the glowing barrier, their cries rising eagerly as if they sense its weakness.

I go well beyond the tree line and set Laia down. The trees sway back and forth behind me, a frantic dance. I must return. But for just this one moment, I let myself look at her. The messy cloud of her hair, her worn boots, the tiny cuts on her face from the Forest, the way her hands grip the dagger I gave her.

"The jinn," she whispers. "They—they told me the truth. But the truth is . . ." She shakes her head.

"The truth is ugly," I say. "The truth of our parents uglier still. But we are not them, Laia."

"She's out there, Elias," Laia says, and I know she speaks of her mother. Of Cook. "Somewhere. I can't—I—" She slips back into the memory again, and though the Forest seethes behind me, it will have done me no good to get Laia out of there if she ends up in the grasp of the jinn again. I take her shoulders, stroke her face. I make her look at me.

"Forgive her, if you can," I say. "Remember that fate is never what we think it will be. Your mother—my mother—we can never understand their torments. Their hurts. We may suffer the consequences of their mistakes and their sins, but we should not carry them on our hearts. We don't deserve that."

"Will it always be chaos for us, Elias? Will things never be normal?"

Her eyes clear as she looks at me, and she is released, for a moment, from what she saw in the Forest. "Will we ever take a walk by the moonlight, or spend an afternoon making jam or making . . ."

Love. My body turns to fire just thinking about it.

"I had dreams about you," she whispers. "We were together—"

"It wasn't a dream." I pull her close. It kills me that she doesn't remember. I wish she could. I wish she could hold on to that day the way I do. "I was there, and you were there. And it was a perfect slice of time. It won't always be like this." I say it like I believe it. But within my own heart, something has shifted. I feel different. Colder. The change is great enough that I speak even more adamantly, hoping that by saying what I want to feel, I will bring it to life. "We will find a way, Laia. Somehow. But if . . . if I change . . . if I seem different, remember that I love you. No matter what happens to me. Say you'll remember, please—"

"Your eyes . . ." She looks up at me, and my breath catches at the intensity in her gaze. "They—they're darker. Like Shaeva's."

"I can't stay. I'm sorry. I have to go back. I have to attend to the ghosts. But I will see you again. I vow it. Hurry—get to Antium."

"Wait." She stands, still unsteady on her feet. "Don't go. Please. Don't leave me here."

"You're strong," I say. "You are Laia of Serra. You are not the Lioness. Her legacy—her sins—they don't belong to you any more than Keris's legacy belongs to me."

"What did you say to me?" Laia asks. "That night before you left months ago, when we were headed to Kauf. I was sleeping in the wagon with Izzi. What did you say?"

"I said, *You are—*"

But Mauth has lost patience. I am wrested back to the Waiting Place, back to Mauth's side, with a force that rattles my bones.

I will find you, Laia. I will find a way. This is not our end. I scream it in my mind. But as soon as I get into the Waiting Place, the thought is dashed from my consciousness. The borders are bending—breaking. I go to reinforce them, but I am a cork in the face of a dam breaking.

All things have a price, Elias Veturius. The jinn speak again, an inexorable truth in their voice. *We warned you.*

A roar cleaves the Waiting Place, a ripping that seems to come from the bowels of the earth. The ghosts scream, their high keen rising as they throw themselves against the border. I have to stop them. They're too close. They'll break free.

Too late, usurper. Too late.

A collective howl goes up, and the ghosts of the Waiting Place, the tortured souls who are my sworn duty, break free of the border and pour into the world of the living, their shrieks like living death carried on the wind.

XLI: The Blood Shrike

"I'm not going to the Augurs," I say to Marcus. I remember well what Cain told me just weeks ago. *I will see you once more, before your end.* "You don't understand, they—"

"Grow a *bleeding* spine, Shrike." Marcus grabs my arm and begins to drag me from the throne room. "Those eerie bastards scare everyone. We have an invasion to worry about, and they can see the future. You're coming with me to their foul little cave. Unless you want to find out if you really *can* heal your sister's shattered kneecaps."

"Damn you—"

He backhands me and grimaces, grabbing his head. I wipe the blood from my mouth and look around as he mutters to himself. The throne room is empty, but there are still guards nearby.

"Pull yourself together," I hiss. "We don't need Keris hearing about this."

Marcus takes a steadying breath and glowers at me.

"Shut it." The softness of his growl does nothing to lessen its menace. "And move."

The pilgrims usually clogging the trail to Mount Videnns have fled, ordered back down to the city to prepare for Grímarr's approach. The path up to the Augurs' cave is empty but for Marcus, me, and the dozen Masks who serve as Marcus's personal guard. The entire way, I try to leash my rage. I must not act on it. As much as I hate them, they are the holy men of the Empire. Hurting one could lead to horrible consequences, and if something happens to me, then Livia and her son go unprotected.

I curse myself. Even now, even when I *loathe* them, some part of me is still trained to respect them. The push and pull of it makes me sick to my stomach. *Just get Marcus up there and let him do the talking. Don't engage. Don't ask questions. Don't let them say anything to you. Tell them you don't want to hear whatever it is they have to say.*

The storm that has raged all morning squats over the mountains, soaking us and turning the path to the Augurs' home into a treacherous, slippery death trap. By the time we make our way across the wide rock bowl that leads to the cave, we are covered in mud and cuts, which puts Marcus in an even fouler mood than usual.

The Augurs' cave is dark, without a hint of life, and I briefly hold out hope that the seers will not allow us within. It is well-known that they can keep out whomever they wish to.

But as we approach the mouth of the cave, blue light flares, and a shadow detaches from the rock, red eyes visible even at a distance. When we draw closer, the shadow speaks. It is the same Augur who let me in last time.

"Emperor Marcus Farrar. Blood Shrike," she says. "You are welcome here. Your men, however, must remain behind."

Like the last time I came here, the Augur walks me down a long tunnel that glows sapphire from blue-fire lamps. I grip my scims as I think back to that day. *First you will be unmade. First you will be broken.*

I was still Helene Aquilla then. Now I am someone new. Though my mental shield didn't work against the Nightbringer, I use it anyway. If the red-eyed fiends want to root around in my head, they should at least know they aren't welcome.

When we get deeper into the mountain, another Augur awaits us, one I cannot name. But from Marcus's sharp intake of breath, it's clear the Emperor knows her.

"Artan." Marcus says the name the same way I snarl Cain's.

"Long have the emperors of the Martials come to the Augurs in times of need," Artan says. "You seek counsel, Emperor Marcus. I am honor bound to offer it. Sit, please. I will speak with you." She gestures to a low bench before clearing her throat and glancing at me. "Alone."

The same woman who escorted us in takes my arm and guides me away. She does not speak as we walk. Distantly, I hear the drip of water and then what sounds like the ping of steel. It echoes again and again, a strange and incongruent tattoo.

We enter a circular cavern, black gems glimmering along its walls, and Cain steps from the shadows. Without thinking, I reach for my blade.

"Nay, Shrike." Cain lifts a withered hand, and my own freezes. "There is no threat here."

I force my hand away from my scim, casting about for something—anything—to distract me from my rage.

"What's that sound?" I say of the strange *ping-ping-ping*. "It's irritating."

"Just the caves singing their stories," Cain says. "A few are filled with crystal, others with water. Many are as tiny as houses, others are large enough to hold a city. But always, they sing. Some days we can hear the horns of the riverboats leaving Delphinium."

"Delphinium is hundreds of miles away," I say. Bleeding hells. I knew there were caves and tunnels under the city, but I didn't know that the Augurs' caves were so extensive. The land to the west of here is solid rock, the only caves inhabited by bears and wildcats. I assumed the mountains to the east are the same.

Cain watches me thoughtfully. "You are much changed, Blood Shrike. Your thoughts are closed."

Satisfaction courses through me—I'll have to tell Harper.

"Did the *Meherya* teach you, as he did the Farrars?" At my mystified look, Cain clarifies. "You refer to him as the Nightbringer."

"No," I snap, and then, "Why do you call him *Meherya*? Is that his name?"

"His name, his history, his birthright, his curse. The truth of all creatures, man or jinn, lies in their name. The Nightbringer's name was his making. And it will be his unmaking." He tilts his head. "Did you come to ask about the Nightbringer, Blood Shrike?"

"I have no desire to be here," I say. "Marcus ordered my presence."

"Ah. Let us make civil conversation then. Your sister—she is well? Soon to be a mother, of course."

"If the Commandant doesn't kill her first," I say. "If she survives childbirth." And even though I do not wish to, I seek the answer to those questions in his eyes. I find nothing.

He paces around the cave, and unwillingly I fall into step with him.

"The Tribespeople say that the heavens live under the feet of the mother," he says. "So great is their sacrifice. And indeed no one suffers in war more than the mother. This war will be no different."

"Are you saying Livia is going to suffer?" I want to shake the answer from him. "She's safe now."

Cain fixes me with his stare. "No one is safe. Have you not yet learned that lesson, Blood Shrike?" Though he sounds merely curious, I sense an insult in his words, and my fingers inch toward my war hammer.

"You wish to cause me pain," Cain says. "But already, my every breath is torture. Long ago, I took something that did not belong to me. And I—and my kin—have spent every moment since paying for it."

At my utter lack of sympathy, he sighs. "Soon enough, Blood Shrike," he says, "you will see my brethren and me brought low. And you shall need no hammer nor blade, for we shall undo ourselves. The time to atone for our sins approaches." His attention shifts to the hallway behind me. "As it does for your emperor."

A moment later Marcus appears, face grim. I nod a curt goodbye to Cain. I hope I never bleeding see him again.

As we walk out of the tunnel and down to our men, clustered between boulders to escape the lashing rain, Marcus looks over at me.

"You will be in charge of the defense of the city," Marcus says. "I will tell the generals."

"Most of them are far more seasoned than I am at dealing with marauding armies, my lord."

"The strength of the butcher bird is the strength of the Empire, for she is the torch against the night. Your line will rise or fall with her hammer; your fate will rise or fall with her will."

When Marcus looks at me, I know for an instant how Cain must have felt when I looked at him. Pure hate radiates from the Emperor. And yet he is strangely diminished. He is not telling me everything the Augur said.

"Did—did the Augur say anything el—"

"That hag hasn't been wrong yet," Marcus says. "Not about me. Not about you. So whether you like it or not, Shrike, Antium's defense is in your hands."

It is deep night by the time we approach the northern gates to the capital. Teams of Plebeians fortify the walls, a legionnaire bellowing at them to work faster. The acrid reek of tar fills the air as soldiers lug buckets of it up ladders to the top of our defenses. Fletchers transport wagonloads of arrows divided into tubs for the archers to grab easily. Though the moon is high, it seems as if there is not a single sleeping soul in the city. Vendors hawk food and ale, and Scholar slaves carry water to those working.

This will not last. When the Karkauns come, the civilians will be forced to retreat into their homes to wait and see whether their brothers and fathers, uncles and cousins, sons and grandsons can hold the city. But in this moment, as all the people come together, unafraid, my heart swells. Come what may, I am glad I am here to fight with my people. And I am glad I am the Blood Shrike charged with leading the Martials to victory.

And I will lead them to victory—over the Karkauns *and* the Commandant.

Marcus appears to notice none of this. He is lost in thought, striding forward without looking at all those who labor for his empire.

"My lord," I say. "Perhaps take a moment to acknowledge the workers."

"We have a bleeding war to plan, you fool."

"Wars succeed or fail based on the men who fight them," I remind him. "Take one moment. They will remember."

He regards me with irritation before breaking away from his men to speak with a group of aux soldiers. I watch from a distance, and from the corner of my eye I notice a group of children. One—a girl—wears a wooden, silver-painted mask over her face as she fights a slightly smaller girl, who is presumably posing as a Barbarian. The clack of their wooden swords is just one more instrument in the frantic symphony of a city preparing for war.

The masked girl spins under the other's scim before delivering a kick to her bottom and pinning her with a boot.

I smile and she looks up, pulling off her mask hastily. She offers a clumsy salute. The other girl—who I realize must be a younger sister—stares open-mouthed.

"Elbow up." I fix the girl's arm. "Hand perfectly straight, and the tip of your middle finger should be at the center of your forehead. Keep your eyes on the space between you and me. Try not to blink too much." When she's got it, I nod. "Good," I say. "Now you look like a Mask."

"Chryssa says I'm not big enough." She looks to her still-staring sister. "But I'm going to fight the Karkauns when they come."

"Then we'll surely defeat them." I look between the girls. "Take care of each other," I say. "Always. Promise me."

As I walk away, I wonder if they will remember the vow they made me ten years from now, twenty. I wonder if they'll still be alive. I think of Livvy, far away, I hope. Safe. That fact is the only thing that gives me comfort. We will defeat Grímarr's army. We are the superior fighting force. But the warlock is a clever adversary and it will be a hard battle. Skies know what will happen in that chaos. Cain's words haunt me: *No one is safe.* Curse the Commandant for bringing this upon us out of her greed. Curse her for caring more about becoming Empress than about the Empire she seeks to rule.

Marcus shouts at me to get moving. When we return to the palace, it is a hive of activity. Horses, men, weaponry, and wagons clog the gates as the palace guards sandbag the outer walls and hammer in planks across the entrance gates. With so many people coming in and out, it will be difficult to keep the place secure against the Commandant's spies—and her assassins.

Come for Marcus, Keris, I think. *Do my work for me. But you'll never get your hands on my sister or her child again. Not while I live and breathe.*

As we approach the throne room, there's a buzz in the air. I think one of the courtiers whispers Keris's name, but Marcus walks too fast for me to linger and listen. The throne room doors fly open as Marcus strides toward them. A sea of Illustrian nobles mills within, waiting to hear what the Emperor will say about the approaching army. I feel no fear in the air, only a grim sense of determination and a strange tension, as if everyone knows a secret they aren't willing to share.

The source of it becomes apparent moments later, as the waves of Illustrians part to reveal a small blonde woman in bloodied armor standing beside a tall, equally blonde woman heavy with child.

The Commandant has returned to Antium.

And she has brought my sister with her.

XLII: Laia

The day Mother gave me her armlet, I was five. Nan's curtains were drawn. I could not see the moon. Pop must have been there. Darin, Lis, and Father too. But I remember Mother's crooked smile most clearly. Her lapis eyes and long fingers. I sat in her lap trying to tuck my cold feet into her warm shirt. *You're not Laia*, she'd said. *You're an efrit of the north trying to turn me into an icicle.*

Someone called out to her. *Time to go.* She whispered to me to keep the armlet safe. Then she wrapped her arms around me, and though she squeezed too tightly, I did not care. I wanted to pull her into me. I wanted to keep her.

We will see each other again. She kissed my hands, my forehead. *I swear it.*

When?

Soon.

The courtyard gate creaked as she slipped through it. She smiled back at me and Darin, huddled between our grandparents. Then she stepped into the night, and the darkness swallowed her up.

«‹«

I reel from what the Nightbringer showed me, from the crawling feeling of him and his kin all over my mind. I hold the armlet Elias gave me and I do not let go. I'm free of the jinn now.

As I stumble away from the Forest, as the voices of the ghosts peak, I move more swiftly. *The Dead will rise, and none can survive.* Shaeva's prophecy rings in my mind. Something has gone terribly wrong within the Waiting Place, and I need to get as far away as possible.

I run, trying to remember again what I am meant to do, trying to get the Nightbringer's voice out of my head.

Musa marked a village on my map. I must get there, meet his contact, and get to Antium. But before then, I need to pull the shards of my mind off the ground and put them back together. I cannot change what is done. I can only move forward and hope to the skies that before I meet Cook again, I've made my peace with what she did to Father and Lis. With what she endured. With what she sacrificed for the Resistance.

I make my way northwest. A pair of hills rises a few miles ahead, with a dip in the middle that should shelter the village of Myrtium. Musa's contact is meant to await me there. Since it's Martial territory, I should use my magic to become invisible. But I cannot bear the thought of more visions, of seeing more pain and suffering.

I cannot bear the thought of seeing *her*. I think of Darin. Did he know about what Mother did? Is that why he tensed up every time I spoke of her? I wish to the skies that he was here now.

Rattled though I may be, I have the wits to wait until dark before I creep toward the village proper. The summer night is warm, the only noise a gentle breeze blowing in off a nearby creek. I feel louder than a horse with bells on as I slink along the walls.

The inn is the central building in the village, and I watch for a long time before getting closer. Musa told me little of his contact, for fear that the knowledge could be extracted by our enemies if I am caught. But I know that he is not a Martial and that he will be waiting within the inn, by the fire. I am to cloak myself, whisper to him that I've arrived, and then follow his instructions. He will take me to the Mariner Embassy in Antium, where I'll get maps of the palace and the city, information about the Blood Shrike and where she will be—everything I'll need to get in, get the ring, and get the hells out.

Gold light spills out into the streets from the inn's wide, rounded windows, and the taproom is full, with agitated conversation drifting out in bits.

"If the Shrike can't stop them—"

"How the bleeding hells is she supposed to stop them with only—"

"—city will never be taken, those pigs don't know how to fight—"

I keep to the shadows, trying to see into the inn from across the street. It is impossible. I must get closer.

The inn has a series of smaller side windows, and the alleys around it are quiet, so I skitter across the square, hoping no one sees me, and climb onto a crate, peeking through one of the windows. It offers a decent view of the room, but so far, everyone here is a Martial.

I peer past the barkeep, through the thicket of serving maids pouring out drinks and lads delivering plates of food. The long bar is crowded with villagers, all of whom seem to be talking at once. How the hells am I supposed to find him in this mess? I'll *have* to cloak myself in invisibility. I have no choice.

"Hello, girl."

I nearly jump out of my skin. When the hooded figure appears behind me, when her voice rasps a greeting, all I can think is that the Nightbringer has somehow followed me here, to this tiny village. That he is playing more tricks on my mind.

But the figure steps forward and lowers her hood to reveal moon-white hair that never belonged on her and midnight-blue eyes too shadowed to be familiar and violently scarred skin that I never noticed was unwrinkled until now. Her fingers are stained a deep, strange titian. Her diminutive height disorients me. All these years, I thought she was tall.

"Girl?"

I reach out a hand to touch her and she shies away. *How can this be real? How can I be staring into Mother's face, after so long?*

But of course, it *is* real. And the Nightbringer somehow knew she would be waiting—why else torment me with her true identity? He could have shown me who she was weeks ago, any time I used my invisibility. But he didn't. Because he knew this is when it would hit me the hardest.

Part of me wants to run to her, feel her hands on my skin, hold them in my own. I wish Darin were here. I wish Izzi were here.

But the part of me that thinks *Mother* is stifled to silence by the darker part of me that screams *Liar!* I want to shout and curse at her and ask her every question that has plagued me since the moment I learned who she is. Understanding dawns on her face.

"Who told you?" Her cold eyes are unfamiliar. "Can't have been Musa. He doesn't know. No one does—except Keris, of course."

"The Nightbringer," I whisper. "The Nightbringer told me who you are."

"Who I was." She draws up her hood and turns to the darkness. "Come. We'll talk on the way."

Marrow-deep panic grips me when she turns from me. *Don't leave!* I want to follow her. And at the same time, I never want to see her again.

"I'm not going anywhere with you," I say, "until you tell me what the hells happened to you. Why didn't you say anything at Blackcliff? You slaved for Keris for *years*. How *could* you—"

She clenches and unclenches her fists. Just like Darin when he is upset.

I dip my head but she will not meet my stare. Her face twitches, her mouth curving into a grimace. "Listen to me, girl," she says. "We have to go. You have a mission, do you not? Don't bleeding forget it."

"The mission. *The mission.* How can you—" I throw up my hands and walk past her. "I'll make my own way. I don't need you. I don't—"

But after only a few steps, I turn back. I cannot leave her. I missed her for so many years. I have longed for her from the age of five, when she was taken from me.

"We've a long road ahead." Nothing about how she speaks sounds like the mother I knew. This is not the woman who called me Cricket, or tickled me until I couldn't breathe, or promised me she'd teach me how to shoot a bow as well as she did. Whoever she is now, she is Mirra of Serra no longer.

"There will be plenty of time for you to scream at me on the way. I'd welcome it." Her scarred mouth lifts in a sneer. "But we cannot delay. The Blood Shrike is in Antium, and Antium is where we must go. But if we don't hurry, we'll never get inside."

"No," I whisper to her. "We settle this first. This is more important, and in any case, you must have a dozen ways of sneaking in—"

"I do," Cook says. "But there are tens of thousands of Karkauns marching on the capital, and all the sneaking in the world won't do us a whit of good if they surround the city before we get there."

XLIII: The Blood Shrike

Faris and Rallius are both pale as ghosts when I meet them in Livia's quarters, rattled by what they have just survived, each bleeding from a dozen wounds. I have no time to coddle them. I need to know what the hells happened out there—and how Keris got the best of us again.

"It was a Karkaun attack." Faris paces back and forth across Livia's sitting room while her women settle her in her bedroom. "Two hundred of those woad-loving demons. They came out of bleeding nowhere."

"They were waiting," Rallius growls as he ties off a bandage on his leg. "Maybe not for the Empress specifically, but for an opportunity, certainly. If Keris hadn't shown up with her men, we'd have been in a bad spot."

"If Keris hadn't shown up," I say in irritation, "Grímarr and his hordes wouldn't have either. She's working with them. She did this so she could get to Livia. Thank the skies for you and the other Masks. She must have realized she couldn't kill you all, so she decided to play the hero instead."

Devious, true, but just like the Commandant. She is always adaptable. And now the Plebeians in the city are hailing her as a hero for saving the life of the half-Plebeian heir—as she probably knew they would.

"Go clean up," I say. "Triple the watch around the Empress. I want her food tasted a day in advance. I want one or the other of you present when it is prepared. She doesn't leave the palace. If she wants to get out, she can take a walk in the gardens."

The men leave, and I go over and over what they have said as I await the arrival of Dex, whom I sent to get Livia's midwife. When he finally returns—

after hours—it is with a different woman from the one I'd personally chosen to tend to Livia.

"The first one is gone, Shrike," Dex tells me as the new midwife bustles into Livia's rooms. "Left the city, apparently. Along with every other midwife I tried to track down. This one only came because she's a Mariner. Whomever the hells Keris Veturia sent to frighten all those women probably didn't have a chance to get to her."

I curse, keeping my voice low. Keris saved my sister from the Karkauns because it suited her needs—the Plebeians sing her praises. Now she'll seek to kill Livia quietly. Plenty of women die in childbirth, especially if they are delivering without a midwife.

"What of the barracks physicians? Surely one of them can deliver a baby."

"They know battlefield wounds, Shrike, not childbirth. That's what midwives are for, apparently. Their words"—Dex winces at my wrath—"not mine."

The new midwife, a skinny Mariner with gentle hands and a booming voice that would put any Martial drill sergeant to shame, smiles at Livia, asking her a series of questions.

"Keep this one alive, Dex," I murmur. "I don't care if you have to put a dozen guards on her and live with her in the Black Guard barracks. You keep her alive. And find a backup. This cannot possibly be the only midwife left in the entire city."

He nods, and though I've dismissed him, I notice his reluctance to leave.

"Out with it, Atrius."

"The Plebeians," he says. "You've heard that they're rising in support of the Commandant. Well, it's . . . gotten worse."

"How the *hells* could it get worse?"

"The story about her murdering the highborn Illustrians who wronged her has been making the rounds," Dex says. "The Paters are infuriated. But the Plebeians are saying that Keris stood up to those more powerful than her. They're saying that she defended a Plebeian man she loved—that she fought for one and took rightful vengeance. They're saying the Illustrians who died got what they deserved."

Hells. If the Commandant now has Plebeian support instead of Illustrian, I haven't hurt her at all. I've just managed to shuffle her list of allies.

"Let the rumor play," I say. At Dex's nod, I sigh. "We'll have to find another way to undermine her."

At that moment, the midwife pokes her head out, gesturing me into Livia's quarters.

"He's strong as a bull." She beams at me, patting Livia's belly with affection. "He'll bruise a rib or two before he joins us, I'd bet my life on it. But the Empress is doing fine, as is the child. A few weeks more, lass, and you'll be holding your precious babe in your arms."

"Should we do anything for her? Some sort of tea or . . ." I realize I sound like an idiot. *Teas, Shrike? Truly?*

"Goldrose petals in goat's milk every morning until her own milk comes in," the midwife says. "And wildwood tea twice a day."

When the woman is finally gone, Livvy sits up, and I am surprised to see a knife clutched in her hands. "Have her killed," she whispers.

I raise an eyebrow. "The midwife? What—"

"Goldrose petals," Livvy says, "are used when a woman is past her due date. They're meant to make a baby come more quickly. I'm still a few weeks away. It wouldn't be safe for him to come now."

I call Dex in immediately. When he leaves, weapons in hand, Livia shakes her head. "This is Keris, isn't it? All of it. The Karkaun attack. The midwives leaving. *This* midwife."

"I'll stop her," I vow to my sister. "I don't expect you to believe it, because all I've done is fail, but—"

"No." Livia takes my hand. "We don't turn on each other, Hel—Shrike. No matter what happens. And yes, we must stop her. But we must also keep the support of the Plebeians. If they support Keris now, you *cannot* speak against her publicly. You must walk that line, sister. We cannot put this child on the throne if the Plebeians don't see him as one of their own. And they won't—not if you cross Keris."

«« «« ««

Evening sees me in Marcus's war room, locked in an argument with the Paters, wanting nothing more than to beat all of them into silence before doing what I wish.

General Sissellius, who is turning out to be as irritating as his twisted uncle, the Warden, paces before the large map laid out on the table, stabbing at it occasionally.

"If we send a small force to stop Grímarr," he says, "we are wasting good men on a lost cause. It's a suicide mission. How can five hundred—even a thousand—men stand against a force a hundred times that?"

Avitas, who has joined me in the war room, gives me a look. *Don't lose your temper*, the look says.

"If we send a large force," I say for the thousandth time, "we leave Antium vulnerable. Without the legions from Estium and Silas, we have only six legions to hold the city. Reinforcements from the Tribal lands or Navium or Tiborum would take more than a month to reach here. We *must* send a smaller attack force to cause as much damage as possible."

It's such a basic tactic that at first I am stunned that Sissellius and a few of the other Paters resist so much. Until I realize, of course, that they are using this opportunity to undermine me—and, by extension, Marcus. They might not trust the Commandant anymore, but that doesn't mean they want Marcus on the throne.

For his part, the Emperor's attention is fixed on Keris Veturia. When he does finally look at me, I can read his expression as clearly as if he shouted the words.

Why is she here, Shrike? Why is she still alive? Those hyena eyes of his flare, promising pain for my sister, and I look away.

"Why is the Shrike leading the force?" Pater Rufius demands of me. "Would not Keris Veturia be a better choice? I do not know if you understand this, my Lord Emperor, but it is highly—" His sentence ends in a yelp as Marcus casually flings a throwing knife at him, missing him by a hair. The sound of Rufius's squeal is deeply satisfying.

"Speak to me like that again," Marcus says, "and you'll find yourself without a head. Keris was barely able to hold Navium's harbor against the Barbarian fleet."

Avitas and I exchange a glance. This is the first time the Emperor has dared to say a word against the Commandant.

"The Shrike," Marcus goes on, "took back the harbor and saved thousands of Plebeian lives. The decision is made. The Shrike will lead the force against the Karkauns."

"But my lord—"

Marcus's giant hand is around Rufius's throat so fast that I almost didn't see him move.

"Go on," the Emperor says softly. "I'm listening."

Rufius gasps his apology, and Marcus drops him. The Pater scurries away, a rooster who has escaped the stewpot. The Emperor turns to me.

"A small force, Shrike. Strike and run. Take no prisoners. And do not waste our forces if you don't have to. We'll need every last man for the assault on the city."

From the corner of my eye, I notice Keris watching me. She nods a greeting—the first time she has acknowledged me since returning to Antium with my sister. My spine tingles in warning. That look on her face—cunning, calculated. I saw it as a student at Blackcliff. And I saw it months ago, here in Antium, before Marcus killed my family.

I know that look now. It is the look she gets when she's about to spring a trap.

«««

Avitas arrives in my office just after the sun has set. "All is prepared, Shrike," he says. "The men will be ready to leave at dawn."

"Good." I pause and clear my throat. "Harper—"

"Perhaps, Blood Shrike," Avitas says, "you are considering telling me that I should not go. That I should remain here to keep an eye on our enemies and to remain close to the Emperor, should he need it."

I open and close my mouth, taken aback. That was exactly what I was going to suggest.

"Forgive me." Avitas looks tired, I notice. I've been leaning on him too much. "But that is exactly what the Commandant would expect. She is, perhaps, counting on it. Whatever she has planned, you surviving isn't a part of it. And you have a much better chance of surviving if you have someone who knows her watching your back."

"What the hells is she *up* to?" I say. "Beyond just trying to take the throne, I mean. I've reports that a man of Gens Veturia was seen at the Hall of Records. She's had the Paters of the three biggest Illustrian Gens over to her villa in the few hours she's been back. She even had the master of the treasury over. She killed that man's son and tattooed her triumph onto her own body, Harper. It was ten years ago, but she still did it. Those men should hate her. Instead they are breaking bread with her."

"She's wooing them back to her side," Harper says. "She's trying to rattle you. You took her by surprise in Navium. She won't be taken by surprise again, which is why I should come with you." At my hesitation, impatience sparks on his face.

"Use your head, Shrike! She had Captain Alistar poisoned. She had Favrus poisoned. She got to the bleeding Empress. You're not immortal. She can get to you too. Be smart about this, for the love of skies. We *need* you. You cannot play into her hands."

I don't consider my next words. They just come out. "Why do you care so much what happens to me?"

"Why do you think?" His words are sharp, lacking his usual care. And when his green eyes meet mine, they are angry. But his voice is cool. "You are the Blood Shrike. I am your second. Your safety is my duty."

"Sometimes, Avitas," I sigh, "I wish you'd say what you're actually thinking. Come along on the raid, then," I say, and at his look of surprise, I roll my eyes. "I'm not a fool, Harper. Let's keep her on her toes. There's something else." A worry has grown in my mind—something no general would publicly speak of before a battle, but something I must consider, especially after talking to Livia of the Plebeians.

"Do we have exit routes mapped out of the city? Paths through which we could move large groups of people?"

"I'll dig them up."

"Do it before we leave," I say. "Give orders—quietly—to make sure those paths are clear and that we protect them at all costs."

"You think we cannot hold back the Karkauns?"

"I think that if they're in league with Keris, it is foolish to underestimate them. We might not know what she's playing at, but we can prepare for the worst."

We move out the next morning, and I force Keris and her machinations from my mind. If I can rout Grímarr's forces—or at least weaken them—before they get to Antium, she'll lose her chance to take Marcus down, and I'll be the hero instead of her. The Karkauns are twelve days from the city, but my force can move faster than theirs. My men and I have five days to make life as hellish as possible for them.

Our smaller force allows us to ride swiftly, and on the evening of the third day, our scouts confirm that the Karkaun force has, as Dex reported, gathered at Umbral Pass. They have Tundaran Wildmen with them—that's likely how Grímarr figured out the way through. Those women-hating Tundaran bastards know these mountains almost as well as the Martials do.

"Why the hells are they just waiting there?" I ask Dex. "They should be clear of the pass by now and out into open country."

"Waiting for more men, perhaps," Dex says, "though their force doesn't seem much bigger than when I saw it."

I send my cousin Baristus out to recon the north end of the pass to see if, indeed, more Karkauns are joining the main body of the army. But when he returns, he brings only questions.

"Bleeding strange, sir," Baristus says. As Dex, Avitas, and I gather in my tent, my cousin paces back and forth, agitated. "There are no more men coming in through the northern passes. Truly, it appears they are waiting, but for what I cannot tell. I thought it might be weaponry or artillery for their siege machines. But they have no siege machines. How the bleeding hells do they plan to get past the walls of Antium without catapults?"

"Maybe Keris promised to let them in," I say. "And they don't yet realize how devious she is. It would be just like her to play both sides."

"And then what?" Dex says. "She lets them lay siege for a few weeks?"

"Enough time for her to find a way to get Marcus killed in the fighting," I say. "Enough time for her to sabotage the birth of my nephew." Ultimately, it is the Empire that Keris wishes to rule over. She will not let the capital of the Empire fall. But the loss of a few thousand lives? That's nothing to her. I've learned that lesson well.

"If we rout the Karkauns here," I say, "then we kill her plan before it draws its first breath." I examine the drawings the aux has given me of the layout of the Karkaun army camp. Their food stores, their weaponry, the locations of their various provisions. They've buried their most valuable goods in the very heart of the army, where they will be almost impossible to reach.

But I have Masks with me. And the word *impossible* has been whipped and beaten out of us.

My force strikes deep in the night, when much of the Karkaun camp is sleeping. The sentries go down swiftly, and Dex leads a force that is in and out before the first flames rise from the Karkaun food stores. We hit perhaps a sixth of their supply, but by the time our enemies sound the alarm, we have retreated back into the mountains.

"I'll come with you for the next assault, Shrike," Harper says to me as we prepare for another. "Something feels wrong to me. They took that attack lying down."

"Perhaps it's because we surprised them." Harper paces nervously, and I put a hand on his shoulder to still him. A spark jumps between us, and he looks up in surprise. Immediately, I let him go.

"I—I need you with the rear guard," I say to cover my awkwardness. "If something does go wrong, I'll need you to get the men back to Antium."

Our next assault comes just before dawn, when the Barbarians are still scrambling from our earlier attack. This time, I lead a group of a hundred men armed with arrows and flame.

But almost before the first volley flies, it is clear that the Karkauns are ready for us. A wave of more than a thousand of them on our western side breaks off from the main army and surges upward in orderly, organized lines that I've never seen in a Karkaun force.

But we have the higher ground, so we pick off as many as we can. They have no horses, and these mountains are not their land. They don't know these hills the way we do.

When we've exhausted our arrows, I signal the retreat—which is when the unmistakable thud of a drum thunders out from the rear guard. Avitas's troops. One deep thud—two—three.

Ambush. We worked out the warnings ahead of time. I spin about, my war hammer in hand, waiting for the attack. The men close ranks. A horse screams—a chilling and unmistakable sound. Curses ring out when the drum sounds again.

But this time, the drum is unceasing, a frantic call for aid.

"The rear guard is under attack," Dex calls out. "How the hells—"

His sentence ends in a grunt as he parries a knife that comes flying out at him from the woods. And then we can think of nothing but surviving, because we are suddenly surrounded by Karkauns. They rise up from well-hidden traps in the ground, drop down from trees, rain down arrows and blades and fire.

From the rear guard, we hear the unholy howling of more Karkauns as they pour down the mountain, from the east. Thousands of them. More still approach from the north. Only the south is clear—but not for long, if we don't clear this ambush.

We're dead. We're bleeding dead.

"That ravine." I point to a narrow path between the closing pincer of the approaching forces, and we make a break for it, sending arrows back over our shoulders. The ravine follows the river, leading down to a waterfall. There are boats there—enough to take the remaining men downstream. "Faster! They're closing!"

We run full force, grimacing at the screams of the rear guard dying swiftly as they are inundated by our enemy. Skies, so many men. So many Black Guards. And Avitas is up there. *Something feels wrong to me.* If he'd been with us, he might have seen the ambush. We might have retreated before the Karkauns attacked the rear guard.

And now . . .

I look up the mountain. He could not possibly survive that onslaught. None of them could. There are too many.

He never told Elias that they are brothers. He never got to speak to Elias *as* a brother. And skies, the things I've said to him in moments of rage, in anger, when all he did was try to help keep me alive. That spark between us, extinguished before I could put a name to it. My eyes burn.

"Shrike!" Dex screams and knocks me to the ground as an arrow cuts through the air, nearly impaling me. We scramble up and stumble on. The ravine finally appears, an eight-foot drop into the remnants of a creek. A hail of arrows comes down as we approach it.

"*Shields!*" I shout. Steel thunks on wood, and then my men and I run again, years of training pushing us into neat rows. Every time a soldier is picked off, another moves to take his place so that when I look back, I can count almost exactly how many are left.

Only seventy-five—of the five hundred Marcus sent.

We hurtle down the path beside the falls, and the thunder of the water drives away any other sound. The path curves back and forth on itself until it drops into a dusty flat where a dozen long boats are beached.

The men need no orders. We hear the chants of the Karkauns behind us. One boat launches, then another and another.

"Shrike." Dex pulls me toward a boat. "You have to go."

"Not until the rest of the boats launch," I say. Four hundred and twenty-five men . . . gone. And Avitas . . . gone. Skies, it was so quick.

The sounds of swords clashing echoes from the path above. My hammer is in my hand, and I am racing up the path. If some of my men are still up there, then by the skies, I will not let them fight alone.

"Shrike—no!" Dex groans, draws his scim, and follows. Just beyond the entrance to the path, we find a group of Martials, three Masks among them, battling the Tundarans but being inexorably shoved back by the sheer number of them. A group of auxes supports a fourth Mask, blood pouring from his neck, from a wound in his gut, from another in his thigh.

Harper.

Dex grabs him from the auxes, staggering under his weight as he carries him down toward the last boat. The auxes arm their bows and fire over and over until the air is buzzing with arrows, and it is a miracle I am not hit. One of the Masks turns—it is Baristus, my cousin.

"We'll hold them off," he shouts. "Go, Shrike. Warn the city. Warn the Emperor. Tell them there's another—"

And then Dex is dragging me away, shoving me down the path and into the boat, sharking through the water as he pushes off. *Tell them what?* I want to scream. Dex rows with all his might, and the boat is through the falls and moving swiftly down the fast-flowing river. I kneel beside Harper.

His blood is everywhere. If it weren't me in this boat beside him, he would be dead in a matter of minutes. I take his hand. If it weren't for Baristus's sacrifice, we'd all be dead.

I expect to search for Harper's song. He is the consummate Mask, his thoughts and emotions buried so deeply that I assumed his song would be equally opaque.

But his song is near the surface, strong and bright and clear as a star-filled winter sky. I delve into his essence. I see the smile of a dark-haired woman with wide-set green eyes—his mother—and the strong hands of a man who looks strikingly similar to Elias. Harper walks Blackcliff's dark halls and endures day after day of the hardship and loneliness I know so well. He aches for his father, a mysterious figure who haunts him with an emptiness he can never quite fill.

He is an open book, and I learn that he *did* set Laia free months ago, when we ambushed her. He set her free because he knew I would kill her. And he knew Elias would never forgive me for it. I witness myself through his eyes: angry and cold and weak and strong and brave and warm. Not the Blood Shrike. *Helene.* And I would be blind not to see what he feels for me. I am woven into his consciousness the way Elias used to be woven into mine. Harper is always aware of where I am, of whether I am all right.

When his wounds have closed and his heart beats strong, I stop singing, weakened. Dex looks at me with a wild, questioning expression but says nothing.

I adjust Harper's head so he is more comfortable, and his eyes open. I am about to scold him, but his harsh whisper silences me.

"Grímarr and the men who hit the rear guard came from the east, Shrike," he rasps, determined to deliver the message. "He attacked me—would have killed me . . ."

All the more reason to hate that swine. "They must have snuck around us somehow," I say. "Or perhaps they were waiting—"

"No." Avitas grabs a strap on my armor. "They *came* from the east. I sent a scout because I had a hunch. There's another force. They split their army, Shrike. They don't have just fifty thousand men marching on Antium. They have twice that."

XLIV: Laia

At first, I don't know what to say to Cook. Mother. Mirra. I watch her with wild eyes, part of me desperate to understand her story and the other part wanting to scream out the pain of a dozen years without her until she throbs with it.

Perhaps, I think to myself, *she will wish to talk*. To explain why she survived. How she survived. I do not expect her to justify what she did in the prison—she is not aware that I know of it. But I hope she will tell me why she kept her identity hidden. I hope she will at least apologize for it.

Instead she is silent, all her thought bent on moving swiftly across the countryside. Her face, her profile are burned into me. I see her in a thousand ways, even if she doesn't see herself. I find myself drawn to her. She was gone for so many years. And I do not wish to hold on to my anger. I do not want a fight with her like the one I had with Darin. On the first night we travel together, I sit down beside her by the fire.

What did I hope for? Perhaps for the woman who called me Cricket and rested her hand on my head, heavy and gentle. The woman whose smile was a flash in the dark, the last joyful thing I could remember for years.

But the moment I get close, she clears her throat and shifts away from me. It's only a few inches, but I understand her meaning.

In her rasping voice, she asks me about Izzi and about what has happened to me since I left Blackcliff. Part of me doesn't want to answer. *You don't deserve to know. You don't deserve to have my story.* But the other part—the part that sees a broken woman where my mother once lived—is not so cruel.

So I tell her of Izzi. Of her sacrifice. Of my foolhardiness. I tell her of the

Nightbringer. Of Keenan and how he betrayed not just me but our entire family.

What must she think of me, to have fallen in love with the creature whose deceit led to those dark days in Kauf Prison? I wait for her judgment, but she offers none. Instead she nods, her hands curled into fists, and disappears into the dark night. In the morning, she says nothing of it.

For the next few nights, every time I so much as move, she flinches, as if worried I will come closer. So I stay far away from her, always on the other side of the fire, always a few yards behind her on the road. My mind churns, but I do not speak. It is as if her silence chokes me.

But finally, the words will no longer stay down, and I find that I *must* say them, whatever the consequences.

"Why didn't you kill her?" The night is warm, and we don't light a fire, instead laying out our bedrolls and looking up at the stars. "The Commandant? You could have poisoned her. Stabbed her. For skies' sake, you're Mirra of Serra—"

"There is no Mirra of Serra!" Cook shrieks so loudly that a pack of sparrows takes flight from a nearby tree, as frightened as I am. "She's *dead*. She died in Kauf Prison when her child and husband died! *I'm not Mirra.* I'm Cook. And you will not speak to me of that murderous, traitorous bitch or what she would or wouldn't do. You know *nothing* of her."

She breathes heavily, her dark eyes sparkling with rage. "I tried, girl," she hisses at me. "The first time I attacked Keris, she broke my arm and lashed Izzi to within an inch of her life. The child was five. I was forced to watch. The next time I got it in my head to try something, the Bitch of Blackcliff took out Izzi's eye."

"Why not escape? You could have gotten out of there."

"*I tried.* But the chances Keris would catch us were too high. She'd have tortured Izzi. And I'd had enough of people suffering for me. Perhaps *Mirra of Serra* would have been willing to sacrifice a child to save her own neck, but that's because Mirra of Serra had no soul. Mirra of Serra was as evil as the Commandant. And I'm not her. Not anymore."

"You haven't asked about Nan and Pop," I whisper. "Or about Darin. You—"

"I don't deserve to know how your brother is," she says. "As for your grandparents . . ." Her mouth splits into a small smile I do not recognize. "I had vengeance on their killer."

"The Mask?" I say. "How?"

"I hunted him. He wanted to die, in the end. I was merciful." Her eyes are black as dead coals. "You're judging me."

"I wanted to kill him too. But . . ."

"But I enjoyed it. And that makes me evil? Come now, girl. You cannot walk in the shadows as long as I have and not become one."

I shift uncomfortably, remembering what the Jaduna said to me. *You are young to stand so deeply in the shadow.*

"I am glad you killed him." I pause, considering my next words. But in the end, there is no delicate way to ask the question. "Why—why won't you touch me? Don't you—" *Long for it,* I want so say. *The way I do?*

"The touch of a child brings a mother comfort." I can barely hear her. "But I'm no mother, girl. I'm a monster. Monsters don't merit comfort."

She turns away from me and falls silent. I watch her back for a long time. She's so close. Close enough to touch. Close enough to hear whispered words of forgiveness.

But I do not think that she would feel the embrace of a daughter if I touched her. And I do not think she would care about being forgiven.

»»»

The closer we get to Antium, the clearer it is that trouble is nigh. Cartloads of carpets and furniture trundle away from the city, their owners surrounded by dozens of guards. Once, we see a heavily armed caravan from afar. I cannot see what they carry, but I count at least a dozen Masks guarding whatever it is.

"They're running," Cook spits. "Too scared to stay and fight. Mostly Illustrians, it seems. Move faster, girl. If the wealthy flee the city, the Karkauns must be close."

We do not stop now, traveling day and night. But by the time we reach the outskirts of Antium, it is clear that disaster has already struck the Martials' fabled capital. We hike over a ridge near the Argent Hills, and the city comes into view below.

As does the enormous army that surrounds it on three sides. Only the north end of Antium, which abuts the mountains, is protected.

"Sweet bleeding skies," Cook murmurs. "If that's not skies-given justice, I don't know what is."

"So many." I can barely speak. "The people in the city . . ." I shake my head, and immediately my thoughts go to the Scholars who are still enslaved in the city. *My people.* "There must be Scholars down there. The Commandant didn't kill all the slaves. The Illustrians didn't let her. What happens to them if the city is overrun?"

"They die," Cook says. "Just like every other poor bastard unfortunate enough to get stuck there. Leave that to the Martials. It's their capital; they'll defend it. You've got something else to think about. How the bleeding hells are we going to get in there?"

"They've only just gotten here." Men stream in to join the Karkaun army from a northeastern pass. "They're staying out of range of the city's catapults, which means they must not be planning to attack. You said you could sneak us in."

"From the mountains north of the city," Cook says. "We'd have to go around the Argent Hills. It would take us days. Longer."

"There will be chaos as they set up camp," I say. "We could take advantage of that. Sneak through at night. They'll have some women down there—"

"Whores," Cook says. "Don't think I'd pass as one of those."

"Cooks too," I say. "Laundresses. The Karkauns are horrible. They'd not go anywhere without their women to scrape and serve for them. I could go invisible."

Cook shakes her head. "You said the invisibility altered your mind. Gave you visions, sometimes for hours. We need to think of something else. This is a bad idea."

"It's necessary."

"It's suicide."

"It's something you might have done," I say quietly. "Before."

"That makes me trust it even less," she says, but I can see her waver. She knows as well as I do that our options are limited.

An hour later, I walk by her side as she hunches over a basket of stinking laundry. We've taken out two sentries who blocked our way into the encampment. Simple enough. But now that we walk among the Karkauns, it is anything but.

There are so many of them. Much like in the Empire, their skin tones and features and hair vary. But they are all heavily tattooed, the top halves of their faces blue with woad so that the whites of their eyes stand out eerily.

There are hundreds of campfires lit but few tents behind which Cook and I can take cover. Most of the men wear leather breeches and fur vests, and I have no sense of which are higher-ranking and which are not. The only Karkauns who stand out are those who wear strange bone-and-steel armor and who carry staffs with human skulls on top. When they walk, they are given a wide berth. But most are gathered around enormous unlit pyres, pouring what looks to be deep scarlet sand in intricate shapes around them.

"Karkaun warlocks," Cook mutters to me. "Spend all their time terrifying the masses and attempting to raise spirits. They never manage it, but they're still treated like gods."

The camp stinks of sweat and rancid vegetables. Huge piles of firewood belie the warm weather, and the Karkauns don't bother cleaning up all the horse dung. Jugs of some pale alcohol are as ubiquitous as the men, and there's a stench of sour milk that lingers over everything.

"Bah!" An older Karkaun shoves Cook when she accidently bumps him with her basket. *"Tek fidkayad urqin!"*

Cook swings her head back and forth, playing the old, confused woman well. The man knocks the basket out of her hands, and his friends laugh as clothes cascade onto the filthy ground. He kicks her in the gut as she tries to gather up the clothes quickly, making lewd gestures.

I quickly help her gather the clothes, trusting that the Karkauns are too drunk to notice an invisible hand helping Cook. But when I crouch, she hisses at me.

"You're flickering, girl! Move!"

Sure enough, I look down to find my invisibility faltering. *The Night-bringer!* He must be in Antium—his presence is snuffing out my magic.

Cook bolts swiftly through the knot of men, making her way steadily north.

"You still there, girl?" Tension is thick on her skin, but she doesn't look back.

"They're not very organized," I whisper in return. "But skies, there are so many of them."

"Long winters in the south," Cook says. "They've got nothing to do but breed."

"Why strike now?" I ask. "Why here?"

"There's a famine among their people and a firebrand warlock who has taken advantage of it. Nothing motivates a man like hunger in the bellies of his children. The Karkauns looked north and saw a wealthy, fat empire. Year after year, the Martials had plenty and the Karkauns had nothing. Empire wouldn't trade fairly with them either. Grímarr, their warlock priest, reminded them of that. And here we are."

We are nearly through the northern end of the camp now. A flat cliff face stretches ahead of us, but Cook makes her way confidently toward it, shedding the basket of laundry as darkness falls and we get farther from the camp. "They're depending entirely on sheer numbers to win here. That or they've got something nasty up their sleeves—something the Martials can't fight."

I glance up at the moon—almost full, but not quite. In three days, it will fatten into the Grain Moon. *By the Grain Moon, the forgotten will find their master.*

Cook doubles back twice to make sure we aren't followed before she gestures me close to the cliff face. She nods upward. "There's a cave about fifty feet up," she says. "Leads deeper into the mountains. Stay here, and stay invisible, just in case."

"How the hells are you going to—"

She crooks her fingers. There is something familiar about the motion, and then suddenly she is climbing the sheer rock face with the spryness of a spider. I gape. It is unnatural—no, impossible. She is not flying, exactly, but there is a lightness to her that is distinctly inhuman.

"What the *hells*—"

A rope falls and smacks me in the head. Cook's face appears from overhead. "Tie it around you," she says. "Brace your feet on the wall, in the wedges, in whatever space you can find, and climb."

When I finally reach her, I am out of breath, and when I ask her how she did it, she hisses at me and starts off through the cave without turning back.

We are deep in the mountains before Cook finally suggests I drop my invisibility.

"It might take me a few minutes to wake up," I say to her. "I have visions, and I'm not sure—"

"I'll make sure you don't die."

I nod but find myself paralyzed. I do not wish to face the visions—not after what the Nightbringer showed me.

Though my mother cannot see me, she cocks her head, as if she senses my discomfort. My face flushes, and though I search for an explanation, I cannot find one. *I'm a coward*, I want to say. *I always have been.* Skies, this is humiliating. If she were just Cook, I would not have cared. But she is my mother. My *mother*. I have spent years wondering what she would think of me.

She looks around the tunnel and finally sits on the earth floor. "I'm tired," she says. "Damn Karkauns. Come. Sit next to an old woman, girl."

I ease down beside her, and for the first time she doesn't flinch away from me—because she can't see me.

"These visions," she says after a time. "They are frightening?"

I think of her in the prison cell. The singing. The crack. Those sounds that meant nothing until they meant everything. And even now, even when I do not comprehend who she has become, I cannot bear to tell her what I saw. I cannot say it, for saying it will make it real.

"Yes." I dig my feet into the ground, sliding them back and forth. "They're frightening." And what will I see now that the visions turn out to be from the past? Something else? Some other horror?

"Best get it done quickly then." Her voice is not exactly gentle, but it isn't harsh either. She hesitates and holds out a hand, palm up. Her jaw is tight, and she swallows.

Her skin is warm. Calloused. And though she might not look like my mother, or sound like her, or act like her, she still has her hands. I squeeze—and she shudders.

I shrug off the invisibility, welcoming the visions because they cannot be worse than holding the hand of a woman who bore me but who is disgusted by my touch.

The visions are upon me, but this time I walk through streets of fire, past walls burned black. Screams echo from blazing buildings and dread fills my bones. I cry out.

When I open my eyes, Cook is hovering over me, one hand on my face, the other still clenched between my fingers. Her face is pained, as if touching me is more than she can bear. She doesn't ask about the visions. And I do not tell her.

« « «

When we approach the entrance to the Mariner Embassy, a wet, crumbling set of steps that lead up to a wooden door, Cook slows.

"There should be two guards here," she says. "It has always been guarded. That lever there—it allows them to collapse the whole damn thing in case of an attack."

I draw my dagger, and Cook draws her bow. She pushes the door open gently, and when we enter, all is silent. In the streets beyond the building, drums thunder, and I am transported back to Blackcliff almost instantly. Carts rumble past, their occupants shouting requests, soldiers bellowing orders. Boots thump, marching in time, and a crisp voice directs a platoon to the walls. Antium prepares for war.

"This isn't right," I say. "Musa had people here. They were to have slaves' cuffs ready for us, maps, the Blood Shrike's movements . . ."

"They must have left before the Karkauns' attack," Cook says. "They can't all have gone."

But they have. I can feel it. This place has been empty for days.

We're on our own.

XLV: Elias

The ghosts explode into the Empire like flaming stones hurtling from a ballista. The border wall is nothing but shreds.

I feel the spirits in the same way that I feel the contours of the Waiting Place. They're bits of winter in a blanket of warmth and they move like a school of fish, closely packed and streaking in one direction—southwest, toward a Martial village I sneak supplies from. The people who live there are decent and hardworking. And they've no bleeding idea what's coming.

I want to help them. But that's also what the jinn want—for it's a distraction from my duty. Yet again, they're trying to use my humanity against me.

Not this time. What matters now is not the humans whom the ghosts will possess and torment. It's the border of the Waiting Place. I have to restore it. There will be more ghosts entering the Forest. They, at least, must be kept within its boundaries.

The thought has scarcely formed in my mind when the magic rises from the earth, winding its way into my body. It's stronger this time, as if sensing that *finally* I understand how I've been manipulated by the jinn. Feeling Mauth, letting the magic consume me, is a relief—but also a transgression. I shudder at Mauth's closeness. This doesn't feel like using my physical magic, which is simply a matter of harnessing something that's already part of me. No—this magic is something alien. It sinks in like a disease and colors my sight. The magic changes something fundamental within. I do not feel like myself.

But my discomfort can wait. I have more pressing work.

The magic allows me to see what the border *should* look like. All I need to do is apply my willpower to rebuild it. I gather my strength.

Far to the south, the ghosts close in on the village. *Don't think about it.*

Mauth's magic flares in response, his presence stronger. Section by section, I rebuild the border, imagining great bricks of light rising all at once, solid and unbreakable. When I open my eyes, the wall is there, glowing as if it never came down. The border cannot call the escaped ghosts back. But it can catch new ghosts who are bound for the Waiting Place.

And there will be many of those.

Now what? Do I go after the rogue ghosts? A nudge from Mauth toward the southwest is my answer. The windwalking comes easily—more easily than it ever has. And though I expect the magic to wear off the farther I get from the Forest, it stays with me, for this is Mauth's magic, not my own.

The ghosts have scattered, splintering among the countryside into dozens of small groups. But I make for the village closest to the Waiting Place. When I am still a mile away, I hear screams.

I slow in a village square, and it is a testament to the havoc the ghosts have created that none of the villagers seem to notice that I appeared out of thin air.

"Thaddius! My son! No!" a white-haired man screams. A younger man twists the old man's arms behind his back and pulls them up with inhuman, inexorable force. "Release me—don't do this—aaa—" An audible crunch sounds, and the father slumps, unconscious from pain. The younger man lifts him up, as if he's nothing but a pebble, and flings him across the village—hundreds and hundreds of yards.

I draw my scims, prepared to attack, when Mauth yanks at me.

Of course, Elias, you idiot, I chide myself. I can't single-handedly beat up everyone inhabited by a ghost. Shaeva tapped my heart, my head. *Mauth's true power is here and here.* The magic nudges me toward the closest group of possessed villagers. My throat grows warm, and I can sense, somehow, that Mauth wants me to speak.

"Stop," I say, but not as Elias. I speak as the *Banu al-Mauth*. I pinion the possessed with my gaze, one by one. I wait for an attack, but all they do is stare balefully, wary of the magic they can sense roiling within me.

"Come," I order them. My voice booms with a supernatural note of command. They *must* listen. *"Come."*

They snarl and yip, and I cast Mauth's magic out like a thin line, wrapping it around each of them, tugging them close. Some come in the bodies they have stolen. Others are still spirits, and they drift toward me with hostile moans. Soon, a small group of a few dozen spirits forms a half circle around me.

Should I rope them together with magic? Send them streaming back to the Waiting Place, as I did with the ghosts that plagued the Tribes?

No. For as I look at these tortured faces, I realize the spirits don't wish to be here. They *want* to move on, to leave this world. Sending them back to the Forest will only prolong their suffering.

The magic fills my sight, and I see the ghosts for what they are: hurting, alone, confused, regretful. Some are desperate for forgiveness. Others for kindness. Others for understanding. Others for an explanation.

But a few require judgment, and those spirits take longer to deal with, for they must suffer the hurt they inflicted on others before they are free. Each time I recognize what a spirit needs, I find myself willing it forth from the magic and giving it to them.

It takes time. Long minutes pass, and I get through a dozen ghosts, then two dozen. Soon, all the ghosts in the vicinity flock to me, desperate to speak, desperate for me to *see* them. The villagers cry out for help, perhaps hoping my magic will offer them respite from their pain. I glance at them and see not humans but lesser creatures who are dying slowly. The humans are mortal, unimportant. The ghosts are all that matter.

The thought feels unfamiliar. Strange. As if it doesn't belong to me. But I have no time to dwell on it, for more ghosts await. I fix my gaze on them, barely twitching until the last of them has moved on, even those who found human bodies to squat in.

When I finish, I observe the devastation they've left behind. There are a dozen dead bodies that I can see and probably dozens more that I can't.

Distantly, I feel something. Sadness? I push it aside quickly. The villagers look at me with terror now—they're simple creatures, after all. In any case, it's only a matter of time before fear transforms into torches and scims and pitchforks. I'm still mortal, and I've no wish to fight them.

A young man steps forward, a hesitant look on his face. He opens his mouth, his lips forming the words *thank you*.

Before he can finish, I turn away. There is much work ahead of me. And in any case, I don't deserve his thanks.

«««

Days pass in a blur of villages and towns. I find the ghosts, call to them, gather them close, and send them on. In some villages, doing so takes only an hour. In others, it takes nearly an entire day.

My connection to Mauth grows stronger, but it's not complete. I know it in my bones. The magic holds back, and I will not be a true Soul Catcher until I find a way to merge with it fully.

Soon, the magic is powerful enough that I can hone in quickly on where the ghosts are. I send hundreds on. Thousands remain. And hundreds more ghosts have been created, for the spirits wreak havoc wherever they go. One evening, I reach a town where nearly everyone is already dead, and the ghosts have already moved on to another town.

Nearly three weeks after the ghosts' escape, when night has fallen and a storm has broken over the land, I take shelter on a grassy knoll free of boulders and scrum, just a few miles from a Martial garrison. The drums of the garrison thunder—unusual this late at night, but I pay them no mind, not even bothering to translate.

Shivering in my soaked leather armor, I gather a bundle of sticks. But the rain doesn't let up, and after a half hour of trying to light the damn fire, I abandon it and hunch miserably beneath my hood.

"What's the use," I mutter to myself, "of having magic if I can't use it to make a fire?"

I expect no response, so when the magic rises, I am surprised. More so when it hovers over me, creating an invisible, cocoon-like shelter.

"Ah . . . thank you?" I poke at the magic with a finger. It has no substance, just a sense of warmth. I didn't know it could do this.

There is so much you do not yet know. Did Shaeva know Mauth well? She was always so deeply respectful of the magic—fearful, even. And like a child who watches his parents' faces for cues, I picked up on that wariness.

Did the magic feel anything when Shaeva died, I wonder? She was bound to that place for a thousand years. Did Mauth care? Did he feel angry at the Nightbringer's foul crime?

I shudder when I think of the jinn lord. When I think of who he was—a Soul Catcher who passed the spirits of humans on with such love—versus what he has become: a monster who wants nothing more than to annihilate us. In the stories Mamie told, he was only ever called the King of No Name or the Nightbringer. But I wonder if he had a true name, one us humans never deserved to know.

Though it's discomfiting, I am forced to admit that the jinn were wronged. Grievously wronged. Which doesn't make what the Nightbringer has done right. But it does complicate my view of the world—and my ability to look on him with unadulterated hatred.

When I finally arise, warm and dry due to Mauth's shelter, it's long before dawn. Immediately, I'm aware of a shift in the fabric of the world. The ghosts I'd sensed lurking in the surrounding countryside are gone. And there is something else—some new fey darkness in the world. I can't see it. And yet I know it exists.

I stand up, scanning the rolling farmland around me. The garrison is to the north. Then there are a few hundred miles of Illustrian estates. Then the capital, the Nevennes Range, Delphinium.

The magic strains north, as if wishing to drag me in that direction. As I reach out with my mind, I feel it. Chaos. Blood. A battle. And more ghosts. Except these do not come from the Waiting Place. They are fresh, new, and imprisoned by a strange fey magic that I've never before seen.

What in the ten hells?

The ghosts are, I know, sometimes drawn to conflict. Blood. Could there be a battle in the north? At this time of year, Tiborum is often harassed by the Empire's enemies. But Tiborum is due west.

Mauth nudges me to my feet, and I windwalk north, my mind ranging out over miles. I finally come across a cluster of ghosts and just ahead of it, another. More of the spirits arrow toward a specific place, wild with hunger and rage. They yearn toward bodies, toward bloodshed, toward war. I know it as surely as if the ghosts tell me themselves. *What bleeding war, though?* I think, bewildered. Are the Karkauns murdering Wildmen in the Nevennes again? If so, that must be where the ghosts are headed.

The drums of a nearby garrison thunder, and this time, I listen. *Karkaun attack imminent. All reserve soldiers to report to South River barracks immediately.* The message repeats, and I finally understand that the ghosts are not, in fact, headed to the Nevennes.

They are headed to Antium.

PART IV

SIEGE

XLVI: The Blood Shrike

The Karkauns have no catapults.

No siege towers.

No battering rams.

No artillery.

"What in the bleeding hells," I say to Dex and Avitas as I look out over the vast force, "is the point of having a hundred thousand men if you are just going to let them sit outside a city, burning through food and supplies for three days?"

Maybe this is why the Commandant plotted with the Karkauns to sneak up on Antium. She knew they'd be stupid enough that we could destroy them quickly—but not so stupid that she couldn't use the chaos they caused to her advantage.

"They are fools," Dex says. "Convinced that because they have such a large force, they will take the city."

"Or perhaps we are the fools." Marcus speaks from behind me, and the men on the wall swiftly kneel. The Emperor gestures us up and strides forward, his honor guard in lockstep behind him. "And they have something else planned."

"My lord?"

The Emperor stands beside me, hyena eyes narrowing as they sweep across the Karkaun army. The sun fades, and night will soon be upon us.

"My brother speaks to me from beyond death, Shrike." Marcus sounds calm, and there is no hint of instability in his demeanor. "He says the Karkauns bring warlock priests—one of whom is the most powerful in their history—and that these warlocks summon darkness. They have no siege weaponry because they do not need it." He pauses. "Is the city prepared?"

"We'll hold, my lord. For months, if need be."

Marcus's mouth twists. He's keeping secrets. *What? What are you not telling me?*

"We'll know by the Grain Moon if we will hold," he says with a chilling surety. I stiffen. The Grain Moon is in three bleeding days. "The Augurs have seen it."

"Your Majesty." Keris Veturia appears from the stairs leading up to the wall. I ordered her to shore up the eastern gates, which are the strongest and which keeps her far from both Marcus and Livia. My spies report that she is not deviating from her assigned task.

For now, anyway.

I'd wanted to get her away from the city, but the Plebeians support her enthusiastically, and getting rid of her will only undermine Marcus further. She has too many damned allies. But at the very least, she's lost much of her Illustrian support. The Paters have, it appears, remained in their own villas the past few days, no doubt preparing for the battle to come.

"A messenger from the Karkauns has arrived," Keris says. "They seek terms."

Though Keris insists on Marcus staying behind—yet another play for power—he waves her off, and the three of us ride out, joined by Avitas at my side and by Marcus's personal guard, who form a protective half-moon around him.

The Karkaun who approaches us rides alone, bare-chested and without a flag of truce. Half of his milk-pale body is covered in woad, the other half in crude tattoos. His hair is lighter than mine, his eyes practically colorless against the woad he's used to blue them out. The stallion he rides on is enormous, and he is nearly as tall as Elias. A necklace of bones circles his thick neck twice.

Finger bones, I realize when we are closer.

Though I only saw him distantly in Navium, I know him immediately: Grímarr, the warlock priest.

"Do you have so few men, heathen"—he looks between Keris and me— "that you must ask your women to fight?"

"I was planning to cut off your head," Marcus says with a grin, "after I'd stuffed your manhood down your throat. But I think I'll let you live just so I can watch Keris gut you slowly."

The Commandant says nothing. She meets Grímarr's eyes briefly, a look that tells me, sure as if she'd spoken it, that they have met before.

She knew he was coming. And she knew he was coming with a hundred thousand men. What did she promise this monster of a man that he would do her bidding and bring a war to Antium, all so she could take the Empire? Despite the fact that the Karkauns appear to have no war strategy, Grímarr is no fool. He nearly bested us in Navium. He must be getting *something* more than a weeks-long siege out of this.

"Deliver your message quickly." Marcus pulls out a blade and casually polishes it. "I'm already wondering if I should change my mind."

"My brother warlocks and I demand that you give up the city of Antium. If you do so immediately, your elderly will be exiled instead of executed, your fighting men enslaved instead of tortured and put to the pyre, and your women and daughters taken to wife and converted instead of raped and debased. If you do not give up the city, we will take it by the Grain Moon. This I vow to you on the blood of my mother and father and unborn children."

Avitas and I exchange a glance. The Grain Moon—again.

"How do you plan to take the city?" I say. "You have no siege machines."

"Silence, heathen. I speak to your master." Grímarr keeps his attention on Marcus even as my hand itches for my war hammer. "Your answer, my lord?"

"You and your corpse-stroking warlocks can take your terms with you to the hells—where we will shortly send you."

"Very well." Grímarr shrugs, as if he expected no less, and wheels his horse away.

When we are back within the city, Marcus turns to Keris and me. "They will strike within the hour."

"My Lord Emperor," Keris says, "how—"

"They will strike, and we must be ready, for it will be swift and hard." Marcus is distracted, head tilted as he listens to whatever secrets his brother's ghost whispers. "I will command the men at the western gate. Keris, the Shrike will inform you of your duties."

His cape whips behind him as he walks away, and I turn to Keris. "Take the eastern wall," I say. "The defense is weakest near the central gate. Hold it, or the first level will be overrun."

The Commandant salutes, and though her face is carefully neutral I can sense the smugness rolling off of her. What the bleeding hells is she up to now?

"Keris." Perhaps this is a lost cause, but I say it anyway. "I know this was you," I say. "All of it. I assume you believe you can hold off the Karkauns long enough to rid yourself of Marcus and Livia. Long enough to rid yourself of me."

She merely watches me.

"I know what you desire," I say. "And this siege you've brought upon the city tells me how badly you wish for it. But there are hundreds of thousands of Martials—"

"You don't know what I want," Keris says softly. "But you will. Soon."

She turns and stalks away, the Plebeians nearby cheering her name as she passes.

"What the bleeding hells is that supposed to mean?" I turn to Avitas, who is at my back. My hand is slick, clenched around the hilt of my dagger. My every instinct screams that something is wrong. That I have irrevocably underestimated Keris. "She wants the Empire," I say to Avitas. "What else could she possibly be after?"

He doesn't get a chance to answer. Panicked shouts rise from the wall. When Avitas and I reach the walkway that runs along the massive structure, I understand why.

The sky is illuminated by the light of scores of pyres. Skies only know how Grímarr disguised them, because I'd have sworn those pyres weren't there moments ago. Now they dominate the field, their flames shooting high into the sky.

Grímarr circles the largest pyre, muttering incantations. From this distance I should not be able to hear him. Yet the malice of his magic taints the very air, the words snaking beneath my skin.

"Ready the catapults." I give Dex the order. "Ready the archers. The Emperor was right. They're making their move."

Down in the Karkaun camp, bound figures are brought toward the pyres, twisting in panic. At first, I think they are animals, part of some sort of ritual sacrifice.

Howls fill the air. And I realize it *is* a sacrifice.

"Bleeding hells," Dex says. "Are those—"

"Women." My stomach churns. "And . . . children."

Their screams echo across the Karkaun camp, and when one of my men retches over the wall, I cannot blame him. Even from here, I can smell burned flesh. Grímarr chants and the Karkauns echo him, soon accompanied by the steady, deep beat of a drum.

The Martials on the wall are well and truly rattled now, but I walk back and forth among them. "Courage in the face of their barbaric ways," I shout. "Courage, lest they bring their darkness upon us all."

The chanting slows, each word drawn out longer until it is one unending low hum that seems to arise from the earth itself.

A distant howl tears through the air, high-pitched, like the screams of those on the pyres but with an unearthly tinge that raises the hair on my arms. The pyres go out. The sudden darkness is blinding. As my eyes adjust, I realize the humming has stopped. Scraps of white rise from the pyres, looking for all the world like—

"Ghosts," Harper says. "They're summoning ghosts."

From the Karkaun camp, screams arise from the men as the ghosts turn on them and plunge into the army, disappearing. Some of the men appear unchanged. Others jerk as if battling something none of us can see, their unnatural movements visible even from here.

Silence descends. Then the thunder of feet, thousands upon thousands of people moving at once.

"They're rushing the walls," I say disbelievingly. "Why would they—"

"Look at them, Shrike," Harper whispers. "Look at how they're moving."

The Karkauns are indeed rushing the walls. But they run with inhuman speed. When they reach the forest of pikes poking out of the ground two hundred yards from Antium, instead of impaling themselves the Karkauns leap over them with unnatural strength.

Shouts of alarm sound from the Martials as the Karkauns come closer.

Even from a distance, their eyes glow a startling, pure white. They're possessed by the ghosts raised by their warlocks.

"Avitas," I say so quietly that no one else can hear. "The evacuation plan. It is ready? All are in place? You have cleared the way?"

"Yes, Shrike." Harper turns from the approaching horde. "All is prepared."

"Then see it done."

He hesitates, about to launch a protest. But I am already moving.

"Catapults!" I call to the drummer, who pounds out the message. "Fire at will!"

Within seconds, the catapults rumble and flaming projectiles fly over the walls toward the possessed Karkauns. Many go down—but more dodge the projectiles, moving with that eerie speed.

"Archers!" I shout. "Fire at will!" With breathtaking swiftness, Grímarr's possessed soldiers have blown past the markers we set out on the field.

A hail of flaming arrows rains down on the Karkauns. It hardly slows them. I order the archers to fire again and again. Some of the Karkauns fall, but not enough. No wonder they didn't have any bleeding siege machines.

An alarm goes up from the men, and less than a hundred yards away, a group of possessed Karkauns lift massive glowing missiles, seemingly unbothered by their flames, and fling them at Antium.

"It's—it's not possible," I whisper. "How can they—"

The missiles fly into the city, smashing into buildings and soldiers and watchtowers. The drummers immediately issue a call for the water brigades. The archers fire volley after volley, and legionnaires reload the catapults as fast as they can.

As the Karkauns close on the walls, I hear their hungry, beast-like snarls.

Too quickly, they are past the trenches, past the secondary forest of pikes planted at the base of the walls to deflect a human army.

We have no defense now. In the space of minutes, the battle will go from strategy and tactics thought up in a distant room to the short, desperate strokes of men fighting for their next breath.

So be it. The Karkauns begin to scale the wall, brandishing their weapons as if they are possessed by demons of the hells. I draw my war hammer.

And then I roar the attack.

XLVII: Laia

The soldier's uniform is far too big, and there's an unpleasant wetness across the small of my back. The previous owner must have taken a blow to the kidney. And he must have spent a long time dying.

Fortunately, the uniform is black, so no one notices the blood as I move through the lines of soldiers along the southern wall of Antium, doling out dippers of water. My hair is tucked tightly into a helm, and I have gloves on to hide my hands. I slump my shoulders beneath the yoke across my back and shuffle my feet. But, tired as they are, the soldiers hardly notice me. I could probably strip down to skivvies and run up and down the wall screaming, "I burned down Blackcliff!" and they wouldn't care.

A light flashes on my helmet. Cook's signal. *Finally.*

It has been two days since we arrived in Antium. Two days since the Karkauns unleashed their hordes of possessed, white-eyed soldiers upon the city. Two days of bone-shaking attacks and streets crumbled to dust. Two days of men with unnatural strength pelting the city with flaming missiles while the air is choked with screams. Above it all, the buzz of arrows as thousands are unleashed on the forces arrayed outside the city's gates.

I have posed as a sweeper, a slops collector, a squire—all in an attempt to get close to the Blood Shrike. I have tried to use my invisibility, but no matter how much willpower I pour into it, I have been unable to harness it.

Which means the Nightbringer must be nearby. He is the only thing that has kept me from drawing on my magic in the past.

Thus the disguises—not that any of them have helped. The Blood Shrike leads the defense of the city, and she is everywhere at once. In the few glimpses I have had of her, her ringed hand has been clenched around her blood-drenched war hammer.

The light flashes on my helm again, this time with an air of impatience. I back away from the line of men, hurrying off as if to get more water, though the buckets attached to the pole across my back are not even half-empty yet.

A missile hits the wall just behind me, and the explosion slams me to my knees, sending the buckets flying. I shudder, every part of my body hurting, a shrill keen in my ears at the sound of the impact.

Get up, Laia! I scramble for the buckets and run from where other soldiers are falling. The missile has left a smoking crater in the earth below the wall, where a group of soldiers and Scholar slaves had been standing only moments ago. The stench makes me gag.

I make my way across the lower level of the wall, up a set of stairs, to the walkway at the top. I keep my head down. This is the closest I've gotten to the Shrike. I cannot make a mistake now.

The mirror flashes again, this time to my left. Cook is telling me which way to go, and I follow the flash, ignoring cries for water, pretending that I have someplace more important to be.

I spy the Shrike ahead of me, blood-drenched and slumped with exhaustion. Her armor is gouged in a dozen places, her hair a mess. Her ringed hand hangs loose.

When I am thirty feet away, I slow my pace. When I am ten feet from her, I clutch at the pole I hold and sling it down, as if preparing to take water to the soldiers around her.

Skies, she is so close, and she has, for once, put down that damned hammer. All I have to do is get my hands on the ring. The moment I do, Cook will launch her distraction—which she has refused to tell me about, for fear of the Nightbringer learning of it and sabotaging us.

Now the Shrike is a mere few feet from me. My mouth is suddenly dry, my feet heavy. *Just get your hands on the ring. Get it off her.*

I should have practiced. Cook spent what little time we had trying to teach me the art of pickpocketing, but in truth, I have no idea how to filch a ring. What if it is tight on her? What if I yank at it and it does not come off? What if she curls her hand into a fist? What if—

A tickle on my neck. A premonition. A warning that something comes. I scurry a few feet farther away from the Shrike and dole out dippers of water to grateful men.

The light ahead shifts strangely, a contortion in the air that births a slice of night's shadow.

The Blood Shrike senses it as I do and stands, her hand fisted around her war hammer once more. Then she takes a step back as the shadows coalesce.

It is him: the Nightbringer.

I am not alone in backing away from him, and it is that that saves me from his gaze. All of the soldiers around the Shrike are in as much of a hurry to escape the jinn's attention as I am.

"Shrike." His grating, grinding voice makes me shudder. "Keris Veturia seeks your counsel, for she—"

I do not hear the rest. I am halfway down the stairs, buckets abandoned, mission aborted.

"What the *hells*?" Cook meets me when I've gotten well away from the wall. I hear the unmistakable whistle of another missile falling.

"We had a *plan*, girl."

"It didn't work." I yank my helm off, not caring who sees, knowing it will not make a difference anyway—not in this chaos. "He was there. The Nightbringer. Right next to her. He would have seen me." I shake my head. "We have to find another way. We need to lure her to us. But short of holding the Emperor hostage, I don't know what would work."

Cook takes my shoulders and turns me toward the wall. "We are going back there right now," she says. "All we have to do is wait for him to leave. Everything is in place, and we won't—"

An explosion tears through the air just yards away, where a group of Scholar slave children are digging through rubble under the watchful eye of a Martial legionnaire.

I find myself flat on the ground, coughing debris from my lungs, trying to wave away the dust.

"Najaam!" A girl cries out. "*Najaam!*" An answering cry, and then the girl's sobbing as she pulls another child from the rubble. With her eyes on the legionnaire, who is still trying to rise from the blast, the little girl grabs the boy, and they begin to run, both of them limping.

Cook sees me watching and drags me to my feet. "Come *on*, girl."

"Those two need help," I say. "We can't just—"

"We can and we will," Cook says. "Move. The distraction I arranged will only work for so long, but it will give you enough time to get to the ring."

But I cannot take my eyes off the child, who spins and searches the city around her, hunting for a way out. Her furrowed brow is far too old for her years, and her younger brother—for they are clearly siblings—looks up at her, waiting for her to tell him what they should do. She spots me and Cook, realizes that we are Scholars, and rushes to us.

"Please," she says. "Can you help us get out? We can't stay. We'll die. Mother and Father and Subhan are already dead. I can't let Najaam die. I promised my parents before they—I promised I'd keep him safe."

I pick up the little boy, and Cook is on my heels. "Damn it, Laia!"

"We cannot get that ring by sneaking it off the Shrike at the wall," I hiss at her. "Distraction or not. But we can save these two lives. We can do *something*. You've seen the tunnels. You know the way out. Get them as far as that. Give them a chance. Because skies know that if they stay in this hellhole, they will die. They'll both die."

"Put the child down, Laia. We have a mission."

"Is that what you told yourself when you left us?" I ask her. "That you had a mission?"

Cook's face goes hard. "You can't help them."

"We can give them a way out."

"So they can starve to death in the forest!"

"So they can have hope!" I scream at her, an eruption born of my guilt over giving up my armlet to the Nightbringer. It is born of my rage at myself for not being able to stop him, frustration at my utter inability to do anything to help or protect or save my people.

"I will get you out," I tell the children. This is one promise I'm going to keep. "Come on. We'll take you through the tunnels. When you come out of them, there will be a forest, and you need to go through it and into the mountains to be safe. You'll have to eat mushrooms and berries—"

The shrill *screee* of a missile rings out, growing louder by the second. It blazes with fire as it arcs downward, graceful as a falling star.

And it's coming right for us.

"Sissy!" Najaam grabs for his sister, panicking. She yanks him from me and runs.

I turn toward my mother in a panic. "Run!" I say. "Ru—"

I feel an arm around my waist, powerful and familiar and searingly hot. The last thing I hear is a deep, scarred voice, growling as if it was born of the earth itself.

"You are a fool, Laia of Serra."

Then I am flung much farther than any human could throw me, and the world goes white.

XLVIII: The Blood Shrike

I do not know how long it has been since the Karkauns descended. I do not know how many I have killed. I only know how many of our men have died. I know where our enemies are starting to push through the wall.

My men roll out pitch and rocks and flames. We throw everything we have at the hordes swarming up ladders and attempting to overrun us. With blood and sweat and unending toil, we hold them back. But they die slowly, if at all. And they keep coming.

The men slump against the wall, bloodied and exhausted. We need a victory. We need something to turn the tide.

I am considering this when Dex arrives, looking as much a mess as I feel. His report is as I expected: too many losses, too few gains. We underestimated the Karkauns and overestimated our own strength in battle.

"Harper says the tunnels are full," Dex says. "He's gotten about five thousand Plebeians up the Pilgrim Road already, but there are thousands left to evacuate. They're all coming out just north of Pilgrim's Gap. That land is hard to travel. It's going to take time."

"Does he need men?"

"He has all he needs."

I nod. At least something in this skies-forsaken city is going right. "And the Paters?"

"Their families have fled. Most of them have holed up in their houses."

We need those men out here, fighting. But it would take more men to drag them out, and we don't have the manpower. The legions from Estium and Silas, which should have been pressing the attack on the Karkaun army's rear guard, have been delayed by storms.

"The Empress?"

"Safe, Shrike, with Rallius and Faris. I still say we need more guards—"

"The Commandant will find her if we move any of her guards from the palace," I say. "With just Rallius and Faris, she can remain hidden. How fare Keris's forces? The Emperor's?"

"The Emperor holds the western gate and refuses to be pulled from battle. They've taken the fewest losses. He's in his element. Keris holds the eastern gate," Dex says. "Pater Rallius and his men are sticking to her like burrs, as you've asked, but they've taken losses. The Karkauns are pushing hard. She's requested more men."

My lip curls. That traitorous hag. *You don't know what I want.* I still haven't worked out what it could be. But I know she won't sacrifice the entire capital. She'll have no one to bleeding rule over if she does. *Everything* that makes the Empire the Empire is here: the treasury, the Hall of Records, the Emperor's palace, and, most importantly, the people. If she allows the city to fall, she'll be Empress of nothing but ash.

I shake my head. We need the damned legions from the south. We need something to stop these monsters.

Work with what you have, not what you want. The Commandant's own words. "What else, Dex?"

"The Karkauns were spotted spreading a white substance around the edges of their army, Shrike. Almost like a border. We've no idea what it is."

"It is salt." The shudder-inducing voice of the Nightbringer behind me doesn't even make me jump. I am too exhausted.

"Salt?" I say. "Why the bleeding hells would they be spreading salt around their camp?"

"Ghosts do not like salt, Shrike," he says, as if this is the most natural thing in the world. "It will not stop the Karkauns who are possessed, for their human hosts make them immune to such tricks. But it will stop attacks from the wild ghosts who approach, ghosts who are not enslaved to the warlocks."

I gape at him. "More ghosts?"

"They have broken free of the Waiting Place and are drawn to the blood and violence of the battle here. Their arrival is imminent."

The Nightbringer reaches a hand to my shoulder and sings a few high notes. Immediately, my body, which burned from a dozen wounds, relaxes, the pain fading. I accept his aid gratefully. He has done this every day since the Karkauns launched their assault, sometimes twice a day, so I can keep fighting. He does not ask questions. He simply arrives, heals me, and disappears again.

As he turns to leave, I stop him. "The day I healed Livia, you said that one day my—my trust in you would be my only weapon." I shake my head at the disaster before me. The flagging men, the unending army of the Karkauns. Antium, the capital, the Pearl of the Empire, slowly crumbling.

"Today is not that day, Blood Shrike." His eyes linger on my face—no, I realize, on my ring, as my hand is propped against my face. Then he is gone.

"Dex," I say. "Find as much salt as you can. Salt the wall, the infirmaries, wherever our fighting men are. Tell the men not to touch it." What does it mean that the ghosts have broken free of the Waiting Place? Have they killed Elias?

When the moon rises, the Karkauns call a retreat. Nothing has changed. Our men are still barely keeping them at bay. Their unnaturally powerful soldiers still wreak havoc. They have the advantage. Why the bleeding hells are they withdrawing?

A ragged cheer goes up along the wall from my men. I do not join them. Whatever is making the Karkauns withdraw cannot be good for us.

Moments later, the wind carries a strange sound to me: wailing. The hair on the back of my neck rises as it draws closer. The cries are too high-pitched to be of this world. *The wild ghosts.*

The men grasp their weapons, stalwart in the face of this new terror. The wailing intensifies.

"Shrike." Dex appears beside me. "What in ten hells is that sound?"

"The salt, Dex," I say. "Did you spread it?"

"Only along the wall," he says. "We ran out before we could spread it in the city."

"It won't be enough." A pale, smoky cloud passes near the Karkauns, veering away from the salt border they have marked around their army, like a trail of ants avoiding a line of water.

The shrieks from the cloud block out every other sound, including the drums, the shouts of the men, the ragged rhythm of my own breath. There are faces in that cloud, thousands of them.

Ghosts.

My men exclaim in fear, and I do not know what to do. I do not know how to kill this enemy. How to fight it. I do not know what it will do to us. *Help,* I scream in my mind. *Father. Mother. Elias. Someone. Help us.* I might as well be calling out to the moon.

The cloud is at the wall now, streaming over. Cold blasts through me as the ghosts shriek past, hissing at the salt along the wall before plummeting down to the unprotected men holding the gates, and into the streets beyond.

The soldiers do not know what hit them. One moment, they gaze at the cloud in wary fear. The next, they twitch and shake, possessed. Then, to my horror, they begin attacking each other like rabid animals.

The Karkauns roar and storm the city gates. We rain down arrows, pitch, rocks, but it is not enough.

I grab Dex by his collar. "We need more salt!"

"It's gone—we used everything we could find."

"If our own men are attacking each other, we cannot hold the gates," I tell him. "We will lose the city. Get to Harper. Tell him to collapse the entrances to the tunnels. We cannot risk the Karkauns getting to our people."

"But what about the people who are still left?"

"Go!"

"Shrike!" Another voice calls to me, and Faris bulls through the soldiers fighting to keep back the Karkauns. Down below, the men tear each other apart, attacking with anything they can find. One of the soldiers on the wall flings handfuls of salt down, perhaps hoping to scare the ghosts out of the bodies they have possessed. But it does nothing.

Any other army would have fled the wall at this sight—Karkauns crawling over the walls, our own men possessed. But the legions hold.

"Shrike." Faris is out of breath, but he still has the sense to speak quietly. "The midwife we found to replace the last one is dead. I just found her swinging from a beam in her own house."

"Well, bloody find another."

"There *are* no others."

"I don't have time for this!"

"You don't understand." Faris crouches down and hisses, and I can see panic that he'd never feel in battle in his shaking hands. "I sought out the midwife because it's time. Your sister is in labor, Shrike. The baby is coming."

XLIX: Laia

C ook does not speak to me for a long time after I wake. Her face tells me what happened to the children I was trying to help. Still, I ask.

"The blast killed them," she says. "It was quick." Her golden skin is pale, but her hunched shoulders and shaking hands tell me of her rage. "Nearly killed you too."

I sit up. "Where are we?"

"The old Scholar's District," she says. "In the slaves' quarters. It's farther from the chaos than the Mariner Embassy, though not by much." She dabs a wound on my face with a warm cloth, careful not to let her skin touch mine. "The skies must love you, girl. That blast threw you thirty feet into a pile of feed."

My head aches, and I struggle to remember. *The skies must love you.*

No. Not the skies. I knew that voice. I knew well the feel of that arm, strange and warped and too hot.

Why would the Nightbringer throw me out of the way of the blast? Why, when he knows what I am trying to do? I had no plan in my head in the moment of the blast—nothing but trying to get the children out. Am I playing into his hands somehow?

Or was it something else?

"Your heroics cost us." Cook stirs a pot of some sort of acrid tea over a cook fire. "Do you know what day it is?"

I open my mouth to respond, but Cook cuts me off.

"It's the day of the Grain Moon," she says. "We lost our chance to get to the Blood Shrike. By tomorrow, the city will be breached. The Martials are stretched too thin, and there's no relief in sight."

She takes a sniff of the tea and adds something else to it. "Girl," she says, "you trained with your"—she takes a deep breath—"grandfather," she spits out, "in healing?"

"For a year and a half or so."

She nods thoughtfully. "As did I," she said. "Before I ran away like a damned fool. When did he take you to meet Nelle, the apothecary?"

"Uh . . ." I am bewildered that she knows about Nelle, until I remember, yet again, that of course she would know Nelle. Pop trained my mother from when she turned twelve until she was sixteen, when she left home to join the Resistance.

"It was at the beginning of my training," I say. "Maybe three months in." Nelle showed me how to make dozens of poultices and teas from basic ingredients. Most of the remedies were things that only a woman needs—for moon cycles and to prevent the getting of child.

She nods. "That's what I thought." She pours the foul tea into a waiting gourd and corks it. I think she is going to give it to me, but instead she stands. "Change the dressing on your wounds," she says. "You'll find everything you need there. Stay inside. I'll be back."

While she's gone, I change the dressings, but I can't stop thinking about the blast, the Nightbringer throwing me out of the way, the brother and sister who died. Skies, they were so young. That little girl couldn't have been older than ten and her little brother—Najaam—no more than seven. *I promised my parents I'd keep him safe.*

"I am sorry," I whisper.

I could have saved them if I had moved faster, if I had not taken the route I did. How many other Scholar children have been ordered to stay in the city? How many others have no way out? How many are expected to die along with their Martial overlords if the Karkauns take Antium? Musa's voice rings in my head. *We need you as a voice for the Scholars. We need you as our scim and shield.*

Though Cook told me not to, I leave the crumbling little shack in which we've taken shelter and walk outside, wincing from the way the movement pulls at the gash on my face.

The house I am in faces a large square. There are heaps of rubble on either side and more dilapidated cottages beyond them. Across the square, dozens of Scholars remove the bricks of a still-smoking shack, trying to get to those trapped inside.

Boots thud beyond the square, their rhythmic tattoo growing louder. Quick as lightning, word spreads. The Scholars disappear into their houses as the patrol marches into the square. The house I am in is set back, but still, I make my way up the stairs, dagger in hand. I crouch beside a window to watch the patrol's progress, waiting for the screams of the Scholars.

I hear only a few, from those the Martials have found and dragged out, whipping them into a line to no doubt save Martial lives from the Karkauns' destruction.

When the Martials are gone, the remaining Scholars emerge again, back at the rubble of the ruined house. I am wondering how they communicated so quickly when the stairwell creaks.

"Girl," Cook rasps, "are you here?"

When I get down the stairs, she jerks her head to the north. "Come with me," she says. "And don't ask questions." She no longer holds the gourd of tea, and I want to know what she has done with it. But I hold my tongue. As we head through the square, Cook does not spare a glance for the Scholars.

"Cook." I run to catch up with her. It's as if she *knows* what I am planning to ask. "These people. We could help them. Get them out of here."

"We could." She sounds utterly unsurprised at my suggestion. "And then you could watch as the Nightbringer takes the ring from the Shrike, sets his accursed subjects free, and destroys our world."

"I am the one who has to get the ring," I say. "Not you. You could rally the Scholars, show them the way out of here. You said yourself that the Karkauns will overrun the city. What do you think will happen to these people when they do?"

As I speak, we slink past a group of Scholars putting out a fire alongside Martial auxes. They are children—teenagers dragging buckets of water when they should be getting the hells out of here.

"That's not our problem," Cook hisses, and grabs me, pulling me away before the aux soldiers see us and press us into service. "I have other things to do while you get the ring."

"*What* other things?"

"Retribution!" Cook says. "That bitch of a Commandant is here, and by the skies, I'll—"

"You'd trade vengeance on Keris Veturia for thousands of lives?"

"Getting rid of her would save thousands more. I have waited years for this. And now, finally—"

"I don't bleeding care," I say to her. "Whatever your vengeance is, whether it works or not, it is not as important as the Scholar children who will die if there is no one to help them. Please—"

"We're not gods, girl. We can't save everyone. The Scholars have survived this long. They'll survive a bit longer. The mission is all that matters. Come now. There's little time." She nods to a building ahead. "That's the Black Guard barracks. The Shrike will be arriving within the hour. When that happens, you'll know what to do."

"What—that's it? How am I supposed to get in? How do I—"

"You need a plan that the Nightbringer can't pick out of your head," she rasps. "I've just given you one. There's a stack of clean uniforms in a basket outside the gates. Take it in and up to the laundry closet on the second floor. Watch the hallway from that closet. When the time comes, you'll know what to do. And if the Shrike threatens you, tell her I sent you. Go."

"You—why would I—do you know her?"

"Move, girl!"

I take two steps, then turn back. "Cook." I look in the direction of the Scholar neighborhood. "Please, just tell them—"

"I'll be waiting here for your return." Cook grabs my daggers from me, including the one Elias gave me, ignoring my protests as she glances about furtively. "Hurry up, or you'll get us both killed."

Uneasy without my blades, I go around to the front of the barracks. What does Cook have planned for me? How will I know what to do? I spot the basket of clean laundry and balance it against my hip. Taking a deep breath, I pass through the front gates and across the cobblestone courtyard.

The ground rumbles, and across the street, a projectile slams into a building, leveling it in seconds. The two legionnaires who guard the barracks entrance take cover, as do I. When it's clear no more missiles are coming this way, I make for the door, hoping the legionnaires will be too distracted to notice me. No such luck.

"You there." One of them holds out a hand. "We need to search the basket."

Oh skies.

"No idea why we even need uniforms," the other legionnaire says. "We're all dead anyway."

"Shut it, Eddius." The legionnaire finishes searching the basket and waves me on. "Go on, girl."

The central room of the barracks is lined with cots, perhaps for men to sleep on while taking shifts at the wall. But they all stand empty. No one in the entire damned city is sleeping through this.

Though it's clear the barracks are almost entirely abandoned, I skirt the cots carefully and skulk up the stairs, unnerved by the silence of the place. At the top of the stairs, a long hallway stretches into darkness. The doors are shut, but from behind one, clothing rustles and someone gasps in pain. I keep walking and get to a laundry closet. The cries continue. Someone must be injured.

After half an hour, the cries transform into screams. It is definitely a woman, and for a moment I wonder, is it the Shrike? Has Cook injured her? Am I supposed to go into the room and take the ring while she lies dying? I creep out of the laundry closet and inch down the hall toward the cries. A male speaks, and it sounds like he's trying to soothe the woman.

Another scream. This time I cock my head. It doesn't sound like someone who is injured. In fact, it sounds like—

"*Where is she?*" The woman wails, and a door in the hallway slams open. I bolt back into the laundry closet just after catching a glimpse of a woman pacing the room. At first, I think she is the Blood Shrike. But she has no mask, and she is very pregnant.

In that moment, I understand the sounds that came from the room. I understand why Cook asked me if I'd met Nelle. Nelle taught me remedies for moon-cycle pain and ways to prevent pregnancy—but she also showed me tricks for relieving pain during childbirth and afterward. I had to learn them because delivering babies was one of the very first things Pop taught me, one of the main things he did as a healer.

And I understand, finally, how I am going to get the ring from the Blood Shrike.

L: Elias

As I come up over the wall, as I force myself to ignore the havoc wreaked by the possessed Karkauns, I hear the lupine snarls of a group of Martial soldiers tearing at each other, completely possessed.

I have always loathed the city of Antium. Everything about it screams *Empire*, from the high, forbidding walls to the streets architected in levels to repel attack. For the first time, I am glad that the city is so quintessentially Martial. Because the forces arrayed against it—and within it—are great, and the defenses are terrifyingly flimsy.

I windwalk down the wall, racing toward the stairs that will take me to the ravening masses of possessed Martial soldiers below. There are hundreds of ghosts to be found, magicked, and set free.

The stairs disappear two by two under my feet, and I am nearly at the bottom when I recognize a head of blonde hair ahead of me, battling through the possessed soldiers. Her face is dark with ash, streaked with tears as she swings a great war hammer, trying to knock her countrymen aside. From the west, a great groan sounds, the splintering of wood and warping of metal. The Karkauns are nearly through the gates of the city.

"Stop!" My voice, amplified by Mauth's magic, explodes across the area beneath the wall. The possessed turn to me as one, my magic drawing them in like a cobra's gaze draws a mouse.

"E-Elias?" the Blood Shrike whispers, but I do not look at her.

"Come to me," I order the spirits forward. "Release those you have possessed."

These ghosts are more feral, and they resist, curling away from me. My anger rises, and I find my hands are on my scims. But Mauth's magic takes hold, and an unnatural calm settles over me. *No*, part of me scrambles against the intrusion of the magic, which is more aggressive than before. Mauth is controlling my body. My mind. *This isn't right.*

But isn't it? I must join with the magic to become the Soul Catcher. First I needed to release my attachments to the human world. And now I must let go of myself. My identity. My body.

No, something deep within screams. *No. No. No.*

But how else will I move so many ghosts on? Their presence here is my fault. The suffering they've brought about is my fault. I can never undo it. All the deaths they have caused will be on my conscience until the day I pass from this earth. But I can stop it. And to do that, I must surrender.

Take over, I tell the magic. *Become me.*

"Release the humans you've possessed." The ghosts shy back at my order, so bewildered at their own deaths that they seek only to hold, hurt, love, *feel* once more. "There is nothing for you here. Only pain."

I draw them all close with the magic. Mauth sinks into my very soul with every second that passes, becoming irrevocably bonded to me. The Blood Shrike and Faris gape, and they do not see their friend Elias Veturius. They do not see the man who escaped Blackcliff, who broke his vows, who defied the Commandant and the Emperor to break into Kauf Prison. They do not see the boy they survived Blackcliff with.

They see the Soul Catcher.

The ghosts sigh and release the bodies they have possessed, passing on from this world. First dozens, then, as I let the magic take over, hundreds. The chaos fades as this small group of soldiers, at least, returns to themselves.

"You came." The Blood Shrike weeps openly now. "You heard me, and you came. Elias, the Karkauns on the wall, they're killing us. They're about to break through."

"I did not come for you." It is my voice she hears—the merciless monotone of a Mask. And yet it is *not* me. It is Mauth. *Stop!* I scream at him in my mind. *She is my friend.*

But Mauth does not listen. "I came," I hear myself saying, "because it is my sworn duty to protect the world of the living from the realm of ghosts. Leave me to my work, Blood Shrike, and I will leave you to yours."

I windwalk away from her, moving swiftly to the next group of possessed soldiers. Why did I do that? Why was I so cruel?

Because it is necessary. I know the answer almost before I ask the question. *Because I must pass the ghosts. Because my duty must come first.*

Because love cannot live here.

I skim over the wall of the city looking for the next group of wayward ghosts, nothing but a flash of darkness to the human eye. Just outside Antium's eastern gate, the Karkauns gather and march forward with a battering ram the size of a Mariner trade vessel. They punch through the ancient gates of Antium like a fist through a paper screen.

No one mans the wall. No pitch comes pouring down. No archers fight back. The Martials have withdrawn. A familiar, pale-skinned figure makes her way from the battle, a group of men at her back. Keris Veturia. She appears calm as she allows the gate to fall.

A great groan echoes through the air, louder than the screams of the dying and the cries of those who still fight. Wood splinters, metal screeches, and a hair-raising howl of victory rises from the ranks of the Karkauns.

The eastern gate sags open, and the Karkauns pour in. The city of Antium, founded by Taius the First, seat of the Imperator Invictus and Pearl of the Empire, is breached. The lives of its people are forfeit.

I turn away. For it is no concern of mine.

LI: The Blood Shrike

I can hear Livvy screaming from the barracks doors and I fly up the stairs. *She might be dying. The baby might be dying. Skies, what do we do—*

When I shove the door open, I find my sister doubled over, Rallius's large hand clenched in hers. Every muscle in my friend's huge body tenses, his dark face turning grim.

"Empress," I say. "Livia, I'm here."

"He's coming, Helly." Livia pants. "Rallius tested my tea this morning, but it tasted funny. I don't know what to do. I don't—I don't feel right—"

Oh hells. I know exactly nothing about childbirth. "Maybe you should sit down."

A knock on the door.

All of us—Rallius, Faris, Livia, and I—go silent. No one but Marcus is supposed to know she's here. But I arrived in such a rush with Faris that though we took pains not to be followed, we might very well have been.

My sister stuffs her fist to her mouth and groans, clutching her belly. Her dress is wet from where her waters have broken, and her sweat-soaked face is sickly gray. Rallius extricates his fingers from Livvy's and approaches the door, scims drawn. I shove Livvy behind me while Faris swipes a crossbow from the wall and points it at the door.

"Who goes there?"

A female voice answers. "I . . . I need to speak to the Blood Shrike. I . . . can help."

I do not recognize the voice, though something about it is strangely familiar. I gesture for Rallius to open the door. In less than a second, he has his scims at the throat of the hooded figure in the doorway.

She doesn't need to lower her hood for me to recognize her. I spot her golden eyes peering out at me from the shadows.

"You!" I snarl, but she raises her hands, and the sheaths at her waist are empty.

"I can deliver the baby," she says quickly. "Cook sent me."

"Why the hells would that old bat send you?" I say.

Livia screams again, unable to stifle the sound, and Laia looks over my shoulder.

"She's close," she says. "She'll have another contraction in only a few moments. The child is coming."

I do not know how in the burning skies she got here. Perhaps it is an assassination attempt. But why would Laia of Serra risk such a thing when she knows that hurting my sister would result in her immediate death?

"I have no wish to harm her," she says. "Fate led me here, Blood Shrike. Let me help you."

"If my sister or the babe die," I say to her as I stand aside, "so do you."

A grim nod is the only response. She knows. Immediately, she turns to Faris, who squints as he looks at her.

"Hang on a minute," he says. "Aren't you—"

"Yes," she says. "Hot water, please, Lieutenant Faris—two pots of it. And clean sheets from the laundry—a dozen of them. Towels too." She goes to my sister, taking her by the arm.

"Let's get you out of these clothes," she says, and there's a gentleness to her voice, a sweetness that immediately calms Livia. My sister sighs, and moments later Laia unlaces her dress, ordering Rallius to turn away.

I shift from foot to foot. "I don't know if this is appro—"

"She's giving birth, Blood Shrike," Laia says. "It is hot, difficult work, and she shouldn't be trussed up for it. Bad for the baby."

"Right," I say, knowing I sound like an idiot. "Well, if it's bad for the baby . . ."

Laia glances at me, and I can't tell if she's irritated by me or laughing at me.

"Once Lieutenant Faris returns with the water," she says, "pour it into the basin, please. Wash your hands well, with soap. Remove your rings. You can leave them there." She nods to the basin and helps a now scantily dressed Livia settle herself at the edge of my simple wooden desk chair.

Faris comes in, takes one look at Livvy, and turns bright red before I take the water from him and he asks, in a choked voice, where Laia wants the sheets.

"Stand watch, Lieutenant Faris," Laia says as she takes the sheets. "There were only two guards outside and they barely searched me. If I got in here with relative ease, so can your enemies."

The drums thunder, and I hear the panic in the order given out. *All units to the second-level gate immediately. Breach imminent.* Bleeding hells, has the first level been breached? "I should go," I say. "The city—"

"I cannot do this alone, Shrike," Laia says quickly. "Though I'm sure your man here"—she nods to a wild-eyed Lieutenant Rallius—"would help if ordered, the Empress is your sister, and your presence will bring her comfort."

"The city—the Karkauns—" But Livvy screams again, and Laia curses.

"Shrike, have you washed your hands yet?"

I do it quickly, and Laia grabs me and yanks me over to Livia.

"Push your fists into your sister's hips, like so." She points to just below the small of my sister's back. "Every time she screams, I want you to push there," she says. "It will give her relief. In between, rub her shoulders, pull her hair out of the way, and help keep her cool."

"Oh skies," Livia says. "I'm going to be sick."

My stomach sinks. "What's wrong?"

"Feeling sick is good." Laia's tone is soothing, but she gives me a look that very plainly asks that I keep my mouth shut. "It cleanses the body."

The Scholar girl gives my sister a bucket and continues to speak to her in low, calm tones as she scrubs her own hands and arms, over and over until her gold-brown skin is red. Then she comes back and feels between my sister's legs. I look away, uncomfortable. Livia shudders again—it's only been minutes since the last time she cried out. I dig my fists into her hips. Immediately, she relaxes.

"How—how many times have you done this?" Livvy asks Laia.

"Enough to know that you're going to be just fine," Laia says. "Now breathe with me."

For the next two hours, with the Scholar girl's calm voice guiding her, Livia labors. Sometimes she walks, sometimes she sits. When I suggest Livvy lie in the bed at one point, both women turn on me with a unified "*No!*" and I cease.

Outside, the drums grow more frantic. I need to get out there—I need to help defend this city. And yet I cannot leave Livia. I must see this child born, for he is our future. If the city falls, I must see him to safety. I am torn, and I pace back and forth, not knowing what the bleeding skies I'm supposed to do. *Why* is childbirth so damned messy? And why didn't I learn anything about it?

"Laia," I finally say to the Scholar when Livia is resting between one of her contractions. "The city—it's about to be breached. I can hear it from the drums. I cannot be here. Rallius can—"

Laia yanks me aside, mouth thin. "It's taking too long," she says.

"You said everything was fine."

"I'm not about to tell a pregnant woman she's not fine," she hisses. "I've seen it happen before. Both times the child died, and the mother did too. They are in danger. I might need you." She gives me a significant look. *I might need your healing.*

BREACH, MAIN GATE. ALL UNITS TO SECOND-LEVEL GATE. The drums thunder frantically now as message after message is passed through, so that troops might know where to go, where to fight.

Livia screams, and this time there is a different quality about it. I turn back to my sister, hoping to the skies that the drums have it wrong.

Laia drapes sheets over the chairs, on the floors. She orders me to bring more buckets of water, and when she asks me to lay a towel on the bed, my sister shakes her head.

"There's a blanket," she says. "It's—it's in the bureau. I—I brought it with me."

I grab it, a simple pale-blue-and-white square that is soft as clouds. I realize suddenly that this child will be my kin. A new Aquilla. My nephew. The moment deserves more than the thunder of Karkaun missiles and my sister's screams. Mother should be here. Hannah.

Instead it is only me. How the hells did it all go so wrong?

"All right, Livia," Laia says. "It's time now. You've been very brave, very strong. Be brave a bit longer and you'll be holding your baby, and I promise that you won't much care about the pain."

"How—how do you know—"

"Trust me." Laia's smile is so convincing that even I believe it. "Shrike, hold her hands." She lowers her voice. "And sing."

My sister grabs on to me with the strength of a Mask in an arm-wrestling competition. With Rallius and Faris watching, I find Livia's song in my mind and sing it, pouring my will into giving her strength, keeping her whole. At Laia's urging, my sister pushes with all of her might.

Childbirth is not something I have wasted much thought on. I do not wish for children. I will never be a midwife. I have a sister, but no female friends. Babies hold no appeal for me, though I was always fascinated by the way my mother loved us: with a fierceness that was almost frightening. She used to call us her miracles. Now, as my sister releases a roar, I finally understand.

Laia is holding a slippery, wet, dirty . . . thing in her hands. She snatches the towels from me, pulling the child into one while using her other hand to unwrap the cord from his neck. She moves quickly, almost frantically, and a strange, unfamiliar terror fills me.

"Why isn't he making any sounds?" I demand. "Why is he—"

Laia puts her finger in the babe's mouth, clearing it, and a moment later, he releases an ear-shattering wail.

"Oh," I squeak as Laia shoves the baby at me. "I—"

"Whisper your hopes for him in his ear," she says. When I stare at her, she sighs impatiently. "It's considered good luck."

She turns back to my sister, doing skies know what, and I stare down at the child. His wails have faded, and he watches me, appearing mildly bewildered. I cannot say I blame him.

His skin is golden brown, a few shades darker than Livia's when she has spent a summer in the sun. His hair is fine and black. He has his father's yellow eyes, and yet they are not Marcus's. They are beautiful. Innocent.

He opens his mouth and vocalizes, and it sounds to me like "Hah," as if he's trying to say the beginning of my name. It is a ridiculous thought, but a burst of pride floods me. He knows me.

"Hail, nephew." I pull him close to me so that he's only inches from my face. "I wish for you joy and a family that loves you, adventures that shape you, and true friends to have them with."

His fist flails, leaving a trail of blood across my mask. I recognize something in him then. Something of me, though it is not in his face. It is deeper. I think of the song I sang him. I wonder how I changed him.

Shouts outside pull my attention away from the child. The angry tenor of a familiar voice rises downstairs. Footsteps thunder up the steps, and the door bursts open. Marcus, along with a half dozen men of Gens Aquilla, enters, scim drawn. The Emperor is covered in blood—his own or that of the Karkauns, I do not know. He does not look at me or Livia or Laia. He reaches me in two steps. Without sheathing his sword, he holds out his left arm for his child. I hand the baby over, hating the feeling, my entire body tense.

Marcus looks into the child's face. I cannot read his expression. Both Marcus and his son are silent, the Emperor's head cocked, as if he is listening to something. He nods once.

"Zacharias Marcus Livius Aquillus Farrar," he says, "I wish you a long reign as Emperor, glory in battle, and a brother at your back." He gives the child back to me, unnaturally careful. "Take your sister and the child, Shrike, and leave the city. That is an order. She's coming for him."

"The Commandant?"

"Yes, the bleeding Commandant," Marcus snaps. "The gates are breached. The Karkauns have broken through the first level. She's left the battle in the hands of one of her lieutenants and is on her way here."

"Shrike." Laia's voice is choked. I notice she's pulled her hood up, and I recall then that she knows Marcus. That he nearly killed her once—after he tried to rape her. I shudder, thinking of it. She is hunched over, her voice raspy as she tries to disguise herself. "Your sister."

Livia is deathly pale. "I'm fine," she murmurs as she tries to stand. "Give him—give him to me."

I am at her side in two steps, her song already on my lips. I do not think of Marcus's soldiers, who will witness this, or of Rallius or Faris. I sing until I feel her body heal. The moment that color returns to her face, Marcus drags her through the door and down to the laundry room, flinging it open. Rallius goes through, then Faris, then my sister.

Marcus does not look at the child again. He gestures me impatiently on.

"My lord," I say, "I cannot leave the city when it—"

"Protect my heir," he says. "The city is lost."

"It—it can't be—"

But he shoves me into the tunnel and closes the door behind me. And it is only there, in the darkness, that I realize I have no idea where Laia is.

«««

We run. From the tunnels, we cannot hear the madness above, but my mind is torn, half of me wanting to go back to fight and the other half knowing that I must get my sister and baby Zacharias out of Antium.

When we reach a way station in the tunnels where Harper has placed soldiers to guard the evacuation routes, I slow.

"I need to go back," I say.

Livia shakes her head, frantic. Zacharias wails, as if sensing his mother's distress. "You were given an order."

"I cannot leave the city," I say. "Not like this. Not skulking through the shadows. There are men back there who were counting on me, and I left them."

"Helly, *no*."

"Faris, Rallius, get her to Harper. You know how to find him. Help him however you can. There are still Plebeians in the city, in these tunnels, and we need to get them out." I lean toward both of them, pinning them with my gaze. "If anything happens to her or the child, I swear to the skies, I will kill you both myself."

They salute, and I turn to my sister, taking one last look at the baby. Upon seeing my face, he goes quiet. "I'll see you soon, young one." I kiss him and Livia, and turn back, ignoring my sister's pleas, then demands, for me to return to her side at once.

When I get back to the Black Guard barracks, I immediately choke on the smoke that fills the laundry closet. Flames roar at the front of the barracks. From a few streets away, the howls of rampaging Karkauns fill the streets. They have not reached here yet, but they will soon.

I draw a scarf up over my face and crouch low to avoid the smoke, my war hammer drawn. When I emerge from the room, I nearly slip on the pools of blood everywhere.

The men of Gens Aquilla, sworn to protect Marcus, lie dead, though it is clear that they took many of the Commandant's men with them. Her body is not among the carnage. But then, I knew it would not be. Keris Veturia would never die in so undignified a manner.

There are other bodies among the dead — Mariners. Before I can understand what the hells they were doing here, a voice calls out.

"Sh-Shrike."

The voice is so quiet that I do not at first know where it comes from. But I hunt through the smoke until I find Marcus Farrar, Imperator Invictus and Overlord of the Realm, pinned against a wall by his own scim, drowning in his own blood, unable to move. His hands are limp over the wound in his stomach. He has hours yet until he dies. The Commandant did this on purpose.

I go to him. Flames lick the wood of the stairwell, and a loud crack sounds from downstairs—a beam falling. I should escape through a window. I should let this monster burn.

How long have I waited for this? How long have I wanted him to die? And yet when I see him pinned here like an animal killed for sport, I feel only pity.

And something else. A compulsion. A need. A desire to heal him. *No. Oh no.*

"Keris moved the Hall of Records, Shrike." He speaks calmly, if softly, saving his breath to relay what he must. "She moved the treasury."

I sigh in relief. "Then the Empire will still stand, even if we lose Antium."

"She did it weeks ago. She wanted the city to fall, Shrike. She knew the Karkauns would bring ghosts. She knew they would win."

A dozen disparate puzzle pieces click into place.

"The Illustrian Paters—"

"Left days ago for Serra," Marcus says. "She evacuated them."

And the master of the treasury met with her despite her murdering his son. She must have told him what was coming. She must have promised to get his family out in exchange for him moving the Empire's wealth.

And the Hall of Records. *The record archivists were preparing for a move.*

Harper told me that when he was getting information on the Commandant. We simply didn't realize what it meant.

Keris knew the city would fall. She was planning for it right in front of me.

Skies, I should have killed her. Whether the Plebeians hated me or not, whether Marcus was overthrown or not, I should have killed that demon.

"The legions," I say, "from Silas and Estium—"

"They aren't coming. She sabotaged the communiqués."

It did not have to be this way, Blood Shrike. Keris's words haunt me. *Remember that, before the end.*

He does not say it is my fault; he doesn't have to. "Antium will fall," Marcus goes on quietly. "But the Empire will survive. Keris has ensured that, though she wishes to make certain that my son will not survive with it. Stop her, Blood Shrike. See him on the throne." He reaches for my hand, his own still strong enough to dig into my flesh so hard that it draws blood. "Swear a blood oath that you will see it done."

"I swear it," I say. "By blood and by bone." The compulsion to heal him comes over me again. I fight it, but then he speaks.

"Shrike," he says. "I have a final order for you."

Heal me. I know he's going to say it. The magic rises in me, ready, even as I shrink away from the thought, disgusted, repulsed by it. How can I heal him, the demon who killed my father, who ordered my torture, who abused and beat my sister?

The fire edges closer. *Leave, Shrike! Run!*

Marcus releases my hand and scrabbles at his side for a dagger, which he thrusts into my hand. "Mercy, Blood Shrike. That is my order. I do not deserve it. I do not even wish it. But you'll give it to me anyway. Because you're *good.*" He spits out the word, a curse. "It's why my brother loved you."

The Emperor meets my eyes. As ever, his are filled with rage, hatred. But beneath that is something I have never seen before in the fifteen years I have known Marcus Farrar: resignation.

"Do it, Shrike," he whispers. "He waits for me."

I think of baby Zacharias and the innocence of his gaze. Marcus too must have looked that way once. Perhaps that's what his twin, Zak, saw when he looked at him: not the monster he had become, but the brother he had been.

I remember my father as he died. My mother and my sister. My face is wet. When Marcus speaks, I can barely hear the words.

"Please, Shrike."

"The Emperor is dead." My voice shakes, but I find my strength in the mask I wear, and when I speak again, it is without emotion. "Long live the Emperor."

Then I drive the dagger into his throat, and I do not look away until the light in his eyes is gone.

LII: Laia

T he ring does not evanesce.

I do not allow myself to look at it until I am outside the Black Guard barracks, tucked in an alcove near the stables, safely away from Emperor Marcus. The baby is strong, and the Blood Shrike's sister is as well. I whispered to her to keep herself clean, to take care of herself to prevent infection. But she saw my face when Marcus entered. She knew.

"Go," she whispered. "Take the towels, as if you are changing them."

I did as she said. Swiping the rings at the same time was only a moment's work. No one even looked my way.

I took both, not knowing which was the Shrike's ring and which was the ring of her family. Now I stand with them in the madness of Antium's streets, staring. Hoping.

Only the Ghost may stand against the onslaught. Should the Lioness's heir claim the Butcher's pride, it will evanesce, and the blood of seven generations shall pass from the earth before the King may seek vengeance again.

The ring should be gone. Why did it not happen? I put it on my finger, pull it off. But there's something wrong with it. It does not feel like my armlet. It just feels like a normal hunk of metal.

I rack my brain trying to remember if I missed something in the prophecy. Perhaps I have to do something to it. Burn it, or break it with Serric steel. I cast about for a weapon—something a soldier might have dropped.

Which is when my neck prickles, and I know instantly that someone watches me. It is a feeling that has become unsettlingly familiar in the past few months.

But this time, he shows himself. "Forgive me, Laia of Serra." The Night-bringer speaks quietly, but the violence latent in his voice still cuts through the shrieks of missiles flying and men dying painfully. "I wished to see your face when you realized that all your work, all your hope, was for nothing."

"It is not for nothing," I say. *It cannot be.*

"It was." He saunters toward me. "Because what you hold is not the Star."

"You lie."

"Do I?" He closes the distance between us and snatches the rings from my hand. I cry out, but he closes his hand around them and, before my eyes, crushes them to powder. *No. Impossible.*

The curiosity that emanates from him is somehow worse than if he simply gloated.

"What is it like, Laia of Serra," he says, "to know that no matter what you do, nothing will stop the war that is coming? The war that will annihilate your people."

He's toying with me. "Why did you save me," I snarl at him, "when the blast hit?"

For a moment, he is still. And then his shoulders ripple, like a great cat shaking itself.

"Run to your brother, Laia of Serra," he says. "Find a ship to take you far away. You do not wish to witness what is to come."

"You know what it means to destroy an entire race. How could you want it when you have survived it?"

"The Scholars deserve destruction."

"You have already destroyed us," I shout. I fight to keep from hitting him—not because I am afraid, but because I know it will do no good. "Look at what the Scholars are. Look at what we have become. We are *nothing*. We are *dust*. Look"—my voice is ragged now—"look at what you did to me. Look at how you betrayed me. Is it not enough?"

"It is never enough." He is angry now, my words poking at something tender that he does not wish to touch. "Do as I say, Laia of Serra. Run. You heard Shaeva's prophecy. The library burned. The dead escaped and marauded. *The Child will be bathed in blood but alive.* I believe you had a hand in that. *The Pearl will crack, the cold will enter.*" He lifts his hands at the chaos around us.

Of course. Antium is referred to as the Pearl of the Empire.

"Jinn prophecies are truth," he says. "I will free my brethren. And we will have our vengeance."

I step back from him. "I will stop you," I say. "I will find *some* way—"

"You failed." He brushes a scorching, flame-veined hand across my face, and though all that is visible of him are those burning suns beneath his hood, I know he's smiling. "Now go, child." He shoves my face away. "Run."

LIII: Elias

In groups of ten and fifty and a hundred, Mauth and I hunt down the ghosts and pass them on. The screams of dying Martials grow more distant, the howl of fire ripping through the city more muted, the cries of civilians and children suffering and dying less important to me with every ghost I attend to.

Once the escaped ghosts are herded, I turn to those enslaved by the Karkauns. The magic used to summon and control them is ancient, but it has a familiar taint to it—the Nightbringer or his ilk taught the Karkauns this magic. The spirits are chained to a dozen or so warlocks—minions of the Karkauns' leader. If I murder those warlocks, the ghosts will be free.

I do not give the killing a second thought. I do not even use my weapons, though they are strapped across my back. Mauth's magic suffuses me, and I call on it as easily as I would my own skills with a scim. We circle the warlocks and choke the life from them one by one, until finally, as the day fades and the drums scream out which parts of the city have fallen, I find myself near an enormous building I know well: the Black Guard barracks.

I feel for more ghosts and find nothing. But as I prepare to leave, I catch a flash of brown skin and black hair.

Laia.

I step toward her immediately; the small bit of my mind that still feels human draws me to her, as ever. As I approach her, I expect Mauth to pull at me or take over my body, as he did when I encountered the Shrike. But though I feel him there in my mind, still a part of me, he does nothing.

Laia has seen me. "Elias!" She runs to me, throwing herself into my arms, almost sobbing. As she does, my arms come up around her of their own accord, as if it's something I've done many times. I feel strange. No, not strange.

I feel nothing.

"It wasn't the ring," she is saying. "I don't know what the last piece of the Star is, but there might still be time to find out. Will you help me?"

Yes, I want to say.

"No" is what comes out of my mouth.

Shock fills her eyes. And then, just like in the Mariner village weeks ago, she goes completely still. Everything does.

Elias.

The voice in my head is not my own, nor is it the jinn's.

Do you know me?

"I—I don't."

Long have I waited for this day, for you to release the last shreds that bound you to the world of the living.

"Mauth?"

The same, Elias. Look.

My body remains before Laia, frozen in time. But my mind travels to a familiar place. I know this sallow yellow sky. This black sea that roils with unknowable creatures just under the surface. I saw this place once before, when Shaeva pulled me from the raid.

A blurred figure approaches, hovering just above the water, like me. I know who he is without him saying so. Mauth.

Welcome to my dimension, Elias Veturius.

"What the ten bleeding hells," I say shakily, pointing to the sea, "are those things?"

Do not concern yourself with them, Mauth says. *They are a discussion for another day. Look.* He waves his hand, and a tapestry of images unspools before me.

The images begin with the Scholars' war on the jinn and unravel from there, threads of darkness blooming like spilled ink, darkening all they touch. I see how the crimes of the Scholar king reached far beyond what he ever imagined.

I see the truth: that without the jinn in this world, there is no balance. They were the destined gatekeepers between the worlds of the living and the dead. And no one, no matter how skilled, can replace an entire civilization.

They must return—even if that means war. Even if it means destruction. For without them, the ghosts will continue to build up, and whether in five years or fifty or five hundred, they will escape again. And when that happens, they *will* destroy the world.

"Why can't you just set the jinn free? Make them . . . forget what happened?"

I require a conduit—a being from your world to harness my power. The amount of power required to restore a civilization would destroy any conduit I chose, human or wraith, jinn or efrit.

I understand then that there is only one path forward: freedom for the jinn. But that freedom will come at a price.

"Laia," I whisper. "The Blood Shrike. They—they will suffer. But—"

You dare to put those you love before all of humanity, child? Mauth asks me softly. *You dare to be so selfish?*

"Why should Laia and the Shrike pay for what a Scholar monster did a thousand years ago?"

There is a price for greed and violence. We do not always know who will pay it. But for good or ill, it will be paid.

I cannot stop what is to come. I cannot change it. Bleeding hells.

You can give those you once loved a world free of ghosts. You can do your duty. You can give them a chance at surviving the onslaught that must come. You can give them a chance to win, one day.

"But not today."

Not today. You have released your ties to strangers, to friends, to family, to your true love. Now surrender to me, for it is your destiny. It is the meaning of your name, the reason for your existence. It is time.

It is time.

I know the moment everything changes. The moment Mauth joins with me so completely that I cannot tell where I end and the magic begins. I am back in my body, in Antium, standing before Laia. It's as if no time has passed at all since she asked for my aid and I rejected her.

When I look down into that beautiful face, I no longer see the girl I loved. I see someone lesser. Someone who is aging, dying slowly, like all humans. I see a mortal.

"E-Elias?"

The girl—*Laia*—speaks, and I turn to her.

"The jinn have a part to play in this world, and they must be set free." I speak gently because she is a mortal, and she will take this news hard. "The world must be broken before it can be remade," I say, "or else the balance will never be restored."

"No," she says. "Elias, no. This is the *jinn* we are speaking of. If they are free—"

"I cannot keep the balance alone." It is unfair to expect Laia to understand. She is only a mortal, after all. "The world will burn," I say. "But it will be reborn from the ashes."

"Elias," she says. "How can you say this?"

"You should leave," I say. "I do not wish to welcome you to the Waiting Place—not yet. May the skies speed your way."

"What the hells has that place done to you?" she cries. "I need your help, Elias. The people need you. There are thousands of Scholars here. If I cannot get the Star, then I can at least get them out. You could—"

"I must return to the Waiting Place," I say. "Goodbye, Laia of Serra."

Laia grabs my face and peers into my eyes. A darkness rises in her—something that is fey, but not. It is more than fey. It is atavistic, the essence of magic itself. And it rages.

"What have you done to him?" She speaks to Mauth, as if she *knows* he has joined with me. As if she can see him. "Give him back!"

My voice, when it comes, is an unearthly rumble that isn't my own. I feel shoved to the side in my own mind, watching as I incline my head. "Forgive me, dear one," Mauth says through me. "It is the only way."

I back away from her and turn east, toward the Forest of Dusk. Moments later, I am through the masses of Karkauns ravaging the city, then beyond them, speeding through the countryside, at last one with Mauth.

But though I know I go now to my duty, some old part of me twinges, reaches out to whatever it is that I have lost. It feels strange.

It is the pain of what you have given up. But it will fade, Banu al-Mauth. You have endured much in a short time, learned much in a short time. You cannot expect to be ready overnight.

"It . . ." I search for the word. "It hurts."

Surrender always does. But it will not hurt forever.

"Why me?" I ask. "Why do we have to change and not you? Why do we have to become less human instead of you becoming more so?"

The ocean waves thunder on, and it is man who must swim among them. The wind blows, cold and brittle, and it is man who must protect against it. The earth shakes and cracks, swallows and destroys, but it is man who must walk upon it. So it is with death. I cannot surrender, Elias. It must be you.

"I don't feel like myself anymore."

Because you are not yourself. You are me. I am you. And in this way, we will pass the ghosts through, that your world be spared from their predations.

He falls silent as we leave Antium far behind. Soon, I forget the fighting. I forget the face of the girl I loved. I think only of the task ahead.

All is as it must be.

LIV: *Laia*

ook finds me beside the stables moments after Elias disappears. I stare after him, disbelieving. He is not the Elias I left even two weeks ago, the Elias who brought me back from the Nightbringer's hell, who told me that we would find a way.

But then I remember what he said: *If I seem different, remember that I love you. No matter what happens to me.*

What in the skies happened to him? What was it inside me that lashed out at him? I think of what the Nightbringer said to me in Adisa: *You know not the darkness that lies within your own heart.*

Deal with Elias later, Laia. My mind reels. The city has fallen. I have failed. And the Scholar slaves—they are trapped here. Antium is surrounded on three sides. Only the north end, built against Mount Videnns, is not overrun with Karkauns.

That is where Cook and I entered the city, and that is how we will escape. That is how we will help the Scholars escape.

Because I know this feeling sweeping through me far too well, the feeling that all my effort, all I have worked for, means nothing. That everything and everyone is a lie. That all is cruel and unforgiving and that there is no justice.

I have survived this feeling before, and I will survive it again. In this fiery hellscape of a world, this mess of blood and madness, justice exists only for those who take it. I'll be damned if I'm not one of them.

"Girl." Cook appears from the streets. "What has happened?"

"Is the Mariner Embassy still clear?" I ask her as we head away from the sounds of fighting. "Have the Karkauns taken that district, or can we escape that way?"

"We can escape."

"Good," I say. "We're getting as many Scholars out as we can—do you understand? I'm going to send them to you at the embassy. I need you to tell them where to go."

"The Karkauns have broken through to the city's second level. They'll be at the embassy in a matter of hours, and then what will you do? Escape with me now. The Scholars will find their own way out."

"They will not," I say. "Because there *is* no way out. We're surrounded on three sides. They don't know there are escape routes."

"Let someone else do this."

"There *is* no one else! There is only us."

"This is a stupid idea," Cook says, "that's going to get us both killed."

"I have never asked anything of you." I grab her hands, and she flinches, but I hold tight to her. "I never had the opportunity. I am asking you to do this for me. *Please.* I'll send them to the embassy. You lead them out."

I do not wait for her response. I turn and run, knowing that she will not say no—not after what I just said to her.

The Scholar's District is in a panic, with people packing and searching for relatives and trying to fathom how they will escape the city. I stop one of the girls I see running across the main square. She looks a few years younger than me.

"Where is everyone going?" I ask her.

"No one knows where to go!" she wails. "I can't find my mother, and the Martials are all gone—they must have started evacuating the city, but no one told us."

"My name is Laia of Serra," I say. "The Karkauns have broken through. They will be here soon, but I'm going to help you leave. Do you know where the Mariner Embassy is?"

She nods, and I heave a sigh of relief. "Tell everyone, every Scholar you see, to go to the Mariner Embassy. A scar-faced woman will take you out of the city. Tell them to go now, to leave their things and run."

The girl nods rapidly and runs away. I grab another Scholar, a man Darin's age, and give him the same message. Whoever will stop, whoever will listen, I tell them to go to the embassy. To find the scar-faced woman. I see recognition in the eyes of a few when I tell them my name, but the sounds of fighting draw closer, and no one is stupid enough to ask questions. The message spreads, and soon the Scholars are fleeing the square en masse.

I hope to the skies everyone in the district gets the message, then I plunge into the city. The girl was right—the only Martials I see are soldiers, all of whom are running toward the fighting. I think of the wagon trains I saw leaving when Cook and I were approaching Antium. The wealthiest of the Martials left here weeks ago. They gave up on their capital and left the soldiers and the Plebeians and the Scholars to die.

I spot a group of Scholars clearing rubble under the direction of two Martials who aren't paying attention because they are listening to drum messages. They discuss the messages in low, urgent tones, as aware of the sounds of nearby fighting as I am. I use the Martials' distraction to sneak up to the Scholars.

"We can't simply run." A woman glances at the Martials fearfully. "They'll come after us."

"You must," I say. "If you don't run from them now, you'll be running from the Karkauns, but by then, you'll have nowhere to go."

Another woman in the group hears, drops her pick, and breaks away, and that is all the other Scholars need. Three score of them scatter, the adults grabbing the few children, all disappearing in a dozen directions before the Martials can even understand what is happening.

I urge the Scholars on and stop to warn any others I see, asking them to pass on the message. By the time I reach the Foreign District, I see hundreds of Scholars streaming toward the embassy.

A fight spills into the streets in front of me. A group of Martial auxes battles a much larger force of Karkauns. Though the Barbarian steel breaks on the auxes' scims, the Martials are hard-pressed, overwhelmed by sheer numbers. If this is happening all over the city, then the Barbarians will be in control of Antium by nightfall.

I skirt around the battle, and when I get to the embassy, Scholars spill out the doors. Cook's grumpy, raspy voice is instantly recognizable as she orders everyone down the steps and into the tunnels.

"About bleeding time!" Cook says when she sees me. "Get down there. A few of these slaves know the way out. Follow—" Cook sees my face and groans when she realizes that I have no plans to leave—at least not until everyone is through.

Even as she speaks, more Scholars arrive. I see Martials now too, most of whom are Plebeians, judging by their clothing. They are drawn by the crowd, assuming rightly that there is a reason so many Scholars flock here.

"Bleeding hells, girl," Cook says. "Do you see what you've done?"

I gesture the Martials in. "I'm not going to tell a mother with a crying child she can't escape through here," I snap. "I don't care if she's Martial or not. Are you?"

"Damn you, girl," Cook snarls. "You're just like your f-f-f-fath—" She presses her mouth closed and turns away in frustration. "Move, you bleeding sloths!" She unleashes her wrath on the Scholars closest to her. "There are hundreds behind you who want to live as badly as you do!"

Urged on by Cook's threats, the Scholars slowly make their way through the tunnels, and the embassy begins to empty—but not swiftly enough. The Karkauns are closing in, pouring through the streets. The Martials are overcome.

As I watch, I see an aux squad go down, blood and viscera spraying the air red. And despite the fact that I know the Empire's evils firsthand, my eyes grow hot. I will never understand the savagery of war, even when it is my foes being destroyed.

"Time to go, girl." Cook appears at my shoulder and shoves me down the steps to the cellar. I do not protest. No doubt there are Scholars still left in the city. But I have done what I can.

"Help me with this." She bars the cellar door, her hands steady. Above, glass breaks, followed by the harsh barks of the Karkauns.

Cook fiddles with something in the door, eventually pulling out what looks like a very long candle wick. Moments later, it is sparking.

"Take cover!" We run to the door that leads to the tunnel, pulling it shut just as the ground begins shuddering. The tunnels groan, and for long moments, I worry that stones above us will collapse. But when the dust clears, the passageway has held, and I turn to Cook.

"Explosives? How?"

"The Mariners had a stockpile," Cook says. "Musa's little friends showed me. Well, girl, that's it. Tunnel's sealed. Now what?"

"Now," I say, "we get the hells out of this city."

LV: The Blood Shrike

The Karkauns flood Antium, breaching gate after gate, the screams of their warriors chilling me to my core. Their ghost-possessed fighters are gone, thanks, perhaps, to Elias.

But the damage is done. They have decimated our forces. Marcus was right. The Empire's capital is lost.

My rage is a pure, glowing flame that drives me to tear through any Karkaun I see. And when, in the distance, I spot a familiar blonde figure making her way through the city with a handful of soldiers at her back, my anger burns white-hot.

"You treacherous bitch!"

She stops when she hears me but takes her sweet time turning around.

"How could you?" My voice breaks. "Your own people? Just for the throne? What is the point of being Empress if you have no love for those you rule? If you have no one to rule over?"

"Empress?" She cocks her head. "To be Empress is the least of my desires, girl. Why stop at Empress? Why, when the Nightbringer would offer me dominion over the Tribes, the Scholars, the Mariners, the Karkauns—over all the world of man?"

No—oh bleeding hells, no.

I lunge for her then, because I have nothing to lose now, no Paters to placate, no orders to follow, just a bolt of wrath that possesses me like a demon spirit.

She steps easily to the side, and in moments her men, all Masks, have me pinned. A knife gleams in her hand, and she runs it lightly down my face, tracing my forehead, my cheeks.

"I wonder if it will hurt," she murmurs.

Then she turns around, leaps onto her mount, and rides away. Her men hold me until she is long gone, before casting me to the side of a road like offal.

I do not chase them. I do not even look at them. The Commandant could have killed me. Instead she left me alive. Skies only know why, but I will not waste this chance. I listen to the drums, and soon enough I am racing toward the men of the Black Guard who still live, along with a few hundred soldiers, as they hold off a wave of attackers from a square in a Mercator district. I search the faces for Dex, hoping to the skies that he's still alive, and nearly crush his ribs when he finds me.

"Where the bleeding hells are our men, Dex?" I shout over the cacophony. "This can't be all that's left!"

Dex shakes his head, bleeding from a dozen wounds. "This is it."

"The evacuation?"

"Thousands make their way through the Augurs' caves. Thousands more are still in the tunnels. The entrances have been collapsed. Those who could get through—"

I hold up a hand. The drum tower closest to us thuds out a message. It is almost lost amid all the noise, but I just make out the end of it: *Karkaun force approaching Pilgrim's Gap.*

"Harper has our people coming out just beyond the Gap," I say. *Livia*, my mind screams at me. *The baby!* "The Karkauns must have scouts up there. If those bastards get through the Gap, they'll slaughter everyone Harper has evacuated."

"Why follow us?" Dex says. "Why, when they know they have the city?"

"Because Grímarr knows we won't let him keep Antium," I say. "And he wants to make damn sure that while his men have the advantage, they kill as many of us as possible so we can't fight them later." I know what I must say, and I make myself say it.

"The city is lost. It belongs to Grímarr now." Skies help the poor souls who remain here under that fiend. I will not forget them. But right now, I cannot save them—not if I want to save those who do have a chance at escape. "Get out this order: Every soldier we have is to report to the Gap immediately. That is our last stand. If we stop them, that is where we will do it."

«««

By the time Dex, my men, and I reach the Gap, just beyond the northern border of the city, the Karkaun force is on the march, bent on crushing us.

As I watch them pour out of Antium's northern gate and up the Pilgrim Road, I know that we will not win this battle. I have with me no more than a thousand men. The enemy has more than ten thousand—and thousands more they can call from the city, if they must. Even with our superior blades, we cannot beat them.

Pilgrim's Gap is a ten-foot-wide opening between two sheer cliffs that sit atop a wide valley. The Pilgrim Road curves across the valley, through the Gap and toward the Augurs' caves.

I glance back over my shoulder, away from the Karkauns. I had hoped when I arrived that the Pilgrim Road would be empty, that the evacuees would have gotten through. But there are hundreds of Martials—and Scholars, I notice—on the road and hundreds more emerging from the tunnel entrances to make their way up to the Augurs' caves.

"Get a message to Harper," I tell Dex. "Take it yourself. White smoke when the last person is through. Then he's to collapse the entrance to the caves. He is not to wait, and neither are you."

"Shrike—"

"That is an order, Lieutenant Atrius. You keep her safe. You keep my nephew safe. You see him on the throne." My friend stares at me. He knows what I am saying: that I don't want him back here. That I will die here today, with my people, and he will not.

"Duty first"—he salutes—"unto death."

I turn to my men—Masks, auxes, legionnaires. All have survived onslaught after onslaught. They are exhausted. They are broken.

I have heard many pretty speeches as a soldier. I remember none of them. So in the end, I dig up words that Keris gave me long ago—and I hope to the skies that they will come back to haunt her.

"There is success," I say. "And there is failure. The land in between is for those too weak to live. *Duty first, unto death.*"

They roar it back at me, and we form up, row upon row of shields and spears and scims. Our archers have few arrows, but they ready what they do have. The rumble in the valley grows louder as the Karkauns surge up the rise toward us, and now my blood sings and I pull out my war hammer and snarl.

"Come on, you bastards. Come for me!"

And suddenly, the Karkauns are a distant rumble no more but a thundering, frenzied horde of thousands who want nothing more than to annihilate all that is left of us. In the pass behind us, my people cry out.

Now, I think, *let us see what the Martials are made of.*

«‑«‑«

After an hour, the Karkauns have ripped through the front half of our forces. All is blood and pain and brutality. Still, I fight, and the men fight beside me, as behind us, those fleeing the city continue up the road.

Faster, I think at them. *For the love of the skies, go faster.* We wait for the white smoke as the Karkauns keep coming, wave upon wave. Our force dwindles from five hundred men to four hundred. Two hundred. Fifty. No smoke.

The gap is too wide for us to hold it much longer. It is piled with bodies, but the Karkauns simply climb over them and down, as if the hill is made of rock and not their dead countrymen.

From the city, a hellish sound rises. It is worse than the silence of Blackcliff after the Third Trial, worse than the tortured moans of Kauf's prisoners. It is the screaming of those I left behind as they face the violence of the Karkauns. The wolves are among my people now.

We cannot falter. There are still hundreds on the Pilgrim Road and dozens emerging from the tunnels. *A little more time. Just a little more.*

But we do not have more time, for to my left, two more of my men fall, cut down by Karkaun arrows. My hammer slips against my palm, slick from the blood that drenches every inch of my skin. But there are more coming— too many. I cannot fight them all. I shout for aid. The only responses are the battle cries of the Karkauns.

Which is when I understand, finally, that I am alone. There is no one else left to fight at my back. All of my men are dead.

And still, more Karkauns surge over the wall of bodies. Skies, are their numbers unending? Will they ever give up?

They will not, I realize, and it makes me want to scream and cry and kill.

They will tear through this pass. They will be on the evacuees like jackals upon injured rabbits.

I search the sky for white smoke—*please, please*. And then I feel a sharp pain in my shoulder. Stunned, I look down to see an arrow sticking out of it. I deflect the next one that comes at me, but there are more bowmen coming. Too many.

This is not happening. It cannot be. My sister is up there somewhere with the hope of the Empire held in her arms. She might not have reached the caves yet.

At the thought of her, of young Zacharias, of the two little girls who said they'd fight the Karkauns, I draw on every last bit of strength I have. I am a thing from the Barbarians' nightmares, a silver-faced, blood-drenched demon of the hells, and I will not let them pass.

I kill and I kill and I kill. But I am no supernatural creature. I am flesh and blood, and I am flagging.

Please. Please. More time. I just need more time.

But I have none. It is gone.

One day soon, you will be tested, child. All that you cherish will burn. You will have no friends that day. No allies. No comrades in arms. On that day, your trust in me will be your only weapon.

I fall to my knees. "Help me," I sob. "Please—please help me. Please—" But how can he help me if he cannot hear me? How can he offer aid if he is not here?

"Blood Shrike."

I whirl to find the Nightbringer standing just behind me. His hand rises and flicks, and the Karkauns stop, held back by the jinn's immense power.

He surveys the carnage with dispassion. Then he turns to me but does not speak.

"Whatever you want from me, take it," I say. "Just save them—please—"

"I want a bit of your soul, Shrike."

"You—" I shake my head. I do not understand. "Take my life," I say. "If that is the price—"

"I want a bit of your soul."

I rack my mind desperately. "I don't—I don't have—"

A memory comes to me, a ghost out of the darkness: Quin's voice, weeks ago, when I gave him Elias's mask.

They become part of us, you know. It is only when they join with us that we become our truest selves. My father used to say that after the joining, a mask held a soldier's identity—and that without it, a bit of his soul was stripped away, never to be recovered.

A bit of his soul . . .

"It's just a mask," I say. "It's not—"

"The Augurs themselves placed the last piece of a long-lost weapon in your mask," the Nightbringer says. "I have known it since the day they gave it to you. All that you are, all that they molded you into, all that you have become—it was all for this day, Blood Shrike."

"I don't understand."

"Your love of your people runs deep. It was nurtured through all the years spent at Blackcliff. It grew deeper when you saw the suffering in Navium and healed the children in the infirmary. Deeper when you healed your sister and imbued your nephew with the love you have of your country. Deeper still when you saw the strength of your countrymen as they prepared for the siege. It fused with your soul when you fought for them on the walls of Antium. And now it culminates in your sacrifice for them."

"Take off my head then, for I cannot remove it," I say, sobbing. "It is *part* of me, a living part of my body. It has sunk into my skin!"

"That is my price," the Nightbringer says. "I will not take from you. I will not threaten you or coerce you. The mask must be offered with love in your heart."

I look back over my shoulder at the Pilgrim Road. Hundreds make their way up, and I know thousands more are in the caves. We have already lost so many. We cannot lose more.

You are all that holds back the darkness.

For the Empire. For the mothers and fathers. For the sisters and brothers. For the lovers.

For the Empire, Helene Aquilla. For your people.

I grab at my face and tear. I claw at my skin, howling, wailing, begging the mask to release me.

I don't want you anymore, I just want my people to be safe. Release me, please, release me. For the Empire, release me. For my people, release me. Please—please—

My face burns. Blood pours from where I have already clawed at the mask. Within, some essential part of me cries out at the recklessness with which I tear it away.

A mask holds a soldier's identity . . .

But I don't care about my identity. I don't even care if I am a soldier anymore. I just want my people to live, to survive to fight another day.

The mask lets me go. Blood pours down my neck, my cheeks, into my eyes. I cannot see. I can hardly move. I retch from the searing agony of it.

"Take it." My voice is as raw as the Cook's. "Take it and save them."

"Why do you offer it to me, Shrike? Say it."

"Because they are my people!" I hold it out to him, and when he does not take it, I shove it into his hands. "Because I love them. Because they do not deserve to die because I failed them!"

He inclines his head, a gesture of deep respect, and I sag to the ground. I wait for him to wave his hand and wreak havoc. Instead he turns and walks away, rising into the air like a leaf.

"No!" Why isn't he fighting the Karkauns? "Wait, I trusted you! Please—you said—you have to help me!"

He looks over his shoulder at something behind me—beyond me. "I have, Blood Shrike."

With that, he is gone, a dark cloud carried away by the wind. The power that held back the Karkauns fails, and they tumble forward toward me, more than I can count. More than I can fight.

"Come back." I have no voice. It wouldn't matter if I did. The Night-bringer is gone. Skies, where is my war hammer, my scim, anything—

But I have no weapons. No strength left in my body.

I have nothing.

LVI: Laia

When I emerge from the tunnels and into the bright sunlight, I grimace at the reek of blood. A massive pile of bodies sits a hundred yards away, at the base of a narrow gap. Through it, I can make out the city of Antium.

And beside the bodies, on her knees with the dark-cloaked Nightbringer standing before her, is the Blood Shrike.

I do not know what the Nightbringer says to the Blood Shrike. I only know that when she cries out, it sounds just like Nan did when she heard about my mother's death. Like I did when I understood how that jinn beast had betrayed me.

It is a cry of loneliness. Of betrayal. Of despair.

The jinn turns. Looks in my direction. Then he disappears on the wind.

"Girl." Cook scrambles up behind me, having swept the tunnels at my side to make sure that no one else lingered. The last Scholars have long since disappeared. It is only us now. "Let's go! They're coming!"

As more Karkauns make their way through the Gap, the Shrike crawls toward her war hammer, attempting to stand. She lurches around to look behind her at the sky—

—where a plume of white smoke curls into the heavens.

She sobs and sinks to her knees, dropping her hammer, bowing her head. I know then that she is ready to die.

I also know that I cannot let her.

I am already moving—away from Cook, away from the path to safety and toward the Blood Shrike. I throw myself at the Karkaun attacking her, and as he snaps at my throat with his teeth, I shove my dagger in his gut and then push him away. I only just manage to pull my knife free in time to shove it into the throat of another Karkaun. A third attacks me from behind, and I stumble and roll out of the way just as an arrow explodes through his head.

My jaw drops as Cook lets arrow after arrow fly, executing the Karkauns with the precision of a Mask. She stops to snatch up a quiver full of arrows from the back of a dead Karkaun.

"Grab the Shrike!" Cook gets her arm under the Blood Shrike's left shoulder, and I take her right. We stagger up the Pilgrim Road as swiftly as we can, but the Shrike can barely walk, and our progress is slow.

"There." Cook nods to a cluster of boulders. We clamber behind it and put the Shrike down. Dozens of Karkauns climb through the Gap. Soon, it will be hundreds. We have a few minutes—if that.

"How the hells do we get out of this?" I whisper to Cook. "We can't just leave her."

"Do you know why the Commandant never fails, girl?" Cook doesn't seem to expect a reply to her bizarrely timed question, because she barrels on. "Because no one knows her story. Learn her story, and you'll learn her weakness. Learn her weakness, and you can destroy her. Talk to Musa about it. He'll help you."

"Why are you telling me this now?"

"Because you're going to take vengeance on that savage demon queen for me," she says. "And you need to know. Get up. Get the Shrike up that mountain. The Martials are going to seal off those caves soon enough, if they haven't already. You need to move quickly."

A group of Karkauns races up the Pilgrim Road toward us, and Cook rises and shoots a dozen arrows. The Barbarians fall. But more come through the Gap.

"I have another fifty arrows, girl," Cook says. "Once I'm out, we're done for. We could fight three or four of those bastards at the most—not hundreds. Not thousands. One of us has to hold them off."

Oh. *Oh no.* I take her meaning now. Finally, I understand what she is saying. "Absolutely bleeding—*no.* I will not leave you here to die—"

"Go!" My mother shoves me toward the Shrike, and though her teeth are bared, her eyes are filled with tears. "You don't want to save me! I'm not worth it. Go!"

"I will *not*—"

"Do you know what I did in Kauf Prison, girl?" There is hatred in her eyes as she says it. Before I knew who she was, I would have thought that hate was directed at me. I understand now that it was never for me. It was for herself. "If you did, you would *run*—"

"I know what you did." Now is not the time to be noble. I grab her arm and try to drag her toward the Shrike. She doesn't budge. "You did it to save Darin and me. Because Father and Lis weren't strong like you, and you knew that they would give us up eventually, and then we'd all die. I knew that the moment I learned of it, Mother. I forgave you the moment I learned of it. But you have to come with me. We can run—"

"Damn you, girl." Cook grabs me by the shoulder. "Listen to me. One day, you will have children. And you will learn that you would rather suffer a thousand torments than let one hair on their heads be harmed. Give me this gift. Let me protect you as I should have protected L-L-L-Lis." The name bursts from her lips. "As I should have protected your f-fath-fath—"

She snarls at her inability to speak and spins away, nocking her bow, letting arrow after arrow loose.

The Ghost will fall, her flesh will wither.

The Ghost was never me. It was her. Mirra of Serra, risen from the dead. But if that's the case, then this is one line of the prophecy I will fight.

Mother spins, grabs the Shrike, and heaves her up. The Blood Shrike's eyes flutter open, and she leans heavily on my mother, who then shoves her at me.

I have no choice but to catch her, my knees nearly buckling at the sudden weight. But the Shrike rights herself, trying to stay steady on her feet, using me as support.

"I love you, L-L-Laia." The sound of my name on Mother's lips is more than I can bear, and I am shaking my head, trying to tell her no through my sobs. *Not again. Not again.*

"Tell your brother everything," she says, "if he doesn't know already. Tell him I am proud of him. Tell him that I am sorry."

She rises up from the rocks and darts away, drawing the Karkauns' fire as she skewers them with more arrows.

"No!" I scream, but she is doing this, and if I don't move, it will be for nothing. I look at her for one more moment, and I know I will never forget how her white hair snaps like a victory banner, and how her blue eyes shine with fury and determination. She is finally the Lioness, the woman I knew as a child—and, somehow, more.

"Blood Shrike!" I call to her as I turn up the Pilgrim Road. "Wake up— please—"

"Who—" She tries to see me, but her ravaged face is drenched with blood.

"It's Laia," I say. "You must walk, do you understand? You must."

"I saw white smoke."

"Walk, Shrike—walk!"

Step by step, we make our way up the Pilgrim Road until we are high enough to see over the bodies and into the Karkaun force, diminished but still enormous. High enough to watch as my mother picks them off one by one, grabbing the arrows the Karkauns are hailing down upon her, giving us as much time as she can.

And then I do not look back anymore. I just move, half dragging, half urging the Blood Shrike onward and upward. But it is too far and the Shrike is too injured, her clothes soaked with blood, her body heavy with pain.

"I'm so-sorry," she whispers. "Go—go on without—"

"Blood Shrike!" A voice from up ahead, and a flash of silver. I know that face. The Mask who helped me at Kauf. The one who set me free months ago. Avitas Harper.

"Thank the bleeding skies—"

"I've got this side, Laia." Harper throws the Shrike's other arm over his shoulder, and together we pull her up the path, then down across a shallow bowl to a cave where a handsome, dark-skinned Mask waits. Dex Atrius.

"Harp—Harper," the Shrike slurs in a whisper. "Told you . . . collapse the tunnels. You disobeyed orders."

"With respect, Shrike, they were stupid bleeding orders," Harper says. "Stop talking."

I twist my head around as we enter the cave. From this height, I can see down the hill to the Gap.

To the Karkauns who are now making their way up the path with no one to block their way.

"No," I whisper. "No—no—no—"

But we are in the cave now, Dex ushering us forward quickly.

"Blast it," Avitas says. "Laia, come quickly. They're not far behind."

I don't want to leave her, I want to scream. *I don't want her to die alone. I don't want to lose her again.*

When we are at the end of a long passage lined with blue-fire torches, an earth-shattering rumble booms out, followed by the unmistakable sound of thousands of pounds of rocks falling.

And then silence.

I slip down onto the ground beside the Shrike. She cannot see me, but she reaches out her hand and takes mine.

"You—you knew her?" she whispers. "The Cook?"

It takes me a long time to answer. By the time I do, the Shrike has lost consciousness.

"Her name was Mirra of Serra," I speak, though no one can hear me. "And yes. I knew her."

PART V

BELOVED

LVII: The Blood Shrike

L aia of Serra cannot hold a tune to save her life. But her hum is sweet
and light and strangely comforting. As she moves around the edges of
the room, I try to get a sense of my surroundings. Lamplight filters through an
enormous window, and I feel a nip in the air—a sign that summer closes in the
north. I recognize the low, arched buildings beyond the window and the large
square it faces. We are in Delphinium. There is a weight to the air. A heaviness.
Distantly, lightning flashes over the Nevennes. I can smell the storm.

My face feels strange, and I reach my hands up. *The mask. The jinn. I
thought it had been a nightmare.* But as I feel my own skin for the first time
in seven years, I realize that it was not a dream. My mask is gone.

And a piece of my soul with it.

Laia hears me move and turns. I see the blade at her waist, and on instinct
I reach for my own.

"No need for that, Blood Shrike." She tilts her head, her face not exactly
friendly but not unkind either. "We didn't drag you through a hundred miles
of caves so your first act upon waking would be to stab me."

A cry sounds from nearby, and I force myself to sit up, eyes wide. Laia rolls
her eyes. "The Emperor," she says, "is *always* hungry. And when he doesn't
get food . . . skies, help us all."

"Livvy . . . they're . . ."

"Safe." A shadow flickers across the Scholar girl's face, but she hides it
quickly. "Yes. Your family is safe."

A whisper of movement at the door, and Avitas is there. Immediately, Laia
excuses herself. I understand her quick smile, and I flush.

For just a second, I see the look on Harper's face. Not the carefully controlled blankness that all Masks wear, but the heartfelt relief of a friend.

Though, if I am being honest, it is not the look of someone who thinks of me as just a friend. I would know.

I want to say something to him. *You came for me. You and Laia dragged me from the claws of Death himself. You have more of your father's goodness in you than you will ever acknowledge.*

Instead, I clear my throat and swing my legs, shaking with weakness, over the side of the bed.

"Report, Captain Harper."

His silver eyebrows flick up for a moment, and I think I see frustration in his eyes. He crushes it, the way I would. He knows me by now. He knows what I need.

"We have seven thousand five hundred twenty Martials who fled Antium," he says. "Another one thousand six hundred thirty-four Scholars. We believe that at least ten thousand more—Illustrians and Mercators—left before the invasion or were siphoned out by the Commandant."

"And the rest?"

"Half died in the siege. The other half remains the prisoners of the Karkauns. The Barbarians have enslaved them."

As we knew they would. "Then we must free them," I say. "What of Keris?"

"She retreated to Serra and established the capital there." Avitas pauses, attempting to get hold of his anger. "The Illustrian Paters have named her Empress—and the Empire has embraced it. Antium's fall is blamed on Marcus, and—"

"And on me." I led the defense of the city, after all. I failed.

"Quin Veturius has pledged his fealty to Emperor Zacharias and Gens

Aquilla," Harper says, "as have the Illustrian Gens of Delphinium. The Commandant has declared your nephew an enemy of the Empire. All who support him or his claim are to be crushed forthwith."

None of what he says surprises me—not anymore. All my plotting and scheming was for nothing. If I'd have known civil war was inevitable, I'd have killed Keris outright, whatever the consequences. At least Antium wouldn't be in the hands of Grímarr.

The storm rolls closer, and rain begins to patter thinly on the cobblestones outside. Harper stares openly at me, and I turn my head away, wondering how my face must look. I wear black fatigues, but without my mask I feel strange. Naked.

I remember what the Commandant said before she fled Antium. *I wonder if it will hurt.* She knew. It's why she left me alive. The Nightbringer must have ordered it.

Harper lifts a hand to my cheek and traces one side, then the other. "You haven't seen yourself," he says.

"I haven't wanted to."

"You have scars," he says. "Two of them, like twin scims."

"Do I—" The words come out a whisper, and I brusquely clear my throat. "How bad is it?"

"They are beautiful." His green eyes are thoughtful. "Your face couldn't be anything but beautiful, Blood Shrike. With or without the mask."

My blush rises, and this time there is no mask to hide it. I don't know what to do with my hands. My hair must look a mess. *I* must look a mess. *Doesn't matter. It's just Harper.*

But it's not just Harper anymore, is it?

He was loyal to the Commandant. He tortured you on Marcus's orders.

But he was never truly loyal to Keris. As for the interrogation, how the hells can I judge him for that after what I ordered Dex to do to Mamie? To Tribe Saif?

He's Elias's brother.

My thoughts are a welter of confusion. I cannot make sense of them. Avitas reaches for my hands, pulling them into his own, examining them with such care.

He draws a line up my forearm with the tip of his finger, from one freckle to another. At that feather-light touch, every nerve ending in my body awakens. I inhale unsteadily, tormented by his scent, by the triangle of skin at his throat. He leans close. The curve of his lower lip is the only softness in a face that looks cut from stone. I wonder, do his lips taste the way I think they must, like honey and cinnamon tea on a cold night?

When I lift my gaze to his, he hides nothing, finally, *finally* unmasking his desire. The power of it is dizzying, and I do not protest when he pulls me close. Avitas stops when he's a hairsbreadth from my lips, careful, always so careful. In that moment of waiting, he lays himself bare. *Only if you want it.* I close the distance, my own need tearing through me with a force that leaves me shaken.

I expected my impatience. I did not anticipate his. For someone who is always so infuriatingly calm, he kisses like a man who will never be sated.

More. I crave his hands in my hair, his lips on my body. I should get up, lock the door—

It is the intoxicating force of that impulse that stops me cold, that compresses my thoughts into two equally clear sentiments.

I want him.

But I cannot have him.

As suddenly as I met Harper's lips, I pull myself away. His green eyes are dark with want, but when he sees my expression, he inhales sharply.

"Look at me." He is about to say my name—my heart's name—the way he did in his mind when I sang him well. And if I let him, I will be undone. "Look at me. Hel—"

"Blood Shrike, Captain Harper." I harness my training and give him my coldest glare. *He is a distraction. Only the Empire matters. Only your people matter.* The Martials are in far too much danger for either of us to allow distractions. I withdraw my hands from his sharply. "I am the Blood Shrike. You would do well to remember it."

For a moment, he is frozen, pain flashing nakedly across his face. Then he stands and salutes, the consummate Mask once more. "Of course, Blood Shrike, sir. Permission to return to duty."

"Granted."

After Harper leaves, I feel hollow. Lonely. Voices rise from nearby, and I force myself to my feet and down the hallway. Thunder growls, close enough to mask my footsteps as I approach the open door to what must be Livia's room.

"—people saved you from the Karkauns, though doing so put them at great risk. I beg you, Empress, begin your son's reign with an act befitting a true emperor. Free the Scholar slaves."

"It's not so simple." I recognize Faris's rumble.

"Isn't it?" The clarity and strength in my sister's voice make me stand up taller. She always hated slavery, like our mother. But unlike Mother, it's clear she plans to do something about it. "Laia of Serra does not lie. A group of Scholars saved us from the Karkauns who infiltrated the tunnels. They carried me when I was too weak to walk, and it was a Scholar who nursed Emperor Zacharias when I lost consciousness."

"We found the mosses that fed your people in the tunnels." Laia's voice is arch, and I scowl. "If not for us, you'd have all starved to death."

"You've made a just case for your people." Livia's voice is so calm that tension dissipates instantly. "As Empress regent, I decree that every Scholar who escaped the tunnels is now a freeman. Lieutenant Faris, pass the news to the Paters of Delphinium. Captain Dex, ensure that the Martial response is not overly . . . emotional."

I step into the room then, and Livia takes a step toward me, stopping short at my warning glare. I shift my attention to the dark-haired bundle on the bed, freshly fed and fast asleep.

"He got bigger," I say, surprised.

"They do that." Laia smiles. "You should not yet be up and about, Blood Shrike."

I wave off her fussing but sit when my sister insists.

"Did you see Elias, Laia? Did you . . . speak with him?"

Something in her face changes, a fleeting pain I know all too well. She has spoken with him then. She has seen what he's become. "He's returned to the Forest. I have not tried to find him. I wanted to make sure you were well first. And . . ."

"And you've been busy," I say. "Now that your people have chosen you as a leader."

Her reluctance is written all over her face. But instead she shrugs. "For now, perhaps."

"And the Nightbringer?"

"The Nightbringer has not been seen since the siege," she says. "It has been more than a week. I expected him to have set his brethren free by now. But . . ." She takes in my expression. The rain pours down hard now, a steady lash against the windows. "But you feel it too, don't you? Something is coming."

"Something is coming," I agree. "He wants to destroy the Scholars—and he plans on using the Martials to do it."

Laia's expression is unreadable. "And will you let your people be used?"

I do not expect the question. Livia, however, appears unsurprised, and I have the distinct feeling that she and Laia have already had this conversation.

"If you plan to take the throne back for your nephew," Laia says, "you will need allies to battle the Commandant—strong allies. You don't have the men to do it on your own."

"And if you don't want your people utterly destroyed by the jinn and the Martial army," I retort, "you will need allies too. Particularly ones who know the Martials well."

We stare at each other like two wary dogs.

"The Augur mentioned something to me about the Nightbringer a few weeks ago," I offer finally. "Before the siege on Antium. *The truth of all creatures, man or jinn, lies in their name.*"

A spark of interest in Laia's face. "Cook told me something similar," she says. "She said that to know the Commandant's story would help destroy her. And I know someone with unique skills who can help us."

"Us?"

"Help my people, Blood Shrike." I can see how much it costs Laia to ask this of me. "And I—and my allies—will help you win back your nephew's crown. But . . ."

She cocks her head, and as I'm trying to puzzle out her look, she whips a dagger from her waist and flings it at me.

"What the *bleeding* hells—" I pluck the blade out of the air on instinct and turn it on her in the time it takes to blink twice. "How dare—"

"If I'm going to carry Serric steel," Laia says quite calmly, "then I'd like to learn to use it. And if I'm going to be an ally to a Martial, I would like to fight like one."

I gape at her, distantly taking note of Livia's quiet smile. Laia looks down at Zacharias and then out the window, and that shadow passes over her face again. "Though I wonder, would you teach me to use the bow, Blood Shrike?"

A memory rises from the haze of the past week: Cook's strong hands as she shot arrow after arrow into the Karkauns. *I love you, Laia*, she'd said. Laia's face as Cook howled at her to get me to the Augurs' cave. And older memories: Cook's fierceness when she told me she'd murder me if I hurt Laia. The way, when I healed that old woman, some distant music within her reminded me of the Scholar girl.

And suddenly, I understand. *Mother.*

I remember the face of my own mother as she went to her death. *Strength, my girl*, she'd said.

Curse this world for what it does to the mothers, for what it does to the daughters. Curse it for making us strong through loss and pain, our hearts torn from our chests again and again. Curse it for forcing us to endure.

When I meet the Scholar girl's stare, I realize she's been watching me. We do not speak. But for this moment, she knows my heart. And I know hers.

"Well?" Laia of Serra offers her hand.

I take it.

LVIII: The Soul Catcher

I t takes many days for the ghost to speak his pain. Listening to it chills my blood. He suffers each memory, a rush of violence and selfishness and brutality that, for the first time, he must feel in all its horror.

Most of the ghosts have passed quickly. But sometimes their sins are so great that Mauth does not let them move on. Not until they have suffered what they inflicted.

So it is with the ghost of Marcus Farrar.

Through it, his brother remains at his side, silent, patient. Having spent the past nine months tied to his twin's corporeal body, Zak has had plenty of time to suffer what he was. He waits, now, for his brother.

The day finally comes when Mauth is satisfied with Marcus's suffering. The twins walk beside me quietly, one on each side. They are empty of anger, of pain, of loneliness. They are ready to pass on.

We approach the river, and I turn to the brothers. I sift through their minds dispassionately and find a memory that is joyful—in this case, a day they spent together on the rooftops of Silas before they were taken for Blackcliff. Their father bought them a kite. The winds were fair, and they flew it high.

I give the brothers that memory so that they might slip into the river without troubling me further. I take their darkness—that which Blackcliff found within them and nurtured—and Mauth consumes it. Where it goes, I do not know. I suspect, however, that it might have something to do with that seething sea I saw when I spoke to Mauth, and the creatures lurking within it.

When I look back at the twins, they are boys once more, untainted by the world. And when they step into the river, they do it together, small hands clasped.

The days go swiftly now, and with Mauth joined fully to me, I cycle through the ghosts, dividing my attention between many at a time as easily as if I am made of water and not flesh. The jinn chafe at Mauth's power, but though they hiss and whisper at me still, I can usually silence them with a thought, and they trouble me no more.

At least for now.

When I have been back in the Waiting Place more than a week, I suddenly feel an outsider's presence far to the north, near Delphinium. It takes me only a moment to realize who it is.

Leave it, Mauth says in my head. *You know she will bring you no joy.*

"I would like to tell her why I left." I have let go of her. But sometimes old images drift to the shores of my mind, leaving me restless. "Perhaps if I do, she will cease to haunt me."

I feel Mauth sigh, but he speaks no more, and in a half hour I can see her through the trees, pacing back and forth. She is alone.

"Laia."

She turns, and at the sight of her, something in me twists. An old memory. A kiss. A dream. Her hair like silk between my fingers, her body rising beneath my hands.

Behind me, the ghosts whisper, and in the ocean tide of their song, the memory of Laia fades away. I draw on another memory—that of a man who once wore a silver mask and who felt nothing when he did. In my mind, I put on the mask again.

"It is not your time yet, Laia of Serra," I say. "You are not welcome here."

"I thought—" She shudders. "Are you all right? You just left."

"You must go."

"What happened to you?" Laia whispers. "You said we would be together. You said we would find a way. But then . . ." She shakes her head. "Why?"

"Thousands across the Empire died not because of the Karkauns but because of the ghosts. Because the ghosts possessed whomever they could and made them do terrible things. Do you know how they escaped?"

"Did—did Mauth—"

"I failed to hold the borders. I failed to uphold my duty to the Waiting Place. I put everything else first—strangers, friends, family, you. Because of that, the borders fell."

"You didn't know. There was no one to teach you." She takes a deep breath, her hands pressed together. "Do not do this, Elias. Do not leave me. I know you're in there. Please—come back to me. I need you. The Blood Shrike needs you. The Tribes need you."

I walk to her, take her hands, look down into her face. Whatever I want to feel is dulled now by the steady, soothing presence of Mauth, the thrum of ghosts in the Waiting Place.

"Your eyes." She runs a finger across my brows. "They're like hers."

"Like Shaeva's," I say. As they should be.

"No," Laia says. "Like the Commandant's."

The words trouble me. But that too will fade. In time.

"Elias is who I was," I say. "The Soul Catcher—the *Banu al-Mauth*—the Chosen of Death—that is who I am. But do not despair. We are, all of us, just visitors in each other's lives. You will forget my visit soon enough." I reach down and kiss her on the forehead. "Be well, Laia of Serra."

When I turn away, she sobs, a soul-deep cry of wounded betrayal.

"Take this." Her voice is wretched, her face streaming tears. She tears a wooden armlet from her bicep and shoves it into my hands. "I don't want it." She turns away then, makes for the horse waiting nearby. Moments later, I am alone.

The wood is still warm from her body. When I touch it, some part of me calls out in rage from behind a shut door, demanding to be set free. But a second later, I shake my head, frowning. The feeling fades. I think to cast the armlet to the grass. I do not need it, and neither does the girl.

Something makes me put it in my pocket instead. I try to turn back to the ghosts, to my work. But I am perturbed, and eventually I find myself at the base of a tree near the spring not far from the ruins of Shaeva's cabin, staring out at the water. A memory rises in my mind.

Soon you will learn the cost of your vow, my brother. I hope you do not think too ill of me.

Is that what this feeling is inside? Anger at Shaeva?

It is not anger, child, Mauth says gently. *It is simply that you feel your mortality. But you have no mortality anymore. You will live as long as you can serve.*

"It's not mortality I feel," I say, "though it is something uniquely mortal."

Sadness?

"A type of sadness," I say, "called loneliness."

There is a long silence, so long that I think he has left me. Then I feel the earth shift around me. The tree's roots rumble, curving, softening, until they fashion themselves around me, into a sort of seat. Vines grow, and flowers burst from them.

You are not alone, Banu al-Mauth. *I am here with you.*

A ghost drifts close to me, flitting about in agitation. Searching, always searching. I know her. The Wisp.

"Hello, young one." Her hand drifts across my face. "Have you seen my lovey?"

"I have not," I say, but this time I give her all of my attention. "Can you tell me her name?"

"Lovey."

I nod, feeling none of the impatience I felt before. "Lovey," I say. "What about you? What is your name?"

"My name," she whispers. "My name? She called me Ama. But I had another name." I sense her agitation and try to soothe her. I seek a way into her memories, but I cannot find one. She has built a wall around herself. When she tilts her head, her profile manifests briefly. The curves of her face strike a deep and visceral chord. I feel like I'm catching a glimpse of someone I've always known.

"Karinna." She sits down next to me. "That was my name. Before I was Ama, I was Karinna."

Karinna. I recognize the name, though it takes me a moment to realize why. Karinna was my grandmother's name. Quin's wife.

But it couldn't be . . .

I open my mouth to ask her more, but her head whips around, as if she's heard something. Immediately, she is back in the air, vanishing into the trees. Something has spooked her.

I run my mind along the borders of the Forest. The wall is strong. No ghosts lurk near it.

Then I feel it. For the second time this day, someone from the outside world enters the Waiting Place. But this time, it is not a trespasser.

This time, it is someone returning home.

LIX: The Nightbringer

In the deep shade of the Waiting Place, the ghosts sigh their song of regret instead of screaming it. The spirits are quelled; the *Banu al-Mauth* has finally learned what it means to be the Chosen of Death.

Shadows emerge from behind me, fourteen in number. I know them and I hate them, for they are the wellsprings of all my sorrows.

The Augurs.

Do they still hear the screams of the jinn children who were slaughtered with cold steel and summer rain? Do they recall how my people begged for mercy even as they were sealed into the jinn grove?

"You cannot stop me," I say to the Augurs. "My vengeance is written."

"We are here to witness." Cain speaks. He is a far cry from the power-obsessed Scholar king of a millennium ago. Strange to think that this withered creature is the same man who betrayed the jinn, promising peace while plotting destruction. "Those who ignited the blaze must suffer its wrath," he says.

"What do you think will happen to you when all the magic you stole from my people is restored to them?" I ask. "The magic that has sustained you in your pitiful forms for all these years?"

"We will die."

"You wish to die. Immortality was a more painful burden than you antici-pated, was it not, snake?" I fashion my magic into a thick, iridescent chain and lash the Augurs to me. They do not fight it. They cannot, for I am home, and here amid the trees of my birth, my magic is at its most powerful. "Fear no more, Your Majesty. You will die. Your pain will end. But first, you will watch as I destroy everything you hoped to save, so that you may know what your greed and violence have wrought."

Cain only smiles, a vestige of his old conceit.

"The jinn will be freed," he says. "The balance between worlds restored. But the humans are ready for you, Nightbringer. They *will* prevail."

"You poor fool." I seize him, and when he unleashes his power to throw me off, the air shimmers briefly before I shake the attack away like a human would a mosquito.

"Look into my eyes, you wretch of a man," I whisper. "See the darkest moments of your future. Witness the devastation I will unleash."

Cain stiffens as he looks, as he sees in my gaze field upon field of the dead. Villages, towns, cities aflame. His people, his precious Scholars obliterated at the hands of my brethren, ground down until even their name is no longer remembered. The Mariners, the Tribes, the Martials all under the bloody, iron-fisted rule of Keris Veturia.

And his champions, those three flames in which he placed all his hopes—Laia of Serra, Helene Aquilla, and Elias Veturius—I smother those flames. For I have taken the Blood Shrike's soul. The Waiting Place has taken the Soul Catcher's humanity. And I will crush Laia of Serra's heart.

The Augur tries to turn away from the nightmare images. I do not let him.

"Still so arrogant," I say. "So assured that you knew what was best. Your foretellings showed you a way to free yourselves and release the jinn while protecting humanity. But you never understood the magic. Above all else, it is changeable. Your dreams of the future only bloom if they have a firm hand to nurture them to life. Otherwise, they wither before they ever take root."

I turn to the jinn grove, dragging the struggling Augurs with me. They push at me with their stolen magic, desperate to escape now that they know what is to come. I wrap them tighter. They will be free soon enough.

When I arrive among the haunted trees, the suffering of my brethren washes over me. I want to scream.

I drive the Star into the ground. Now complete, it bears no sign of its splintering and stands as tall as I do, the four-pointed diamond harkening to the symbol of Blackcliff. The Augurs adopted the shape to remind themselves of their sins. A pathetic, human notion—that by drowning in guilt and regret, one can atone for any crime, no matter how despicable.

When I place my hands on the Star, the earth stills. I close my eyes. A thousand years of loneliness. A thousand years of deceit. A thousand years of plotting and planning and atonement. All for this moment.

Dozens of faces flood my mind, all those who possessed the Star. All those I loved. *Father-mother-brother-daughter-friend-lover.*

Release the jinn. The Star groans in response to my command, the magic within its metal twisting, warping, pouring into me and drawing from me, both at once. It is alive, its consciousness simple but thrumming with power. I seize that power, and make it mine.

The Augurs shudder, and I bind them tighter—all but Cain. I weave a shield from my magic, protecting him from what is to come.

Though he will not thank me for it.

Release the jinn. The trees moan awake, and the Star fights me, its ancient sorcery sluggish and unwilling to bend. *You have held them long enough. Release them.*

A crack echoes through the grove, loud as summer thunder. Deep in the Waiting Place, the soughs of the spirits transform into screams as one of the trees splits, then another. Flames pour from those great gouges, bursting forth as if the gates to all of the hells have been breached. My flames. My family. My jinn.

The trees explode into cinders, their glow painting the firmament an infernal red. Moss and shrubs curdle to soot, leaving an acres-wide black ring. The earth shudders, a tremor that will shatter glass from Marinn to Navium.

I taste fear on the air: from the Augurs and the ghosts, from the humans that infest this world. Visions flash across my mind: a scarred soldier cries out, reaching for daggers that will not help her. A newborn babe awakes, howling. A girl I once loved gasps, wheeling her horse about to gaze with gold eyes at the crimson sky over the Forest of Dusk.

For an instant, every human within a thousand leagues is united in a moment of ineffable dread. They *know*. Their hopes, their loves, their joy— all will soon be naught but ash.

My people stagger toward me, their flames coalescing into arms, legs, faces. First a dozen, then two score, then hundreds. One by one, they tumble from their prisons and gather near me.

At the edge of the clearing, thirteen of the fourteen Augurs silently collapse into heaps of ash. The power that they siphoned from the jinn flows back to its rightful owners. The Star crumbles, dusty remnants swirling restlessly before disappearing on a swift wind.

I turn to my family. "*Bisham*," I say. *My children.*

I gather the flames close, hundreds and hundreds of them. Their heat is a balm on the soul I thought I had long since lost. "Forgive me," I beg them. "Forgive me for failing you."

They surround me, touch my face, pull away my cloak, and release me into my true form, the form of flame, which I have repressed for ten centuries.

"You freed us," they murmur. "Our king. Our father. Our *Meherya*. You did not forget us."

The humans were wrong. I had a name, once. A beautiful name. A name spoken by the great dark that came before all else. A name whose meaning brought me into existence and defined all I would ever be.

My queen spoke my name long ago. Now my people whisper it.

"*Meherya*."

Their long-banked flames blaze brighter. From red to incandescent white, too bright for human eyes, but glorious to mine. I see their power and magic, their pain and rage.

I see their soul-deep need for vengeance. I see the bloody reaping to come.

"*Meherya*." My children say my name again, and the sound of it drops me to my knees. "*Meherya*."

Beloved.

ACKNOWLEDGMENTS

To my incredible readers all over the world: Thank you for laughing at my talking vegetables and hooting owls, and for all the love. I am lucky to have you.

Ben Schrank and Marissa Grossman: You helped me transform this strange fever dream into an actual book. I've run out of words to say thanks, so I'll keep sending you weaponry and socks, and hope that suffices.

Kashi, thank you for teaching me how to vanish into the attack, for cheering the loudest when I did so. Your patience with my flinty-eyed, gunslinger ways is saintly. God only knows what I'd do without you.

Thank you to my boys, my falcon and my sword, for knowing I need coffee in the morning. I hope you read this book one day, and I hope you are proud.

My family is my scim and my shield, my own little fellowship. Mama, thank you for your love and grace. Daddy, bless you for assuming that I am more awesome than I actually am. Boon, you are one tough brother and I am proud of you. Also, you owe me dinner. Mer, next time I won't call you quite as much, ha-ha, lying, I'll probably call you more. Heelah, Auntie Mahboob, Maani, and Armo—thank you for the hugs and duas. Aftab and Sahib Tahir, I am so blessed to have you.

Alexandra Machinist—here's to bullet journals, philosophizing on the phone, and flailing over the things we cannot control. I adore you and I am forever grateful for you.

Cathy Yardley—I would not have survived writing this book without your calm wisdom. You're a badass.

Renée Ahdieh—your friendship means more to me than all the croissants in the galaxy. Nicola Yoon, bless you for being the sane one. Our calls are the highlight of my week. Abigail Wen, Thursdays at 10 are my happy place—I am lucky to know you. Adam Silvera—I am so damn proud to be one of your tattoo lines. Marie Lu, all the hugs for your friendship, and for the most diabolical pedicure ever. Leigh Bardugo, you lovely, wise goth owl, long may we eat s'mores whilst laughing evilly. Victoria Aveyard—no one better to be in the writing trenches with; we survived! Lauren DeStefano, DRiC forever.

A big, sock-filled thank-you to: Jen Loja for your leadership and support; Felicia Frazier and the sales team; Emily Romero, Erin Berger, Felicity Vallence, and the marketing team; Shanta Newlin and Lindsay Boggs, who deserve all the chocolate; Kim Wiley for putting up with the lateness; Shane Rebenschied, Kristin Boyle, Theresa Evangelista, and Maggie Edkins for all their work on the covers; Krista Ahlberg and Shari Beck for saving me from some genuinely horrifying mistakes; Carmela Iaria, Venessa Carson, and the school and library team; and Casey McIntyre, Alex Sanchez, and all the folks at Razorbill. Great thanks to mapmaker Jonathan Roberts, whose talent is gobsmacking.

My foreign rights agents, Roxane Edouard and Stephanie Koven, have made my books world travelers—thank you. To all of the foreign publishers, cover artists, and translators, your dedication to this series is a gift.

Hugs and great thanks to Lilly Tahir, Christine Oakes, Tala Abbasi, Kelly Loy Gilbert, Stephanie Garber, Stacey Lee, Kathleen Miller, Dhonielle Clayton, and Liz Ward. Much appreciation to Farrah Khan for all your support and for letting me use the line about being a visitor.

Music is my home, and this book wouldn't exist without it. Thank you to: Austra for "Beat and the Pulse," Matt Maeson for "Cringe," Missio for "Bottom of the Deep Blue Sea," Nas for "War," Daughter for "Numbers," Kings of Leon for "Waste a Moment," Anthony Green for "You'll Be Fine," and Linkin Park for "Krwlng." Chester Bennington, thank you for singing your pain, so I didn't have to be alone with mine.

As ever, my final thanks to the One who witnesses the seen and unseen, and who walks with me, even on the darkest roads.

SABAA TAHIR is a former newspaper editor who grew up in California's Mojave Desert at her family's eighteen-room motel. There, she spent her time devouring fantasy novels, listening to thunderous indie rock, and playing guitar and piano badly. Her #1 *New York Times* bestselling An Ember in the Ashes series has been translated into more than thirty-five languages, and the first book in the series was named one of *TIME*'s 100 Best YA Books of All Time. Tahir's most recent novel, *All My Rage*, won the National Book Award for Young People's Literature, the Michael L. Printz Award, and the *Boston Globe–Horn Book* Award for Fiction and Poetry, and was an instant *New York Times* bestseller.

Visit Sabaa online at SabaaTahir.com
and follow her on Instagram @SabaaTahir
and TikTok @SabaaTahirAuthor.

WHO WILL SURVIVE THE STORM?

TURN THE PAGE FOR A PEEK AT THE JAW-DROPPING
CONCLUSION TO THE *NEW YORK TIMES*
BESTSELLING EMBER QUARTET.

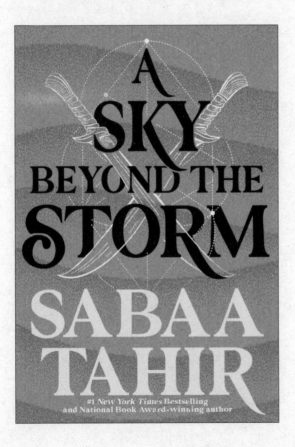

"A masterclass example of how to wrap up a series."
—THE NERD DAILY

I: The Nightbringer

I awoke in the glow of a young world, when man knew of hunting but not tilling, of stone but not steel. It smelled of rain and earth and life. It smelled of hope.

Arise, beloved.

The voice that spoke was laden with millennia beyond my ken. The voice of a father, a mother. A creator and a destroyer. The voice of Mauth, who is Death himself.

Arise, child of flame. Arise, for thy home awaits thee.

Would that I had not learned to cherish it, my home. Would that I had unearthed no magic, loved no wife, sparked no children, gentled no ghosts. Would that Mauth had never named me.

"Meherya."

My name drags me out of the past to a rain-swept hilltop in the Mariner countryside. My old home is the Waiting Place—known to humans as the Forest of Dusk. I will make my new home upon the bones of my foes.

"Meherya." Umber's sun-bright eyes are the vermillion of ancient anger. "We await your orders." She grips a glaive in her left hand, its blade white with heat.

"Have the ghuls reported in yet?"

Umber's lip curls. "They scoured Delphinium. Antium. Even the Waiting Place," she says. "They could not find the girl. Neither she nor the Blood Shrike has been seen for weeks."

"Have the ghuls seek out Darin of Serra in Marinn," I say. "He forges weapons in the port city of Adisa. Eventually, they will reunite."

Umber inclines her head and we regard the village below us, a hodge-podge of stone homes that can withstand fire, adorned with wooden shingles that cannot. Though it is mostly identical to other hamlets we've destroyed, it has one distinction. It is the last settlement in our campaign. Our parting volley in Marinn before I send the Martials south to join the rest of Keris Veturia's army.

"The humans are ready to attack, Meherya." Umber's glow reddens, her disgust of our Martial allies palpable.

"Give the order," I tell her. Behind me, one by one, my kin transform from shadow to flame, lighting the cold sky.

A warning bell tolls in the village. The watchman has seen us, and bellows in panic. The front gates—hastily erected after attacks on neighboring communities—swing closed as lamps flare and shouts tinge the night air with terror.

"Seal the exits," I tell Umber. "Leave the children to carry the tale. Maro." I turn to a wisp of a jinn, his narrow shoulders belying the power within. "Are you strong enough for what you must do?"

Maro nods. He and the others pour past me, five rivers of fire, like those that spew from young mountains in the south. The jinn blast through the gates, leaving them smoking.

A half legion of Martials follow, and when the village is well aflame and my kin withdraw, the soldiers begin their butchery. The screams of the living fade quickly. Those of the dead echo for longer.

After the village is naught but ashes, Umber finds me. Like the other jinn, she now glows with only the barest flicker.

"The winds are fair," I tell her. "You will reach home swiftly."

"We wish to remain with you, Meherya," she says. "We are strong."

For a millennium, I believed that vengeance and wrath were my lot. Never would I witness the beauty of my kind moving through the world. Never would I feel the warmth of their flame.

But time and tenacity allowed me to reconstitute the Star—the weapon the Augurs used to imprison my people. The same weapon I used to set them free. Now the strongest of my kin gather near. And though it has been months since I destroyed the trees imprisoning them, my skin still trills at their presence.

"Go," I order them gently. "For I will need you in the coming days."

After they leave, I walk the cobbled streets of the village, sniffing for signs of life. Umber lost her children, her parents, and her lover in our long-ago war with the humans. Her rage has made her thorough.

A gust of wind carries me to the south wall of the village. The air tells of the violence wrought here. But there is another scent too.

A hiss escapes me. The smell is human, but layered with a fey sheen. The girl's face rises in my mind. Laia of Serra. Her essence feels like this.

But why would she lurk in a Mariner village?

I consider donning my human skin, but decide against it. It is an arduous task, not undertaken without good reason. Instead I draw my cloak close against the rain and trace the scent to a hut tucked beside a tottering wall.

The ghuls trailing my ankles yip in excitement. They feed off pain, and the village is rife with it. I nudge them away and enter the hut alone.

The inside is lit by a tribal lamp and a merry fire, over which a pan of charred skillet bread smokes. Pink winter roses sit atop the dresser and a cup of well water sweats on the table.

Whoever was here left only moments ago.

Or rather, she wants it to look that way.

I steel myself, for a jinn's love is no fickle thing. Laia of Serra has hooks in my heart yet. The pile of blankets at the foot of the bed disintegrates to ashes at my touch. Hidden beneath and shaking with terror is a child who is very obviously *not* Laia of Serra.

And yet he feels like her.

Not in his mien, for where Laia of Serra has sorrow coiled about her heart, this boy is gripped by fear. Where Laia's soul is hardened by suffering, this boy is soft, his joy untrammeled until now. He's a Mariner child, no more than twelve.

But it is what's deep within that harkens to Laia. An unknowable darkness in his mind. His black eyes meet mine, and he holds up his hands.

"B-begone!" Perhaps he meant for it to be a shout. But his voice rasps, nails digging into wood. When I go to snap his neck, he holds his hands out again, and an unseen force nudges me back a few inches.

His power is wild and unsettlingly familiar. I wonder if it is jinn magic, but while jinn-human pairings occurred, no children can come of them.

"Begone, foul creature!" Emboldened by my retreat, the boy throws something at me. It has all the sting of rose petals. Salt.

My curiosity fades. Whatever lives within the child feels fey, so I reach for the scythe slung across my back. Before he understands what is happening, I draw the weapon across his throat and turn away, my mind already moving on.

The boy speaks, stopping me dead. His voice booms with the finality of a jinn spewing prophecy. But the words are garbled, a story told through water and rock.

"The seed that slumbered wakes, the fruit of its flowering consecrated within the body of man. And thus is thy doom begotten, Beloved, and with it the breaking—the—breaking—"

A jinn would have completed the prophecy, but the boy is only human, his body a frail vessel. Blood pours from the wound in his neck and he collapses, dead.

"What in the skies are you?" I speak to the darkness within the child, but it has fled, and taken the answer to my question with it.

II: Laia

The storyteller in the Ucaya Inn holds the packed common room in her thrall. The winter wind moans through Adisa's streets, rattling the eaves outside, and the Tribal *Kehanni* trembles with equal intensity. She sings of a woman fighting to save her true love from a vengeful jinn. Even the most ale-soaked denizens are rapt.

As I watch the *Kehanni* from a table in the corner of the room, I wonder what it is like to be her. To offer the gift of story to those you meet, instead of suspecting that they might be enemies out to kill you.

At the thought, I scan the room again and feel for my dagger.

"You pull that hood any lower," Musa of Adisa whispers from beside me, "and people will think you're a jinn." The Scholar man sprawls in a chair to my right. My brother, Darin, sits on his other side. We are tucked by one of the inn's foggy windows, where the warmth of the fire does not penetrate.

I do not release my weapon. My skin prickles, instinct telling me that unfriendly eyes are upon me. But everyone watches the *Kehanni*.

"Stop waving around your blade, *aapan*." Musa uses the Mariner honorific that means "little sister" and speaks with the same exasperation I sometimes hear from Darin. The Beekeeper, as Musa is known, is twenty-eight—older than Darin and I. Perhaps that is why he delights in bossing us around.

"The innkeeper is a friend," he says. "No enemies here. Relax. We can't do anything until the Blood Shrike returns anyway."

We are surrounded by Mariners, Scholars, and only a few Tribespeople. Still, when the *Kehanni* ends her tale, the room explodes into applause. It is so sudden that I half draw my blade.

Musa eases my hand off the hilt. "You break Elias Veturius out of Black-cliff, burn down Kauf Prison, deliver the Martial Emperor in the middle of a war, face down the Nightbringer more times than I can count," he says, "and you jump at a loud noise? I thought you were fearless, *aapan*."

"Leave off, Musa," Darin says. "Better to be jumpy than dead. The Blood Shrike would agree."

"She's a Mask," Musa says. "They're born paranoid." The Scholar watches the door, his mirth fading. "She should be back by now."

It is strange to worry about the Shrike. Until a few months ago, I thought I would go to my grave hating her. But then Grímarr and his horde of Karkaun barbarians besieged Antium, and Keris Veturia betrayed the city. Thousands of Martials and Scholars, including me, the Shrike, and her newly born nephew, the Emperor, fled to Delphinium. The Shrike's sister, Empress Regent Livia, freed those Scholars still bound in slavery.

And somehow, between then and now, we became allies.

The innkeeper, a young Scholar woman around Musa's age, emerges from the kitchen with a tray of food. She sweeps toward us, the tantalizing scents of pumpkin stew and garlic flatbread preceding her.

"Musa, love." The innkeeper sets down the food and I am suddenly starving. "You won't stay another night?"

"Sorry, Haina." He flips a gold mark at her and she catches it deftly. "That should cover the rooms."

"And then some." Haina pockets the coin. "Nikla's raised Scholar taxes again. Nyla's bakery was shuttered last week when she couldn't pay."

"We've lost our greatest ally." Musa speaks of old King Irmand, who's been ill for weeks. "It's only going to get worse."

"You were married to the princess," Haina says. "Couldn't you talk to her?"

The Scholar offers her a wry smile. "Not unless you want your taxes even higher."

Haina departs and Musa claims the stew. Darin swipes a platter of fried okra still popping with oil.

"You ate four ears of street corn an hour ago," I hiss at him, grappling for a basket of bread.

As I wrest it free, the door blows open. Snow drifts into the room, along with a tall, slender woman. Her silvery-blonde crown braid is mostly hidden beneath a hood. The screaming bird on her breastplate flashes for an instant before she draws her cloak over it and strides to our table.

"That smells incredible." The Blood Shrike of the Martial Empire drops into the seat across from Musa and takes his food.

At his petulant expression, she shrugs. "Ladies first. That goes for you too, smith." She slides Darin's groaning plate toward me and I dig in.

"Well?" Musa says to the Shrike. "Did that shiny bird on your armor get you in to see the king?"

The Blood Shrike's pale eyes flash. "Your wife," she says, "is a pain in the a—"

"Estranged wife." Musa says. A reminder that once, they adored each other. No longer. A bitter ending to what they hoped was a lifelong love.

It is a feeling I know well.

Elias Veturius saunters into my mind, though I have tried to lock him out. He appears as I last saw him, sharp-eyed and aloof outside the Waiting Place. *We are, all of us, just visitors in each other's lives*, he'd said. *You will forget my visit soon enough.*

"What did the princess say?" Darin asks the Shrike, and I push Elias from my head.

"She didn't speak to me. Her steward said the princess would hear my appeal when King Irmand's health improved."

The Martial glares at Musa, as if he is the one who has refused an audience. "Keris *bleeding* Veturia is sitting in Serra, beheading every ambassador Nikla has sent. The Mariners have no other allies in the Empire. Why is she refusing to see me?"

"I'd love to know," Musa says, and an iridescent flicker near his face tells me that his wights, tiny winged creatures who serve as his spies, are near. "But while I have eyes in many places, Blood Shrike, the inside of Nikla's mind isn't one of them."

"I should be back in Delphinium." The Shrike stares out at the howling snowstorm. "My family needs me."

Worry furrows her brow, uncharacteristic on a face so studied. In the five months since we escaped Antium, the Blood Shrike has thwarted a dozen attempts to assassinate young Emperor Zacharias. The child has enemies among the Karkauns as well as Keris's allies in the south. And they are relentless.

"We expected this," Darin says. "Are we decided, then?"

The Blood Shrike and I nod, but Musa clears his throat.

"I know the Shrike needs to speak to the princess," he says. "But I'd like to publicly state that I find this plan far too risky."

Darin chuckles. "That's how we know it's a Laia plan—utterly insane and likely to end in death."

"What of your shadow, Martial?" Musa glances around for Avitas Harper, as if the Mask might appear out of thin air. "What wretched task have you subjected that poor man to now?"

"Harper is occupied." The Shrike's body stiffens for a moment before she continues inhaling her food. "Don't worry about him."

"I have to take one last delivery at the forge." Darin gets to his feet. "I'll meet you at the gate in a bit, Laia. Luck to you all."

Watching him walk out of the inn sends anxiety spiking through me. While I was in the Empire, my brother remained here in Marinn at my request. We reunited a week ago, when the Shrike, Avitas, and I arrived in Adisa. Now we're splitting up again. *Just for a few hours, Laia. He'll be fine.*

Musa nudges my plate toward me. "Eat, *aapan*," he says, not unkindly. "Everything is better when you're not hungry. I'll have the wights keep an eye on Darin, and I'll see you all at the northeast gate. Seventh bell." He pauses, frowning. "Be careful."

As he heads out, the Blood Shrike harrumphs. "Mariner guards have nothing on a Mask."

I do not disagree. I watched the Shrike single-handedly hold off an army of Karkauns so that thousands of Martials and Scholars could escape Antium. Few Mariners could take on a Mask. None is a match for the Blood Shrike.

The Shrike disappears to her room to change, and for the first time in ages, I am alone. Out in the city, a bell tolls the fifth hour. Winter brings night early and the roof groans with the force of the gale. I ponder Musa's words as I watch the inn's boisterous guests and try to shake off that sense of being watched. *I thought you were fearless.*

I almost laughed when he said it. *Fear is only your enemy if you allow it to be.* The blacksmith Spiro Teluman told me that long ago. Some days, I live those words so easily. On others, they are a weight in my bones I cannot bear.

Certainly, I did the things Musa said. But I also abandoned Darin to a Mask. My friend Izzi died because of me. I escaped the Nightbringer, but unwittingly helped him free his kindred. I delivered the Emperor, but let my mother sacrifice herself so that the Blood Shrike and I could live.

Even now, months later, I see Mother in my dreams. White-haired and scarred, her eyes blazing as she wields her bow against a wave of Karkaun attackers. She was not afraid.

But I am not my mother. And I am not alone in my fear. Darin does not speak of the terror he faced in Kauf Prison. Nor does the Shrike speak of the day Emperor Marcus slaughtered her parents and sister. Or how it felt to flee Antium, knowing what the Karkauns would do to her people.

Fearless. No, none of us is fearless. "Ill-fated" is a better description.

I rise as the Blood Shrike descends the stairs. She wears the slate, cinch-waisted dress of a palace maid and a matching cloak. I almost don't recognize her.

"Stop staring." The Shrike tucks a lock of hair beneath the drab kerchief hiding her crown braid and nudges me toward the door. "Someone will notice the uniform. Come on. We're late."

"How many blades hidden in that skirt?"

"Five—no, wait—" She shifts from foot to foot. "Seven."

We push out of the Ucaya and into streets thick with snow and people. The wind knifes into us, and I scramble for my gloves, fingertips numb.

"Seven blades." I smile at her. "And you did not think to bring gloves?"

"It's colder in Antium." The Shrike's gaze drops to the dagger at my waist. "And I don't use poisoned blades."

"Maybe if you did, you would not need so many."

She grins at me. "Luck to you, Laia."

"Do not kill anyone, Shrike."

PREPARE FOR THE
NEXT GENERATION OF
EPIC FANTASY BY SABAA TAHIR
WITH . . .

COMING TO BOOKSTORES
FALL 2024